'Why should I help you?' said the Crab.

'Out of mercy,' said Justina.

And Shabble said, brightly:

'I've found a cockroach.'

Nobody took any notice.

'I will be eternally grateful for any help you give me,' said the Empress Justina, still speaking to the Crab.

'You will not live for eternity,' said the Crab. 'You will be lucky if you live another forty years. Your rhetoric is empty.'

'Forty years is hardly emptiness,' said Justina.

'It's a big cockroach,' said Shabble.

Still poor Shabble was ignored.

Shabble tried again. 'He's—'

'Quiet!' said Chegory Guy, addressing himself to Shabble.

'Chegory has given you a very wise command,' said the Crab, pretending it thought the Ebrell Islander had been addressing the Empress Justina.

Chegory blushed profusely.

Also by Hugh Cook

THE WIZARDS AND THE WARRIORS
THE WORDSMITHS AND THE WARGUILD
THE WOMEN AND THE WARLORDS
THE WALRUS AND THE WARWOLF
THE WICKED AND THE WITLESS

and published by Corgi Books

THE WAZIR AND THE WITCH

Hugh Cook

CORGI BOOKS

THE WAZIR AND THE WITCH
A CORGI BOOK 0 552 13537 2

First publication in Great Britain

PRINTING HISTORY
Corgi edition published 1990

This book is set in 10/11pt Times by County Typesetters,
Margate, Kent

Corgi Books are published by Transworld Publishers Ltd.,
61–63 Uxbridge Road, Ealing, London W5 5SA, in Australia
by Transworld Publishers (Australia) Pty. Ltd., 15–23 Helles
Avenue, Moorebank, NSW 2170, and in New Zealand by
Transworld Publishers (N.Z.) Ltd., Cnr. Moselle and
Waipareira Avenues, Henderson, Auckland.

Printed and bound in Great Britain by
BPCC Hazell Books
Aylesbury, Bucks, England
Member of BPCC Ltd.

CHAPTER ONE

Begin at the beginning.

Bolfrigalaskaptiko.

A curse word?

No, it is not a curse word, though it comes within a couple of syllables of being obscene in the extreme.

Bolfrigalaskaptiko.

Is this perhaps a dish of fried seagull livers mixed with a touch of basilisk gall and served with side helpings of baked yams and diamond-shaped segments of dried jelly-fish?

A good guess.

But wrong.

For tolfrigdalakaptiko is the word which denotes the above-mentioned dish of seagull livers, and the mystery which here confronts us is bolfrigalaskaptiko.

Give up?

Very well.

All will now be revealed, and your education will thus be made complete.

Take down your atlas and open it to a map of the continent of Yestron. Run your finger down the western coast of that continent until you reach the equator. Here you will find the huge lagoon known as Manamalargo. What vast and slovenly river of fever fogs and predatory crocodiles empties itself into this lagoon? Why, the River Ka, of course. And what is the city of marshlands and malaria which lies just upstream from the estuary of that river?

Look!

If the atlas you are using is worth the price you paid for it, your finger will now be resting upon a blob (or at

5

least a flyspeck) which is labelled 'Bolfrigalaskaptiko'.

Thus the mystery is solved.

Bolfrigalaskaptiko is a city.

A city which lies upon the River Ka.

A city just upstream from the great lagoon of Manamalargo.

A city on the western coast of the continent of Yestron, that sprawling land mass which has for so long been dominated by the Izdimir Empire.

Now this has been learnt, it can all be forgotten, for the history which this text deals with has nothing whatsoever to do with the great lagoon of Manamalargo, the city of stilts and sewage canals known as Bolfrigalaskaptiko, or with the River Ka. Manamalargo, Ka and Bolfrigalaskaptiko are equally irrelevant to the action which follows, for this tome deals not with the history of Yestron but with Untunchilamon.

And Untunchilamon, as your atlas will doubtless reveal, is far from Bolfrigalaskaptiko; it lies in the deeps of Moana, many horizons from the furthest shore, and is but a piece of rock beset on all sides by the rolling seas. A piece of rock? A considerable piece of rock, for Untunchilamon measures its length in leagues by the hundreds. Untunchilamon, then, is an island marooned in the middle of the ocean, a great many leagues from the nearest continental mass.

It is to Untunchilamon that this tale must go, and there remain until the intricacies of a political crisis upon that island have been properly explicated, together with the tragedies, betrayals, murders, killings, manoeuvres, heartbreaks, traumas, loves and loyalties so richly entangled in the web of that crisis.

Yet Bolfrigalaskaptiko remains an excellent place to start, even though we have already agreed that this city and its attendant geography may be conveniently forgotten. For it is here that an important meeting takes place. A meeting? Yes. A meeting between a heart specialist and a young man.

The heart specialist?

His name will not be given here, for he is of the Ola caste which is unique to the city of Bolfrigalaskaptiko; and, as any standard text of ethnology will tell you, names of male members of that caste never run to fewer than seven thousand syllables. Furthermore, it is considered culturally offensive to give such names in any abbreviated form, and were this text to take such a liberty it would doubtless be prosecuted; so, bearing in mind the length of the name, the limitations of paper and patience, and the sensitivities involved, it is best that the good doctor remain anonymous.

As for the patient?

The patient declares himself to be Jean Froissart, a name which at once identifies him as a child of Wen Endex. The patient gives his age as thirty-two, which is correct; therefore, while he thinks of himself as being young, he has already attained a maturity which beardless striplings and their giggling and newly nubile mates would look upon as being close to antiquity.

The patient complains of sharp stabbing pains, sometimes in the region of his heart, sometimes in his arms or shoulders. At times he also experiences a vicious pain which makes it impossible to breathe except shallowly. He fears himself to be in danger of a heart attack, which is why he has presented himself to this medical specialist of the inordinately long (and hence ungiveable) name.

The good Doctor Anonymous takes a detailed case history then declares that the young man known to him as Jean Froissart is suffering from symptoms of anxiety rather than cardiac delinquency. As for the stabbing pains which sometimes force this fearful patient to breathe as shallowly as possible, why, these are most unlikely to be connected with the heart.

Doctor Anonymous puts it this way:

'The lungs exist within a sac known to medical science as the plad'dnog'k'qara. This sac has two layers. There is an outside layer, which medical science in its genius has

7

chosen to call the outer layer. Then there is an inside layer, the name of which you can guess for yourself.'

Doctor Anonymous smiles, then sits back in his creaking chair of mangrove wood as if all has already been explained. His office shakes alarmingly as a punt collides with one of the struts which hold it clear of the sewage canal over which it is built; the monkey breeder who shares the premises gives vent to strident vituperation.

'And?' says Jean Froissart.

'It is simple,' says Doctor Anonymous, rubbing his hands together.

He is endeavouring to help his patient to discover the truth for himself.

But Froissart is in no mood for discovery. He is oppressed by the suffocating heat of Bolfrigalaskaptiko, the stench of rotten dogs and decayed sewage, the furious chatter of half a thousand caged monkeys and the persistent ministrations of the flies which he no longer bothers to brush from his face. With some disappointment, Doctor Anonymous accepts that his patient lacks an inclination to intellectual endeavour; the good doctor therefore proceeds with his lecture.

'It is simple, as I have said already,' says Doctor Anonymous, once more rubbing his hands together. 'As you breathe, so the inner and outer layers of the plad'dnog'k'qara rub against each other. Sometimes, for reasons unknown to us, they stick together. This occasions pain upon breathing. Hence your symptoms.'

'Perhaps,' says the patient reluctantly. 'But surely my other symptoms are . . .'

Froissart pauses.

Hesitates.

'Trust me,' says Doctor Anonymous. 'In some patients, some of the symptoms you complain of are associated with angina or impending myocardial infarction. However, my careful elucidation of your own personal medical history assures me that in your case these symptoms indicate nothing but anxiety. However, if it would set your mind at rest, I will give you a clearance test.'

'A clearance test?'

'Yes,' said Doctor Anonymous, beaming. 'It is a seven-day test. On the first day, you join the crew of a galley. From dawn to dusk you row upstream against the flow of the River Ka. On the second day, the swelter bath. On the third day, exposure to controlled doses of medicinal alcohol. The forced march comes on the fourth day, the fifth is spent in the smoke chamber, the wrestling match follows on the sixth, then we finish with the sledgehammer test on the seventh.'

On receiving this intelligence, Froissart finds that it is too hot to indulge in anything as athletic as a shudder. So he contents himself by asking:

'Is there not some . . . some element of danger in this test?'

'Oh yes, oh yes indeed,' says Doctor Anonymous, beaming all the more. 'The mortality rate can run as high as fifty per cent. But for those who survive, the clearance test is infinitely reassuring. Their health is certified and assured. I believe you would pass this test, young man, and pass with honours. In any case – consider! If my diagnosis is incorrect, is not a swift death infinitely preferable to a long life as an invalid? One way or another, the clearance test will put your mind at rest.'

Jean Froissart declined to participate in the clearance test, but thanks the good Doctor Anonymous, pays the good Doctor Anonymous, then hails a water taxi and sets off for his ship. On the way, the taxi sinks, miring its young passenger in the sludge of a foul and pestilential sewage canal. Hence Froissart is both foul-tempered and foul-smelling by the time he reaches the brig which is to take him to Untunchilamon.

Aboard that ship is the man who has recently (and briefly) acted as the wazir of Manamalargo. This is Manthandros Trasilika, who expects to depart from

Bolfrigalaskaptiko without futher delay. Already he has thrice practised a speech in which he announces himself as the rightful wazir of Injiltaprajura. In this speech, a speech which the orator plans to make as soon as he sets foot upon the island of Untunchilamon, he denounces Justina Thrug as a witch. Yes. He denounces Justina Thrug as a witch. And proclaims that justice demands her immediate death.

But the first trouble which will befall Justina Thrug will come not from Manthandros Trasilika but from the Inland Revenue Department of the island of Untunchilamon.

CHAPTER TWO

Mention of the Inland Revenue Department may lead some people to think this will be a horror story.

Certainly, horror and the Inland Revenue walk hand in hand. This you must admit. For, unless you were born blind or live with your eyes shut, you must have seen the headless corpses hanging by their heels outside the offices of your local taxation department; and, unless you have gone deaf or habitually stuff your ears with beeswax, you must on occasion hear the screams of the damned issuing from that grim building as the auditors go about their work.

However – and here the sensitive will doubtless breathe a sigh of relief – as little as possible will be said of the activities of the Inland Revenue Department. Furthermore, even were the affairs of that department to be explicated in full, nothing too hideous would appear in these pages.

You may find this claim startling, for the Inland Revenue Department of Untunchilamon is in many places synonymous with horror.

Untunchilamon: island of Norbik the Auditor!

Untunchilamon: island of Max the Inquisitor!

Untunchilamon: island of blood!

If your reaction is as above, doubtless the person to blame is Greven Jing. While Jing is doubtless a horror writer of exceptional talent, his treatment of certain historical events is far from accurate. Take for example his book *The Bothopody*, which purports to be a history of Injiltaprajura's Inland Revenue Department. Despite Jing's claim that 'this is a true story', *The Bothopody* is a book which has little more than a random relationship to the truth.

True, Norbik the Auditor lived and worked on Untunchilamon, and did extract teeth in the manner described by Jing; and those extractions were every bit as painful as Jing would have us believe. It is equally true that Max the Inquisitor used to shark people in the lagoon for the pure pleasure of it; and the number of tax defaulters thus disposed of cannot be fewer than two and a half thousands.

Even so, *The Bothopody* is a work of fiction rather than a work of fact.

For Norbik the Auditor worked for the tax department during the reign of Wazir Sin, he who was overthrown by Lonstantine Thrug; and the end of Sin's wazirate saw the end of Norbik himself. On the other hand, Max the Inquisitor did not land on Untunchilamon until some time after the reign of the Empress Justina. It follows that the activities of these two men are separated (as far as Injiltaprajura is concerned) by a good seven years and more of peace and reason, yet Jing has written thus:

'Trob the Lobble stared in horror as Norbik the Auditor fastened him to the table with the razor-sharp spikes of his steely gaze. There was an inhuman gleam of rabid lust in Norbik's drug-crazed eyes. Merely to look into those eyes was unendurable torture. They spoke of the fiendish brutality of which only an accountant is capable. Trob the Lobble spat out another piece of his tongue. He tried to scream. He could not.

'He was close to death. The heat of Injiltaprajura clogged his arteries and sweated through his bones. Malarial fevers shook his shuddering limbs. The drums, the drums, the pulsing drums of Untunchilamon throbbed in his skull like the pulse of hell itself. He wanted to die. But he could not. He was cursed with the constitution of a shark. After ten days of torture, he was still far, far away from the blessed release of death.

'The sound of the devilish drumming intensified as the door opened. In through the door came Max the Inquisitor. Max carried a wooden bucket in his hands. Steam rose from the bucket, which was full of boiling water. Max smiled a gloating smile, raised the bucket on high, then began to empty its contents over Trob the Lobble's bleeding face. Outside, the drummers screamed in manic glee.'

To the above one may object on many grounds. As has been stated already, it is false to history, since Norbik the Auditor and Max the Inquisitor never worked together on Untunchilamon. It is also unfair to accountants. Jing implies that accountants are the most inhuman monsters known to civilization, whereas in fact this description is rightly applied to lawyers.

Furthermore, the 'drumming' cult was not known to Norbik the Auditor, who died roughly seven years before that cult came into existence; and it had ceased entirely by the time Max the Inquisitor came to power. The 'drumming' cult obsessed the adolescents of Injiltaprajura for a very short time, that being the final days of the rule of the Empress Justina.

Let it be recognized, then, that the horrors of life on Untunchilamon have been grossly exaggerated by certain mercenary fabulists who have distorted history in the interests of personal profit; and, furthermore, that the 'fiendish' and 'diabolical' nature of the short-lived drumming cult is entirely the creation of such fabulists.

It is true that 'drummers' and 'drumming' existed. That is to say, young people sat around in groups and drummed the sun from dawn to dusk. Sometimes they also drummed right through undokondra and bardardornootha as well, only ceasing their activities when exhaustion set in. It is true that some of these 'drummers' also engaged on occasion in sexual intercourse, but such behaviour is not unknown even in those cultures where not a single drum is to be heard from one sunbirth to another.

It is also true that more than one 'drummer' committed suicide. Which has led the eminent psychologist Yumbert Qipty to assert that the beating of drums is itself a dehumanizing process which, by a complicated process of auto-hypnosis, encourages a person to self-destruct.

Qipty's thesis has been seized upon, and enlarged, and exaggerated, by writers such as Greven Jing. Qipty's thesis (whether in its original form or that elaboration of it which has been created by Jing) has won popularity because it is so reassuring.

Reasssuring?

Yes!

To contrast externalized sources of horror with the sane and sensible values of a putative 'normality' – and such a process is the essence of the analytical science espoused by Qipty and the fables created by Jing – is infinitely reassuring. For it allows us to indulge ourselves in a totally irrational delusion: namely, that such a 'normality' exists at all.

The great attraction of Qipty's theories, and of Jing's drummers, demons, rabid flying fish, killer worms and blood-sucking ghosts is that (always) the horror is generated by 'the other'; by the abnormal presence, or influence, or trend; by something trespassing on the safe, kind, loving and lovable world of the 'normal'.

In fact, the 'normality' which is posited by Qipty and Jing alike does not exist. Never has existed. Never will exist.

In proof of this, we need make no mention of the horrors of a world ruled by the threat of war; we need say nothing of the starvation which squalors in the backstreets behind prosperity's mansions; we need make no mention of mortality, that great doom which threatens one and all with ultimate oblivion; we need say nothing of the cold wastelands between the stars and the heat-death of the universe which promises the destruction of all the works of man and woman alike.

We need make no mention of any of the above, for those who are alert to reality have realized the true horrors of everyday reality already; and it is a waste of time trying to convince the worshippers of 'normality' of the emptiness of their beliefs.

So, while 'drumming' truly existed on Untunchilamon, and while 'drummers' sometimes committed suicide, the realist will surely not join the eminent Yumbert Qipty in thinking the mere beating of drums to be the cause of adolescent self-destruction.

Rather, the realist will recognize that the world is a much harsher place than the self-deluded followers of the 'normality' cult would have us believe. Realists will recognize that it is very tough being an adolescent, and the problems of this age of life sometimes compound themselves to the point of causing suicide.

While it is difficult to be an adolescent, this fact is often obscured by another fact: namely, that it is exceptionally difficult (few things could be harder) to be a mature adult trying to deal with the insolence, foolishness, insensitivity and unconscious selfishness of children who are between the ages of thirteen and twenty-three. In despair, adults often seek a simple answer for the monstrous behaviour of such children, and find it comforting to pretend that it is abnormal, and to blame it on some simple external source of horror such as a 'cult'.

But the fact is that every younger generation is destined to be a trial to the older generation. Thus it has always been, and always will be, though it is denied by professional myth-makers like Yumbert Qipty, he with his much-loved concept of 'normality'. Qipty would have us believe that children 'at the age of the blood's turmoil' (as the poet puts it) can be sane, rational, loving and law-abiding human beings. Qipty declares that in a 'normal' world, the young are polite, and considerate, and clean the dirt from beneath their fingernails without being told, abjure alcohol and other strong drugs, and unflinchingly cleave to truth, justice and the imperial way.

It is true that this desirable state of affairs has sometimes been obtained in certain closed societies where severe sanctions (not excepting banishment and death) are available for the chastisement of the young, and where adults unite to impose upon their progeny a degree of authoritarian control which even Aldarch the Third would envy. However, the strenuous nature of such social engineering is itself sufficient to refute the contention that the happy state of affairs thus obtained (a younger generation meek, quiet, obedient and fearful) is in any sense 'normal'.

Rather, the realist recognizes that the young are by nature unruly and discontented; not least because they wish for the same freedoms their elders enjoy in the realms of action (and in sexual action in particular) but largely lack the means, money, skill, ability and power to make such wishes come true. This discontent expresses itself in many ways, with 'drumming' being but one such way; and one which arguably (though your sensationalist would have it otherwise) should not be greeted by hysterical fear on the part of their elders.

So, while this text does touch upon 'drumming' on occasion, please do not get the wrong idea. This is not a lurid assemblage of horrors designed to titillate and excite. Rather, this is a sober history which will proceed largely by careful analysis and exegesis, not by exclamation marks. Here you will find no gaudy tales of monsters and maidens; and, likewise, no breathbating stories of midnight raids, of cannibalism and torture, of blood-spouting torsos and amputated ears.

This – this is a work of scholarship, not to be confused with trite and trifling books about swords and slaughter, rapine and rape, battle and barrat. If you have an appetite for such, then you are advised to flee from the presence of these civilized pages, and find refuge from the world of reality in a romance like Chulman Puro's famous magnum opus, *The Bloodstained Dream*.

In those pages of ill fame, you will be able to indulge your purile appetites by following at length the exploits of Vorn the Gladiator, who bellows his defiance to the world as he is driven into the Grand Arena at Dalar ken Halvar. A jeering crowd cheers for his destruction. But he is yet to be destroyed!

'A hero's weapon!' he roars, holding aloft the great sword Zaftig.

Huge is that sword, a weapon too heavy for any mortal to lift from the sands. But Vorn the Gladiator bears its weight with ease; and, indeed, twirls it between two of his fingers as if it were a wieldy drumstick rather than a humungous weapon of murder.

Then the Great Gates of the Great Arena are opened, and the crowd screams for murder as a huge malatothapus lurches out on to the burning sands. The brute is a ghastly red. It is hideous to look upon, for it looks like an obscenely mutated Ebrell Islander grown to historic size, like the worst nightmares of prejudice made flesh. The thing is so huge that its shadow alone would crush any ordinary mortal to death.

But Vorn the Gladiator holds his ground.

The malatothapus advances.

The brave sword Zaftig gores the monster. But it sneers at the wound. Vorn is barely able to throw himself to one side to avoid his immediate extinction. Down to the burning sands he falls. He rolls sideways. Not away from the malatothapus but—

Under it!

He grabs at the brute's testicles and fastens his teeth in its scrotal sac. Mad with rage and pain, the malatothapus charges the wall of the arena. It rams that wall, which is made of huge slabs of iridescent opal – wealth which is typical of Dalar ken Halvar, a city where the streets truly are paved with gold, and the buildings made of silver and ever-ice.

The slabs split, crack and crumble. Unfortunately, the ornamental chair which sustains the delicious rump of the Princess Nuboltipon is seated upon the uppermost of the slabs so destroyed. She falls screaming to the sands. She stands up, still screaming. Then she runs, fleeing across the burning sands like a common slave doomed to die for some unpardonable crime, like spilling soup over her master's robes.

The malatothapus snorts with fury.

It starts after the Princess Nuboltipon.

Following behind is Vorn the Gladiator. His feet are braced upon the shield of a lesser warrior who died earlier in the day. He is clutching the short tail which waggles behind the malatothapus. Sand spurts out from either side of the shield as it furrows its way across the sands of the arena, as the tail-holding hero is dragged along by the monster.

The Princess Nuboltipon stops, for she can run no longer.

She turns.

She sees the malatothapus bearing down on her.

She screams.

The impact of her scream shatters every crystal wineglass brought to the Grand Arena by the wealthy members of the leisure class.

Then Vorn the Gladiator acts. He has noticed an orifice at the rear end of the malatothapus. Keeping hold of the brute's tail with his left hand, he plunges the right into this orifice, driving his right arm into the hot and humid flesh until it is buried to the shoulder. Vorn claws at the monster's innards with his fingernails, which are specially sharpened so he can gouge out eyes in close quarters combat.

The malatothapus bellows with agony, then faints from a surfeit of pain. As the monster swoons, Vorn pulls his arm free. He recovers the great sword Zaftig and hacks off the head of the brute.

'My hero!' says the Princess Nuboltipon, running to him with open arms.

Von embraces her, though one arm is smeared with

hot brown dung from fingertips to shoulder, and the other is much besplattered with the blood of the malatothapus. He crushes her to his breast. And, that night, duly reprieved and happily married, he crushes her to the bed, her perfume swooning around her as he thrusts an unmentionable part of his anatomy into a princessly orifice of hers which is equally unmentionable.

If you have an appetite for tales of such things, then by all means turn to the indulgent pages of the books of the above-mentioned Chalman Puro. But do not expect to find any such frivolous amusement here! The historian is happy to say that no such lurid incidents will be recorded in this tome. Instead, here we have a sober book of history, complete with statistical analysis where appropriate. Here is one such analysis:

It has been reliably computed that if the eyeballs of all the inhabitants of Untunchilamon were pulped together in a barrel, this would yield enough fluid to provide three baths for Aldarch the Third, Mutilator of Yestron. With equal reliability, it has been computed that the same amount of eyeball juice could provide the formidable Al'three with an infinite number of baths were he prepared to reuse the substance indefinitely.

This statistic has been derived from firm experimental evidence obtained by torturers working in the employ of the Mutilator of Yestron, and is mentioned here in order to indicate something of the character of Aldarch the Third to anyone who may by chance be unfamiliar with his history.

That character is part of the necessary background to this history, for virtually everything that was done in, on, around and underneath the city of Injiltaprajura in the final days of the reign of the Empress Justina was done with reference to the tastes, manners and mores of Al'three.

Even people's dreams were conditioned by the activities of the Mutilator. Though that tyrant was many leagues from Untunchilamon, it was customary for the blood spilt by his armies to pour in smoking rivers through the dreams of the people of Untunchilamon. Blood smoking, stinking, drenching, drowning – of such things is nightmare made.

Of such we will not speak again, trusting that the reader will hold it in mind throughout the rest of this history, and will not need to be reminded from paragraph to paragraph that 'when x did y he had the rightful expectations of Aldarch the Third very much in mind'.

However, while we trust the intelligence and intellectual powers of our readership, repetition of some thematic motifs will be necessary if only because pattern (and, hence, repetition) is an unavoidable part of life. Therefore it will (for example) be recorded (more than once) that the sun rose; and, again, that it set. From this, only the rash will presume that the historian presumes his readers to be so imbecilic that they need to be regularly reminded of the behaviour of the sky's major luminary. Likewise, only a harebrained speculator would presume that the succession of night by day and day by night speaks of some hidden symbolic scheme.

The historian makes mention of this because the world is not free from either the rash or the harebrained.

With particular regard to the harebrained, it needs to be stressed that this is a history written with painstaking regard to fact, and the historian has nowhere indulged in any poetic flights of fancy or invention. Thus, while blood is necessarily one of the dominant thematic elements of this text, no 'symbolic scheme' is intended or implied, for such nonsense belongs to the province of the poets. Rather, it happens that the ruling colour of Untunchilamon is lifeblood red, and this is a fact of geography which the historian did not invent and cannot alter.

The island of Untunchilamon has red rock known as bloodstone, reefs of red coral, seas of red seaweed, intermittent plagues of red plankton, beaches of red sand (ground coral and bloodstone mixed), and tropical sunsets which tend to be of a singularly sanguinary nature. The historian might therefore in fairness say:

Untunchilamon: island of blood!

But to say this is not to imply (after the style of Greven Jing, whom we have neatly disembowelled above) an atmosphere of horror. True, what one remembers most after a prolonged incarceration upon the island is the oppressive bloodstone, the sweltering heat, and the edible fires of the heavily spiced food in which the local inhabitants tend to indulge themselves.

But the fact is that, overall, Untunchilamon is a tolerably pleasant place. One can escape the heat by retreating to the labyrinthine underground mazes Downstairs. Or, if you do not care to venture Downstairs yourself, you can ameliorate the effects of heat by indulging in ice which others have rescued from those ancient machineries which fabricate that useful substance in the depths. Apart from ice, hidden machines also make (or so we presume, for it is the simplest of available explanations) the potable water which feeds Injiltaprajura's eversprings.

Injiltaprajura is, of course, the capital city (the only city) of Untunchilamon, and is sited where it is (on the shores of the Laitemata Harbour) expressly because of the water, ice, dikle and shlug manufactured by the machines of Downstairs.

On the Laitemata one might find (at night) Shabble admiring Shabbleself in the nightwater lightmirror. One would also find (at any time of day or night) the island of Jod. This was (and, doubtless, is still) a small island notable chiefly for one building in spectacular white marble, that building being the Analytical Institute which housed Jod's Analytical Engine.

On a hot day on the island of Jod, we find the master chef Pelagius Zozimus preparing a platter of tolfrigdalakaptiko, that dish which consists of fried seagull livers plus a dash of basilisk gall, the said dish being served with side helpings of baked yams and lozenges of dried jelly fish.

The perceptive reader will recall that the very same dish was mentioned in the first chapter of this history, and may suspect the existence of an unpardonable coincidence.

The true explanation is that the historian is working with a complete set of Pelagius Zozimus's favourite recipes on his desk, and is interleaving the labour of composing this history with the pleasures of trying out those recipes (to the extent to which the ingredients are obtainable in this region of the island of Quilth).

Thus, when the historian came to record the departure of Jean Froissart from the city of Bolfrigalaskaptiko on the River Ka (just upstream from the great lagoon of Manamalargo on the western shores of the continent of Yestron) it happened that tolfrigdalaptiko infiltrated the text because the recipe for the dish was on his desk; the very taste of the stuff was on his tongue; the pan in which he had cooked it was sitting in a washing barrel together with all those pans, pots and casserole dishes used by the historian over the last ten days; and the historian's favourite cockroach was feeding on one stray seagull liver which, having fallen to the floorboards, had failed to slip between the cracks between those boards.

In addition to all the above, the notes for this second chapter were on hand when the first was written, and tolfrigdalaptiko was much on the historian's mind because Pelagius Zozimus is recorded to have cooked it for the Empress Justina on no fewer than ten separate occasions; and, when working in the premises of the Analytical Institute on Jod, to have prepared it on every second day for the Crab.

The historian trusts that the reader's mind has been set at rest. A coincidence exists; but, rather than undermining the validity of this text, it serves merely to emphasize and underline the stringent research which has gone into this work of surpassing scholarship.

Let would-be critics further note that any attempt to studiously avoid coincidence would result in the most perverse perversion of history. For it is a statistical truth that, when Aldarch the Third sits upon his throne in the city of Obooloo and drinks wine or water (or blood, or the juice crushed from the eyeballs of his enemies, or the semen of his favourite dog), there will simultaneously be other people elsewhere who are also drinking wine or water (or other substances); and the historian cannot reasonably ask all these people to cease and desist from their activities merely to avoid the occurrence of a coincidence, that entirely natural pattern of synchronic correspondences which some schools of criticism find so intensely distressing.

Readers raised on histories of the weird and the wonderful raise another serious objection to the events of this narrative; namely, that the events it deals with are so close to those of their own lives and their own times.

This objection can only be answered by stating an unpalatable truth: the weird and wonderful histories which gratify the appetites of such readers are nothing but a tissue of untruths.

It is a great principle of historical philosophy (though one as yet far from universally acknowledged) that all lives are but variants of one common pattern; to the point that, were all the lives of all people from the beginning of time to be compounded into one Life Experience then divided by the number of the whole, the statistically accurate Average Life thus produced would be little different from the one the reader is living now.

While those who deal in weird and wonderful untruths are reluctant to admit it, the truth is that all the lives of all the peoples of all of humanity are, were and always will be very much alike.

Wherever we look, we find the same patterns repeating themselves. The gods are (and were, and will be) always distant, bad tempered and less than perfectly understood. The younger generation is always a trial to the older. Slaves are always idle and stupid, and a cause of exasperation to their masters. Chastity is everywhere preached, and the preaching is nowhere a solution to venereal disease. Youth acts in haste and age repents at leisure. Inflation prospers everywhere. Everywhere, scholarly talent starves while Chulman Puro and Greven Jing grow rich. And all cultures (regardless of what superficial differences exist between them) recognize that very special and peculiar difficulties inevitably exist between a man and his mother-in-law.

As this is a sober history, it follows that nothing is recorded in these pages which cannot happen in your own life, or at least in your own lifetime. The Empress Justina is not the first person to struggle valiantly to secure the liberties of her kingdom against the oppressions of a foreign empire; and the fact that her best efforts ended in general disaster merely indicates a principle well known to all historians, which is that might is might and right is easily forgotten.

One final comment.

Great differences will be found between this history and others now extant.

The greatest difference is that of treatment; for this is a singularly intimate history.

It is intimate largely because of the very special advantages enjoyed by the historian. Personal experience is one of these; for the historian was actually on Untunchilamon when the events herein recorded took place. Furthermore, since the historian writes late and last, he has access to the documents of all those who have written earlier.

But the historian's greatest advantage is that he was for long a confidante of Shabble; and Shabble was everywhere, and saw everything, or at least learnt of it thereafter by way of confession or hearsay.

Shabble was in the kitchen attached to the Analytical Institute when Pelagius Zozimus was preparing that platter of tolfrigdalakaptiko. Shabble was there listening

to one kitchen slave telling another about the delinquencies of her grandmother's neighbour's daughter's
son, who had run away from home and was living on the
streets as a drummer.

Later, Chegory Guy came into the kitchen to collect
that tolfrigdalakaptiko, and Shabble went with Guy to
the cave where the Hermit Crab lived, and watched as
that formidable monster ate its way though its meal with
a pair of chopsticks which its huge claws handled with
the most exquisite delicacy imaginable.

Olivia Qasaba was present at that same meal, for she
had made herself the Crab's servant. This she had done
in order to have an excuse to associate with Chegory on a
regular basis.

In truth, the Crab needed no services apart from the
regular provision of its meals. The Crab was a philosopher of a singularly unambitious kind, and did very
little apart from sitting still, thinking, and waiting for the
inevitable onslaughts of those human beings who from
time to time (for selfish reasons of their own) would try
to kill it.

However, Olivia had invented a great many jobs for
herself to do. Early on in her service, she had taken to
adorning the Crab with flowers. Daily, she brought fresh
frangipani blooms for the Crab, and glued them to its
carapace (the Crab being possessed of no human-style
ears behind which such flowers might have been stuck).
Later, thinking the Crab in need of some more permanent form of adornment, Olivia went to work with a
stronger kind of glue, and began to cover the Crab with a
mosaic of white marble, cowrie shells, chips of bloodstone, old fish-hooks, brass rings, worn-out cogs from
the Analytical Engine, fragments of blue and yellow
glass and rags of silk.

Thus festooned, the Crab looked more than a little
ridiculous. Olivia was taking a fearful risk, for, had the
Crab resented its transformation, it might have lost its
temper; and in its incontinent rage it could easily have

destroyed Injiltaprajura, if not Untunchilamon as a whole.

But Olivia Qasaba never worried her head about that, because it never occurred to her for even a moment that the Crab might not take kindly to the programme of beautification on which she had embarked. As for Chegory Guy, he never sought to restrain the hand of his beloved Olivia; though surely concern for the common good (if not for Olivia's safety) should have led him to veto her artistic efforts.

Chegory's dereliction of duty – the insouciant manner in which he allowed his true love's whim to endanger his whole world – is easy to understand when we note that he was an Ebrell Islander. The Ebrell Islanders have never been noted for caution, reason or responsibility.

That explains Chegory's actions; or, rather, his inaction. But how are we to account for the fact that Injiltaprajura allowed a feckless Ashdan Lass and a reckless Ebrell Islander to minister to the most powerful and most dangerous entity to be found anywhere west of Yestron and east of Argan?

In explanation of this incongruity, the historian has a duty to explain that everyone else on Untunchilamon was far too scared of the Crab to go anywhere near the thing. And with good reason! Among other things, the Crab had perfected a method for turning people inside out; and such topological rearrangement is compatible with neither sanity nor survival.

So Chegory and Olivia had the Crab to themselves.

Chegory regularly brought the Crab those meals cooked for it by the master chef Pelagius Zozimus, and Chegory relayed to the kitchen any demands the Crab might have with respect to its menu.

And Olivia adorned the Crab in the manner described above, polished the unadorned parts of the Crab's carapace with coconut oil, and persuaded Shabble to act as a globular mirror so the Crab could admire its changed appearance.

26

For her own amusement, Olivia recovered the frail shells of lesser crabs from the shore, and arranged them in niches around the cave 'so you can pretend they're statues of your mummy and daddy and all your brother crabs and sister crabs'. Often she sat beside the Crab, comfortably embraced by Chegory's arms, and made up stories about those lesser crabs, telling of their loves and lusts, their griefs and sorrows, their victories and triumphs, their counters with malicious seagulls and hungry octopuses, their heroic quests and territorial disputes, and their secret love for the great Crab of the island of Jod.

The Ashdan lass also made the Crab a set of wind-chimes out of coconut twine and cards of copper stolen from the Analytical Institute. She even got the Crab its own drum, in case it wanted to participate in the latest youth cult; and, since the Crab had no hands, Olivia got the thing its very own drumstick.

'Or,' she said, 'you could beat it with your chopsticks.'

This should not be taken as implicating Olivia Qasaba herself in active participation in the 'drumming' cult, for there is no evidence that she herself ever beat upon a drum; though it is inevitable that she was sometimes in close proximity to adolescent youths who were 'drum-ming'.

By now the reader may be getting restless, and may be wondering why the historian has chosen to adduce so many trivialities concerning the Crab and its servants.

The answer is that these trivialities are not trivialities at all. Rather, they are important items of evidence which help explain why the Crab, this Power of Powers, played such a slight role in the politics of Injiltaprajura.

The Crab was not one of your active Powers which daily demand homage and sacrifice; which lust for praise, and burn incense, and the flesh of virgins; which build palaces and organize empires; which like to get drunk and be jolly; which collect gold and diamonds and all things rare and precious.

27

No, the Crab was not like that at all.

The Crab was a singularly retiring person, its demands being merely that it be fed at regular intervals and otherwise left in peace. While it was prepared to permit Olivia's ministrations, it had never demanded them, nor did it praise or encourage them. And as for homage, or gold, or virgins, or palaces, or other such materialistic rubbish – why, the Crab had no use whatsoever for any such frivolities.

While this eremitic and philosophical Crab was loathe to take an active claw in Untunchilamon's politics, it was nevertheless manipulated on occasion by the devious Justina Thrug and others – as we shall see in due course.

You will be assisted in seeing this if you will now clear from your field of vision all those distorted images and outright hallucinations practitioners of fiction and even other 'historians', so-called, have brought forward to gratify a debased public taste.

Pay no attention to the gross distortions of Greven Jing, the rambling inaccuracies of Thong Sai Stok, the pretentious pedantry of Morton Plum or the romantic mistiness of the anonymous author of *Untunchilamon: An Account of the Isle of Many Splendours and the Unfortunate Contretemps which Occasioned Sundry Lapses of Public Order and Good Discipline in that Paradigm of Paradise*.

This is the true history of the final days of the rule of Justina Thrug upon the island of Untunchilamon, and it is the only such history which is worth the price of the fooskin upon which it is written.

And remember: your historian was there!

Your historian will not, as a rule, intrude upon this narrative. I will not mention my arthritic fingers, for instance; or the outrageous price of fooskin; nor complain about the racket from the craftshop next door, where, from the sound of it, they are trying to reinvent the skavamareen.

But I will say this:

28

I was on Untunchilamon when the great troubles beset Justina Thrug. I myself have stood upon the balcony of the pink palace atop Pokra Ridge; I myself have looked down Lak Street to the waters of the Laitemata, and across those waters to the island of Jod where the white marble of the Analytical Institute stands like a block of chalk riding atop a bank of congealed blood.

And I have been to those places elsewhere mentioned in this history.

I myself have been to Manamalargo; and have ventured up the River Ka to the city of Bolfrigalaskaptiko. In that city, I myself have sat within a tent of mosquito netting, enjoying a meal of roast crocodile meat while watching a professional child beater clean the blood from his whips. In that same city, I have enjoyed the delights of non-insertive ecstasy in the House Without Fleas.

And, more to the point, I have interviewed many inhabitants of Bolfrigalaskaptiko. Their testimony justifies and supports the claim made in the first chapter of this history:

That Jean Froissart, a man of 32 who was much worried about his heart, left Bolfrigalaskaptiko in the company of Manthandros Trasilika.

The fat and fleshy Manthandros Trasilika planned to sail to Untunchilamon, to land at Injiltaprajura, to declare himself the rightful wazir of the place, to denounce Justina Thrug as a witch, and to order her immediate execution.

But, as stated at the end of the first chapter, the first trouble which would befall Justina Thrug would not come from Manthandros Trasilika but from the Inland Revenue Department; and nothing written above should be taken as altering or modifying that fact.

CHAPTER THREE

The head of the Inland Revenue was Dui Tin Char, a man of much mana and influence. He pretended loyalty to the Family Thrug, but his true loyalties were actually quite elsewhere.

Dui Tin Char was equipped by nature and breeding to take his place in the court of Aldarch the Third, the dreaded Mutilator of Yestron. But it was Tin Char's misfortune to dwell far from Al'three's sphere of influence. For, as our history opens, Aldarch the Third was busy laying waste to the continent of Yestron; whereas Tin Char was marooned upon Untunchilamon, that equatorial island which lies half an ocean away from Yestron.

Untunchilamon.

Island of blood!

Island of—

But we have been through all that. So, enough of the atmospherics. It is time for some solid facts and figures, some honest statistics, and as many of them as possible.

Well then:

Untunchilamon is an equatorial island which lay (and lies still) midocean between the continents of Argan and Yestron. Ships approach from the north, enter Untunchilamon's circumferential lagoon by the Galley Gate, then navigate through a maze of coral to the Laitemata Harbour at the island's southern tip.

On the Laitemata lies Injiltaprajura, Untunchilamon's sole city, a metropolis of some 30,000 souls. Here there is life; and water; and greenery; and mosquitoes by the millions; and caterpillars with stinging legs which sometimes drop from the trees to agonize the necks of the unwary. The rest of Untunchilamon is a wasteland desert known as Zolabrik.

To Injiltaprajura, then, come the ships; and they can only approach that city as described above because the shallows of the Green Sea lie to the south. Canoes can travel the Green Sea, and often do; but a ship would find no water deep enough to permit it a safe passage.

With that clearly stated (your encyclopedia will doubtless supplement this account should you wish to know more) let us return to the matter of Dui Tin Char, head of the Inland Revenue, and his relationship with the Family Thrug.

The Family Thrug had ruled Untunchilamon for seven years. Their rule had begun when civil war broke out in the Izdimir Empire, for Lonstantine Thrug seized his opportunity, overthrew the local governor and installed himself as emperor of this isolated island. In due course, the unfortunate Lonstantine became incapable of discharging the responsibilities of government, and was thereafter succeeded by Justina, the elder of his twin daughters.

While the outcome of Yestron's civil war remained uncertain, none disputed the right of the Family Thrug to rule. But in the seventh year of Talonsklavara (this being the name which dignified the protracted internecine conflicts of the Izdimir Empire), it became increasingly apparent that Aldarch III was likely to triumph. A coup was then launched against Justina by her Master of Law, the albinotic sorcerer Aquitaine Varazchavardan, who had no wish for personal power but who did wish to demonstrate his loyalty to Aldarch Three.

Great was the peril which the Empress Justina then endured, but she survived thanks to the loyalty of many of her subjects and the intervention of the Hermit Crab.

The Hermit Crab, a being with powers at least equal to those of any wizard or sorcerer, dwelt on a small island in the harbour of Untunchilamon's capital city.

31

The Crab took exception to the violent political disputes which had disturbed the peace of its domicile; to restore the peace, the Crab commanded Justina and Varazchavardan to declare a truce and resolve their differences.

This they did.

Had they disobeyed, they would have been turned inside out by a wrathful Crab; therefore the matter of their compliance is scarcely a mystery. Furthermore, the same threat of gross physical disconcertment similarly compelled the compliance of all others on Untunchilamon, at least for the moment; some who thought the Crab could read minds (it could not) almost went mad as they endeavoured to suppress their inner yearnings for the end of the regime of Thrug and the imposition of the rule of Aldarch Three.

However, while peace again prevailed for the moment, the crisis had served to teach Justina a salutary lesson; which was, that her power was almost at an end, and that she would most surely die if she tarried on the island for any longer than was absolutely necessary.

At that time, Untunchilamon lay in the doldrums; for the season of Fistavlir was upon the island, and that season, also known as the Long Dry, is a time when both wind and rain are denied to this equatorial region. Lack of wind means lack of shipping, but for those canoes of the Ngati Moana which travel even during Fistavlir, riding the Coral Current which flows through the shallow and treacherous waters of the Green Sea.

Justina considered making her escape in such a canoe, drifting with the currents through those shallow southern waters which are interdicted to ships of any size and substance. But the dangers of such a voyage were great; the Ngati Moana might well be reluctant to carry her, lest long-term repercussions deny them their favourite trading routes; and such an escape would have been selfish.

Selfish?

Yes.

For a canoe could carry no more than a few passengers, whereas a great number of people stood in danger thanks to their association with Justina – her loyal advisers; her friends; her lovers (a category most definitely plural); her ex-lovers (a body of athletes who could certainly not have been accommodated in but a single canoe); certain of her servants; various Ashdans and Ebrell Islanders; and Aquitaine Varazchavardan himself, now tainted by the protestations of loyalty which the Crab had forced him to make to Justina.

When Justina had made a full list of all those who stood in danger, she concluded that nothing would serve but for her to seize a bare minimum of a dozen ships to carry the endangered ones to foreign shores.

Two problems then confronted her.

First, there were not a dozen ships in the Laitemata Harbour. There were but three, all three imprisoned by the absence of wind. Never mind. The end of Fistavlir would bring the winds, and the winds would bring the Trade Fleet; if Justina had but patience, in time there would be a dozen ships in her net.

However, the second problem was more serious, and was this: when the time came to seize these ships, would her soldiers be for her or against her? Most of Justina's soldiers were not of her own people, the children of Wen Endex; instead, they were grey-skinned Janjuladoola warriors who owed her little love and less loyalty.

The solution?

Bribery.

Injiltaprajura's treasury was rich in gold. And silver. And diamonds, jade, emeralds, ultramarines, opals, japonica, turquoise, celestine, carnelian and so forth; and in coinage, for it boasted dragons and damns by the sackload, dalmoons by the bushel, and a surfeiting overflow of spings, flothens, zeals and ems. The imperial hoard reflected the wealth of Untunchilamon, and Justina was prepared to squander all of it to bribe her soldiers.

The Empress Justina made careful plans along these lines as the season of Fistavlir drew to a close, and she was full of hope by the time the rule of the doldrums finally ended, the Long Dry coming to an end in an outbreak of wind and of rain.

But hope soon changed to something remarkably like despair when the Inland Revenue raided Justina's pink palace.

As has been stated, the head of the Inland Revenue was the redoubtable Dui Tin Char, who had long pretended loyalty to Justina. But Tin Char (so we must name him, for Dui is a personal name, and to refer to him merely by the family name of Tin would be ever so slightly insulting) was of Janjuladoola race like Aldarch the Third. Tin Char longed to see the rule of Aldarch Three triumph on Untunchilamon, and to see Justina and her cohorts punished for their various acts of repression and usurpation.

To give but one example of Tin Char's grievances, he had long lamented the suppression of the rites of his dearly beloved Temple of Torture. Under the reign of Wazir Sin, Tin Char had been a most enthusiastic priest of that temple; when the Family Thrug had outlawed his religion, Tin Char had abandoned the priesthood for the bureaucracy with the specific idea of rising to a place of eminence from which he could exact revenge.

Now Tin Char was eminent indeed.

Treachery, blackmail and poison had made him head of the Inland Revenue in scarcely seven short years, and he was ready to move against the Family Thrug.

But . . .

What would be the reaction of the Hermit Crab?

The potential dangers from this quarter were so great that they gave even Tin Char cause for thought; accordingly, he did not begin by chopping off Justina's head, but contented himself with looting her treasury. His logic was very simple. If the Crab objected, he could always return the treasure and make apologies, whereas decapitation could not be so easily reversed; on the other hand, if the Crab proved compliant, Justina's head could then be removed without trouble.

Tin Char offered immense bribes to Justina's soldiers, who then co-operated with the raid in which every bit of treasure in the pink palace was removed to the premises of the Temple of Torture. The legal pretext for this move was very simple. According to Tin Char, Untunchilamon was still a part of the Izdimir Empire, and Justina Thrug was still a subject citizen of that empire and hence liable to penalties under imperial law; which meant that, as she had paid no taxes for the last seven years, all her assets could be confiscated.

Justina's dismay can easily be imagined.

The winds were blowing; the Trade Fleet would in due course arrive; but she would never get her twelve ships unless she had money for bribes. Unless suitably bribed, her soldiers would prevent her escape: and now Tin Char had all her money.

What was Justina to do?

A direct move against Tin Char was of course impossible. Except for a trifling handful of fanatical Thrug loyalists, Justina's soldiers would rather fight for the Inland Revenue than against it; and, besides, Tin Char had the tacit support of most of Untunchilamon's resident sorcerers.

In the end, Justina realized there was only one thing she could do. She would have to go to the island of Jod, confront the Crab face to face, and register her protest. She knew she might get turned inside out if she thus disturbed the denizen of Jod. But she had no choice in the matter! So she girded her loins (precisely how I do not know, for I am not privy to all the feminine mysteries), summoned certain of her retainers who were both loyal and reliable, then set forth for the island of Jod.

CHAPTER FOUR

The Empress Justina did not allow herself to be carried to the waterfront in a litter. No. She walked down Lak Street on her own two feet. This fact may well amaze some of my readers, particularly if they come from one of those cultures where the wealthy traditionally regard walking as evidence of sin, to the point where the Watch will often arrest and interrogate people solely because they have been caught in an act of perambulation.

But the facts are the facts, and the historian has a duty to record the facts even when they may seem to call the veracity of these annals into question. The truth is that Justina Thrug habitually walked about her city on her own two feet, even though she was an imperial ruler with many slaves at her command; and, unbelievable though this may seem to many of my readers, she actually enjoyed walking.

Here we must remember that Justina Thrug was the daughter of a Yudonic Knight, and hence a child of Wen Endex; and the children of Wen Endex are possessed of a culture which is in many ways singular and unique.

After walking down Lak Street to the waterfront, Justina did not embark upon an outrigger canoe. For a start, she did not like canoes; for she was a fleshy woman, and found the constrictions of such craft nearly intolerable. Besides, she preferred to walk. So, with her loyal and reliable retainers, she strode along the embankment of crushed red coral and broken bloodstone until she came to the harbour bridge, and this she crossed.

Those who accompanied the Empress across the Harbour Bridge to the island of Jod were the corpse-master Uckermark, his woman Yilda, the conjuror Odolo, the lawyer Dardanalti and the bullman Log Jaris.

Notably absent from this expedition was Juliet Idaho, a warrior of unimpeachable loyalty but dubious reliability. Unfortunately, Idaho was a Yudonic Knight who tried to out-knight all other knights real and imaginary, living and dead; and, consequently, he had but small skills as a diplomat. If Idaho had come along, there was a danger he might have attacked the Crab; and such were the Crab's powers that such foolishness would only have served to secure a hero's death for the Yudonic Knight.

As Justina and her trusty few made their way across the harbour bridge, their progress was observed by a number of people. Among these was Threp Sodakik, an innocent fisherman. He was fated to be torn to pieces by sharks, and his relevance to this history is precisely zero, so no more will be said of him.

Other observers included a group of drummers based on four outrigger canoes which were rafted up together in the middle of the Laitemata. Despite the heat and the suffocating humidity, the drummers were pounding their instruments of delusion with an unabated frenzy, sweat drenching from their faces as they did so. For these juvenile delinquents, drumming was life; hence their political impact was zero, and no more will be said of them either.

The Empress Justina was also scrutinized by several of the many spies who those days infested Injiltaprajura. At this time, fear and suspicion had reached such a pitch that virtually every power in the city had its spies, so it is certain that the Empress was under observation. However, as it has proved impossible for the historian to unravel the intricacies of espionage and counter-espionage which played such an important part in the final days of imperial rule on Untunchilamon, nothing more will be said of these spies.

The oncoming band of petitioners was observed from

the Analytical Institute. Artemis Ingalawa (Jon Qasaba's sister-in-law, and hence Olivia Oasaba's aunt) looked up from her work and saw them approaching. But, as the algorithmist's attention was engaged by a complicated problem in binary logic, she returned to her labours and thought no more about it.

Thus it would have appeared to the casual observer that nobody was paying any attention whatsoever to the progress of the imperial party, who might have been mistaken for an idle group of tourists on their way to gawk at the Analytical Engine.

Of course the reality was entirely different.

Many people were watching Justina, either directly or by proxy; and her mission was one of the utmost delicacy, danger and importance, which was why she had very carefully chosen her companions.

The bullman Log Jaris had been brought along precisely because he had the head, horns and fur of a bull, for all that he walked along on two feet like a man. Justina suspected that the Crab knew that many people feared and hated it merely because it was in Crab shape rather than human. Justina personally found the crustacean configuration aesthetically pleasing, but doubted that the Crab would believe her if she simply stated this fact; so, by way of practical demonstration of her lack of prejudice where form was concerned, she was bringing along Log Jaris.

Quite apart from that, Justina was these days going to great lengths to cultivate Log Jaris's acquaintance, because the bullman was an expert on the geography of the mazeways Downstairs. Since Justina might not be able to get off Untunchilamon, she might one day have to flee Downstairs to preserve her own life; in which case, the help of experts such as the bullman would be indispensable.

Yilda had been brought along because Justina had recruited her as a spy, and was setting her many tests of observation and recall. When they got back to the pink

38

palace (presuming they were not eaten or otherwise destroyed by an irritated Crab) the Empress would debrief Yilda and make any recommendations needed to improve the woman's observational talents.

The corpse-master Uckermark, a man richly tattooed and grossly scarred by burns, had been brought along as extra muscle, for he was a handy man in a fight. Justina feared assassins – and with reason – and hence seldom went anywhere without the company of loyal fighting men.

Uckermark was not actually all that loyal.

Furthermore, the Empress Justina knew as much.

She knew Uckermark to be a man very much engaged in the furtherance of his own ends. He was an individual of piratical inclinations, who had once (he did not know she knew, but she knew it right enough) gone so far as to steal Injiltaprajura's precious wishstone on the occasion of a royal banquet. Even so, Justina felt she could safely make use of him, at least for the moment.

Perhaps she was right, perhaps she was wrong, but . . . either way, she had very little choice in the matter. A year ago, she had felt she could trust almost everyone on Untunchilamon. But, since an attempted coup by Aquitaine Varazchavardan, Justina's hold on the affections of her people had become very shaky indeed. Why? Simply because the valuable illusions of invulnerable power which had long supported the reign of the Family Thrug had been rudely shattered.

These days, all Injiltaprajura knew that Justina Thrug ruled only by the good graces of the Crab, which had intervened to restore her to the throne after Varazchavardan's coup. Injiltaprajura knew too that, were the Thrug to lose the Crab's support, she would swiftly be overthrown by the wonderworkers of the Cabal House, or the Inland Revenue, or her own soldiers, or a priestly conspiracy acting in the name of the Izdimir Empire, or by some whim of the mob.

With Justina went Dardanalti, the lawyer who had

first entered her life on the recommendation of Log Jaris.

Also with the Empress was the conjuror Odolo, whom she brought along for the sole purpose of confusing her enemies. She knew her enemies wasted much time and effort wondering (and seeking to discover precisely) what dark part the ever-present conjuror played in the imperial power plays. The mundane truth (a truth which the imperial enemies never suspected) was that Odolo was no more than he appeared to be, that is to say, an entertainer and a personal friend of the Empress.

(And in this connection let us say that the olive-skinned Odolo is not to be confused with the professional jester or fool whom you will find at many courts imperial, for the Empress Justina had no need for such; she was her own fool, and maintained a sense of proportion without the professional assistance of a jester.)

On reaching the island of Jod, the Empress Justina conducted her expeditionary force to the cave where Chegory Guy and Olivia Qasaba were attending to the needs of the Crab.

When discovered by the Empress, Chegory and Olivia were locked together in a close embrace. Given the heat of the day, this embrace must have been extremely uncomfortable; and, as the mouths of those two young people were in intimate communication, it must have been rather difficult for them to breathe. Perhaps this combination of this discomfort and difficulty accounts for the fact that both were distinctly heard to be moaning.

For its own part, the Crab was doing very little. To be more precise, it was doing precisely nothing; and looked for all the world like a statue of itself.

Justina was startled to see the chips of glass, the rags of silk and other junk collaged across the Crab's carapace. The Empress did not receive regular intelligence reports on the hermit of Jod because fear made people give the thing the widest berth possible. It was the imperial startlement which prompted her first question:

'Blood of the Gloat! What has happened to you?'

'What has happened to me?' said the Crab. 'I appear to have been disturbed by a crowd of uninvited visitors led by the daughter of a Yudonic Knight. That is what has happened to me.'

'That's not what I meant,' said Justina. 'I meant – oh, never mind. I have to talk to you about something important.'

'Nothing is important,' said the Crab.

Whether the Crab really believed this is a moot point, and my own opinion is that it did not. However, rather than arguing the point, Justina began to pour out her sorrows. She told the Crab all about the depredations of Dui Tin Char and the uncertainties which now attended her grip on life and power alike.

While Justina was thus lecturing the Crab, a juvenile delinquent arrived to see what had drawn this great crowd to the domicile of Injiltaprajura's most distinguished eremite. The delinquent was Shabble.

'Hello,' said Shabble brightly. 'What's going on?'

'Hush,' said Chegory Guy, who had ceased his slow-motion wrestling with the delectable Olivia Qasaba.

'But why?' said Shabble.

To this, Chegory made no answer.

So Shabble drifted closer.

'. . . and after all,' said the Empress Justina, 'it was you who imposed the present peace upon Injiltaprajura. When Dui Tin Char moves against the pink palace, that's really an offence against your dignity.'

'Dignity,' said the Crab heavily, 'is a vanity. I am not partial to the vanities.'

'There's more to it than questions of vanity,' said the Empress, with a note of desperation in her voice.

And she went on to elaborate.

While the Empress was elaborating, an ant of the red

and biting kind (a very Ebrell Islander in its humours) was doing its best to circumnavigate Shabble's surface. As Shabble had temporarily made Shabbleself a mirror, this surface reflected the tense and anxious spectators, notably the hard-bitten Yilda (a woman somewhere between the ages of forty and sixty), the corpse-master Uckermark (he of the many tattoos) and the conjuror Odolo (he of the olive skin and the hooked nose).

Shabble, who was no respecter of persons (or of much else, for that matter) rubbed Shabbleself against Justina's neck in order to be rid of the ant. This was a merciful way to dispose of this nuisance, since Shabble could just as easily have heated Shabbleself until the ant was burnt alive, or (alternatively) could have made Shabbleself's surface as cold as ice (or colder), thus freezing the poor thing.

Unfortunately the insect, when let loose upon the neck imperial, failed to appreciate either the honour which had been done to it or the dangers of its present position; and, irritated or enraged by some ant-style emotions which it is beyond the power of the historian to elucidate, the small hymenopterous insect launched a sanguinary assault upon the mistress of the pink palace.

Now it happens that Justina Thrug was great in mercy; and, had she realized that she was under attack from such a source, she might have asked Yilda or Log Jaris to remove the thing. But such was the stress of the moment that Justina merely brushed the beast away, crushing it without consciously realizing she had felt the thing bite her.

'. . . and,' said Justina, 'given your help, I could secure ships sufficient to remove myself and my supporters from Untunchilamon for ever. All I need is help sufficient to maintain my power until the Trade Fleet comes.'

'Why should I help you?' said the Crab.

'Out of mercy,' said Justina.

And Shabble said, brightly:

'I've found a cockroach.'

Nobody took any notice.

'I will be eternally grateful for any help you give me,' said the Empress Justina, still speaking to the Crab.

'You will not live for eternity,' said the Crab. 'You will be lucky if you live another forty years. Your rhetoric is empty.'

'Forty years is hardly emptiness,' said Justina.

'It's a big cockroach,' said Shabble.

Still poor Shabble was ignored.

Shabble tried again.

'He's—'

'Quiet!' said Chegory Guy, addressing himself to Shabble.

'Chegory has given you a very wise command,' said the Crab, pretending it thought the Ebrell Islander had been addressing the Empress Justina.

Chegory blushed furiously.

And Shabble said:

'He's hiding under a rock. He has to hide there because there's nowhere safe for him to go.'

'Yes,' said Justina, at last turning her wrath upon the floating bubble of brightness, 'but there's plenty of places both safe and unsafe for you to go. Leave us!'

Such was the imperial anger that Shabble sideslipped through the air and hid behind Odolo. Shabble, as cold as chilled crystal, pressed Shabbleself against the conjuror's neck and whispered:

'Please won't you help me. With my cockroach, I mean.'

'Shabble!' said Odolo, with a note of warning in his voice.

'As I was saying,' said the Empress Justina, a note of stridency entering her voice. 'Dui Tin Char is—'

'I know what Dui Tin Char is doing,' said the Crab. 'You've told me twice and thrice already.'

Then one of the Crab's huge claws opened. Then closed. With a crunch. This was a danger sign.

'I think,' said Chegory Guy, pulling Olivia to her feet, 'that, um, you'd be more private without us, all you, um, ah, politicians and people.'

Without further ado, the Ebrell Islander and the Ashdan lass absquatulated. The corpse-master Uckermark, the least reliable member of Justina's expeditionary force, sensed danger, and wished himself elsewhere.

'My cockroach,' said the plaintive Shabble. 'Won't anyone help me with my cockroach?'

Not having any desire to be turned inside out by a wrathful Crab, Uckermark seized his opportunity to escape:

'All right, my friend,' said Uckermark. 'Let's go and see this cockroach of yours.'

Then he looked at Yilda. And she, realizing the reasons for Uckermark's decision, made her apologies to her Empress and followed her mate and the free-floating Shabble.

'So,' said the Empress Justina, 'it seems my people wish to desert me. Very well! Be gone, the lot of you! Off you go! Now! Vanish!'

Thus spoke Justina, driving her people from her despite their protests. She too had realized that the Crab was on the verge of doing something unfortunate.

Once the crowd had left, the Crab seemed to calm down a little. At least it stopped claw-crunching. So Justina ventured to say:

'All I'm asking is a very little favour. I'm asking you to bring Dui Tin Char into line, that's all.'

'I am no longer interested in your politics,' said the Crab. 'If you haven't paid your taxes that's your problem, not mine.'

'But I'm the Empress!' protested Justina. 'I don't have to pay taxes.'

'I have heard that legal opinion is divided on the matter,' said the Crab. 'In any case, I am no longer interested. Go away, leave me alone.'

Further argument convinced Justina that this entity

was speaking the truth. The Hermit Crab had entered one of those deep depressions to which it was prone; it wished nothing more than to be left alone and in peace. Justina did her best to rouse the Crab's interest, appealing to its pride, curiosity, vanity and fear, to its philanthropic inclinations and its desire for human fellowship. All to no avail.

For many millennia, the Crab had pursued a policy of quietism; it seldom intervened in human politics, which it had found singularly unrewarding, for the greatest labours in that field of endeavour are likely to be undone overnight by the thoughtless violence of the mob or the cunning machinations of unscupulous power-seekers. Justina was battling against habits deeply entrenched over the centuries, and she was losing. At last the Empress Justina withdrew in confusion.

'Well?' said Log Jaris, when the Empress met up with her expeditionary force at the steps of the Analytical Institute.

'It's no good,' said Justina. 'The Crab won't help us.'

Then she looked around and said:

'Where's Uckermark? And Yilda?'

'Still with Shabble,' said Odolo. 'And Shabble's cockroach.'

'That Shabble!' said the Empress. 'Can Shabble help us?'

'Shabble,' said Odolo, 'is notoriously difficult to work with. But I suggest we . . . I suggest we work on the problem.'

45

CHAPTER FIVE

In the days that followed, the Empress Justina and the conjuror Odolo did work very hard on the problem of converting Shabble to their cause; but unexpected difficulties supervened, and their best efforts met with failure.

Then the Empress Justina despaired of her life.

She had virtually no power of any description at her disposal, and the power of her enemies was great. At the moment, her enemies feared her to be protected by the Crab. That fear was restraining them. But the illusion of such protection surely could not be maintained for ever.

While Justina did truly despair, this condition did not last long, for the Empress was possessed of a strong streak of constitutional optimism. After a secret conference with Log Jaris, Dardanalti and other advisers, she initiated an extremely dangerous strategy, risking the total destruction of Injiltaprajura.

Justina Thrug said nothing directly to Tin Char, and refused to speak to the head of the Inland Revenue when he asked for an audience so they could discuss 'the matter of your unpaid taxes'.

While Dui Tin Char tried to persuade his allies to launch a direct assault on the pink palace, Justina arranged for the Crab to be tormented most unmercifully. At her instigation, parties of school children toured the island of Jod, with a visit to the lair of the Crab being the highpoint on their itinerary. Since the Crab was known to have an aversion to bells, Justina arranged for a bell-swinging ghost to walk that island thrice nightly. As the Crab was a dedicated gourmet, its personal chef – the eminent Pelagius Zozimus – was poisoned with opium then kidnapped, and held incommunicado in a helpless drug stupor.

If there was one person who possessed a degree of empathy with the Crab, one person who could possibly be thought of as a friend of that entity, then that was the Ebrell Islander Chegory Guy. But Justina removed young Chegory from the Crab's presence by the simple expedient of commanding him to her bed then keeping him there. Chegory's abrupt disappearance left the delectable Olivia Qasaba quite hysterical. She retired to the Dromdanjerie, where she took to her bed and wept as if the world were ending.

That left the Crab completely alone in the world.

Meanwhile, Justina arranged for a series of conflicting rumours and ambiguous documents (variously marked SECRET, TOP SECRET, MOST URGENTLY SECRET, EYES ONLY, BURN AFTER READING and BURN UNREAD) to be leaked to Dui Tin Char. She then told her sister Theodora (in the greatest confidence) that the Crab planned to boil Tin Char alive when the Trade Fleet arrived, and was only permitting him to live so he would still be available for this ceremony. As Justina had expected, this intelligence was common knowledge in less than three days.

Naturally, Dui Tin Char took fright at this intelligence.

But Tin Char was no coward, and hence did not commandeer a canoe and flee from Untunchilamon forthwith.

So what were his other options?

He could have sat tight and done nothing.

Had he done so, then a messenger would have arrived bearing a summons (ostensibly from the aforesaid Crab) commanding Tin Char to the presence of that dignitary, thus precipitating a confrontation between two great Powers.

As it happened, no such subterfuge was necessary. For Tin Char was true to his courage. He thought Justina

Thrug might be feeding him lies in an effort to scare him off Untunchilamon; so, taking his life in his hands, he went to the island where the Hermit Crab dwelt, meaning to ask that dignitary what the truth was.

Justina had expected as much.

The timing was perfect.

By the time Dui Tin Char ventured to Jod, the Crab was in the worst of moods imaginable. Its companions had deserted it; in place of gourmet meals it was being fed buckets of slops; its sleep had been disturbed nightly by bells; it had been brought close to murder by the attentions of giggling schoolchildren.

When Tin Char arrived, the Crab refused to communicate with the head of the Inland Revenue. That courageous individual continued to pester the continent one. The Crab told Tin Char to go away, for such importunate attentions were unwelcome in the extreme. Tin Char did not go away. The Crab lost its temper.

The Crab did not turn Tin Char inside out. (To Justina's great disappointment. She had been certain that this would be the minimum misfortune which would befall her enemy.) Instead, the Crab merely exerted a fraction of its power, causing Tin Char to be set upon his backside. Then, as the head of the Inland Revenue staggered to his feet, the Crab caused Tin Char's arms to be forced backwards and upwards.

Until both shoulders were dislocated.

At that, Tin Char fled the island. Or, to put it more precisely, he staggered over the harbour bridge which led from the island of Jod to the mainland of Untunchilamon, and was carried from there to the Temple of Torture.

Tin Char then gave urgent orders, and the contents of the treasure (minus certain irretrievable bribes which had been paid out to Justina's soldiery) were returned to the pink palace forthwith.

This incident had a very salutary effect, for it led most people on Untunchilamon to believe that Justina Thrug truly did have the Crab on her side. Respect for her increased enormously. But Justina and her trusted advisers knew the dreadful truth. The Crab's brief-lived interest in the politics of Injiltaprajura had ceased; it was no longer an ally but a neutral power. If this secret were to get out, then Tin Char would surely have no hesitation in slaughtering Justina immediately.

However, at least Justina once again had her money.

At least she could still hope to bribe her soldiers when the time came to seize her dozen ships.

But, for the moment, there were not a dozen ships to seize. There were only the same three, the three which had sat in the Laitemata throughout Fistavlir. And, as the days went by and no new ships manifested themselves, Justina began to consider a dreadful possibility: what if, this year of all years, the Trade Fleet never came?

The Empress Justina was not the only one considering dreadful possibilities. The Hermit Crab had dislocated Tin Char's shoulders. It indicated that the Crab was not pleased with him. That he could live with. But . . . what if the Crab was seriously angry with him? Tin Char brooded about the possible consequences of such anger as he lay awake at nights listening to the disconsolate drumming of a group of adolescents, the drums of their cult singing thus:

Tok – tok – tuk. Tok – tok – tuk. Tok – tok – tukata tok. Tok – tok – tuk. Tok – tok – tuk. Tok – tok – tukata tok.

Ah yes.

I remember.

Night.

Night, hot night, with the bloodstone of Untunchilamon clotted to absolute black. The shimmering stars reflected by the sharktooth silence of the black lagoon. The hulking shadow of a ship looming dark against the doom-black waters of the Laitemata. A brief burst of hubbub as the heavy soundproof door of a speakeasy swings open. That noise abruptly silenced. No noise now but the drums. The drums throbbing through the heat.

The heat!

The heat of Injiltaprajura, a moist enfolding heat, a sweating embrace, smelling of armpits and coconut musk, of woodsmoke and rotting drains. A positively vaginal heat. Heat, yes, and the mosquitoes whining through deliriums of dark, and the relentless punctuation of the drums speaking of the oppressions of the present, the past and the future . . .

CHAPTER SIX

To know of the Crab, and to know of the Crab's crucial role in the affairs of Injiltaprajura, is to know much. The historian believes that the ruling dynamic of those affairs has now been explicated: while Justina's enemies believed the Crab to be on her side, they would obey her; but, once they realized that she had in fact been deprived of such protection, they would fall upon her and overwhelm her.

Justina's problem, then, was threefold:

First, to maintain the illusion that she was still supported by the Crab;

Second, to avoid death at the hands of assassins and such until the arrival of the Trade Fleet;

Third, to seize the ships of that Fleet and thus make her escape.

All this is very easily stated.

Bu of course the realities are somewhat more complex, because there did not in fact exist a clear-cut division between 'Justina Thrug and her allies' and 'Justina's enemies'.

Rather, there were many shades of political affiliation and intention within Injiltaprajura; and to explain fully the political complexities of the last days of the reign of the Empress Justina, it would be necessary for the historian to analyse the thoughts and actions of all 30,000 of the inhabitants of Injiltaprajura. Some mention might also have to be made of the interactions between those individuals and the animals which then inhabited Untunchilamon's capital, the said animals consisting of 1,946 monkeys, 3,101 pigs, 6,429 dogs, 10,111 snakes, 17,942 cats, 30,000 people, 246,995 vampire rats, 456,831,887 mosquitoes, and numbers of billipedes, millipedes, centipedes, scorpions and other creatures.

When one considers the difficulties attendant upon the exercise thus suggested, one must surely allow the historian the right to generalize upon occasion. On occasion? It is more reasonable to say that generalization must be the rule, and particularization the exception; else the creation of this account will become impossible for logistic reasons alone, the historian being a mortal creature with strictly limited supplies of ink, pens and fooskin at his disposal.

A generalization, then:

It was a quiet, peaceful day on Untunchilamon, where Frangoni was having intercourse with Dub, and Dub with Janjuladoola, and Janjuladoola with Toxteth, and Toxteth with Ashmarlan, and Ashmarlan with Slandolin, without any sign of riot or civil disturbance.

Even so, it was not, of course, quiet and peaceful for everyone.

It was not, for example, peaceful for the conjuror Odolo, who was having yet another painfully frank interview with his bank manager. Nor was it quiet and peaceful for Threp Sodakik, a hapless fisherman, who was being torn to pieces by sharks in the lagoon waters just south of Island Scimitar. Others embroiled in turmoil, strife and barrat include Yilda, the mate of the corpse-master Uckermark, for Yilda was busy driving a group of teenaged drummers from her doorstep with the help of a gutting knife and a kraken club.

As for the Princess Sabitha, why, she had been kidnapped – snatched in the streets by a group of adolescent drummers from Marthandorthan – and was being held in a captivity which she bitterly resented.

(Do not worry. The princess will escape, even though this history will not chronicle the event; and we will meet her later in these pages, and find her aristocratic beauty unmarred and her matchless hauteur as imposing as ever.)

52

Furthermore, if we were to attempt an exhaustive catalogue of those currently unquiet and unpeaceful, we would have to mention the bullman Log Jaris, who was arguing with the drug dealer Firfat Labrat about the question of alleged non-payment of certain beer-buying debts; and Ox No Zan, who was thrashing and screaming in his sleep as he endured nightmares in which Doctor Death the dentist played a prominent role; and Dolglin Chin Xter, who was struggling to stay alive as hepatitis and malaria did their best to overwhelm him; and the market gardener Pa Po Pep who was staring at a chancre on his shaft and wondering if it was syphilis (it was, and in due course he would die of it); and Dunash Labrat, who was berating his son Ham for misplacing his favourite bee-smoking pot.

And other individuals could be mentioned, for the above list is far from complete.

However, if the historian can be allowed a generalization:

It was a quiet, peaceful day on Untunchilamon. It was quietest and most peaceful of all in those parts of Untunchilamon which were uninhabited; but even the most populous region of the island was tranquil and unagitated. That most populous region was of course Injiltaprajura, the city to be found (then and now) on the Laitemata Harbour at the southern end of the island.

It was a quiet, peaceful day on Untunchilamon, and it was also hot.

It was a hot day?

It was a day on Untunchilamon, so what else could it have been if not hot?

It was a hot day, and Master Ek was in a bad mood.

But it was not the sweating humidity which had put Master Ek in a bad mood, nor the restless night occasioned by the repeated onslaughts of vampiric insects which had taken advantage of a tear in his mosquito net.

Nor was it the drumming, the relentless drumming of the discontented adolescents of Injiltaprajura.

Ah, the drums! The drums!

Tok – tok – thuk! Tok – tok – thuk . . . !

The drums!

Tok – tok – thuk! Tok – tok – thuk . . . !

Mesmeric pulse of monomania and menace.

Tok – tok – thuk! Tok – tok – thuk . . . !

The horror! The horror!

Dui Tin Char, head of the Inland Revenue, felt the pulse of those infernal instruments in the marrow of his bones as he tried to sleep by day after a sleepless night. The bull-man Log Jaris heard those drums as he (having finished his argument with the drug dealer Firfat Labrat) quit the Xtokobrokotok and stumped away through the streets of Marthandorthan. The inimitable Yilda heard those drums as she looked for blood on the kraken club she had used to such good effect; for, though she had driven a pack of drummers from her doorstep, they had not gone far, and were drumming again just around the corner.

Tok – tok – thuk! Tok – tok – thuk . . . !

Tok – tok – toketa – toketa – toketa – tok!

Will they not stop that infernal noise? Will they not—

But enough of this atmospheric backgrounding! It is totally irrelevant to our present purpose, which is to introduce Master Ek into this history; and the reason it is irrelevant is that Nadalastabstala Banraithanchumun Ek heard those drums not at all.

Not because he was deaf.

But because the drums were not there to be heard.

Not where he was.

And where was he?

Why, he was exactly where we would expect to find him; which is to say, he was in his house on Hojo Street, that road which follows the line of Pokra Ridge. That thoroughfare was the site of Injiltaprajura's prime real estate. Naturally the pink palace is there. Also, Aquitaine Varazchavardan had a villa there. And a great many temples were there located. And adolescent drummers were not to be found anywhere along that road, for temples and villa-keepers alike had servants with sticks who were quite prepared to sally forth to assault any drummer should a single 'tok – tok – tuk' or 'tok – tok – thuk' be heard.

So, while it is disappointing to have to abandon the attractively melodramatic line which we began to develop so nicely above, the historian must favour truth over drama; and the fact is that Master Ek was singularly untroubled by drums or by drummers. First, because there was none to be heard anywhere near his house. And second because, if the truth be told, Ek rather liked drums; and, when they were to be heard, Ek found their rhythms comforting rather than disturbing.

So we must seek elsewhere for the source of Ek's discomfort.

After seeking elsewhere, the historian presents the world with the following datum: the proximate cause of the discontent experienced by Nadalastabstala Banraithanchumun Ek was the Empress Justina's undisturbed enjoyment of life, health and liberty.

'The female Thrug is a witch.'

So said Master Ek, whose audience consisted of selected members of Injiltaprajura's Cabal House. These individuals listened with every appearance of attentive respect; and in this case appearances were not at all deceptive. Ek was not a prepossessing figure, for he was a gnarled and diminutive man with age-twisted features and hunched shoulders; nevertheless, he was one of the most dangerous power brokers on Untunchilamon, and hence was comfortably seated while the sorcerers stood before him like supplicants or penitents.

'Not only is she a witch,' continued Ek, 'she is monstrous in her habits and her appetites.'

While Ek did not specify the object of his displeasure, all knew that he referred to Justina Thrug, and not to her libidinous twin sister Theodora.

'She must,' continued Ek, 'be killed.'

The assembled sorcerers received this in silence. Their apparent apathy was encouraged by the stifling heat of the day. The end of the Long Dry had been marked by the advent of strenuous winds, which on some days had reached gale force; but today there was no wind but for a shuffling waffling breeze which merely served to shunt the air from one corner of the room to the next.

The room in question was large and high-gabled; it occupied the entire upper storey of Master Ek's mansion atop Pokra Ridge, and afforded outlookers with the most marvellous views. Today nobody had any appetite for those views.

'If no action is taken against the female Thrug,' said Ek, 'then Aldarch the Third will no doubt display his displeasure in due course. It is known that inertia annoys him. This is but one of the reasons why the Thrug must be killed.'

'Do you order as much?' said one of the wonder-workers from the Cabal House.

A foolish question, which Master Ek did not bother to answer. He was not going to order anyone to murder the Thrug. Not when the Hermit Crab might take exception to such orders. The misfortune which had befallen Dui Tin Char lay some time in the past; Tin Char's dislocated shoulders were once again functional. Nevertheless, nobody had forgotten what had been done to the head of the Inland Revenue. And tales of people who had in the past been turned inside out were also fresh in the minds of Injiltaprajura's inhabitants.

'There is,' said another of the sorcerers, 'the matter of the protector who guarantees Justina's flesh.'

This was of course an oblique reference to the dangers posed by the Crab.

'Forgive me if I am mistaken,' said Ek, 'but I have heard that the Thrug's protector lives on the island of Jod. Unless my informants are mistaken, its primary interest in life is its belly. Apart from that, it wishes only

56

solitude and silence. Are those modest needs so difficult to guarantee?'

'If I may venture to say so,' ventured one of the bolder sorcerers, 'the Crab is not amenable to bribery.'

'What I meant,' said Ek, 'is that it displays remarkably little curiosity. It has no spies and agents. It receives no reports. It listens to no gossip. It eats. It meditates. One may presume it also defecates. That is the sum of its existence.'

'So?'

'Are you familiar,' said Ek, 'with the principle of quarantine?'

He smiled, showing black teeth. Then he fumbled with a small and equally black pouch. His gnarled, arthritic fingers opened it with difficulty and extracted a quantity of tobacco, an addictive narcotic herb personally imported by Ek at immense expense. The Janjuladoola grey of his fingers, darkened already by liver spots, was further stained with the yellow-orange of nicotine, one of the minor symptoms of this rare addiction.

'Do you propose . . .'

So began one of the wonder-workers, but a look from Master Ek silenced him. Ek wished to propose nothing. He desired the wonder-workers to do their own thinking; he sought to avoid taking explicit responsibility for generating Crab-defeating stratagems, lest the Crab some day call him to account for his misdemeanours.

Ek rolled himself a 'cigarette', which is a quantity of tobacco compressed by finger-strength and rolled in a tube of paper. Standing by Ek's chair was a tri-table, one of the notoriously rickety and unstable pieces of furniture favoured by Janjuladoola culture; this civilization considers the gross bulk of the earth to be unclean, hence scorns any object which is or which appears to be solidly rooted to the earth. Atop the tri-table was a casket of green bamboo. Ek opened this, withdrew a hot coal with a pair of soot-tipped tweezers, blew upon the coal until it glowed cherry-red, then lit his cigarette.

While Master Ek smoked, the wonder-workers considered the possibility of placing the island of Jod under quarantine. It was certainly not impossible. A quarantine would cut off all news to the Crab; and, providing its suspicions were not aroused, those forces loyal to Aldarch Three could do as they wished with the monstrous Thrug.

'One anticipates,' said one of the sorcerers carefully, 'that meticulously planned quarantine regulations could resolve many of our present difficulties.'

'However,' said another, 'there is a danger that a certain person will escape justice before such quarantine measures could be put in place.'

Ek smoked impassively. A casual observer might have thought that the nicotine of his addiction had somehow succeeded in staining his eyes, for these were a pale orange strangely flecked with green. However, this oddity had a genetic foundation. Ek was a mutant, though his divergence from the Janjuladoola norm began and ended with his eyes. He had never passed on this trait, and indeed was doomed to die without progeny; which was unfortunate, since those eyes had proved their superiority by retaining their acuteness right into his old age.

(Ek was seventy. Is this old age? His flesh would answer in the affirmative. And, while many of the old complain that they inwardly feel as fresh as they did at twenty, Ek himself felt worn, weary and infinitely ancient.)

While Ek thus smoked, his audience waited in an uncomfortable silence. Ek's strategic silence tempted them to take further risks, to propose plots, schemes and conspiracies; but even the boldest spirits amongst the wonder-workers felt they had dared sufficient dangers already.

Ek pursed his lips, as if to speak. The sorcerers waited for revelation. Ek blew a smoke-ring.

'Thrug,' said one of the sorcerers, pushed into speech by the tensions generated by silence, 'may escape.'

58

Ek stared at him through a haze of grey smoke. Slowly, slowly, the curling-coiling smoke dissipated. Ek outbreathed again, once more veiling his face.

'She may escape,' continued the sorcerer, 'because her tame wizard is building her a ship. A special ship. An airship, we believe. It looks like a – a bird's nest. It is being constructed atop the pink palace.'

The end of Ek's cigarette glowed red as he drew upon it. A crinkling brown line moved fractionally, eating its way down the cigarette. Ek breathed out, studied the lengthening ash at the end of his cigarette, tapped the ash into a clam shell, coughed harshly, spat, then said:

'Priests have no powers. No temporal powers. That may change. When Aldarch the Third triumphs in Talonsklavara, it may change with remarkable rapidity. For the moment we priests merely watch. What others do is their business. But what they do and what they do not will be noted. Noted and remembered. In time.'

At the conclusion of this speech, Ek folded his hands in his lap and studied the sorcerers assembled in his presence. Studied them as if he were committing their faces to memory. He had given them a clear message. He had not told them to move against Justina Thrug; fear of the Crab had restrained him, though the letter of the law was his excuse. But he had given them clear warning that he would remember everything they did or did not do.

And, in due course, would give evidence.

'Go,' said Ek. 'You are dismissed.'

The sorcerers made reverence to Master Ek then departed with troubled minds. Ek had made his wishes clear. They were to move against Justina Thrug. Furthermore, he had indicated how it could be done without arousing the wrath of the Crab; a meticulously maintained cordon sanitaire around the island of Jod would suffice to keep the Crab in ignorance. As for the question of the flying ship, that was something for the sorcerers to attend to themselves.

It could be done.

But the prospect of a head-on clash with Justina and her allies was scarcely something the wonder-workers welcomed, for they feared her abilities greatly, and suspected that moves against her might well compromise their own health and happiness.

Not to mention their lives.

As the sorcerers departed, the idling winds strengthened to a purposive breeze which held the promise of better things yet to come; but this good omen failed to lift the spirits of those upon whom Ek had laid such a heavy burden.

While Master Ek had been conducting his lengthy and theatrical audience with certain senior wonder-workers, a much younger and comparatively inexperienced sorcerer, Nixorjapretzel Rat by name, had been waiting for a personal interview with Ek. When Ek dismissed the wonder-workers, Rat heard them depart, their footsteps clunking down the stairs on the southern side of the house, their querulous voices raised in unintelligible conversation which faded out of earshot as they trooped along Hojo Street.

But Rat himself was not called to Ek's presence.

Instead, he was left to stew.

Nixorjapretzel Rat was sitting on a chair. The chair was on a verandah. This shaded portico was on the northern side of Master Ek's mansion atop Pokra Ridge, and afforded the outlooker with a view across Master Ek's back garden, across a steeply descending slope largely given over to market gardens, and then across a great many leagues of the wastelands of Zolabrik.

Nixorjapretzel Rat had scant appetite for the view.

Another desire temporarily dominated his existence.

Nixorjapretzel Rat wished to urinate.

This urge possessed him sixty times a day, though until the present troubles he had scarcely needed to relieve himself more than twice or thrice between the sounding of the sun bells and bat bells. Young Nixorjapretzel had already taken himself off to a quack, who had pronounced him the victim of boblobdidobaltharbi (for which read nervous enuresis). The quack had recommended a long holiday combined with a programme of massage and sunbathing. Unfortunately Rat had no time for a holiday, had suffered a slipped disk on his first and only visit to a professional masseur, and already endured regrettable side effects as a result of his exposure to the sun.

'Excuse me,' said Rat to a passing servant, 'is there a place where I might avail myself of the second minor pleasure?'

The grey-skinned servant expressed incomprehension in the Janjuladoola manner; that is to say, he raised his hands to nipple-height and twiddled his fingers.

'Have you no ears?' said Rat, mortally offended.

It happened that Nixorjapretzel Rat was of the Janjuladoola people. Not only was he of that race: he also had the honour of having been born in Obooloo itself. While he had dwelt in the cold and mountainous realms of Ang, his skin had always displayed the luxuriant grey which was his birthright. But Untunchilamon's harsh and relentless sun had wrought curious changes in his pigmentation, giving his skin a slightly reddish tinge. In consequence, young Nixorjapretzel was sometimes mistaken for an Ebrell Islander, which led members of the Superior Race to pretend that his efforts to speak the Superior Tongue fell short of comprehension.

The servant twiddled his fingers some more. Then departed. Rat raised his hands, pointed in the direction of the retreating racist, and muttered:

'Vo. Vo bigamo. Vo bigamo skoreeth. Japata!'

On an instant, the back of the servant's shirt disintegrated into a mass of seething colours. The servant cast a startled glance at Rat. Then fled. Leaving a cloud of harlequin butterflies flicker-floating in the air. Nixorjapretzel Rat was somewhat disappointed, for he had

61

meant the servant to be incinerated on the spot. On reflection, though, the sorcerer was inclined to be glad that his magic had gone wrong, for Master Ek might have been annoyed had one of his servants been reduced to a heap of smouldering ashes, and Ek's annoyance might swiftly have proved lethal for Rat.

The butterflies scattered on the ship-shifting winds now blowing across the city of Injiltaprajura. The same winds stirred through the shrubbery of the gardens of Mansion Ek; but with much reduced force, since walls sheltered those gardens. In those gardens, some thin and stunted sprite bamboo struggled for survival. This cold-climate plant had been imported to Ang from the northern continent of Tameran; it thrived in the cold uplands which surrounded Obooloo, but barely survived in Untunchilamon's realms of fever heat and sunstroke. Still, Master Ek's gardeners did their best to make the plant grow, for it was greatly prized for its grey foliage.

The paltry plantings of sprite were overtopped by luxuriant stands of fist-thick green bamboos native to the tropics. The tight-furled spears of fresh upthrusts of green spoke of fervent growth, of prodigal fecundity, of life imbued with a positively copulatory passion. Such brazen spear-thrust lust roused uneasy thoughts in the fidgeting Rat, who had committed himself to celibacy for fear of contracting some of the lethal venereal diseases which ran rife amongst Untunchilamon's population.

Standing clear of both species of bamboo were plantings of banana trees, their broad leaves shredded to fronds by recent fraughts of bad weather. Like the bamboos, they too yielded to the whims of the light-lilting flirts and quirks of wind which stooped beneath the guardian walls; but the paw-paw trees, on the other hand, seemed to dwell in a different climate, for their close-stacked leaves were reluctant to answer to such cajolery. As for the lone needle-rose, pride and joy of Master Ek's gardener, that spine-spiked monstrosity remained stubbornly immobile; for no freak of weather could move a needle-rose, not the occasional whisper-winds of Fistavlir nor the massed force of those full-fledged hurricanes which sometimes (once a century on average) descended upon the city of Injiltaprajura.

Nixorjapretzel Rat began to contemplate a quick expedition down to the garden so he could piss upon the needle-rose, or hide himself in among the banana trees and relieve himself in their comparative privacy. While he vacillated, the opportunity was lost, for Master Ek at last put in an appearance.

'Jan Rat,' said Ek. 'How nice that you could put in an appearance.'

At that, Master Ek smiled. His smile was not a pretty one, for his teeth were blackened by the mercury treatment used in Obooloo to cure syphilis. To cure? In a manner of speaking. Statistically, the outcome is that one-third are cured, one-third are killed and one-third are left half-dead from mercury poisoning but with the vibrant life of their affliction unaffected.

'I came as soon as I could,' said Rat.

'I'm sure you did, Jan Rat.'

Young Nixorjapretzel was already intensely irritated by Ek's use of the slighting 'Jan', a Janjuladoola title properly applied only to children. But he durst not complain, for he was in the presence of the most powerful and most dangerous man on Untunchilamon. So he said:

'My Master knows I am ever at his service.'

'You claim to read my mind, do you?' said Ek. 'Are you always so free in taking liberties with your superiors?'

'I meant no offence,' said Rat, taking a backward step.

He bumped against an amphora seated upon a rickety tri-table just behind him. The amphora fell, shattered, scattering a mix of pulped paw-paw and mashed banana across the verandah. With many protestations of innocence and apology, a grovelling Rat began to clean up the soft and slushy mess, or at least to try to.

63

'Stop that,' said Master Ek impatiently. 'Sit! There, in that chair! Sit, and do nothing.'

Nixorjapretzel Rat immediately precipitated himself into the cane chair indicated by Ek. Who wasted no further time, but flourished a sheet of paper in front of his incontinent victim.

'What is this?' said Ek.

'Ricepaper,' said Rat. 'Ricepaper washed with purple.'

'It's writing, fool. Is it not? What says this writing?'

'Something, something,' gabbled Rat. 'Something in, oh, Toxteth maybe. Dub? Ashmarlan?'

'Slandolin,' said Ek coldly. 'I am reliably informed that you read that language. Am I in error?'

'I . . . I . . .'

'I knew your father,' said Ek. 'He was a translator, was he not? A man of great scholarship. He was very fond of you, too. It is fortunate that the Great Enfolding claimed him before you grew to the estate of manhood, for surely the sight of your quivering flesh and incompetent tongue would give him the greatest displeasure. The language is Slandolin, and what it says is known to me, for I have had it translated into the Superior Tongue for my own enlightenment. Read!'

Nixorjapretzel Rat obeyed. With every appearance of the greatest care imaginable, he studied the single sheet of ricepaper which Ek had given him, a piece of paper so clogged with miniscule purple-penned letters that at a glance it looked as if it had been washed with ink.

'Tell me now,' said Ek, treasuring the words on his tongue as if they were portentous in the extreme, 'what says this text?'

'It is a madman's garbling of a fragment of recent history,' said Rat.

'A madman wrote this?' said Ek. 'An interesting hypothosis. What brings you to believe as much?'

'Because none of this is true,' cried Rat. 'It's libels, that's all. It has me dealing with Varazchavardan, running for him, walking for him, doing his errands, bringing him news. Whereas I repudiate the man.'

Ek looked upon the babbling Rat with disgust.

'Save your lies for the courts of law,' said Ek. 'You're not on trial yet, least of all for treason. So we've no need for pretence. Your association with Varazchavardan is long, and my informants tell me that it continues yet. You've no need to dissemble, least of all with me. As yet, the time for punishment lies in the future. Some as yet may hope to avoid their just desserts.'

'Just desserts?' said the quivering Rat.

'Torture,' said Ek. 'Torture to the point of death and then to the place beyond. This is the fate which will befall those who have leagued with traitors, with the enemies of the State, the enemies of our dearly beloved Aldarch Three. All such will suffer their doom unless they can earn themselves a pardon.'

'Oh, earning,' said Rat. 'I'll work, I'll work, anything, I'll do anything for pardon.'

'So you admit it,' said Ek. 'You admit yourself a traitor or the associate of traitors, which amounts to the same thing.'

Rat gaped in dismay.

'But – but you said—'

'Fool!' said Ek. 'No! Stay in the chair. This is no time for grovelling, least of all at my feet.'

In the years of his increasing age, Ek no longer took pleasure in the grovellings of underlings, for his feet had lost the strength to kick them effectively.

'What is it time for, then?' said Rat, emboldened by the fact that Ek had spared him a kicking.

'For work,' said Ek. 'Hard work for one who wishes to earn himself a pardon. Your mission, should you decide to accept it, is to seek out the rest of this manuscript.'

'The rest?' said Rat.

'This piece of ricepaper is but a fraction of what I suspect to be a much greater whole. *A Secret History of Untunchilamon*. I suspect this Secret History has been written by one whose motives as yet remain a mystery, but who nevertheless appears to have sources of information which have disclosed to him at least something of the extent of the treason which pervades the ranks of high and low alike on Untunchilamon. Your mission, then, is to find the rest of this text and the person who wrote it, and bring both of them to me.'

'And if I don't accept?' said Rat. 'Don't accept the mission, I mean?'

'A treason trial this very day and your execution on the morrow,' said Ek.

'Oh, I accept, I accept!'

'Then go!' said Ek.

Rat went.

In his haste, young Nixorjapretzel slipped on the still-spreading ooze of mushed banana and paw-paw and sprawled flat on his face. Provoked beyond endurance, Ek kicked him, albeit ineffectually. Rat scuttled away on all fours, found the stairs, precipitated himself down them then fled.

Once the Rat had gone, old master Ek stumped away to his favourite smoking chair where he rolled himself a cigarette and endeavoured to relax. But relaxation did not come easily, for Ek was in the grip of a great excitement.

What had roused this old and arthritic man to such a passion? Why, it was the manuscript which he had discussed with Nixorjapretzel Rat. But why should this in itself prove a source of such stimulation? Because of what was written on one fragment of that manuscript, a short and incomplete fragment which Ek had not shown to Rat.

Now that Rat had gone, Nadalastabstala Banraithanchumun Ek once again pulled that secret fragment of ricepaper from his tobacco pouch. He unfolded it slowly, for his arthritic fingers felt as if splinters of bone were floating loose in the joints, and this condition did not encourage speed.

Ek read it greedily for the thousandth time, his eyes of green-flecked orange deciphering the miniscule script with ease. Ek had once been a translator, and his decreptitude had as yet left him with his mastery of a dozen languages still intact. As a matter of strategy, he kept this mastery secret, which encouraged the unwary to betray themselves in his hearing as they discoursed in foreign tongues; one such language was Slandolin, which Ek could read with ease, though he pretended complete ignorance of this argot.

This was what was written on that piece of paper:

'. . . to become immortal. Immortality is easily achieved if one has possession of an organic rectifier. On Untunchilamon . . .'

On Untunchilamon what?

Once again, Master Ek cursed the fact that his precious fragment ended where it did. Though Ek was old and wise, his frustration was scarcely different from that experienced by an eager adolescent who has bought the first book of one of those dreadful gladiator yarns peddled by the shameless Chulman Puro.

Our adolescent has reached the final page of this yarn, Vorn the Gladiator is in a dungeon which is lit only by the phosphorescence from the fifty rotting corpses which share his imprisonment. Gouts of dirty water are flooding into this oubliette from a breach in the wall. Vorn is chained to the floor with unbreakable shackles. Already the water has reached his mouth, and—

And here the story ends, with Chulman Puro grinning like a pirate, for he knows his victims have no alternative but to pay out good gold for the continuation of the story, or suffer the pangs of unsatiated curiosity ever afterwards.

Master Ek, not having any access to the continuation of the text, suffered absolute agonies of curiosity. What did the missing portion of the MS say? That Untunchilamon possessed one of these mysterious organic rectifiers? Or that it lacked such an arcanum?

As a matter of urgency, Master Ek intended to find out.

For Ek was staring mortality in the face.

And Ek did not wish to die.

Death is the common fate of all men. The fisherman Threp Sodakik lies dead in the lagoon with starfish browsing upon the bloody rags of his corpse. The market gardener Pa Po Pep looks at the emblem of death which adorns his shaft, then rubs it first with ice and then with fertilizer, but rightly suspects that neither of these desperate experiments will save him from ultimate extinction. Ox No Zan, moaning as he rubs his aching jaw, knows he will die of pain unless he goes to the dentist, but may quite possibly expire from sheer terror if he actually submits himself to Doctor Death's probes and pincers.

Death is everywhere; and inevitable; and inescapable.

Or so it had always seemed to Master Ek.

But now, in a passion of hope, he imagined himself uncovering an 'organic rectifier', whatever that might be, and using that to make himself immortal.

From the above, it will be seen that Master Ek had seriously misled young Rat. Ek had no need of any mysterious manuscript to tell him who the traitors were; he had already drawn up a comprehensive schedule of tortures and executions which would commence as soon as the Thrug was overthrown. What interested him, what excited him to the point of frenzy, was the question of immortality.

And here the historian must once again call the reader's attention to the proposition which introduced this chapter: namely, that there did not exist a clear-cut division between 'Justina Thrug and her allies' and 'Justina's enemies'. In the case of Nadalastabstala Banraithanchumun Ek, we have a man divided even within his own mind. On the one hand, he wished to destroy the Thrug because he hated her, and because Aldarch the Third would look favourably on such destruction. On the other hand, the temptations of immortality were such that, if this 'organic rectifier' came into his hands, he might wish to keep it from being confiscated by Aldarch the Third. And it was possible, just possible, that such defiance of the Mutilator of Yestron might ultimately force Master Ek into an alliance with the Empress Justina.

CHAPTER SEVEN

What lures the trade fleet to Untunchilamon? What calls
the ships across the waters of Moana? What makes them
dare the dangers of the Kraken Deep and the coral teeth
of Untunchilamon's lagoons? What draws mariners to
this sweating hell of rapturous mosquitoes, rabid vampire rats and magnanimous sharks?

Why, in fact, would anyone come to such a place?

Let us look at some people and their motives.

The red-skinned Chegory Guy, lover of Olivia Qasaba
and confidant of the Crab, came to Untunchilamon
because he wished to escape from his mother's womb,
and this necessitated a head-first dive from the clutching
humidity of the uterus into the deliriums of a heatwave
in Injiltaprajura. In other words, he was born there, and
had no choice about the matter.

Olivia Qasaba, she of the intimate giggle, the fearless
thighs, came to Untunchilamon because her father
brought her there from Ashmolea; and she was too
young at the time to protest.

The Crab came there—

But we will hear later how the Crab reached Untunchilamon, and with the price of fooskin being what it is,
your historian cannot afford to tell the story twice.

The corpse-master Uckermark, he of the many scars
and the intricate tattoos, came to the island with a pirate
band which tried to loot Injiltaprajura's treasury, and
achieved but partial success. His friend Log Jaris arrived
for identical reasons, and chose not to leave after being
unfortunately transmogrified into a bullman.

The conjuror Odolo, dexterous prestigitator and
public entertainer, came to Untunchilamon (according

to his bank manager) so he could be the bane of honest citizens. Or, to go by his own account—

But enough of this!

We have established what needed to be established; which is, that nobody came to Untunchilamon for the sake of pleasure. Rather, needs, greeds, fears and lusts of all descriptions drove them to that place.

As for the ships of the trade fleet, why, they chiefly came to purchase dikle (a thixotropic fluid widely used as a lubricant) and shlug (a grey grease most excellent for preserving metals). Both dikle and shlug flow (intermittently) from the mysterious wealth fountains of a small island in the harbour of Injiltaprajura, Untunchilamon's capital. Fountains elsewhere located provide Injiltaprajura with the bounteous supply of fresh water which allows the city's market gardens to be irrigated to such excellent effect.

The journey the trade fleet makes is arduous and hazardous in the extreme. Hence Master Ek was not the only one staring mortality in the face, for Manthandros Trasilika and Jean Froissart had their own worries on that score. The sea voyage from Yestron to Untunchilamon had its fair share of lethal dangers, including storms, those rare but hideously powerful monsters known as krakens, and the coral shadows of the lagoon passage from the north of Untunchilamon to Injiltaprajura itself. But what perturbed Trasilika and Froissart was not so much the voyage (the dangers of which have greatly been exaggerated by most travellers) as the reception they would receive on arrival.

They were not worried about the drumming cult, for news of this novelty had yet to escape Untunchilamon. Instead, they worried about the reception they might receive from the island's politicians.

Manthandros Trasilika was coming to Injiltaprajura to take over Untunchilamon in the name of Aldarch the Third, and feared the task might prove difficult. Justina Thrug? She was only a woman, so Trasilika had left her

71

out of his calculations. Rather, he worried about the many enemies of Aldarch Three who had fled to Untunchilamon during the years of Talonsklavara. He feared such opponents of the Mutilator might choose to dabble in assassination; as he loved to eat, he particularly feared poison. Furthermore, while Trasilika's documentation was in good order, there was always a chance that some diehard Janjuladoola bureaucrats on Untunchilamon would not accept him as their new governor.

Indeed, Trasilika was a most unlikely choice for such an important and sensitive post. When one considers his appointment, the first question which arises is this: why would a xenophobe like Aldarch Three grant a man like Trasilika the wazirship of Untunchilamon? Trasilika was not of the Janjuladoola people. Instead, he was of the same racial group as the children of Wen Endex; that is to say, his skin was naturally possessed of a pink-tending-towards-pallor which tanned to brown (or broiled to red) on exposure to the tropic sun.

Furthermore, Manthandros Trasilika was not a citizen of the Izdimir Empire. Generations previously, the children of Wen Endex had established a colony on the shores of the northern continent of Tameran. This was Port Domax, a free port which in time became notorious for the rapacity and rascality of its merchants. Here Trasilika had been born; here he had been raised; here he had lived until his thirtieth year.

So how did Trasilika come to be, at the age of forty-five, a wazir of the Izdimir Empire, with ornate documents to prove it? Here a mystery, a mystery compounded by the fact that Trasilika was fat. While the Janjuladoola people are given to private debauch, their culture frowns upon outwardly visible signs of dissipation, and in particular upon any overburden of flesh. While excess weight does not technically disqualify one from holding high office in the Izdimir Empire, it does act as an impediment to promotion.

Not only was Trasilika fat, he was also verbose: a

strutting, posturing man who was wildly over-fond of his own loud and windy voice. This was a trait sure to serve him ill when he had dealings with the Janjuladoola; for the people of that culture place a high value upon silences, the Janjuladoola version of a skilled orator being the man who can 'say without saying, command without speech'.

As Manthandros Trasilika was (though admittedly to a strictly limited extent) conscious of his personal limitations, he experienced some unquiet when he contemplated the dangers which lay ahead.

As for Jean Froissart, he was in better shape than he had been on departure from Bolfrigalaskaptiko, for he had experienced a complete remission of the symptoms which had then afflicted him. No longer did he suffer stabbing chest pains or twinges of lacerating agony in his arms and shoulders; furthermore, his intermittent breathing problems had disappeared entirely. He was inclined to think that his doctor had been right: his symptoms had been consequent upon anxiety.

But, while the physical symptoms were in remission, Froissart remained anxious still, and his anxiety increased tenfold when Manthandros Trasilika called him to a private shipdeck conference.

'Do you know who this is?' said Trasilika, displaying a miniature portrait.

Trasilika's fleshy palm engulfed the oval-shaped miniature, hiding it fom all scrutiny but their own. It was a picture of an old, old man with a cruel mouth parted in a smile which showed black gravestone teeth. Froissart surmised these fuliginous fangs to be dentures; he was wrong, but the mistake was pardonable, for few men as old as this retained their own teeth. The age of the sitter, more than the limitations of the portraitist, made the subject's race hard to decipher; for it is one of the peculiarities of humanity that those differences which evidence themselves so stridently in youth (contrasts of race, health and gender) soften and blur with increasing age, all but vanishing in extreme senescence, that time of life when all flesh displays its common ancestry in the universal processes of wasting, shrivelling and depigmentation. However, Jean Froissart had spent many years in the Izdimir Empire, and hence was hypersensitive to matters of race; accordingly, he swiftly identified this gnarled ancient as a member of the Janjuladoola people. Only one thing made Froissart hesitate before pronouncing that diagnosis, and that was the eyes. Those ocular orbs, animating the wizened flesh as they did with such intelligent malice, were pale orange flecked with green, like undercooked eggs sprinkled with mint; they deviated so much from any human norm that Froissart momentarily wondered if the painting was of a real person at all, or whether the subject was a creature of legend or myth.

'Well?' said Trasilika. 'Are you delaying the delivery of your wisdom till your ninetieth birthday adds the authority of age to its native credibility?'

'No,' said Froissart. 'No, it was the eyes that gave me pause, that's all. What I think is . . . here we have an old man. One of the Janjuladoola. Eighty, perhaps. Or older. That's all. What else is there to say?'

'Much,' said Trasilika, closing his spongy fingers around the miniature. 'The man is not eighty. He is in his youth still, for his years do not exceed seventy. He is a priest of Zoz the Ancestral. A High Priest. He is . . . the High Priest on Untunchilamon.'

Froissart was startled.

'But,' he said, 'but, but you said . . .'

'I know what I said.'

Before their departure from Bolfrigalaskaptiko, Trasilika had told Froissart (in the strictest confidence) that the latest intelligence (allegedly brought from Untunchilamon by the canoes of the Ngati Moana) confirmed earlier rumours which had declared Justina Thrug to be guilty of a massacre of all priests of Zoz the Ancestral who had the misfortune to dwell upon her island.

Obviously, Trasilika had lied.

'So . . . so this is a priest,' said Froissart, his 'this' referring to the miniature which Trasilika had already pocketed. 'May I know his name?'

'Nadalastabstala Banraithanchumun Ek,' said Trasilika.

'Ek?' said Froissart in alarm.

'The same.'

'But – but you said he was dead.'

'I lied,' said Trasilika simply.

'How could you?' said Froissart.

He was horrified, and with good reason. Law and custom decreed that no wazir could be officially installed in his office without the ceremonial assistance of a High Priest of Zoz the Ancestral. In the absence of such a High Priest, Froissart himself would have conducted the necessary religious ceremony. But now that right, duty and privilege would automatically be claimed by Master Ek himself.

Jean Froissart knew much of Master Ek already, and none of what he knew was pleasant. Ek was as much a xenophobe as Aldarch the Third. He preached the supremacy of the Janjuladoola people, and despised all other races, particularly the children of Wen Endex; and, as both Trasilika and Froissart belonged to the despised group, Ek would doubtless be reluctant to give them his cooperation.

On the perilously unstable island to which the two men were venturing, lack of cooperation might mean their deaths; and surely there was a possibility that Ek's displeasure might take a more active, more dangerous form.

As Froissart and Trasilika confronted each other in the shipdeck sunlight, a fight broke out between two sailors, matelots whose tempers had been strained beyond endurance by the stresses of this much-feared voyage to the waters of Untunchilamon. Without hesitation, both men plunged into the fray and sorted out the miscreants. No dignitary of the Janjuladoola people would even have contemplated joining such a brawl, but Froissart and Trasilika could not resist it.

Though Jean Froissart had lived for years in Obooloo, he still retained from his youth a love of physical conflict. He had been raised to be a Yudonic Knight of Wen Endex, and thus in his early years his every impulse toward reckless violence had been lauded and applauded. The results of such training in one's formative years are not easily altered.

As for his companion:

Though he was travelling to Untunchilamon to be the new wazir of that island, Manthandros Trasilika was at heart a merchant; and a fat merchant; and a rapacious, rascally merchant. But he was not a cowardly merchant. The traders of Port Domax are noted for their ferocity in battle and the unmerchantlike joy which they take in the same; which helps explain the long and uninterrupted independence of their city.

When the sailors had been separated, pummelled and dismissed to the brig, a sweating Trasilika said to a panting Jean Froissart:

'Cheer up,' said Trasilika. 'Soon I'll be wazir and we'll all be rich.'

'Or dead,' said Froissart. 'Ek could be the death of us.'

'Not Ek,' said Trasilika. 'Ek could be many things to us, but death is not one of them.'

'How can you be so certain?'

'Relax! I've a gift for Ek. Something he wants. Something he wants really, really badly. Something which will sweeten his heart till he sings to us as a lover.'

'What?' said Froissart.

'A death warrant,' said Trasilika. 'A death warrant for the witch of Injiltaprajura. Justina Thrug, whom he so bitterly hates. My first act as wazir will be to have the bitch slaughtered. Then Ek, oh, Ek will love us indeed.'

76

Manthandros Trasilika was the very picture of confidence, but Froissart was not entirely convinced. He worried. And his worries were worsened when, that very day, he experienced a perturbing new symptom. Not the stabbing chest pains he had previously suffered with such anguished apprehension, but something equally ominous, if not more so. It felt like a heaviness in the region of his heart, as if that organ had been lumbered with a burden of lead. For the rest of that day he lived in fear of a massive, crushing heart attack.

'Nonsense,' muttered Froissart to himself. 'Hypochondriacal hysteria. I've the constitution of an ox and a clearance from a heart specialist.'

The force of such self-reassurance was strengthened toward evening, when the weight at last eased from his chest, and he was almost able to persuade himself that the whole incident had been a figment of his imagination.

But, while fears of heart attack could be attributed to hypochondria, fears of Nadalastabstala Banraithanchumun Ek were not so easily dismissed.

CHAPTER EIGHT

The Empress Justina woke in the depths of bardardornootha, that quarter which starts at midnight and ends at dawn. She woke alone, for she had gone to bed unpartnered; the current political crisis had almost ended her customary indulgences, for she needed all her wit and energy to ensure her own survival.

Her twin sister Theodora was not as continent. Nightly, Theodora was holding revels with Troldot 'Heavy-Fist' Turbothot, a trader from Hexagon who owned and captained one of the ships which had been anchored in the Laitemata all through the Long Dry. But Justina herself slept solo, except when she took the Princess Sabitha to bed.

On waking, the Empress listened for drums. She had banned all 'drumming' in the precincts of the pink palace, but someone was disobeying her orders. At odd moments of night and day, she had heard the ominous tok – tok – thuk of a small hand drum echoing through her hallowed halls. The culprit might be a young soldier; or a waiter; or someone else. Whoever it was, Justina wanted them caught and stopped.

Justina listened.

She heard . . .

A mosquito.

The clicketing of some unidentifiable night insect.

And:

Her own heavy breathing.

Apart from that, nothing.

The night was not ruled by sound but by heat, the ever-heat of the tropics, the soft wet suffocation of the island nights. Justina felt as if she was wrapped in warm

wet dishcloths. Her folds and clefts were swampy with
sweat, with the hot ooze of fluid, the slow spralpablan-
darakatarla of a woman's bloodsea waters.

Justina Thrug scratched at her sweating armpits,
digging her fingers into her tousled axillary hair as if
trying to dislodge lice, then lay back on the damp sheet
and pondered her dreams, as was her habit. She was a
child of Wen Endex, and her own culture lacked a
formal theory of dreams; nevertheless, Justina had
developed her own personal oneirocritical methods, and
applied them regularly to her own reveries.

What had she dreamed of?

Of home.

Of Wen Endex, land of upthrust rock and watersky
winds, of sea-shocked dunes and horizon to horizon
swamp-lands, of gloating quicksands and whirlpool
rivers, of black-boughed forests where only the brave or
the foolish dared to venture. Of the slopes of Mobius
Kolb and the battlements of Saxo Pall, of the dark
gutterals of the Riga Rimur and the uncanny flirtation of
the zana. Red, gold, green, blue and pink were the zana.

'Ah,' said Justina, breathing her loss.

Tears filled her eyes. She was – for the moment –
utterly homesick. She longed for the mud of Galsh
Ebrek and the shores of the Winter Sea. And, possessed
by such longing, Justina found it impossible to get back
to sleep. Did Tromso Stavenger still rule the Families?
Did Qa still lord it over Island Thodrun? Did heroes still
quest for the saga swords, the brave blades Kinskorn,
Edda and Sulamith's Grief?

'Enough of that,' said Justina firmly.

If she survived the dangers of Untunchilamon, then
one day she would return to her homeland. But for the
moment she must concentrate on the struggle for
survival.

So thinking, the Empress did her best to get back to
sleep. But insomnia defeated her. At last, abandoning
the struggle, she rose from her bed, the shadows of her

nakedness wallowing in her bedroom mirrors as she hunted for a silken robe of spiderweb silver, that shade known to the Janjuladoola tongue as rolabalibolifontasdima. Once dressed, she left her room, the fluent fabric of her robe slick-sliding against her flesh as she strode down darkened corridors.

The Empress Justina, ruler of the hearts and ribs of many, ascended some stairs and ventured out on to the roof. The night was possessed by a sweltering heat despite the steady breeze; it was moonless but bright-pricked by stars.

Justina looked out over her city of dreams and nightsweats. Somewhere, a cockerel screamed, its arrogant challenge abrupting through the dark without warning. Somewhere, a dog barked, then was silent. Apart from that, the city was quiet.

Green, blue and white shone the stars; red and purple; yellow and mauve. Were stars related to the zana? And if so, then how? Were there any black stars? And supposing there were, how would one see them against the night? Those stars low on the horizon trembled incessantly, as did the night-lights of the fishing canoes out on the Laitemata Harbour. There is a Janjuladoola myth which says the night sky is a sea fished by a race of lesser gods, and that the stars are the fishing lights of those gods; Justina knew that myth, but preferred the tale native to Wen Endex which declared the stars to have been cast into the sky at whim by a spirit of frivolous inclination. To play with such conceits was particularly pleasing at a time like this when life had become, for the most part, so very very serious.

Justina stalked the rooftop in her silver robe, and was pleased to be challenged by the sentries posted in each of the four belfries. The bells themselves had been removed and destroyed on the orders of the Hermit Crab. No longer did they ring out to announce the start of bardardornootha, istarlat, salahanthara and undokondra. The day's four quarters merged into each other

80

without formal announcement; and for some obscure reason this seemed to increase the oppressiveness of the heat, the humidity of the air, and the zest possessed by that great tormenter, the mosquito.

Ah, the mosquito!

Lord of blood, master of—

But I must restrain myself; for, once started on the subject of the mosquito, I would be unable to stop until my scorpioned handwriting had covered both sides of a full quire of fooskin. That I would have done when I was younger and not so sane as I am now. But increasing age and sanity have given me a better sense of proportion. And, besides, the price of fooskin is monstrous, and likewise the opium needed to subdue the pains of my arthritis; and both these factors encourage me to adopt the terse concision of this present text, so different from the expansiveness of my earlier years.

Therefore I here say nothing whatsoever about the mosquito, that winged vampire which the Dagrin say is the creation of the devil-god.

(And here please note that the devil-god in question is the Evil One, Storpandif the Stone Fish, the death-lurker of the coral reefs; and is not to be confused by that mightier deity of the Dagrin, the formidable Elasmokar-charos, who is identified with the shark.)

Avoiding the subject of the mosquito – that beast with the teeth of a cactus, the whine of a woman and the morals of a pirate – I continue my account of the Empress Justina, who, having identified herself to her guards, ventured to her pool, the rooftop swimming pool which alone made these days of waiting bearable.

Waiting?

Yes, that was how the imperial days were largely spent.

Unlike Vorn the Gladiator, Justina could achieve nothing by careering around the universe trying to lop off heads. Those decisive destructions in which Vorn so casually indulges himself were forbidden to the Empress, for incontinent violence would serve only to secure her own death and ruin for ever her hopes of evacuating her supporters from Untunchilamon.

Until the Trade Fleet came, Justina's best strategy was to preserve the status quo; and that she could best do by bluff, which meant carrying on the routines of her life with every appearance of imperturbable confidence. Until the Trade Fleet came, heroic action of any description was quite out of place; and nothing Justina could do would hurry the advent of that Fleet.

Justina, her modesty (such as it was) preserved by night, slipped off her robe and lowered herself into the water. Though dawn was not far off, the water was still warm. It would be strange to return to Wen Endex, where wet and damp were always so chilled that they must be feared as life-threateners. If she returned to Wen Endex . . .

If all else failed, a very swift return might be possible, at least for Justina herself. If the flying ship worked.

The flying ship?

This fantastical construction looked for all the world like a gigantic nest constructed by an untidy and brain-damaged bird. It sat atop the roof of the pink palace near the swimming pool; the wizard Hostaja Sken-Pitilkin had spent days working on this weird contraption, and averred that he would shortly make it fly. But Justina had her doubts. She had little acquaintance with wizards, hence was inclined to accept the sorcerers' valuation of the breed; the wonder-workers of Injiltaprajura were adamant that the magic of wizards was weak stuff, slow to work if it ever worked at all. Still, they would very shortly see one way or another, for the ship's maiden flight was scheduled for that very morning.

Such was the length of Justina's leisurely swim that dawn was breaking before she at last hauled herself from the water.

Dawn!

Mosquito torment ceases. The sun rises red on the far

horizon, staining sea and shore alike with the colours of blood and over-ripe cherries. Flies and maggots alike stir to industrious life. Monkeys scream in the jungle undergrowth which chokes the steep gullies which finger their way through portside Injiltaprajura. The sullen heat of night is stoked and steamed anew by the powers of the sauna-making sun.

As the sun rises, Pelagius Zozimus busies himself in the kitchens of the Analytical Institute, preparing a special flying fish sauce for the Crab's breakfast. In the cave of the Crab, Chegory Guy awakes in the arms of his true love Olivia. Both are tired, for they spent very little of the night sleeping. Neither slept well when they did sleep, for only some coconut matting separated them from the rockfloor. But both look remarkably happy, and their yawns are interrupted by silly grins, and then by blissful kisses.

Elsewhere, in the docklands of Marthandorthan, in the warehouse known as Xtokobrokotok, the corpse-master Uckermark wakes with his wife Yilda. They have slept in Xtokobrokotok (rather than in their own house in the slumlands of Lubos) because Uckermark is a corpse-master no longer. Instead, he has risen to a position of especial power and influence, for he is—

But I get ahead of myself, and must cure myself of the habit, for it eats up the fooskin alarmingly, and my own bank manager is no more understanding than the monster who tormented the days of the conjuror Odolo. Therefore, abandoning the overview of Injiltaprajura by dawn upon which I almost launched myself in earnest, let me return to the rooftop of the pink palace, and to the sight of the Empress Justina, who is squeezing the water from her hair and is saying:

'I wish.'

That she said, and then:

'I wish the Trade Fleet would come.'

Then, as she straightened up after slipping herself into her silken robe, she saw the Fleet had come indeed.

Or, at least, the first two vessels of the Fleet.

Yes, there were two ships creeping into the harbour. They must have taken hair-raising risks to navigate the coral-clogged reefs in the dark. But there were always a couple of skilled and confident navigators prepared to dare such dangers in order to reap the profits available to the first ships of the Trade Fleet.

Justina watched the ships with mingled fear and excitement. At the very least, they would bring news. News of Talonsklavara. Had the civil war in Yestron been decisively settled? Or would the military turmoil continue for yet another year? Another year was the best Justina could hope for. Hope she did, though her analysis told her the civil war was almost certain to be at an end, and that Aldarch the Third was by far the most likely victor.

As Justina watched, the two ships dropped anchor; their sails were shortly brailed up, leaving the spars skeleton-bare. Already canoes and paddle-boats were crowding round the ships. Hearing what? Learning what? Justina would know soon enough; her spies were efficient, and all knew that incoming news had the highest priority for the Empress.

In a deliberate exercise of self-discipline, Justina turned her back upon Injiltaprajura's portside, the Laitemata Harbour and the freshly arrived ships. She turned just in time to see Hostaja Sken-Pitilkin's eccentric creation start to dismantle itself.

The dismantling began with a single stick which detached itself from the crow's nest confusion of the airship. It hung hesitantly in the air then spindled upwards. Then, in slow motion, the rest of the ship began to discard to the sky as Justina watched in open-mouthed astonishment. As she gaped, Hostaja Sken-Pitilkin himself arrived. The wizard was there to conduct the first flight-trials of his skycruiser, and he was as astonished as the Empress to see the thing tearing itself apart.

'Molst!' shouted Sken-Pitilkin. 'Molst, molst!'

But the sticks paid no heed to this frantic command in Toxteth. So the wizard switched to the High Speech of the eight orders of Drangsturm's Confederation. In that tongue he commanded the fragments of his swiftly disintegrating ship. But to no avail, for a brisk and gathering wind scattered the sticks across the landscape.

Hostaja Sken-Pitilkin greeted this disaster with horror-struck anguish. The Empress Justina, though angry (this must be the work of those perfidious sorcerers!) was comparatively phlegmatic. Sken-Pitilkin's airship could scarcely have carried a dozen people at best, whereas she needed to remove a dozen ship loads to safety. She was less concerned with the loss of the airship than with any immediate danger which might be posed by the incoming ships.

What news did they bring?

Unfortunately, the answers to Justina's many questions would have to wait until her spies brought their reports to the pink palace. So the Empress took herself from the roof to her dining room, there to breakfast upon the delicate fragrance of papaya lightly laced with lime juice, upon the fibrous sweetness of fresh-chopped pineapple liberally dosed with the sap of crushed sugar cane, and upon the white flesh of hot fried flying fish.

As Justina savoured her papaya, munched down her pineapple and anatomized the flesh which lay beneath the freckled skin of her flying fish, spies loyal to her regime (or as loyal as anyone could be expected to be in those chancy times) were already making their way toward her palace with ambiguous intelligence.

In shouted conversations with shipboard crews, the spies had been told that Talonsklavara had still been in progress when the two vessels departed from Yestron. The civil war might have ended by now, for a major battle (perhaps a decisive battle) had been taking place even as the ships set sail from the continent. However, for the time being the status quo prevailed.

One of the ships had declared itself to be a general trader, here to exchange tea, opium and iron for dikle, shlug and slaves. Prices for the last commodity were high in Yestron. In particular demand were male slaves who could be sold as soldiers to the rival armies contending for possession of the Izdimir Empire; and Untunchilamon, blessed with peace for the last seven years, was a reliable source of such.

The other ship had announced itself as the *Oktobdoj*, brothel ship extraordinaire. A claim which had provoked the following dialogue between inquisitive water rats and decktop sailors:

'What does a brothel ship so far from Manamalargo?'

'Why, sailing for profit, of course.'

'Then you've come to the wrong place. We've whores aplenty ashore, aye, and poxes too. We've no need of yours.'

'There you're wrong. For we have aboard sophisticated delights unknown to these the provinces.'

This and other such advertising propaganda had aroused a tepid enthusiasm among the water rats, an enthusiasm which had dissipated rapidly when they had been told there was a two-dragon fee merely to climb aboard to inspect the merchandise.

Justina's spies had taken this brothel-ship claim at face value, and none had been inclined to spend two dragons to confirm it. Which was unfortunate, for officials had now climbed aboard that very ship, and were being told a very different tale.

The officials were the plague inspector (who was due a fee for giving the ship its health clearance); the pilot (who must by regulation be paid for guiding the ship into harbour, for all that he had been in his bed when it put into port); the ladipti man (a sinecurist of obscure function but certain charge); the harbour master (who was due a fee of his own, besides receiving a tithe of the emoluments disbursed to the other officials) and a representative of the Combined Religious Guild who was there to extract what was owing to the gods.

When these officials were assembled upon the deck of the good ship *Oktobdoj*, two children of Wen Endex came forth to meet them. One was a heavyweight in his forties, a confident brute with a cauliflower ear. The other was younger (in his early thirties), lighter in build (indeed, he was positively slender) and less confident (much less, for his watering eyes blinked nervously at the too-bright sunlight).

Had these two men been of Janjuladoola breed, their dealings with the officials might have been delicate and protracted. But, as they were children of Wen Endex, their approach was blunt, direct and unsubtle. It was the heavyweight who did most of the talking.

'I am Manthandros Trasilika,' said he. 'I am here for a reason.'

'So am I,' said his slender companion. 'I am Jean Froissart, a priest of Zoz the Ancestral.'

'A priest of Zoz?' said the Janjuladoola-skinned harbourmaster. 'You a child of Wen Endex yet you claim yourself for Zoz?'

'He is,' said the heavyweight, answering before his companion had time to hesitate. 'For a wazir needs a priest, and I stand before you as your new wazir.'

This pronouncement was so abrupt and unexpected that it was greeted with total silence among the ranks of the officials. The heavyweight betrayed a momentary and uncharacteristic nervousness by tugging at his cauliflower ear. Then his ever-confident voice rolled on:

'Aldarch the Third has triumphed in Talonsklavara. All dispute in the Izdimir Empire is at an end. To celebrate his victory, Aldarch Three has sent me to Injiltaprajura to assume command of Untunchilamon and to punish those who have usurped rightful authority during the years of civil war.'

'Then,' said the representative of the Combined Religious Guild, the first of the officals to adapt to this startling intelligence, 'you should by rights report to Master Ek immediately.'

So said the worthy Guild representative, then waited. This was the first test. If the newcomers did not know who Master Ek was, then they could hardly be the wazir and priest they claimed to be.

'Nadalastabstala Banraithanchumun Ek has long been in my thoughts,' said the heavyweight. He pulled a miniature from his pocket and tossed it to the Guild representative. 'That's him, isn't it?'

The Guild representative fielded the miniature. It hurt him to do so, for such an abrupt athletic gesture was not consonant with dignity; nevertheless, he caught the portrait adroitly, moving with an agility which betrayed his secret and shameful addiction to the outlawed sport of ping-pong. The Guild representative studied the miniature. There was no mistaking that face. Gnarled, wizened features. Black teeth. Eyes of pale orange flecked with green. It was without a doubt Master Ek himself. The newcomers had passed the first test.

'Manthandros Trasilika,' said the Guild representative. 'I am Hoboken Ik Tau. In the name of the Combined Religious Guild, I bid you welcome. Welcome to the Laitemata. Welcome to Injiltaprajura. To the shores of Untunchilamon, welcome. Thrice welcome you are. And to you also, Jean Froissart, to you, welcome.'

That was the start of the speech made by Ik Tau, a long speech which it would be tedious to relate in full. But the upshot is that in due course the newcomers were conducted to the presence of Master Ek himself. They took with them a present for that formidable dignitary: a death warrant commanding the immediate execution of Justina Thrug.

CHAPTER NINE

Aquitaine Varazchavardan, wonder-worker of Injilta-prajura, woke late after bad dreams. He had slept beneath a mosquito net without so much as a sheet across his naked body; nevertheless, his skin was greased with sweat as if he had laboured all night at the oars of a galley. He had dreamt that his leucodermic flesh had become tainted with the bloodstone red of Untunchilamon's native rock. Why? Because he had been hanging suspended from a million spider-threads, each attached to a microscopic fish-hook. While he dangled in agony, a torturer—

'Enough!' said Varazchavardan, dismissing the memories of nightmare as he slid out of bed.

Varazchavardan stood upright. A mistake, for the blood escaped from his head. As all colours swooned toward ebony, Varazchavardan sank to a crouch, his right knee protesting with an ominous grikle-grakle-gruk. He squatted like a foetus in the womb. Perfume-padded heat enfolded him. A choking, sweating heat which made him claustrophobic, which made him want to shout and hit out, to rip the air and claw his way to freedom. He felt as if he had been swallowed by a carnivorous flower which was even now crushing the last remnants of sanity from his psyche.

The crisis ebbed, receded.

His moment of near-blindness passed.

Cautiously, he stood.

Then, barefoot and naked, padded across his bedroom's rough coconut matting to the smooth and slightly slippery wooden slats of the bathroom. Even though the day was so advanced, the bathroom was nevertheless pleasantly cool. Its moist shadows had found favour with a mosquito, an insect swollen by vampiric night-feeding; it clung to dank wooden panelling with a stillness which mimicked paralysis. Varazchavardan, resentful of the Janjuladoola grey of its skin, that grey which had been denied to him by his unfortunate albinism, crushed it with the heel of his hand. Such was the delicacy with which Varazchavardan approached this exquisite task that he actually felt the momentary, slightly rubbery resistance of the mosquito's tumid flesh. Then the carbon-charcoal of its integument gave way and its body burst asunder, flesh becoming corpse as Varazchavardan smeared a miniscule bloating of someone else's blood across the panelling.

Varazchavardan smiled slightly, his mood marginally improved by this first pleasure of the day. A second pleasure followed as he pissed upon the shower slats, taking an obscene and somewhat guilty delight in offending against one of the taboos of his people. Then he stepped beneath the first of three gravid shower-sacks, reached up, gripped a plunger between two knuckles and pushed it upwards. This unplugged the nozzle of the shower-sack, aborting its contents. Cold water began to sprinkle down around Varazchavardan. As delightful shocks thrilled through his flesh, he eased the sweat from his skin, careful lest his talons tear his own chalk-white epidermis.

The first shower-sack shrivelled, slackened and collapsed in on itself. The water-flow diminished to a dribble-drip. The pink-eyed albino began lathering his wet, hairless body, whistling as he sent a slippery amber egg glissading over his skin. This egg was pure (unscented) palm oil soap, bought at considerable expense since the product requires considerable chemical ingenuity for its formulation. Despite the pleasure Varazchavardan took in this daily ritual, his whistling was on one note; it sounded for all the world like a monotonous mountain wind lancing through a crack in the roof of a mountain shelter in the high snows of the uplands of Ang.

The second shower-sack served to wash off the soap suds, while the third was reserved for pure sybaritic bliss, letting Varazchavardan devote himself entirely to the exquisite raptures of actually being cold, a sensation which allowed him to pretend he was back in Obooloo in winter, a world away from this accursed island of fever dreams and suffocating heat.

He dried himself on a towel of rough cotton then stepped from the cool of his bathroom to the heat of his bedroom. Outside his shuttered windows there bloomed a much-flowering vine, profligate with aromas, one of the myriad plants of the tropics whose names he had never bothered to learn. Once again he considered having it cut down. Once again he rejected the notion, for the cloying, oppressive scent of the plant at least kept him from imagining (as he did at times when his fears took him unawares) that he smelt hot wet blood guttering down the walls.

Varazchavardan dressed, adorning himself in silken ceremonial robes most marvellously embroidered with serpentine dragons ablaze with goldwork and argentry, with emerald and vermilion, with incarnadine and ultramarine. He had once had five such robes, each identical to each, but one had been stolen and three others damaged beyond repair in sundry alarms, confrontations and disasters of the last year.

Then the wonder-worker left his bedroom and ascended to the uppermost storey of his villa, which was devoted to one single room of prodigious size. Shutters had been taken from the windows, giving him uninterrupted views to the east (a street of grand mansions, including Master Ek's), the west (Justina's pink palace), the north (market gardens and the wastelands of Zolabrik beyond) and the south (portside Injiltaprajura and the Laitemata Harbour).

The view gave Varazchavardan no pleasure, for,

though this was his sixteenth year on Untunchilamon, he could not look upon its landscapes without aesthetic discomfort. The colours were too hot, in particular the red of bloodstone, the red of red coral, the red of red seaweed, the red sands of Scimitar and the malevolent reds of bloodshot dawns and the slaughter-bath sunsets. Varazchavardan feared that another year with such reds would send him mad. In contrast, the greens (the exuberance of market gardens and deep-gashed overgrown gullies) and blue (sea and sky at times other than dawn and dusk) were minor discomforts.

Nevertheless, while the outlook was not pleasurable, it was most marvellously informative. Varazchavardan saw at a glance that the number of ships in the Laitemata had increased from three to five. A slave was kneeling by Varazchavardan's breakfast table, and the wonderworker addressed the slave thus:

'What news of the ships?'

'Nixorjapretzel Rat waits to make report,' answered the slave.

'Show him in once I am finished,' said Varazchavardan, who had never found young Rat to be an asset to his digestion.

Breakfast was papaya. One papaya. The big, bulbous, yellow-skinned fruit yet awaited the knife. Varazchavardan liked to cut. He felt a special pleasure when he butchered the thin-skinned fruit, quartering its substance to reveal the smooth and succulent orange flesh. Once he had toyed with the idea of dispatching Justina Thrug and her father Lonstantine with equal ease; but when, after long meditation, he had finally tried to realize his fantasy, the task had proved impossible. And now it was too late. Now his reputation was irretrievably soiled and stained by the protestations of loyalty he had been forced to make to Justina.

Varazchavardan dug into the helpless flesh of the papaya. It yielded with much less protest that is made by the surprisingly muscular pulp of an eye when a torturer scoops it from its socket with a sharpened spoon.

'Ah, Justina, Justina,' crooned Varazchavardan. And then, adjusting his fantasy: 'Or shall we say, my dearest beloved Crab.'

'My lord?' said his still-squatting slave, not quite catching the import of these words.

'Ice,' said Varazchavardan, raising his voice; he did not want even a slave to know that he had taken to talking to himself. 'Ice, that's what I want.'

'My lord,' said the slave, and erranded away for the desired substance.

On ate Varazchavardan, imagining he was eating crab, or, more precisely, Crab. It was the dreaded Hermit Crab who had compelled him to swear loyalty to Justina. Had Varazchavardan refused, then the Crab would have played unpleasant topological games with the wonder-workers's flesh. But Aldarch the Third, notoriously stubborn in anger, was unlikely to heed such niceties; as far as Aldarch Three was concerned, Varazchavardan was most surely a traitor. Hence the news brought by the incoming ships was of vital interest and importance to Varazchavardan.

Nevertheless, the sorcerer ate slowly. Surely the ships had brought no news to upset the status quo. For surely any decisive settlement of Talonsklavara (in favour of Aldarch Three or against him) would already have been greeted by public uproar, general riot, arson and execution as adherents of the victorious faction celebrated their triumph at the expense of those loyal to the losers.

Varazchavardan finished his papaya.

Unlike Justina Thrug, the wonder-worker did not proceed to pineapple and flying fish, but crunched some freshly arrived ice and ordered that Nixorjapretzel Rat be shown into his presence. This was done.

Rat, Varazchavardan's erstwhile apprentice, was now (in theory, at least) a fully fledged sorcerer in his own right. Wonder-working, however, was not young Nixorjapretzel's strong suit. His endeavours in this direction

93

tended to be disastrous; to give but one example, when Rat had first joined the members of Injiltaprajura's Cabal House in their traditional quest to turn lead into gold, he had managed to turn every piece of gold in the building into fragmented lead.

Rat had lately found employment with the Empress Justina; he was working as her liaison officer, which at least had the advantage of keeping him too busy to get into mischief. Furthermore, this arrangement gave Varazchavardan yet another source of intelligence, albeit a somewhat unreliable source.

'Greetings, achaan Varazchavardan,' said Rat, making reverence to his teacher.

Varazchavardan made no reply whatsoever. He merely crunched some more ice.

'The Empress Justina has received reports of the latest arrivals,' said Rat. 'One is a general trader; the other, a brothel ship.'

So said Rat. However, he spoke in Janjuladoola, therefore his report was not as brief and blunt as it may appear in translation. For Janjuladoola is a language which lends itself to studied elegance and considerable prolixity; and Rat availed himself of both those features, using for 'general trader' a circumlocution which translates literally as 'dealer-in-all-from-lapis-lazuli-and-fresh-spinach-to-the-aroma-of-mountain-clouds-of-the-Singlaramonoktidad-region-and-ballast-of-that-type-in-which-conglomerate-rock-predominates'.

Varazchavardan's reply was similarly embroidered, though it can be translated very simply, thus:

'Whence comes this knowledge?'

'Canoes were on the water when the ships arrived,' said Rat. 'They asked, they were answered.'

'And what of the Izdimir Empire?' said Varazchavardan.

'Of that they say only that it is as it was,' said Rat.

The ships had claimed they departed from Yestron shortly before a decisive battle, a battle which must surely have become a part of history by now. Rat had heard this rumouring yet failed to report it to Varazcha-vardan. No deep plot, conspiracy or manoeuvring was here involved; the Rat had simply forgotten this detail.

'Is that all?' said Varazchavardan. 'Or is there some small yet important detail which you have forgotten?'

Rat thought about it then answered:

'Oh yes. That's right. The brothel ship is called the Oktobdoj and there's a two-dragon fee just to get aboard to inspect.'

'Then,' said Varazchavardan, 'I suggest you exert yourself by turning ice cubes to dragons. Or damns at least.'

'My master flatters me with his confidence,' said Rat, entirely missing the ironic force of this invitation.

Rat, intending to attempt the transformation on the spot, focused his attention on the amphora which held Varazchavardan's ice cubes, extended his hands and said:

'Bamaka! Ba—'

'Not here!' said Varazchavardan in unconcealed alarm.

'Oh,' said a somewhat crestfallen Rat. 'Then where?'

'I suggest you make the experiment on Island Scimi-tar,' said Varazchavardan. 'That way, if it should succeed, your wealth will be less likely to come to the attention of the Inland Revenue.'

'Oh,' said Rat. 'I hadn't thought of that. Oh, and there's one more thing. The conjuror Odolo waits without, whatever for I've no idea. He craves an audience.'

'Then show him in,' said Varazchavardan moodily.

Whereupon Justina's messenger boy withdrew, returning shortly with the conjuror Odolo, an olive-skinned foreigner of unknown nationality.

'Your mission?' said Varazchavardan bluntly.

'I come from Justina on a mission of some sensitivity,' said Odolo, glancing at Rat.

'Nixorjapretzel!' said Varazchavardan. 'Vanish!'

'As you wish,' said Rat, somewhat offended by this abrupt dismissal.

Then the young sorcerer raised his hands and cried out in his most imposing of voices:

'Foo! Fa-brok! Fajanthamoglostima! Ka!'

Thunder burped, lightning fizzled through the air with a sound similar to that made by a fire when it is abruptly extinguished by a bucket of water, and Nixorjapretzel Rat vanished. Where he had stood, nothing whatsoever could be seen except a boiling cloud the colour of octopus ink.

'Oh, get out of here!' said Varazchavardan in disgust.

'As you wish,' said the cloud in a muffled voice.

Then it perambulated away to the stairs and descended. Perhaps it could not see properly, for its departure was followed by the heavy sound of someone falling downstairs and a brief cry of pain (or was it surprise?). Then there was the sound of loud-voiced argument between cloud and house slaves, a hiatus, the sound of a door slamming emphatically, another hiatus, then the confused sounds of combat between a purple cloud and a bewildered but belligerent mange dog.

All that time, Aquitaine Varazchavardan sat chewing ice cubes, endeavouring to intimidate Odolo through application of silence. Odolo displayed no anxiety, but waited patiently until Varazchavardan deigned to speak.

'Now,' said the wonder-worker, as the noise of that battle receded into the distance, 'what was it you wished to talk to me about?'

Odolo then explained about the destruction of the airship.

'The Empress Justina saw it,' said Odolo. 'The thing came apart and was carried into the sky.'

'It was poorly made, then,' said Varazchavardan.

'The wizard who built the thing protests that such spontaneous destruction is impossible,' said Odolo. 'He declares it must have been masterminded by the Cabal House.'

'Very likely,' said Varazchavardan sourly.

He did not elaborate. He had no need to. Both Odolo and Varazchavardan knew that Injiltaprajura's wonderworkers were largely loyal to Aldarch Three, the dreaded Mutilator of Yestron. It was an open sécret that Varazchavardan would have liked to give his loyalty to the said Mutilator. Unfortunately, the Hermit Crab of the island of Jod had forced Varazchavardan into an alliance with the Empress Justina. And Aldarch Three, a notable exponent of unreason, was most unlikely to forgive that alliance.

Is it tedious to have this twice remarked upon? If so, then spare a thought for poor Varazchavardan, who remarked upon this calamity not twice a day but fifty times at least. As the advent of the Trade Fleet had drawn nearer, his apprehension had steadily increased; hence his nightmares, his angers, and his waking visions of drenching blood.

There was a pause; and this time it was Odolo's turn to maintain a disconcerting silence.

'Well,' said Varazchavardan at length, 'so the flying thing is dead.'

He said it blandly, as if this were a matter of no importance; whereas in fact he had hoped to escape from Untunchilamon by air, paying for his passage with a small quantity of the considerable treasure he had amassed during his stay on that island. While the blow was a heavy one, Varazchavardan had endured many dreadful blows in his life (the death of his much-beloved friend Wazir Sin, for example) and so had experience in absorbing shocks and sorrows.

'Yes,' said Odolo. 'We have no hope of escape by air. Furthermore, Justina says the destruction of the airship proves that Master Ek is ready to move against us. She declares that we must attack Ek first. Today. Lest we be arrested by Ek. He has the support of the Cabal House.

He could do it. He will do it. Unless we move. First. Attack, you know, is the best means of defence.'

Varazchavardan received this extraordinary declaration in complete silence. Then he thought about it. The scheme was lunacy, of course. Flight was possible. Difficult, dangerous and uncertain. But at least possible. They had possessed a hope of getting away by air. They might yet leave the island by sea. But to dare an armed confrontation with Master Ek? No. That was lunacy.

Ek had no Powers.

Ek was but a priest, albeit the High Priest of Zoz the Ancestral on the island of Untunchilamon.

However, Nadalastabstala Banraithanchumun Ek had the support of most of the wonder-workers of Injiltaprajura's Cabal House, for most of those worthies were worshippers of Zoz the Ancestral. Justina's soldiers were largely disloyal and untrustworthy, and far more likely to fight for the Janjuladoola-skinned Ek than for a child of Wen Endex like the female Thrug. As for the populace, at least half would support Ek rather than the empress.

Varazchavardan clawed more ice from his amphora. He rubbed it between his hands. Ice-melt lubricated the palms of his hands. Then, abruptly, Varazchavardan crammed the ice into his mouth and smashed it with his teeth. His jaws bit, savaged, crunched. The ice broke, splintered, shattered. Varazchavardan swallowed convulsively. Then smiled sweetly upon the disconcerted Odolo and said:

'This is not Justina's plan. Justina is not a lunatic.'

Odolo said nothing.

So Varazchavardan went on:

'A plan such as this, a jejune and bloodthirsty plan based on senseless, hopeless violence, could only have been hatched by Juliet Idaho.'

Odolo did not deny it.

'However,' said Varazchavardan, 'even Idaho would never come up with something so witless unless he was truly desperate. Which means things are as I have long feared. The Crab is no longer prepared to support Justina Thrug against her enemies.'

'You are correct insomuch as the plan originates with Juliet Idaho,' said the conjuror Odolo, choosing his words with great care. 'I must admit that I am his messenger. That, as you have doubtless suspected, Justina knows nothing of this plan. However, as for your surmisals about the Crab, of this I know nothing, for I am not privy to any information so sensitive.'

'I should hope not,' said Varazchavardan. 'You're not fit to be trusted, not if you let a mad Yudonic Knight entangle you in schemes so witless.'

'Juliet Idaho,' said Odolo, 'threatened to remove my head from my shoulders if I failed to bear you this message.'

'Extravagant,' said Varazchavardan, 'but in character. Very well. Tell that madman of a Yudonic Knight I wish to see him.'

'Why?' said Odolo.

'That,' said Varazchavardan, 'is for me to know and for you to wonder about. Go!'

So Odolo went.

Leaving Varazchavardan to ponder the strategy he would pursue when he met with Juliet Odaho. It was difficult, difficult. As he laboured with the problem, his hands began working in an insidious rhythm, thrap-patting against his thighs, thus:

Thrap – thrap – thrup!

Thrap – thrap – thrup!

Abruptly, Varazchavardan realized what he was doing.

He was drumming!

'Stop that,' he said to himself.

Then went back to work on his problem.

It was possible, just possible, that Idaho might have devised a scheme which would give them some slim hope of overwhelming Ek and his allies by an act of force majeure. If so, then Varazchavardan wanted to know about it. Might even go along with it. For . . . such a possibility would be very, very tempting.

Suppose all those loyal to Aldarch Three were slaughtered. Then Untunchilamon would be safe from the Mutilator for ever. The island was far from Yestron, the seas dangerous, the approaches narrow and easily defended. A resolute population loyal to its leaders could make any conquest of the island impossibly expensive. All nightmare would be at an end.

'Idaho may have a scheme,' muttered Varazchavardan. 'And if not, for my own protection I should at least know what madness is on his mind.'

Thus muttered Aquitaine Varazchavardan as he analysed the conversational gambits he would use to extract the truth from the ferocious Yudonic Knight he planned to interview.

Varazchavardan, who was born to plot and scheme, soon began to take pleasure in this planning. His pleasure was enhanced by the fact that he was totally ignorant of the crucial meeting which was taking place elsewhere in Injiltaprajura. This meeting was between Master Ek and two newcomers from the good ship *Oktobdoj*. The newcomers had just identified themselves as Jean Froissart (a priest of Zoz) and Manthandros Trasilika (the new wazir of Untunchilamon).

Even as Varazchavardan was crunching the twenty-fourth piece of ice in which he had that day indulged, Trasilika was saying:

'It was Aldarch the Third who appointed me. And, as I am sure you will be glad to hear, he gave me a death warrant for Justina Thrug. And this is that death warrant.'

CHAPTER TEN

The Temple of Torture, as such, had ceased to operate shortly after the death of Wazir Sin. In the seven years which had followed, the Temple had usually stood empty. Sometimes it had been used as a quarantine station, and sometimes as a detention centre; apart from that it had been untenanted. More recently, the Inland Revenue had taken over the premises; and, thanks to the patronage of that organization, the torture chambers of the Temple had been restored to their former glory.

Shortly before dawn, Master Ek was carried to the Temple of Torture in a litter; he could have walked, but such was his decrepitude that any such exercise would have taken him the better part of the day. Once in the Temple, Ek began his morning by watching the final stages of the torture of a vampire rat. His old friend Dui Tin Char (now head of the Inland Revenue) had begun the torture five days earlier. The exercise was a demonstration of the art of the Temple of Torture: a hint of delights yet to come should the temple be once again legalized.

When the vampire rat finally expired, Ek had to admit that he was impressed. He had not known that such a small animal possessed such a capacity for suffering.

'With humans,' said Dui Tin Char, 'the experience is immensely more rewarding.'

Dui Tin Char was a trained Exponent of the Grand Method of the Temple of Torture. He had participated in the Temple's daily Rites of Revelation for five years during the reign of the late and much-lamented Wazir Sin. Then Lonstantine Thrug had murdered Sin and had closed down the Temple. Since then, Tin Char had derived a considerable degree of satisfaction for his work in the field of tax collection; but, somehow, it was not quite the same.

'I must say,' said Ek, 'I find it hard to see where the extra reward can come from. Never have I seen anything suffer as this creature suffered before its death. Any elaboration or exaggeration of such pain is hard to imagine.'

'Ah,' said Tin Char softly. 'It is not pain which provides the pleasure. It is fear. Oh yes, fear. And humiliation. A vampire rat, you see, cannot be humiliated. Its psyche is not sufficiently developed. But humans are an altogether different proposition. You must always remember that Justina Thrug is the daughter of a Yudonic Knight. These people have considerable reserves of pride, hence their destruction upon the torture table is all the more pleasurable.'

'And Ashdans?' said Ek.

'I . . . I have never destroyed an Ashdan,' said Tin Char. He considered his lack of experience in this field then smiled cheerfully. 'But I am most certainly ready to make the experiment.'

Master Ek and Dui Tin Char had intended to devote their morning to the destruction of another rat, this time using the comparatively rapid quick-shock-bone-smash method. However, they were interrupted by a servant bearing slightly alarming news: a party of officials was on its way to the Temple of Torture.

'For what purpose?' said Dui Tin Char.

'To see Master Ek.'

'How,' said Ek, 'do these officials know that I am here?'

'One is the ladipti man,' said the servant, as if that explained all.

It did explain all, for the ladipti man was another of Ek's old and trusted friends, and had in Ek's company observed a part of the five-day death of the vampire rat which had so recently expired.

'Who else is coming here?' said Ek.

'That I know not,' said the servant.

'Then,' said Dui Tin Char softly, 'find out. Quickly!'

The servant hastened away, but the officials had reached the Temple of Torture before any fresh intelligence could be supplied to Master Ek and Tin Char. So they were none the wiser when their visitors were shown in.

Ek and Tin Char recognized the officials at once. Plague inspector, pilot, ladipti man, harbour master and a representative of the Combined Religious Guild. All, to a man, were of the Janjuladoola people. But with them were two children of Wen Endex, one a heavyweight in his forties, the other a slender and nervously blinking individual in his thirties.

'Greetings,' said the harbour master, making reverence to both Master Ek and Tin Char.

Ek observed the appropriate silence, emphasizing his own superiority and the harbour master's comparative inferiority. Then he said:

'And to you, greetings.'

Other formalities followed, then the harbour master got down to business:

'Behold, Master Ek. I bring you two most welcome newcomers. They are from one of the new ships.'

'These new ships which I hold in my lap,' said Ek, spreading apart his gnarled, arthritic hands as if he was measuring an invisible fish.

The harbour master was thrown into confusion. Not because he had any difficulty understanding Ek's idiom (he understood it perfectly) but because he realized he had made a social gaffe. He had assumed Ek knew all about the recently arrived ships, but obviously he had assumed in error. Now the harbour master would have to instruct Ek. And, in the Janjuladoola culture, a social inferior does not lightly undertake to instruct a superior in the presence of strangers.

At this point one of those strangers, the heavyweight

with the cauliflower ear, broke into grammatically imperfect and badly-accented Janjuladoola.

'We be the ship *Oktobdoj*. I be Trasilika. Fresh arrived we be and are from Yestron.'

'Yestron, yes,' said Master Ek acidly, switching from Janjuladoola to Toxteth as he did so. 'Yestron, in whose northern reaches they speak an argot different from that of Ang, do they not?'

'Indeed, Master Ek,' said the heavyweight gratefully, pleased to be able to converse in his native Toxteth.

'So you come from Yestron,' said Ek. 'What news?'

'Talonsklavara is at an end. Aldarch the Third has triumphed. I am Manthandros Trasilika, one whom Aldarch Three has sent to Injiltaprajura to do his bidding. I am—'

Ek gestured for silence then pointed at the heavyweight's slender companion.

'You?' said Ek.

'Jean Froissart, that's who I am, Froissart,' said the quick-blinking man, who was so nervous one might believe him to be on the edge of a nervous breakdown, or a heart attack, or both.

Ek hawked, then spat.

'So,' said Ek. 'Talonsklavara is at an end. Aldarch Three has won. Excellent. Excellent.'

Yet, even as he said it, Master Ek found himself curiously unelated, strangely unexcited. Depressed, almost. True, he was a loyal servant of Aldarch Three. He longed to see the family Thrug overthrown and the rule of the True Law restored to Untunchilamon. But . . .

'One presumes,' ventured Dui Tin Char, 'that Aldarch the Third will shortly appoint a new wazir to rule on Untunchilamon.'

'He has already,' said the heavyweight blandly. 'For I am that wazir.'

'And I,' said his nervous companion, 'am the priest of Zoz sent to accompany him.'

Master Ek and Tin Char positively goggled. Two children of Wen Endex, yet they claimed to be wazir and priest? This was unheard of! It was almost – not quite, but almost – impossible.

'Trasilika,' said Ek, 'I understand you to declare yourself to be the new wazir of Untunchilamon.'

'Yes. It was Aldarch the Third who appointed me. And, as I am sure you will be glad to hear, he gave me a death warrant for Justina Thrug. And this is that death warrant.'

Ek opened the warrant with difficulty, inwardly cursing the pains that shot through his fingers as he grappled with the parchment. Strange. His hands had been free of pain all morning till now. He studied the death warrant. Genuine? Probably. He passed it to Tin Char, then, to conceal his inward turmoil, took out his black tobacco pouch and began rolling a cigarette.

A long and most embarrassing silence then began, for Ek said nothing as he smoked his way through a cigarette then rolled himself another. That was his privilege. In the Janjuladoola system, the High Priest of Zoz the Ancestral was superior to everyone else on Untunchilamon except the wazir.

And, as yet, Untunchilamon did not have a wazir.

For, though Manthandros Trasilika claimed to have been appointed to that position, he needed to be ceremoniously installed by Master Ek himself. Until then, Trasilika's appointment had no legal force. Until then, he was wazir in name only, and not in fact.

As Ek sat smoking, he looked for all the world like a smoke-shrivelled corpse. Only his eyes betrayed the bright life of his intellect. But even the eyes failed to hint at the confusion which currently reigned in that intellect.

The source of Ek's confusion was the scrap of ricepaper hidden in his tobacco pouch, the tantalizing fragment of purple-scripted manuscript which said just this:

'. . . to become immortal. Immortality is easily

achieved if one has possession of an organic rectifier. On Untunchilamon . . .'

On Untunchilamon?

Maybe there was such an 'organic rectifier' on Untunchilamon. Maybe Ek had a chance of immortality.

So thinking, Master Ek had sent Nixorjapretzel Rat in search of the rest of this purple passage. But Ek had yet to profit from the Rat's pursuit of this Secret History. And, now, it was too late. For, if one of these 'organic rectifiers' was to be somehow uncovered, the new wazir would doubtless claim it on behalf of Aldarch Three.

Was that a problem? An outsider would probably have answered 'no'. For Aldarch the Third was a worshipper of Zoz the Ancestral. Why then should the Mutilator deny immortality to the priesthood of Zoz? Ek, who was an insider's insider, knew the answer to that all too well. An immortal Mutilator would doubtless prefer a mortal priesthood, fearing political threats from priests who had all of eternity in which to indulge in political manoeuvring.

'Is there a problem?' said the heavyweight at last, intruding on Ek's silence.

'Yes,' said Ek.

'May we . . . may we know the nature of this problem?' said the slender man in his thirties who had identified himself as Jean Froissart.

Ek coughed, hawked, spat, ground out his cigarette then said:

'I am old. I am seventy years old and I will never again set eyes on Obooloo. My bones bite, my spine twists, my bowels cramp, and my flesh lacks the appetite for the fourth major pleasure.'

The High Priest of Zoz the Ancestral indulged yet again in the first minor pleasure, then continued:

'So there is a problem. There are several problems. But they are mine, not thine. Let us proceed with the consecration. I will install you as wazir here and now.'

'What?' said Tin Char, startled.

106

This was unheard of. The consecration of a new wazir was a very formal ceremony rightly carried out in public after the appropriate sacrificies and preliminaries.

'You heard me,' said Master Ek.

He knew he was offending against protocol and tradition; he knew Obooloo would take umbrage at his actions; ultimately, he might be reprimanded, or chastised, or recalled to Ang to be removed from the priesthood and executed. But he no longer cared. He was sick at heart and a great bitterness was upon him. His recent days had been brightened by the chance of life eternal; but now that chance had been taken from him, and all was blighted.

Therefore the ceremony of consecration was carried out in the Temple of Torture. It was a rushed, squalid affair which offended all those who participated in it. But, for legal purposes, it sufficed. By the end of the ceremony, the heavyweight had been installed as the new wazir of Untunchilamon, and his lightweight companion had been confirmed as the wazir's personal priest.

'Just one last thing remains,' said Master Ek. 'By what means do you choose to be called?'

'Why, Manthandros Trasilika, of course,' said the heavyweight promptly. 'So I was born, so I will live, so I will die.'

This was an offence against custom, for a new wazir usually takes a new name when assuming his post. But Ek was too far gone to be troubled by such trifles.

'So be it,' said Ek. 'As Manthandros Trasilika you will be known. And you? Do you claim the name Jean Froissart?'

'It is my own,' said Trasilika's companion, 'so what other should I claim?'

This question was both ignorant and rude, but Ek let it pass without comment, and said:

'Then go forth into the world as wazir and priest, Trasilika and Froissart your names.'

'Go forth we will,' said Mathandros Trasilika. 'First to secure the execution of Justina Thrug. Are there loyal troops we can call upon?'

'That is for you to find out,' said Ek, then walked away.

This was a display of breathtaking, almost suicidal insolence. Mathandros Trasilika was now the wazir of Untunchilamon. And no priest, not even a High Priest, treats a wazir with open contempt. Not if he values his head.

'Hey!' said Trasilika. 'You can't walk out on us like this!'

Ek, who for the moment did not value his head, went on walking. And Dui Tin Char said, smoothly:

'Master Ek has been troubled of late, as have we all, for the island has been beset by nightmares of all descriptions. The drumming has been getting on his nerves of late.'

So spoke Tin Char; though in truth it was not Master Ek who was disturbed by Injiltaprajura's drummers but Tin Char himself.

'Drumming?' said Trasilika.

'Yes, yes, drumming,' said Tin Char. 'A hideous cult of diabolical inspiration which has the entire younger generation in its grip. And this is the least of the problems which have been worrying Master Ek. Be easy on the old man, for he has need of your mercy.'

'Mercy!' said Trasilika. 'That's as may be. But I have need of fighting men that justice may be done.'

'Yes, yes,' said Froissart eagerly. 'The witch must die.'

'And die she will,' said Tin Char. 'Today. For the troops are ready and waiting. They have been waiting only for the arrival of the new wazir.'

So spoke Tin Char. And he was as good as his word. For, very shortly, arrangements were being made to secure the arrest and execution of Justina Thrug, self-styled empress of Untunchilamon.

CHAPTER ELEVEN

On the fateful day which was marked by the arrival of the good ship *Oktobdoj*, the Empress of Untunchilamon began her routine with a swim, followed by a breakfast of papaya, pineapple and flying fish. Even as she took her breakfast, her spies were proceeding toward the pink palace with news of the ships lately arrived in the Laitemata, one a general trader and the other a brothel ship.

However, Justina was not a dainty eater, and she had demolished her breakfast long before her spies reached the portals of her palace. She then proceeded to a meeting with her legal counsel.

Dardanalti was Justina's lawyer, and a very good one he was. While he was of the Janjuladoola race, he was conscientious in his service to the usurper Thrug; for Dardanalti was one of those men for whom money takes precedence over prejudice, and Justina served him well. He was young, energetic, efficient, knowledgeable and cunning; better still, he did not belong to any of the Janjuladoola faiths, but adhered to the evolutionary heresy. This made him remarkable, for heretics of this breed were to be found almost exclusively among the Ebrell Islanders. Equally remarkable was Dardanalti's ability to look crisp and cool regardless of the extremes of heat and humidity he, like every other inhabitant of Injiltaprajura, had necessarily to endure.

Justina met regularly with Dardanalti in a bid to find a legal solution to her difficulties. If all else failed, she planned to seize a dozen ships by brute force and flee from Untunchilamon. But was there a way for her to take those ships legally, without going to war against their crews?

Furthermore, what would happen if a new wazir came to Injiltaprajura aboard one of the ships of the Trade Fleet? If Aldarch Three had already triumphed in Talonsklavara – a strong possibility – then an Aldarch appointee might be on his way to Untunchilamon with a death warrant commanding the execution of Justina Thrug.

Long had Justina and Dardanalti wrestled with these problems, but without coming any nearer to a solution. Justina had no great hopes for this latest meeting, but, to her surprise, Dardanalti announced that he had finished his analysis of her predicament.

'Surprise me,' said Justina.

'By exhaustive research,' said Dardanalti, 'I find there is no way you can legally seize twelve ships or avoid the wrath of any incoming wazir.'

'That,' said Justina severely, 'surprises me not at all. I'm not paying you to tell me what I can't do. What's the matter with you? Isn't the success bonus big enough? If it isn't, maybe you're getting a little too greedy.'

'My lady,' said Dardanalti hastily, 'you misjudge me. I know this matter to be dear to your heart.'

'To put it mildly,' said Justina.

'So,' continued Dardanalti, 'once the search for legal methods was exhausted, I began to explore those which, ah, are not strictly in accordance with legislated guidelines.'

'Illegal methods,' said Justina, who always wished to simplify.

'Um, well, in a manner of speaking,' said Dardanalti, his customary fluency failing him. 'Let us say, perhaps . . . how shall I put this? I began to contemplate a variety of manoeuvres, the legality of which has yet to be tested by the courts. That is one way of putting it.'

'You mean for us to become partners in crime,' said Justina. 'Very well. If that is what we must do to survive, that is what we will do. But I can't afford to sit here for six months or more while you dream up some wild and woolly scheme. I need something soon. Now, in fact.'

'Then you have it,' said Dardanalti.

'Explain,' said Justina, her brusqueness betraying something of the pressure she was under.

So Dardanalti did explain.

His scheme was daring, ambitious and very dangerous. Therefore it had a certain natural appeal for the Empress Justina, who was, after all, a child of Wen Endex and the daughter of a Yudonic Knight. Dardanalti proposed that they intercept one of the incoming ships of the Trade Fleet and place a false wazir aboard.

'The false wazir would be your creature,' said the young lawyer, growing enthusiastic as he enlarged on this scheme. 'He would give you authorization to seize a dozen ships.'

'But what if there was a real wazir with the Trade Fleet?' said Justina.

'Then things would get very sticky,' admitted Dardanalti. 'But we might yet win. After all, who could tell our wazir from the real thing? There's forgers on Untunchilamon who could make the necessary seals, warrants and authorizations.'

Justina began to smile.

But only momentarily.

'You seem,' she said, 'to have overlooked one vital point. Where is the candidate for this false wazirship to come from?'

She had a point. Injiltaprajura was a city of barely 30,000 souls, most of whom had been on the island for the last seven years or more. How could they find a face unknown to the city's power brokers?

'There is Jal Japone,' said Dardanalti.

'There is,' said Justina, and left it at that.

The outlawed warlord Jal Japone effectively ruled the northern wastelands of Untunchilamon. He was of Janjuladoola race, and Justina trusted him not at all.

'There is also,' said Dardanalti, 'the Dromdanjerie.'

'Hmmm,' said Justina.

111

Her lawyer had a point. The Dromdanjerie was Injiltaprajura's lunatic asylum. It held the usual range of howling madmen, slobbering morons, helpless dements, autistic bone-bags, schizophrenic demon-angels, alcoholic degenerates and syphilitic idiots; but also imprisoned within its walls were a few very intelligent psychopaths, some of whom had not been seen in public for decades.

'Candidates?' said Justina.

'Pardon?' said Dardanalti.

'Have you any specific candidates in mind?' said Justina. 'For our fake wazir, I mean?'

'No, my lady,' said Dardanalti.

'Then,' said Justina, 'I propose that we go together to the Dromdanjerie. The sooner the better. Now being better than any time later.'

But before Justina and Dardanalti could depart, a manservant intruded upon their privacy.

'What is it?' said Justina.

'We have news of the latest arrivals,' said the manservant, referring to the two ships which had come into the Laitemata at dawn.

'Good,' said Justina, pleased to see that her orders were being obeyed; it was most important that the palace had intelligence about each new vessel that arrived in the harbour.

'One is a general trader,' said the manservant, retailing the information freshly delivered by Justina's spies.

'And the other?' said Justina.

'It is a cruise ship, ma'am.'

'A what?' said Justina.

'A – a ship of ill repute,' said the manservant.

'He means a brothel ship,' said Dardanalti.

'Oh,' said Justina. 'I didn't know there really were such things. I thought that was just a story.'

'Manamalargo is famous for such cruise ships, ma'am.'

'Well, well,' said Justina. 'One lives and learns. What news of Yestron?'

112

'Talonsklavara wages still. The war is undecided.'

'Good,' said Justina. 'You are dismissed.'

The manservant departed, and Justina smiled.

'That seems to solve our immediate problems,' said Dardanalti.

'It gives us time in which to manoeuvre,' said Justina. 'But no more. The sooner we choose and train our wazir the better. Come! The bedlam awaits.'

The impetuous haste with which Justina set forth for the Dromdanjerie is best explained by the agonies of impotent waiting which she had endured for so long. At last she had a plan of action: risky, uncertain, perhaps lunatic. But a plan regardless. Something she could do. And this fired her frame with energy. So forth she went with Dardanalti at her side.

But Justina had got no further than the front steps of her palace when she was intercepted by Juliet Idaho, who demanded to see her in private. Immediately.

Justina sighed, commanded Dardanalti to wait, then walked Idaho to her office. Juliet Idaho was a warrior's warrior, a hero who would have made a fitting companion for Vorn the Gladiator on any of the missions of peril undertaken by that lusty swordsman; but Justina was not a gladiator, and sometimes (just sometimes) Idaho got on her nerves.

Once in her office, Justina sat.

'What is it?' said she.

'This,' said Juliet Idaho, passing over a document.

'And what is this?' said Justina.

'That's what I want to know,' said Juliet Idaho, seating himself without invitation.

Justina studied Idaho's offering, a single sheet of ricepaper nearly obliterated by a million chicken-scratchings in vermilion ink.

'It appears to be writing,' said she, squinting at the miniscule letters so painfully executed in a crabbed and scorpioned hand. 'But in what language I cannot say. The words are like our dummer's drums: they

113

say something, but say nothing intelligible to me.'

'The text is written in Slandolin, my lady,' said Idaho.

Justina had never got round to learning that language. She supposed she should have; but then, there were so very many tongues that the learning of them could easily have overwhelmed a lifetime.

'What is your interest in this . . . this Slandolin?' said Justina. 'What have we here? A work of scholarship?'

'In a manner of speaking,' said Idaho. 'It purports to tell of the creation of a dragon. A new kind of dragon. A dragon no longer than your finger.'

'This dragon?' said Justina.

So saying, she pointed at the little nest of cat's fur and feather-fluff which sat upon her desk. Within was the dragon Untunchilamon, so named by the Empress Justina. This was a beast of heroic lineaments but decidedly unheroic physical capacities; seven days previously it had been mobbed by a squabble of seagulls on the island of Jod, and would have died but for the personal intervention of the imperial veterinarian, who had been upon Jod to give the Hermit Crab a medical check. The poor mite of a dragon had been half-dead when brought to the palace, but had been recovering steadily ever since; indeed, the veterinarian averred that it would soon be fit to fly.

For those who lack knowledge of alien tongues, it should here be noted that the dragon Untunchilamon was so named for the same reason that cats are so often called 'Cat'. In the Janjuladoola of the Izdimir Empire, 'Untunchilamon' means 'dragon', hence many firedrakes have thus been called, and doubtless many more will thus be denominated hereafter.

Why then was Justina's island named 'dragon' in Janjuladoola? Here there is no great mystery. The ruling rock of the island was and is the sunset-tinged bloodstone, its red colour oft associated with fire and hence with dragons.

'The document,' said Idaho, 'would appear to speak of

114

the creation of this dragon, yes. However, there is a fractional notation of greater interest at the very bottom of the page. A translation reads thus.'

He handed the Empress a piece of paper, rough stuff incorporating patent splinters of wood. The Slandolin of the purple script had been translated into Janjuladoola and set down in large letters of lamp-black ink written in a bold, confident hand. The translation read thus:

'A neat trick, this creation of dragon from cockroach. But greater feats have been done in the past. Take for example the attainments of the organic rectifier, that magnanimous piece of machinery which allowed selected citizens of the Golden Gulag to make themselves immortal. Such was the jovial vigour of its accomplishments that it could jest a man to woman in less time than a twinkling wave takes to break from curves as smooth as haunch and hip to a flurry of foam and galactic scintillations, which is certainly less time than it takes to write these words which seek to encapture that motion. Damn this light! And how is a man to work with the dogs so wrath? Anyway: the rectifier. It could easily have delighted the Crab by converting that frustrated dignity to human form. Furthermore, though Untunchilamon knew it not, there was—'

Justina frowned.

She read through the translation a second time.

The implications made her head spin.

'Are we to imagine that there might be a . . . a device of some kind?' said she. 'Here, I mean? On Untunchilamon? A device to magic Crab to human?'

'I'm a Yudonic Knight,' said Juliet Idaho. 'I don't imagine things. I kill things. I vote we find the person who wrote the original. Find, interrogate, torture, kill. That strikes me as better work than any labour of imagination.'

'Julie, darling,' said Justina, smiling upon her trusted retainer. 'Your energy and enthusiasm are a constant inspiration to me. Verily, we shall seek the author of

115

the original text. Where did that text come from?'

'It was thieved from the Cabal House by one of our spies,' said Juliet Idaho. 'He knew not the value of what he had carried away, for he could read no Slandolin. In truth, he is illiterate; he reads nothing.'

'What else did he steal?' said Justina.

'A great many bills, most of them invoices for deliveries of medicinal alcohol. A book of bad poems, a lampoon upon Aquitaine Varazchavardan, a street map of Obooloo, the plans for a twenty-oar galley, the deeds to the title of Ganthorgruk and a letter addressing birthday greetings to Jal Japone.'

'Try to find another thief,' said Justina. 'A literate one. With such a thief found, send him into the Cabal House to steal some more of this purple writing. Meanwhile: who did our translation?'

An obvious question, since Juliet Idaho knew no more of Slandolin than did the Empress herself. Furthermore, since no imperial business was conducted in that Ashmolean tongue, no official translators of such were on tap.

'A soldier,' said Idaho. 'I knew it for an Ashdan tongue so I sought out an Ashdan to read it. Shanvil Angarus May.'

'May!' said Justina. 'I know him well. But he tells himself to be from Ashmolea North. Are not the secrets of Slandolin the sole possession of the south?'

'Of livers and kidneys and buckets of blood, of such is my teaching,' answered Idaho, speaking with unabashed violence. 'I asked as a soldier will. I asked: can you do it. He answered: yes. So I told him: do it.'

'Well!' said Justina, sounding slightly miffed. 'I'm sorry I asked!'

'Forgive me, my lady,' said Idaho.

That much he said in a stiff and formal manner which entirely failed to suggest remorse. But Justina replied with grace and gratitude, for all the world as if he had made an impassioned and extended apology on bended knees:

116

'Julie, my love, of course I forgive you. I know what a strain you've been under. You've been working so terribly hard and doing such a darling job. I couldn't possibly ask more of you. What say you fetch me Shanvil May so we can talk over the translation in detail?'

Whereupon the doughty Juliet Idaho – 'Julie' to his Empress but 'Thugboots' to his troops – was much mollified. He bowed to his Empress, though such was not his custom, then departed to search for Shanvil May.

While the Empress Justina ruled Idaho with velvet, it would be wrong to suppose that all her dealings with the world were thus. Some she flattered; some she urged to her assistance by feigning that melting weakness which your romantic and misogynist alike will describe as being womanly. But others she bent to her will by exercise of brute force and unprincipled violence, for the strenuous demands of keeping order in her faction-fraught kingdom did not allow her to eschew these standard weapons of stateswomanship.

Then Justina rang for a manservant and told him to fetch Dardanalti.

While the Empress still intended to visit the Dromdanjerie, and soon, she first wanted to discuss the latest development with Dardanalti himself. Was there really an 'organic rectifier' on Untunchilamon? An immortality machine? A device which could translate Crab flesh to human? Justina thought she had better find out, and quickly.

Unfortunately for the Empress, her time for research was going to be strictly limited. For the day had advanced while she conferred at length with her lawyer and with Juliet Idaho. Unbeknownst to Justina, Untunchilamon already had a new wazir. A heavyweight uitlander had been confirmed in that position by the High Priest of Zoz the Ancestral.

Soldiers disloyal to the Empress had been hastily

117

summoned by Dui Tin Char, and were even then on the way to the pink palace, seeking to arrest Justina Thrug so she could be brought before Manthandros Trasilika and summarily executed.

CHAPTER TWELVE

The disloyal soldiers summoned by Dui Tin Char marched into the pink palace and sought out the Empress Justina. The men were led by Coleslaw Styx, a ruthless guard marshal.

The soldiers were soon at the door to Justina's office. They knocked. Then knocked the door down. Then stormed into the office and seized the Empress.

'Stop!' cried Dardanalti. 'You can't do this!'

But his protests did no good whatsoever.

Justina Thrug was dragged out of the pink palace and hauled away down Lak Street without any ceremony whatsoever. Few of the citizens of Injiltaprajura observed her plight. As yet, few people knew that Untunchilamon had a new wazir, let alone that the Empress had been arrested and was being taken to the Temple of Torture to be executed.

Here we long for a hero to intervene, a hero built along the lines of Vorn the Gladiator. But, to the historian's regret, it must be recorded that no hero was on hand; and those citizens who observed the passage of the Empress were content to gawk at the spectacle like so many disinterested tourists.

Justina did not see a single friendly face until she had been marched down Lak Street as far as its intersection with Goldhammer Rise and Skindik Way. There Justina glimpsed an Ashdan lass she remembered from the past. The girl was loitering by a group of drummers who were tub-thumping their instruments of diabolical intoxication in the shadow of the Cabal House itself. The girl's name? That escaped the Empress. But Justina knew the young female to be the lover of a rock gardener who had the trust and confidence of the Crab.

The Crab!

Could the Crab help the Empress on this her day of greatest need?

Justina had no time to speculate, no time to formulate a cunning strategy to pass a Crab-petitioning message to the Ashdan lass. For the soldiers turned down Goldhammer Rise: and the rock gardener's girlfriend was left behind.

Justina was possessed of a sense of unreality. She had long anticipated such a disaster, but the precipitate haste of its enactment had taken her by surprise. The world around her seemed too large. The heads of the soldiers gross, swollen. Their weapons huge, the razorblade sunlight of their armaments brighter than reality. She found it hard to pay attention to Dardanalti who was walking beside her, rattling out instructions as if they were going to an auction or a town planning hearing.

Then she saw the Temple of Torture, which lies on the left-hand side of Goldhammer Rise as one descends from Lak Street towards Manthandorthan. She remembered once reading an autopsy report which the corpse-master Uckermark had done on a victim of that temple. She felt sick.

With the temple in sight, the soldiers quickened the pace. Orders were shouted. The syllables jagged through the air, echoed, fractured, buckled in the heat. Dardanalti said something. Gafoblik? Choglik? Moglig? His urgent utterances floundered into unintelligibility. Justina tripped, stumbled, was caught by an iron-grip soldier. Her feet hurt. Beads of sweat swarmed between her flouncing breasts, stung her eyes, hummed in her ears. The sky was pale yellow, was grey, was black.

Justina fell.

Fainting.

Down on her face she went and the boots were in, quick, quick, no chance to rape but a chance yet to hurt, bruise, break, crush. Dardanalti shouted. Threatened. A lawyer, Janjuladoola nuances on his tongue. His skin the same grey as that of the soldiers. Their anger ebbed, and two helped haul a groaning Empress to her feet.

The soldiers marched the Empress to the door of the Temple, a door on which two artists were busy painting a much-wounded human body. Dui Tin Char had wasted no time whatsoever. The Temple of Torture was back in business. From within came persistent screaming, a horrific outcry which intensified as the doors opened. Dardanalti darted inside. Justina, shoved from behind, stumbled in after him. The air stank. The stench was that of diarrhoea tinged with curry.

Then the Empress was hauled into the naos of the Temple, and there was Dui Tin Char, and there were two strangers, and weird sounds were being made by the mouths of these strangers, and there was a bulky man whom she recognized as an executioner, and she tried to speak but her mouth was full of vomit, and there was darkness, again there was darkness, darkness flooding her eyes as once more she fainted.

CHAPTER THIRTEEN

Earlier that day, the airship built by Hostaja Sken-Pitilkin had dismantled itself. The disgruntled wizard had shortly thereafter departed from the pink palace, and had made his way to the island of Jod to confer with the master chef Pelagius Zozimus, who happened to be his cousin.

These days, Jod was assuming something of the aspect of a fortress. Earlier that year, Pelagius Zozimus had been kidnapped by persons unknown, dragged away from the Analytical Institute, stuffed full of opium and held for several days in a helpless drug stupor. Why? He knew not, but was determined that the same thing would not happen again.

As Zozimus was the master chef who served the Crab, that dignitary was equally determined that there would be no repetition of this incident, and so had supported moves to build a defensive wall to guard the approaches of the Analytical Institute.

Ever since, slaves and servants had been labouring to construct that wall, working under the supervision of Chegory Guy. Young Chegory was an Ebrell Islander possessed of a formidable musculature. Until recently, he had been officially employed as a rock gardener – even though ever-increasing amounts of his time had been spent in direct association with the Crab. Now, Chegory still served the Crab its meals and, with help from the delectable Olivia Qasaba, did his best to stop the poor thing from getting lonely in the evenings. However, he was discharging his new wall-supervising responsibilities admirably.

Chegory himself had also suffered in the previous

year. After Zozimus had been kidnapped, Chegory had been ordered to the pink palace and there detained by the Empress Justina for a matter of days. What unspeakable things had happened to him? And why? Chegory ever after refused to say. In particular, he refused to discuss the matter with his beloved Olivia, the love of his heart; but his refusal had been couched in terms which had made it abundantly clear to that Ashdan lass that her sledgehammer swain had endured near-unendurable tortures in that palace.

When Hostaja Sken-Pitilkin arrived on Jod, he was soon admitted to the kitchen. The Crab's breakfast had already been cooked and served, and Zozimus was organizing its lunch. The Crab was going to dine upon centipede soup, shark steaks marinated in a mixture of red wine and dog's blood, fried octopus wrapped in tendrils of fresh seaweed, the meat of twenty coconuts and thrice thirty mangos, riceballs piqued with cayenne pepper, baked yams and a pie incorporating the eyeballs of five hundred fish.

Sken-Pitilkin told his cousin of the destruction of the flying ship, and thereafter the two wizards sat long together in earnest conference. Both were gravely worried, for the airship's destruction was the first sign that Injiltaprajura's sorcerers might be ready to actively move against them. If that happened, the wizards would have two chances: slim and none. For they could not hope to withstand an onslaught by the combined powers of the wonder-workers of Injiltaprajura's Cabal House.

The two were still dialoguing in helpless circles when a servant ventured to interrupt their conference. Someone was coming across the harbour bridge which linked Jod to the mainland. Someone in a great big hurry.

Now, nobody runs on Untunchilamon. Not unless they absolutely have to. Climate and custom both oppose the practice. Hence a runner stands in danger of collapsing from the heat and humidity; or alternatively, being mistaken for a lunatic and hustled into the

Dromdanjerie. So, while there were no psychics on Jod, those on the island were sure the hastening messenger must be bearing tidings of the utmost urgency.

Zozimus and Sken-Pitilkin thanked the servant for the interruption and made sure they were on hand to intercept the messenger and hear the burden of his panic.

The messenger – a her, as it happened – was none other than Olivia Qasaba. She came hammering across the harbour bridge, raced to the wall so slowly rising in front of the white marble magnificence of the Analytical Institute, and promptly collapsed at the feet of her true love, young Chegory Guy.

The Ashdan lass was in a sorry state after her flight from the Cabal House to Jod. Her face was shining with sweat, her bosoms heaving as she gasped for air. She tried to get up. She managed to get up. Then promptly bent double and was sick, for the force of her flight had overstressed her. Chegory, the very incarnation of concern, yelled for someone to bring water, then knelt beside the distressed young woman.

Water was brought; Olivia's breathing eased; and, to Chegory's relief, the Ashdan lass found herself capable of speech.

'Justina,' said Olivia.

'She – she's dead?' said Chegory.

Olivia shook her head wordlessly. Chegory wiped a little vomit from her lower lip and served her some water in a clean-scraped coconut shell.

'Don't drink,' he said. 'Just swill and spit.'

Olivia obeyed. Then began to explain. She had been on her way to a jeweller's shop on Lak Street to get a broken locket fixed. But she had got no further than the Cabal House when soldiers had gone past, dragging Justina with them.

'Where were they taking her?' said Chegory.

'I – I don't know,' said Olivia. 'But they went down Goldhammer Rise.'

124

Everyone knew what lay on Goldhammer Rise. Memories of the history of the Temple of Torture had been stirred to full and vigorous life by the recent renovations. Immediately a babble of blabbermouthed speculation broke out among the bystanders.

Even as they were speculating, another messenger came across the harbour bridge. This one was not running; instead, he was stumping along stolidly in the mounting heat of the day. He was a mechanic who worked on the Analytical Engine, and he brought grim tidings.

This was the first pronouncement which the mechanic made once he had the attention of the denizens of Jod:

'Aldarch the Third has won the war.'

Did Chegory feel the day grow cold despite the heat of the sun? He did. Did his vision darken though the sky's major luminary yet shone bright? It is a pity to answer in the affirmative, for such a response verges on cliché. However, his vision did thus darken. On reflection, we must acknowledge that humans demonstrate a strictly limited repertoire in the face of disaster. Upon deprivation of food, they hunger; when starved of water, they thirst; and when, after months of dread, a long-awaited disaster befalls them, they do for the most part greet such disaster with a stoic's ataraxia, a drunkard's braggadocio, a warrior's defiance, a child's hysterical panic or with a sudden descent into invalidism.

In the face of disaster, Chegory on this occasion tended to the invalidism school of reaction. But his constitution was sound and solid; and, besides, his concern for Olivia prevented him from indulging in a fainting fit.

So he pulled himself together and listened as the mechanic made all plain.

The mechanic (Joy Wax by name) had been finishing off a late breakfast in his favourite speakeasy when sailors had entered. These matalots had proved to be from the good ship *Oktobdoj*, and soon they had been

125

drinking up large, earning free drinks with the remarkable tale they had to tell.

When Joy Wax had retailed that tale in turn, there was consternation all round. A new wazir on Untunchilamon! Justina arrested! Aldarch III victorious! Where would it all end?

'I think, um, I think we'd better do something,' said Chegory. 'It's like, Justina, she, they, they'll chop her, that's what I think. Unless we do something.'

'Yes,' said a much-recovered Olivia Qasaba. 'We must rescue her.'

While Olivia had been given to understand that Chegory had been arrested, imprisoned and tortured at Justina's behest, Chegory was nevertheless wont to opine that the Empress was essentially good. His loyalty was understandable. For it was the Family Thrug which had halted the pogrom against Chegory's Ebrell Island breed; and an isolated aberrant incident was pardonable when set against the racial debt. Hence Olivia's expressed loyalty to the Empress; this loyalty being no less than an aspect of Olivia's love for Chegory himself.

While Olivia spoke with confidence, she failed to bend her audience to her point of view.

'Rescue her?' said Joy Wax in open derision. 'Thrug is finished. That's all there is to it. Al'three has won. We've a new wazir, the Empress already in his grip. Chegory's right. It's head-chopping time. Doubtless the Empress has greeted the widest grin already.'

However, the wizards Pelagius Zozimus and Hostaja Sken-Pitilkin were not so swift to write off Justina.

'We must at least try to preserve the Empress,' said Zozimus.

'Indeed we must,' agreed his cousin.

Their attitude owned nothing to altruism. The two wizards were sorely isolated on an island dominated by sorcerers, and hence hostile to wizards. Their allies were

126

few. Few? Two! Keeping them company on Untunchilamon was a cut-throat by name of Thayer Levant and a barbarian called Guest Gulkan.

This little band of foreigners had come to Untunchilamon to seize a bauble known as the wishstone, a triakisoctahedron of obscure origin which was one of the minor ornaments of Justina's treasury. They had failed. They now wished to leave Untunchilamon with at least their lives: something far easier to arrange if Justina remained on the throne.

'Yet,' said Sken-Pitilkin, 'we lack the strength to win in war against the wonder-workers.'

'Then,' said Zozimus, 'Shabble must help us.'

'Shabble?'

'Shabble! Send for Ivan Pokrov!'

Joy Wax was sent to fetch Pokrov, while other mechanics, servants and slaves were dispersed in other directions with different messages. Some were sent to warn selected Ebrell Islanders that a victorious Aldarch Three had sent a new wazir to Untunchilamon, and that a fresh pogrom might shortly begin. One was sent to summon a lawyer to the Temple of Torture to act for Justina (for they were ignorant of the fact that the redoubtable Dardanalti was already with the Empress). Others were sent to warn Theodora Thrug (Justina's twin sister) and Troldot Turbothot (Theodora's latest boyfriend) that it would be best if they went into hiding.

'You must also go into hiding,' said Olivia to Chegory.

Reasonable advice, for Chegory was an Ebrell Islander, and hence a potential victim of pogrom. But Chegory demurred, saying he must first consult with the Crab. Hand in hand, Chegory and Olivia made their way to the cave where the eremitic dignitary dwelt that Chegory might receive orders from Jod's true ruler.

Meanwhile Ivan Pokrov came hastening out of the Analytical Institute, and was soon deep in urgent discussion with Zozimus and Sken-Pitilkin.

'Shabble would at this stage appear to be our only hope of rescuing Justina,' said Zozimus.

'What exactly do you know of the Shabble breed?' said Pokrov.

'I know,' said Zozimus, 'that Shabble can throw flame sufficient to disgrace a dragon. With that power on our side, all Untunchilamon will necessarily yield to us. Furthermore, I have heard it said that you have the power to command Shabble.'

'Me?' said the olive-skinned analytical engineer, doing his best to appear innocent.

But Zozimus was right.

Ivan Pokrov knew the secret of commanding Shabble.

There is no great mystery about Shabble or Shabble's past. The free-floating ball which had made Injiltaprajura its playground was no more than an analytical engine left over from the days of the Golden Gulag. It drew its energies directly from a sun located in a different cosmos entirely, hence would have no trouble burning Injiltaprajura to the ground if the necessity arose. Against such a weapon, no wazir would be able to survive: not even if he had an army at his back.

Furthermore, Ivan Pokrov was an immortal survivor of the Golden Gulag, and knew the secret of commanding Shabble. Which, again, was very simple. Shabble lived in dread of being sent to a therapist. And Shabble could always be commanded against Shabble's will by a threat of impending therapy. All Pokrov needed to say was this:

'Do what I tell you or I'll send you to the therapist!'

By such commands, Ivan Pokrov had long bent Shabble to his will. Thus Shabble worked in the Analytical Institute when Pokrov commanded it, designing complex machinery capable of processing algorithms. Better still, Shabble even worked out Pokrov's income tax. Pokrov had never tried to command Shabble to kill someone. But surely Shabble would obey if commanded.

'Very well,' said Pokrov, coming to a decision. 'I admit it. I can and will command Shabble. But first we have to find our floating bubble. Shabble has not been seen on Jod these many days. I propose that we begin by looking in the Dromdanjerie. Well, shall we be going?'

'Pelagius will go with you,' said Sken-Pitilkin. 'Not me.'

A wise decision, for, though the two cousins were of equal age, Pelagius Zozimus looked at least a thousand years younger and was far more athletic. Sken-Pitilkin's wizardry could not protect him from the crushing heat and humidity of the day, and there was a danger that if he hastened up and down the steep-rising streets of Injiltaprajura he would shortly fall victim to heat-stroke.

So Pelagius Zozimus and Ivan Pokrov set forth to seek out Shabble, first making their way to the Dromdanjerie, the lunatic asylum where the globular master of mischief so often went for interesting conversation with a wide range of people who had plenty of time on their hands.

Pelagius Zozimus and Ivan Pokrov did not run. Nevertheless, their pace evidenced a certain haste as they went across the harbour bridge, through the slumlands of Lubos, then up steep-rising Skindik Way. Past the slaughterhouse they went, a trickle of monkey blood running into the street as they stalked past. Next came the huge rotting doss-house known as Ganthorgruk, and then the Dromdanjerie.

Into that bedlam they went. It was cool within, and quiet, but for the ominous beating of a drum.

Tok – tok – tuk!

Tok – tok – tuk . . .!

The pulse of a remorseless madness!

Zozimus and Pokrov paid no heed to the drumming, but enquired after the master of the place (the eminent Ashdan known as Jon Qasaba). At their request, a servant sought him out. They then interrogated him as to Shabble's whereabouts.

129

'You'll find friend Shabble in Marthandorthan,' said Jon Qasaba.

Pelagius Zozimus raised one eyebrow. This raising of one eyebrow was a speciality of his. Though Zozimus was an uitlander who had spent very little of his life on Untunchilamon, he nevertheless knew Marthandorthan to be a singularly insalubrious area, a slumland of warehouses, speakeasies, gangster lairs and over-populated tenement blocks notorious for the delinquency of the children spawned with them.

Pokrov knew this also.

'Marthandorthan?' said the analytical engineer, frowning. 'What would Shabble be doing there?'

'Do you by chance know of a drug dealer by name of Firfat Labrat?' said Qasaba.

'Well . . . yes,' conceded Pokrov with some reluctance. 'Labrat is a cousin of an employee of mine.'

'So he is,' said Qasaba. 'So he is. And unless I am misinformed, you once had occasion to shelter in the Xtokobrokotok.'

'The Xtokobrokotok?' said Pokrov.

'That,' said Jon Qasaba, 'is the name of Firtat Labrat's warehouse in Marthandorthan.'

'Oh,' said Pokrov. 'So. What are you trying to tell me? That I'll find Shabble there?'

'Shabble, yes,' said Qasaba. 'And Labrat. Did you by chance introduce the pair?'

'In a manner of speaking,' said Pokrov. 'When I was in this – what is the name of the place?'

'Xtokobrokotok.'

'Yes, well, when I was there, Forfat Labrat asked for some help with his income tax. As a matter of courtesy I was compelled to oblige, and naturally I asked Shabble to give me some help. It's an excellent accountant, this Shabble, whatever its other failings may be.'

'Then you must bear some of the responsibility for what has happened,' said Qasaba ominously.

'Responsibility?' said Pokrov in bewilderment. 'What

130

are you talking about? What's Shabble done now?'

'If I was to tell you,' said Qasaba, 'you'd be most unlikely to believe me. It's best that you go and see for yourself.'

'This is no time for games,' said Zozimus.

And elaborated, swiftly outlining the need for urgency. Qasaba remained unmoved.

'Go,' said Qasaba, 'and see for yourself.'

'Well,' said Pokrov, 'well, if you say so. We will. We will. Don't worry, friend Zozimus. Shabble will soon be a convert to our cause. I guarantee it.'

'You speak of converts?' said Qasaba, with a wry smile. 'You mean to convert Shabble? I believe it is Shabble who is doing the converting these days.'

'What precisely is that supposed to mean?' said Pokrov.

'Go to Marthandorthan,' said Qasaba. 'Dare your way to Xtokobrokotok. Then you'll find out.'

Since the eminent Ashdan therapist declined to say more, regardless of the urgencies of the moment, his two visitors had no option but to remove themselves from the Dromanjerie and set forth for the lair of the drug dealer Firfat Labrat, there to find out for themselves precisely what mischief was presently amusing the feckless and ever-reckless Shabble.

They feared, of course, that by this time Justina might well be dead.

CHAPTER FOURTEEN

There were at this time some 30,000 souls in the fair city of Injiltaprajura, which means that a comprehensive history of even a single day in the life of the metropolis would be encyclopedic in bulk and mind-boggling in complexity. Fortunately, this is not such a comprehensive history; it is selective in the extreme, which is why only a very few of the inhabitants of Untunchilamon's capital have been mentioned by name.

Reference has been made to Lonstantine, Justina and Theodora Thrug; to Juliet Idaho and Shanvil May; to the wizards Pelagius Zozimus and Hostaja Sken-Pitilkin; to the formidable Aquitaine Varazchavardan and his erstwhile apprentice Nixorjapretzel Rat; to certain survivors of the Golden Gulag, these being the bright-bouncing Shabble, an engineer called Ivan Pokrov and a conjuror going by the name of Odolo; to Jon Qasaba and to his daughter Olivia, lover of the Ebrell Islander Chegory Guy, himself a friend of the Crab of the island of Jod; to Manthandros Trasilika, Jean Froissart and Nadalastabstala Banraithanchumun Ek; to the lawyer Dardanalti and to others.

Now, all of these people know (or will know) all of the others; and each must take the actual or potential actions of all into account when manoeuvring for survival or advantage. Unfortunately, this tends to make for complexity; and there is a danger that some few readers unversed in the ways of history will find the interplay of even this carefully thinned selection of protagonists a trifle bewildering.

But what is the poor historian to do?

Were this a fiction instead of a history, certain obvious

solutions could be entertained, most of them involving a general massacre to simplify the outline of events. A glorious and spontaneous bursting of brains, for example; or a sudden plague of meningococcal meningitis; or a rain of rocks from the sky to shatter an appropriate number of heads; or a swarm of killer scorpions invading from Zolabrik to sting, chew, bite and scrabble their way through a living nightmare until Injiltaprajura was suitably depopulated; or evil elves with phosphorescent eyes arriving by the shipload to hack the city's population down to a thousandth of its original magnitude.

But facts are as they are; and the fact is that no unnatural disaster beset the island of Untunchilamon in the final days of the reign of Justina Thrug. Furthermore, anyone who grew to maturity in the time of Talonsklavara was by definition a survivor; therefore the advent of a new wazir and the political instability thereby produced did not automatically result in large numbers of people conveniently curling up their toes and disappearing from the historical panorama.

Be assured, however, that all key players in the politics of Untunchilamon have now been identified, and will be identified yet again should the need arise. Nevertheless, there remains a need to make mention of one more person. This is Bro Drumel, captain of Justina's palace guard.

On the fateful day on which the good ship *Oktobdoj* arrived in the Laitemata, Bro Drumel began his morning by attacking some of the paperwork which had piled up in his office in the Moremo Maximum Security Prison. He was still hard at work in that office when he received news of the arrival of a brothel ship in Laitemata.

'Such rumour is false,' said Drumel to the messenger who so informed him. 'If drums could talk, they'd rumour thus, but tongues have no less excuse for ignorance. No brothel ship would sail across Moana.'

'But it is true, my lord,' insisted the messenger, as

politely as he knew how. 'I have seen the bark myself.'

'How absurd,' said Drumel. 'A brothel ship ! Here! They'll lose money on that, and badly.'

Then he thought no more about it, which was easy to do as Moremo was located on Injiltaprajura's desert side, and hence insulated from any immediate knowledge of developments (excitements, alarums, arrests, confrontations and such) taking place portside.

Bro Drumel was currently running the prison (as well as Justina's palace guard) because the Governor of that institution had died after being attacked and bitten by a rabid pig. The Governor's deputy was in the Dromdanjerie suffering from delirium tremens and the deputy's deputy was illiterate; so the Empress Justina, after considering the lack of available talent, had lumbered Bro Drumel with this job in addition to his other duties.

Drumel suspected he was being punished.

Punished?

Why, yes.

For, earlier in the year, Bro Drumel had joined a coup against the Empress, a coup which had almost cost Justina her life. Much had thereafter been forgiven, but not all; hence Bro Drumel's labours.

His paperwork was finally interrupted by the advent of Juliet Idaho, who was searching for Shanvil Angarus May.

'What do you want him for?' said Bro Drumel.

'To kick in his head,' answered Idaho.

Which was in keeping with Idaho's character; though the truth was rather different, the truth being that the Empress Justina had commanded Idaho to produce Shanvil Angarus May so they could discuss a certain translation which May had made from the Slandolin.

'Why,' said Drumel, 'seek him here?'

'Because May is your deputy, is he not?' said Idaho.

'Technically, yes,' said Drumel. 'But he's yet to show his face in the prison. I think he lacks a taste for paperwork.'

So saying, Drumel pointed at his own paperwork in distaste. Petitions; ration requisitions; authorizations for routine maintenance work; calculations for release dates; certificates of birchings, beatings and brandings; and stacks of similar bureaucratic impedimenta.

'But,' said Idaho, in extreme irritation, 'I was specifically told he would be here.'

'You were lied to,' said Drumel.

'It was a soldier who told me,' said Idaho.

'Soldiers are not universally truthful,' said Drumel dryly.

'I'll beat him till his bones are bare and bloody,' said Idaho savagely. 'He told me a deliberate lie. To my face!'

'Who was it?' said Drumel.

Idaho named the miscreant, then said:

'I'd been looking for May in the palace. Then I . . . I met these—'

He stopped.

Something unusual had happened.

Juliet Idaho had begun to think.

Idaho thought hard. He had left Justina. He had gone in search of May. He had failed to find May. Then he had met a party of soldiers entering the palace. He had asked after May. He had been lied to: had been misdirected to the desert side prison.

Which meant . . .

'You!' roared Idaho, drawing his sword.

'Don't chop me!' screamed Bro Drumel, throwing up his hands in horror.

'It's a plot, isn't it?' shouted Idaho.

'Plot?' said Drumel in bewilderment. 'Plot, what plot? What are you talking about?'

'To kill Justina. It must be. That's what they came for. Too scared to kill me on the spot so they sent me haring off to Moremo. And you're mixed up in it!'

Bro Drumel protested his innocence, but Idaho was not placated. Drumel had participated in one attempted coup already, so was unlikely to be innocent if a second was in progress.

Shortly, Juliet Idaho was making for the pink palace with a much-sweating Bro Drumel stumbling in front of him. Idaho's sword was drawn. Bro Drumel's hands were tied behind his back, and Idaho had already promised the man that he would be killed immediately if any terminal misfortune had befallen Justina Thrug.

CHAPTER FIFTEEN

On departing from the Dromdanjerie, Pelagius Zozimus and Ivan Pokrov followed Jon Qasaba's advice and made their way to Marthandorthan, Injiltaprajura's ill-reputed dockland area, where they hoped to find Shabble. The most direct route would have been via Goldhammer Rise, but they felt it wisest to avoid the vicinity of the Temple of Torture until they had recruited Shabble to their cause; hence they took a back-cut route which avoided possible embarrassments.

Zozimus and Pokrov reached Marthandorthan. As they strode through this quarter of slumland tenements and brooding warehouses, the feverish pulse of the drums of Injiltaprajura assailed them from all sides.

When they located the Xtokobrokotok, the insalubrious warehouse belonging to the drug dealer Firfat Labrat, they found a group of teenage drummers camped in the street outside it, beating repetitively upon their instruments of diabolical intoxication.

Tok – tok – thuk!

Tok – tok – thuk . . .!

Ignoring the drummers, Zozimus and Pokrov advanced upon the Xtokobrokotok and begged leave to enter. But the doorman who guarded the portal of the place refused to admit them unless they stated their business; and this both wizard and analytical engineer declined to do. Instead, they overpowered the doorman and forced an entrance.

They found themselves in a large, high-gabled hall studded with doors opening into offices and strong-rooms. The light of a few feeble oil lanterns was supplemented by some high-placed slit windows which had lately been cut in the far wall of the warehouse. The air was heavy with the scent of joss, incense and burnt rice.

To his surprise, Pokrov saw a gallows had been erected in the centre of the warehouse. From it there hung a cage. A birdcage? He could not tell, for the cage was distant and the gloom murky. Round the gallows there sat some four or five dozen people of various ages, sexes and classes. They sat cross-legged, and from them there arose a monotonous chanting. What were they saying? If Pokrov heard aright, the chant went thus:

'Holy holy holy. Holy is thy presence. Holy is the day which thou dost grace. We will worship thee now, and tomorrow, and on tomorrow's morrow, and on into eternity. Holy holy holy. Holy is thy presence . . .'

Floating above the gallows was a bright-shining bubble about the size of a clenched fist. Or, to be slightly more specific, about the size of the Standard Fist affixed to the end of those lethal clubs wielded by the rubble boxers of the city of Obooloo.

'They're worshippng Shabble!' said Pokrov in tones of mingled astonishment and outrage.

'That will never do,' said Zozimus. Then raised his voice to a shout: 'Shabble! Come here!'

'At once,' said Pokrov. 'Or I will send you to a therapist!'

The chanting ended abruptly. The worshippers around the gallows turned in startlement to see who had intruded upon their sacred ceremony. And Shabble, with a wail of terror-stricken panic, bobbled through the air toward Pokrov and Zozimus.

As Shabble approached, a side door was flung open, and forth from that side door there came Firfat Labrat himself and a much-scarred and much-tattooed man whom Pokrov recognized as the corpse-master Uckermark. Behind them were half a dozen men with crossbows.

Shabble came to a halt just above their collective

heads and brightened marginally, throwing all into sharp focus.

'Hello,' said Shabble, brightly.

Shabble's momentary fear and panic were over, and Shabble's customary high spirits had once again regained the ascendancy.

'Shabble!' said Pokrov. 'I've got a job for you. You must—'

'Silence!' said Firfat Labrat. 'One more word and you're dead.'

Half a dozen cocked and loaded crossbows were immediately levelled at Ivan Pokrov and Pelagius Zozimus. If this confrontation disintegrated into violence, then Pokrov and Zozimus would surely be killed. Pokrov had no combat skills. Zozimus, on the other hand, was an accomplished warrior, and a wizard to boot. But Zozimus could scarcely hope to dodge half a dozen crossbow bolts fired at point blank range. And as for his wizardry, that was unfortunately somewhat specialized; Zozimus was a wizard of the order of Xluzu, and hence dealt largely with the animation of corpses, an ability scarcely apposite at the moment.

As Zozimus and Pokrov maintained a studied silence, the corpse-master Uckermark cleared his throat.

Then said:

'Allow me to introduce myself. I am Shabble's lawyer.'

This was news to Ivan Pokrov. Uckermark was certainly no stranger to the law, for his work with human flesh had brought many charges of blasphemy upon his head; however, while Uckermark had always defended himself in court with panache and success, he had never before laid claim to any legal qualifications.

Despite the threat of the crossbows, Pokrov could not help but expostulate:

'You are no lawyer!'

'Ah, but I am,' said Uckermark, with a grin of great cunning. 'I have a degree from Injiltaprajura's leading university.'

139

'Your fraudulent farce does not amuse us,' said Pelagius Zozimus coldly. 'Injiltaprajura has no university.'

'You stand in error,' said Uckermark. 'In point of fact, it has three. The Temple of Torture was formally constituted as a university in the time of the late Wazir Sin. Furthermore, standing beside you is the head of a second university, our dearly beloved Ivan Pokrov. Under interrogation, I'm sure he would admit that his Analytical Institute had a similar legal status. The Cabal House of the wonder-workers is another such seat of learning, and it is from there that my degree derives.'

'You have not the look of a scholar,' said Zozimus. 'So, as for this degree, I suppose you bought it.'

'I did,' said Uckermark, unabashed by this accusation. 'But my knowledge of the law is firm regardless. This restraint order is valid.'

So saying, Uckermark produced an ornate parchment with a flourish, and presented it to Ivan Pokrov.

'We knew you'd show up sooner or later,' said Uckermark, 'so we went to the trouble of getting this court order. It restrains you from interfering in any way whatsoever with the Cult of the Holy Cockroach, or with the High Priest of that Cult.'

'The holy what?' said Pokrov in amazement.

'Cockroach,' said Firfat Labrat.

'You know,' said Uckermark. 'The shabiti. The veko-veko. The loqualadibimosqantarka.'

'Yes,' said Shabble in great excitement. 'He's holy, that's what he is, holy as ever was. And I'm His Priest, His High Priest, that's what, so no more accounting, not ever, no more algorithms, no nothing. Just playing with cats and chasing seagulls, that's all, for ever and ever. Lawyers, that's what I've got, lawyers, court orders, freedom of religon, isn't it exciting?'

'Shabble!' said Pokrov sharply. 'This has gone quite far enough. If you don't come to order promptly, I'll—'

'Die,' said Uckermark.

Pokrov shut his mouth abruptly. He could be killed before he could command Shabble to kill the potential Pokrov-killers.

'Yes,' said Uckermark. 'That's more sensible. Silence is a much more sensible course of action under the circumstances. Now why don't you leave?'

'We cannot leave,' said Pelagius Zozimus, 'because Injiltaprajura stands in grave danger.'

Then Zozimus quickly explained that Aldarch Three had triumphed in Talonsklavara; that a new wazir had come to Untunchilamon; that Justina Thrug had been arrested and was believed to be imprisoned in the Temple of Torture, and, in all probability, to be in immediate danger of losing her life; and that the new wazir would probably shortly kill a great many other people unless he was overthrown immediately.

'You mean to bring civil war to the streets of Injiltaprajura,' said Uckermark.

'With Shabble's help we can win such a war,' said Pokrov.

'Maybe,' said Uckermark.

And maybe not. For, as Uckermark knew well from long acquaintance with Shabble, the shining one was prone to musical fits in which Injiltaprajura's bright spark was totally deaf to all pleas and orders, however couched. Anyone who had Shabble as an ally could prosecute a war with fearful effect; but might lose regardless if an untimely fit befell poor Shabble.

'We have no option,' said Zozimus, 'for if we go not to war then we will likely die.'

'Then die in your own time,' said Uckermark.

'You will die with us,' said Zozimus.

'Oh, I don't think so,' said the much-scarred corpse-master. 'We belong, you see, to a Protected Religion. The Cult of the Holy Cockroach and all its adherents are under the protection of the High Priest of Zoz the Ancestral.'

'But,' said Pokrov in amazement, 'that's impossible!

That's an honour almost unheard of. Master Ek would never give his protection to a – cockroach, of all things!'

'Master Ek!' said Uckermark smoothly, 'is not unaware of Shabble's desire for independence. Nor is Master Ek unsympathetic to that desire. In long discussions with Master Ek, I myself made the advantages of the afore-mentioned Protected Religion perfectly clear.'

Zozimus and Pokrov looked at each other.

Obviously, they had been out-manoeuvred.

Nadalastabstala Banraithanchumun Ek, a long-time resident upon Untunchilamon, was fully aware of Shabble's potential for mayhem; moreover, Ek may well have heard rumours to the effect that some people were able to command Shabble for their own purposes. So Ek had neutralized Shabble by, in effect, allowing Shabble to raise a private army to protect Shabble's desire for independence.

'This . . . this Cult of the Cockroach,' said Pokrov.

'The Holy Cockroach,' said Firfat Labrat by way of correction.

'Holy Cockroach, then,' said Pokrov. 'You say its adherents are under Master Ek's protection. How . . . how precisely does one join this religion?'

Pokrov was already thinking, and thinking fast. Since Ek had neutralized Shabble, there was no way that enemies of Aldarch Three could triumph in civil war in Injiltaprajura. So Pokrov might well be advised to join this new Protected Religion to secure his own safety. After all, if it admitted villainous drug dealers like Firfat Labrat, why should it refuse entry to a reputable Analytical Engineer?

'I regret to say,' said Uckermark, with remarkably little regret in his voice, 'that the entrance rolls are closed. This is a Closed Congregation. That was part of our agreement with Master Ek. The High Priest of Zoz the Ancestral is scarcely a fool, is he?'

'No,' said Pokrov bleakly.

'And neither are we,' said Zozimus brusquely, 'so we'll waste no more time here trifling with cockroaches holy or otherwise. Come! Let's be going.'

And the wizard hustled the Analytical Engineer out into the street, where they faced each other in the hot and sweating sunlight.

'Where will we run to?' said Ivan Pokrov, in something like despair.

'Run?' said Pelagius Zozimus. 'We're running nowhere. We're going to the Temple of Torture. To attack!'

CHAPTER SIXTEEN

As the Empress Justina was hustled towards the Temple of Torture she collapsed, she went down, and the boots went in. Then Dardanalti was shouting, his lawyerly threats restoring order. Justina was hauled to her feet and marched into the Temple, into a blood-cooking heat where the air stank of curry-flavoured diarrhoea, where screams of agony bucked and contorted, where writhing smoke singed nostrils and rasped within throats.

Then the Empress was hauled into the naos of the Temple, and there was Dui Tin Char, and there were two children of Wen Endex – but both men were strangers, and their faces denied her all hope of help. An executioner bulked forward and wrenched back her head.

'Stop!' said Dardanalti. 'I demand—'

Someone hit him, and he demanded no more.

Justina tried to plead, to protest. But vomited instead.

The executioner raised his blade.

Justina fainted.

'Hold!' cried Dui Tin Char.

Obediently the executioner stayed his hand.

'Come on, man,' said Manthandros Trasilika testily. 'Get on with it.'

Dardanalti picked himself up from the ground, wiped a thread of blood from his mouth, and decided that for the moment his client would best be served by his silence.

'The Thrug has fainted,' said Tin Char.

'What of it?' said Trasilika, he of the heavyweight build and the cauliflower ear.

'Your colleague will explain,' said Tin Char, glancing at Jean Froissart.

The priest of Zoz the Ancestral stammered, looked around as if seeking an escape hatch, saw there was no getting out of the place, then said defiantly:

'I don't know what you're talking about.'

'It is Written,' said Tin Char, 'that Delight depends on Desire, and the heights of Desire upon a studied Postponement. Is that not so?'

'Verily,' said Froissart weakly.

The sweat was bulging from his forehead and furrowing down his face. His eyes blinked furiously.

'Are you ill?' said Tin Char.

'It's the heat,' said Froissart.

'He's had malaria,' added Trasilika.

Whether heat or malaria was to blame, the great and ever-increasing distress of Jean Froissart was a sight to see. Tin Char found it a most delicious sight. Tin Char was a Janjuladoola racist who hated the children of Wen Endex; therefore he found Froissart's suffering worth savouring. How could that suffering be prolonged?

The answer came to Tin Char almost immediately.

'Friend Froissart,' said Tin Char, 'I'm most concerned to see you suffering so badly. We will therefore dedicate this sacrifice to the cause of your improved health. You are conscious of the honour, I hope?'

'Yes,' said Froissart weakly.

'Then,' said Tin Char, 'we will proceed, but in the leisurely way that this most honourable ceremony demands. We will start with the Torture of the Thousand Scorpions. Ah, Justina! Are you awakening? You are? Good. You will be happy to hear that your execution has been postponed. Instead, we are going to commence with some preliminary delights.'

Tin Char explained, and his explanation left Justina Thrug so sick with fear and horror that her vocal chords were temporarily paralysed. As she was strapped down in a torture chamber, Dardanalti intervened on her behalf, saying:

'By what authority do you bring Justina here?'

'By the authority of this warrant,' said Tin Char, flourishing Justina's death warrant before her lawyer.

Dardanalti snatched it, read it, then said:

'This warrant is good, valid and legal. On behalf of my client, I demand that this warrant be executed immediately. I demand that my client be killed on the spot.'

'You are in no position to demand anything,' said Dui Tin Char, starting to get angry.

How dare this prating attorney interfere?

'I demand,' said Dardanalti, 'what Aldarch the Third demands. This warrant is from Aldarch Three. He demands and commands the immediate execution of Justina Thrug. Immediate. As in now. Executioner, proceed!'

'Yes,' said Froissart, who wanted to get out of that sweltering place of blood and shadows, to escape before he fainted. 'Yes, kill her.'

'Oh yes,' said Justina faintly, as she found her voice at last. 'Kill me.'

The Empress Justina knew death to be far preferable to the horrors offered as an alternative, particularly when those horrors would in any case ultimately lead to her demise.

'What say you?' said Tin Char, looking at Manthandros Trasilika. 'As wazir, you have wide discretionary powers. Even in the face of a direct order such as this warrant. Well. Are you wazir, or are you not?'

'I am,' said Trasilika, with more emphasis than was strictly necessary.

The vehemence of Trasilika's insistence startled Tin Char. It consolidated a dozen half-felt suspicions into a series of most definite questions. Was there more to Froissart's mounting panic than a surfeit of heat? Were these two children of Wen Endex the wazir and priest they claimed to be?

What an interesting line of thought!

Dardanalti, whose mind was as sharp as a meat skewer, observed Tin Char's speculative scrutiny of Jean

Froissart and guessed its cause. Here was hope!

'May I humbly suggest,' said Dui Tin Char, 'that you establish your authority by granting me permission to vary the terms of this warrant.'

Dardanalti was disappointed. He had expected Tin Char to denounce Jean Froissart as a false priest. But Tin Char had not. Why not? Maybe his suspicions were too slight. Maybe, thought Dardanalti, Tin Char actually did not have such suspicions. Or maybe he suspected but reserved those suspicions for later exploitation.

'We all know from historical example,' continued Tin Char, 'that Aldarch the Third is very lenient in his attitude to death warrants. It would seem to me that he cares not how they are executed, as long as the subject of the warrant ends up dead.'

Tin Char then cited several historical cases to back up his judgement. Then he made a little speech.

'Manthandros Trasilika. Untunchilamon has long suffered the lack of legal leadership. We are ready for a true wazir. We hope you show yourself to be such a man. But . . . may I venture a small observation? Untunchilamon is far removed from the heartland of the Izdimir Empire. Our wazirs have traditionally been chosen for their initiative, independence and self-sufficiency. All qualities unacceptable in Obooloo, as we know. But our isolation demands that we have a true leader in our midst, lest our island be paralysed by a bureaucracy with its brain seated half an ocean away. Manthandros Trasilika. I beg you. Grant me this boon. Show yourself to be a wazir true. Show your initiative. Your independence. Your confidence. Show us we have the leader we desire. Grant us a variance to the terms of this warrant. Allow me to torture the Thrug before she is killed.'

There was a pause.

Jean Froissart swayed on his feet, as if he would faint.

But Manthandros Trasilika was made of sterner stuff. He looked Tin Char in the face and he said:

'Dui Tin Char, I speak to you as the rightful wazir of Injiltaprajura. The witch must die. That is the law. But, as wazir, I grant a variance to the terms of her death warrant. You may torture the Thrug before you kill her.'

'Excellent!' said Tin Char. 'May the pleasures both major and minor delight your years till the very end, and may your hereafter join your ancestors amidst the fragrance of the nine million lotus flowers of the seventy-fifth heaven. May you—'

But there is no need to give the rest of Tin Char's speech of gratitude, for it is one of those formalized speeches which most cultivated people know by heart; the uncultivated but curious student will find the complete text (plus an account of the appropriate accompanying hand gestures) in Lady Jade's *Book of Common Etiquette*.

With the speech complete, Dui Tin Char ordered that ten hundred scorpions be produced so the Torture of the Thousand Scorpions could commence. Unfortunately, there were not a thousand scorpions to be found. Indeed, there was not even one. A furious Tin Char swiftly extorted the truth from two shamefaced acolytes: they had sold the delectable arachnids to Jarry the chef, Ganthorgruk's master of cookery.

The acolytes had thought it safe to make this deal because, under the rule of the Empress Justina, the Temple of Torture was not supposed to exist at all; hence no legal remedies could have been pursued against them had they been caught out. To their great discomfort, the sudden advent of a new wazir had altered their situation diametrically.

'I'll deal with you later,' said the wrathful Tin Char to his trembling acolytes. 'If you wish to redeem yourself, find me some scorpions. Or some centipedes at least.'

So the acolytes fled from the Temple of Torture. Proceeding with a haste most unsuited to the climate, they rushed to the waterfront, where a path of crushed coral and broken bloodstone stretched all the way from Marthandorthan to the harbour bridge. Along this path lay the markets of Untunchilamon where one could buy all products and services imaginable, from a bunch of bananas to the tender attentions of Doctor Death the dentist.

Everything was on sale.

Except scorpions.

And centipedes.

Scorpions had always been hard to come by in Untunchilamon, since Jarry the chef had always made great demands upon the available supply. Whether Ganthorgruk's clientele actually liked eating scorpions is a moot point; nevertheless, the fact is that bits and pieces of these predators went into every hash, curry and pie that was served to the denizens of that enormous doss house. As for centipedes, Injiltaprajura had suffered a great shortage of these myriads ever since the Crab had been introduced to this addictive delicacy; for the quantities of centipede soup which can be consumed on a daily basis by a gourmandizing Crab are nothing short of prodigious.

While the acolytes were desperately questing for scorpion and centipede, there was a disturbance at the Temple of Torture. The perturbation of the smooth flow of events was caused by the intrusion of a soldier, Shanvil Angarus May. This warrior was an Ashdan from Ashmolea North, which explains the impetuous manner in which he tried to storm the Temple single-handed to rescue his Empress.

Shanvil Angarus May was overpowered and disarmed. Then he was taken to the naos of the Temple so he could watch the destruction of his Empress before suffering a similar fate himself.

Shortly, the wizard Pelagius Zozimus arrived at the Temple in the company of Ivan Pokrov. The wizard and the analytical engineer hoped to free Justina by bribe or bluff, or, if all else failed, by carefully timed violence. A

149

desperate dare: and a dare which failed. For they were overpowered, bound, gagged and then dragged to the naos of the Temple, where they were tied to iron rings set in the walls. They too were doomed to wait, witness then die.

There was then a somewhat more prolonged disturbance – a regular stramash, in fact – when a furious Juliet Idaho burst in upon the Temple with mayhem on his mind. He too was disarmed, though not without difficulty. Then he was taken to join the other captives. His feet were tied to iron rings set in the floor; his hands were bound behind his back; and a noose was strung around his neck and tightened till Idaho had to stand on tiptoe lest he strangle.

It will be seen, then, that four formidable residents of Injiltaprajura were loyal enough or desperate enough to dare all in an effort to free their Empress. Had they been able to combine, conspire and agree on a concerted effort, they might have succeeded. Possibly. But the speed of events, the difficulties of communication and the failure of intelligence-gathering activities had prevented such combination.

Strangely, the accumulation of so many prisoners did not hearten Tin Char. Rather, he began to worry. He began to suspect he had been rash in proposing to indulge himself in acts of extended torture. The politics of Injiltaprajura would remain unstable until Justina Thrug was quite dead.

It was the acolytes who were to blame.

If they had not dabbled in thievery, then the torture would already be well on its way to a terminal conclusion.

As Tin Char was so thinking, the acolytes at last returned with two centipedes in a wickerwork cage. Only two? A pair would suffice, for these were malevolent monsters of purple hue, each as long as a man's forearm.

'At last,' said Tin Char. 'Fetch me the centipede

150

tongs, or have you perchance pawned them?'

'Master,' said the younger of the acolytes, 'the centipede tongs will be with you instantly.'

A protracted delay followed, a delay in which Tin Char became so agitated he felt quite sick; but at last the tongs were produced. Tin Char took the tongs.

'Out of my way!' he said, giving one of the acolytes a push.

Both acolytes squeezed in beside Juliet Idaho. The Yudonic Knight looked sideways at them and whispered:

'Cut me free.'

Unfortunately, the naos was far too small for private conspiracy. Tin Char heard the whisper and gave Idaho a dirty look; whereafter the helpless Yudonic Knight said no more.

Tin Char already had to hand the pry-levers which he planned to use to open a certain portion of the imperial anatomy so the scorpions could be inserted into a particularly sensitive part of the body.

But first, the preliminary sacrifice must necessarily be made. The rites of the Temple of Torture require the sacrificing priest to drink the blood of whatever animal is slaughtered in such a ceremony. Tin Char, however, was in no mood for drinking fresh hot blood, never a pleasant beverage on a humid day in Injiltaprajura. He wondered if he could inflict this duty on the quick-blinking Jean Froissart.

'Friend Froissart,' said Tin Char in his sweetest tones, 'do I have your permission to invite you to take part in this ceremony of torture?'

Froissart hesitated. He had conceived a great terror of this cramped, hot, shadowy place, a bloodstone tomb ever infiltrated by screams from some agonized creature enduring great trials elsewhere in the Temple, a close-packed place crowded with the rank and hot-breathing bodies of prisoners, guards and terrified acolytes.

'Of course we wish to participate,' said Manthandros

151

Trasilika, annoyed by Froissart's hesitation. 'What do you want us to do?'

'I would be greatly honoured if your priest would consent to make an initial sacrifice for me,' said Tin Char.

'Of course he will,' said Trasilika, before Froissart had a chance to protest.

Whereupon Tin Char lifted the lid from a copious covered dish. Within lay a vampire rat, its paws tied together with threads of gold and silver. Despite these cords of bondage, it had thrashed around inside the dish. And, as it had befouled its place of imprisonment, streaks of brown smeared its luxuriant orange fur.

The vampire rat screamed in agonies of intelligent anticipation. Froissart grabbed it. The rat twisted, snapped, bit. Blood streamed from Froissart's hand. If this rat was rabid – and rabies was endemic amongst the vampire rats of Injiltaprajura – then Jean Froissart was going to endure a very unpleasant death.

'Gath!' said Froissart, swearing in his native Toxteth.

Then the child of Wen Endex smashed the rat with his fist, grabbed the knife and cut its throat. Blood streamed forth into the dish, mixing swiftly with urine and excrement.

'There,' said Froissart, smearing blood across his forehead as he wiped away a lathering of sweat. 'It's dead.'

At that point, a servant intruded. A low-browed young man who had but one eye, the other being covered with a black patch.

'Master,' said the servant.

'Silence!' said Tin Char. 'You have the manners of a drummer.'

'Master, I—'

'Silence!' roared Tin Char.

And resolved to have the man beaten as soon as the ceremony was finished. To thus intrude on holy ceremony was perilously close to blasphemy.

'But master,' said the servant desperately. 'I must—'

'You must be quiet!' said Tin Char. 'If he speaks again, gouge out his other eye!'

The servant did not speak again.

Instead, the man started to wring his hands in frustrated anguish.

Dui Tin Char waited for Froissart to proceed with the next step demanded by ritual. The drinking of the blood. But Froissart did no such thing.

'That was well done,' said Manthandros Trasilika, when nobody else seemed inclined to speak.

Trasilika's ignorance was pardonable. But Froissart's inaction was something else again. Perhaps Froissart had forgotten how to proceed. An unlikely event, for all priests of Zoz the Ancestral familiarized themselves with the rites of the closely associated Temple of Torture. Unlikely, yes, but not impossible. Or perhaps Froissart was in no condition to drink the blood. The child of Wen Endex was bleeding from a bite from a possibly rabid animal. His face had assumed an unnatural pallor; he looked shocked, exhausted, close to collapse.

One way or another, the ritual must be brought to its proper conclusion. Any other course would be blasphemy.

'There is the matter of the blood,' said Tin Char carefully, thinking that would suffice.

'The blood?' said Froissart.

'Yes,' said Tin Char. 'The blood.'

'Oh,' said Froissart.

He picked up the big dish. He breathed the fumes of blood, excrement and urine. Sweat dropped from his chin and splashed in the unorthodox cocktail he now contemplated. The fluid trembled as Froissart's hands shook. He opened his mouth as if to say something. Then, quite calmly, he vomited into the bowl. He stood looking at the vomit. The heavy dish started to slide in his sweat-greased hands. Froissart tried to put it down. But the dish was going, going, gone, a slosh of filth and vomit splurping over the side. Impact! The dish smashed down, spraying its contents across Trasilika's feet.

'Jean Froissart!' said Tin Char in shocked surprise. 'You disgrace yourself!'

Froissart grovelled in the mess of muck and vomit.

'It blasphemes,' said Dardanalti, affecting shock. 'It sins against our faith with malice. What makes it priest? It has not the Skin.'

So spoke Justina's lawyer, speaking of Jean Froissart with all the resources of racial hatred at his disposal. Then the lawyer dared a most unlawyerly thing. He kicked the cringing priest.

'This is no priest,' said Dardanalti, kicking the thing again. 'This is a fraud.'

Dardanalti was making the greatest gamble of his life. He suspected – but was not certain – that Jean Froissart was a false priest. But he had no proof of that whatsoever. There was therefore every possibility that Dardanalti might shortly find himself entertaining five million red ants with a most extraordinary generosity, or, to detail just one of the many alternative fates which might befall him, taking his ease on a sharpened roasting spit.

Dardanalti, then, gambled with his life.

Froissart sat up.

'I,' he said, 'I'm—'

Outside, someone screamed, as screams a man of nervous disposition when a dentist wrenches an ulcerated wisdom tooth from the living flesh of the gums and, gripping this trophy in a pair of rusty pliers, holds it aloft in all its gory glory.

Froissart opened his mouth.

Closed it.

Began to cry.

'Pull yourself together,' said Manthandros Trasilika roughly, as blubbering tears streamed down Froissart's face, washed through his sweat then dropped to the disgraced flagstones.

154

'I . . . I'm sorry,' said Froissart.

Then he could no longer help himself. He broke down altogether. He wept, then smashed his head against the stones. Once, twice, thrice. Hammering his forehead against that obstinacy with full force. As if to fracture his skull.

'A false priest,' said Dardanalti. 'I knew as much.'

'No!' said Trasilika.

But there was not one person in the room who doubted Jean Froissart's guilt. He was an imposter. A fake. A blaspheming charlatan.

'He – he's mad,' said Trasilika, speech starting to blunder as panic took grip.

'Not mad,' said the Empress Justina, speaking up from her torture table. 'Not mad, but guilty. A false priest with a false wazir.'

Thus spoke Justina, effectively pronouncing Trasilika's death sentence. For if Jean Froissart was a fraud, then Manthandros Trasilika must be a criminal imposter likewise.

'He's – it's the voyage,' said the heavyweight would-be wazir. 'It's, it's the, the malaria, or rabies, the rat which bit, it bit, he's blood, blood, he's bleeding, he—'

Trasilika was babbling.

But Juliet Idaho was perfectly calm as he said to the Temple acolytes standing alongside of him:

'Cut me loose.'

They obeyed. Knives they had. In moments they triced through his bonds, the neck-noose included. Then Juliet Idaho said to the nearest soldier:

'Give me your weapon.'

Wordlessly, the soldier handed over his scimitar.

'Stop him!' said Trasilika in panic. 'A blade, he's got a blade, he's going to—'

'Foreign filth,' hissed Dardanalti.

Trasilika rushed for the exit door. The acolytes met him, punched him, threw him back. He crashed into the torture table. Went down, but got to his feet again. Too

155

late! For Juliet Idaho was already upon him. In that enclosed space, there was precious little room to manoeuvre. But there was room enough to swing a scimitar.

Trasilika's head went bouncing to the floor. The headless body swayed. Sprayed the ceiling with blood. Then toppled. And Idaho was already moving, arm striking, blade plunging, steel ripping, fingers delving. Moments later, Juliet Idaho stood in triumph with a trophy in his fist. A beating heart. Jean Froissart's heart.

'Bravo,' cried Justina faintly.

Then faint voice gave way to fainting fit.

And, at a nod from Tin Char, guards disarmed the still-panting Juliet Idaho.

'Well,' said Tin Char, wiping some of the much-splattered corpse blood from his face, 'this is not a good start to the day. Nevertheless, we've profited from the experience. We know that Aldarch Three has victory in Yestron.'

'We know no such thing,' said Dardanalti, confronting probabilities with possibilities as a lawyer must. 'Two liars we have for certain. Two shiploads of liars, possibly. But as for Al'three, why, he may be dead, and his enemies victorious.'

'I'll take a chance on that,' said Tin Char, who doubted that a couple of frauds could have suborned two whole shiploads of sailors. 'As Aldarch Three has triumphed in Talonsklavara, the time has come for the rule of the rightful to be restored to Untunchilamon. In the absence of any other appropriate candidates, I therefore declare myself wazir of Injiltaprajura.'

'Master,' said the one-eyed servant, venturing at last to speak again. 'That's what I came to tell you about. We have a new wazir.'

'Yes,' said Tin Char. 'Me.'

'But Master, there's an Ebrell Islander in the court-yard outside. It's got a sledge hammer. Guy, it's called

156

Guy, Chegory Guy. It's got an Ashdan with it, a girl Qasaba. They – they—'

'They what?' said Tin Char. 'They want to be a two-headed wazir? What madness is this?'

'Not madness, master. Messages. They bring a message from the Hermit Crab. The Crab has declared itself the wazir of Injiltaprajura.'

Dui Tin Char gave a little moan. He remembered his last encounter with the Crab. Without laying so much as a claw upon Tin Char's flesh, the Crab had exerted a Power which had wrenched Tin Char's arms back further and further until both were dislocated.

'Show them in,' said Juliet Idaho decisively.

Two acolytes moved to obey.

In came a redskin, the heavily muscled Chegory Guy, with Olivia Qasaba beside him.

'We're here with a, a message,' said Chegory, holding tight to his sledge hammer, his sole source of comfort and reassurance in this most difficult of situations.

'Yes,' said Olivia, in a firm though girlish voice. 'The Crab brings pardons for those who obey. As long as . . . as . . .'

'If it's now,' said Chegory. 'Now that they obey, I mean. If they obey later, it'll be too late.'

'That's right,' said Olivia.

'The Crab's wazir,' said Chegory. 'Hence should command obedience. Yes, wazir, that's what the Crab is. Wazir of Untunchilamon. And it orders, uh, the immediate release of the Empress Justina. Of course. And Juliet Idaho, Shanvil May, Pokrov and, uh, the wizard here.'

'Or else,' said Olivia.

'So get moving,' said Chegory. 'Zozimus, he's the most important. The Crab is hungry. It wants its next meal. And fast. Oh, you've got centipedes! Good, we'll take those. And, um, there was someone we had to, what was it?'

'Bring along,' said Olivia. 'Tin Char, wasn't it?'

'Yes, that's right,' said Chegory. 'Dui Tin Char. That's

157

you, isn't it? Come along then. The Crab wants to see you.'

Dui Tin Char howled in anguish and then, reluctantly, submitted to the inevitable.

For the Crab was a Power which none on Untunchilamon durst disobey.

CHAPTER SEVENTEEN

Naturally, there was consternation in Injiltaprajura when it was known that the Crab had declared itself wazir. But, in the days that followed, remarkably little changed. Decrees were published in the name of the Crab, saying that Justina Thrug should remain in the pink palace for the time being as its custodian; that religious freedom should prevail as before; and that all civil and uncivil servants were temporarily confirmed in their positions.

Thus consternation was soon replaced with disappointment; for the mob saw that there were to be no wholesale torturing or executions, no mass arrests or persecutions, no opportunities for looting and rampage; and a sense of anticlimax prevailed in the city.

Nevertheless, while there was no major public drama in those days, there were private dramas in plenty, as there always are in any great city. And, turning our attention to one of those dramas, let us record the following:

This was the number:

011010100001.

And this was the demand:

One thousand dragons.

And the lever was a page of the *Injiltaprajuradariski, The Secret History of Injiltaprajura*, a work now gaining a certain underground fame on Untunchilamon.

Bro Drumel read the page through yet one more time. Was it really as dangerous as he had thought at first blush? He was inclined to think that it was.

So what was he to do?

Pay the thousand dragons?

He could. But doubtless there would be further demands to follow the first. For such was the nature of blackmail. So what was the alternative? Hunt down the blackmailer and kill him. Obviously. But much easier said than done. In fact, it might well prove impossible.

Bro Drumel, captain of Justina's palace guard and Governor of Moremo Maximum Security Prison, began to work on his fingernails, easing the overgrowth of skin back from each moon in turn. While his skin was Janjuladoola grey, the fingernails themselves were a blood-flushed pink. Pink nails. White moons. He found them fascinating. And beautiful. Indeed, Bro Drumel had little eye for the sculptural masses which make up the body as a whole. What delighted him was the elegant finishing touches. Fingernails. Earlobes. Eyes.

Those oh-so-elegant finishing touches which so delight the torturer.

Bro Drumel looked out of the window of his office in Moremo. He closed his right eye experimentally. And, as he had expected, the view dimmed.

Year by year, the colours perceived by his left eye had slowly been growing darker and dimmer. He supposed that in the fullness of time he would go blind in that eye. He could live with that. He could face the thought of such idiosyncratic failures of the flesh, and the inevitable generalized degeneration of old age which must one day follow.

But the horror that would befall him if he became a victim of the rage of Aldarch Three . . .

Bro Drumel squeezed both eyes tight, trying to close out light, thought and vision together.

If he did yield to blackmail, his persecutor would hand certain documentation to Master Ek, High Priest of Zoz the Ancestral. Then certain doom would in due course befall him. So what should he do?

Bro Drumel fought with panic.

And, finally, decided to go and see the Empress Justina.

The Empress had been restored to the pink palace five days earlier, after her release had been ordered in the name of the Crab. Since she had the Crab's favour, perhaps – just possibly – she could give Bro Drumel some help. Or reassurance at least.

But, first, he should shave.

Soon Bro Drumel was at work, soothing the steel across his skin. He paused in his work. Slid two fingers to the carotid artery which lay beside his windpipe. The skin was hot. Hot and slightly sweaty. The pulse beat beneath his fingers. A rhythm strong and slow. He made his resolution. Both jugular veins and both carotids and the windpipe too. A single sweep. A grin.

That's all it takes.

He would do it.

Yes, if torture threatened, he would do it.

And, now that he knew he would never be taken alive, Bro Drumel felt stronger, calmer and more confident. The game was not over yet. And, while the game yet ran, life was still sweet, and had many, many satisfactions.

Shortly, a clean-shaven Bro Drumel was at the pink palace and deep in conference with the Empress Justina and Juliet Idaho. Both the Empress and her untame Yudonic Knight examined the blackmail documents with interest.

What particularly attracted their attention was the page from the *Injiltaprajuradariski* which had been sent to Bro Drumel. The page was a sheet of ricepaper covered with scorpioned Ashdan orthography scripted in purple ink. The words were in Slandolin, the literary language of Ashmolea South. While neither Justina nor Idaho could read this tongue, both by now could recognize a text written in that argot.

'You've had it translated, I take it,' said Justina.

'I have,' said Bro Drumel.

'What does it say?' said Idaho.

'It . . . well . . .'

'Out with it!' said Idaho, harshening his voice.

'Peace, Julie,' said Justina, laying one heavy and sweaty hand upon Idaho's wrist.

'But we must know what it says,' growled Idaho. 'Or must we call in our own translator?'

'It . . . it tells of a . . . a relationship between myself and our Empress,' said Bro Drumel. 'My blackmailer threatens to send a duplicate copy to Nadalastabstala Banraithanchumun Ek.'

'And what if he does?' said Justina.

'It . . . this would damn me in the eyes of Aldarch Three,' said Bro Drumel.

The Empress snorted.

'You're damned already if that's all it takes for damnation,' said she. 'Your close connection with me is no secret. Come! You helped Varazchavardan when he sought to coup against me. If I remember correctly, your help was so strenuous I had need to hit you with my handbag.'

'Yes,' said Drumel, remembering the shattering impact of that blow.

'So this blackmailing is no more than a nonsense,' said Justina briskly. 'But I would dearly like to catch the blackmailer, for capture might give us a clue to the source of the *Injiltaprajuradariski, The Secret History of Injiltaprajura*. You know it, I take it.'

'Well . . .'

'You must have heard rumours,' said Justina.

'A few,' said Bro Drumel cautiously.

'Come, let's not be so close-mouthed,' said Justina. 'It's no secret. Untunchilamon's a place too small for that. Someone has written a Secret History. We know not who. What we do know is that pieces of it are scattered all over Injiltaprajura. The Cabal House had a piece.'

'How do you know that?' said Bro Drumel.

'The knowledge came to me by powers which are mine to possess but not to discuss,' said Justina.

Of course, she knew because a thief in her pay had stolen the purple-scripted document in question, thieving it from the Cabal House under the noses of the resident wonder-workers.

'Also,' said Idaho, 'Masker Ek has a piece of that document.'

'You read his mind also?' said Drumel to Justina.

'I have my methods,' said Justina severely.

She had recently debriefed young Nixorjapretzel Rat, her liaison officer, and it was in the course of this debriefing that she had learnt something of Master Ek's interest in the Secret History.

'So you see our interest,' said Idaho. 'We must find this Secret History.'

'Actually, I don't,' said Drumel, now puzzled. 'You tell me no document matters since nothing is secret. If nothing is secret, what matters this history? First you tell me not to worry about it, that blackmailing makes things no worse. Then you say we have to find the blackmailer.'

Justina Thrug and Juliet Idaho glanced at each other.

'Either you trust me or you don't,' said Bro Drumel.

'We don't,' said Idaho.

'But we could,' said Justina. 'Oaths solemn enough might bind you.'

Bro Drumel realized he had to make a choice. Swear binding oaths of loyalty to the Empress and throw in his lot with hers. Or trust to the justice of the Izdimir Empire.

Drumel had no faith in justice.

Justina was not of the Janjuladoola race. She was a hated foreigner from Wen Endex. But seven years of close association with the family Thrug had taught Bro Drumel that the word of a Thrug could be trusted. If he made a common cause with Justina, the alliance would last till the point of death; the Empress would not betray him.

163

'I will swear myself to your service,' said he.

Then did, a process which took some time, as no solemn oath can be sworn in Janjuladoola without the expenditure of at least a thousand words.

Once Bro Drumel had pledged his fealty to the Thrug, Justina revealed the truth.

'There is more to this Secret History than a recital of common fact,' said she.

'Much more,' said Juliet Idaho.

'Julie,' said Justina, again laying her hand on Idaho's wrist. 'This is my story.'

'My lady,' said Idaho, acknowledging the rebuke.

And Justina continued:

'The Secret History also speaks of something truly exceptional. An immortality machine. An organic rectifier, so called. We have seen fragments which tell us something of this organic rectifier. That it exists. That it can grant humans the gift of immortal life. That it can change female form to male. Or vice versa. That it could make a human of a Crab.'

Justina paused.

'And . . . and where is this machine?' said Bro Drumel. 'It must be Downstairs, surely.'

'Perhaps,' said Justina. 'But where are we to look? And what would we be looking for? That we know not. We suspect that the Secret History has much, much more to say about this organic rectifier. What it looks like, where it hides, how to use it. We know your blackmailer came into possession of a fragment of the Secret History. The blackmailer may have the whole. So let us catch the blackmailer.'

'You . . . you say the organic rectifier could change Crab to human,' said Bro Drumel. 'Is this something the Crab would desire?'

'It is,' said Justina. 'I have discussed it with the Crab's ambassadors.'

She had no need to specify the names of those ambassadors, for all Injiltaprajura knew the Crab's official representatives to be Chegory Guy and Olivia Qasaba.

'And?' said Drumel.

'And the Crab would welcome a human form,' said Justina. 'If we provide it with such, it guarantees the safety of Injiltaprajura for ever.'

'You mean it won't if we don't?' said Drumel.

'It is no secret that the Crab is too inhuman to demonstrate a sustained interest in human politics,' said Justina. 'It rules Injiltaprajura now, but it does so at a whim. It could lose interest in our island's fate as early as tomorrow.'

Bro Drumel could not help himself. He shuddered.

'So,' continued Justina briskly, 'we have no time to lose. We must find the blackmailer, locate the Secret History, discover the truth about the organic rectifier, find that device if it is anywhere within finding range, take it to the Crab and win our safety.'

'After using it ourselves,' said Juliet Idaho.

'For what?' said Bro Drumel. 'To become Crab ourselves?'

'No,' said Idaho. 'To become immortal. Weren't you listening?'

'It . . . it's rather a lot to take in at once. Have I got this right? You say – what? That Ek has some of this Secret History?'

'Yes,' said Justina.

'And the Cabal House?'

'Yes.'

'Then . . . do they know of this . . . this organic contraption?'

'The Cabal House has most definitely seen written mention of the organic rectifier,' said Justina. 'They may know more of it than we do. Our spies are trying to find out. As for Master Ek, he has a part of the *Injiltaprajuradariski* in his possession, and may know more than we would like him to know.'

'So,' said Idaho. 'Enough blathering. Let's see how

your blackmailer plans to get money off you.'

The three then studied the blackmailer's written demands.

'As you see,' said Drumel, 'my blackmailer says I must pay a thousand dragons into this numbered account at the N'barta.'

'N'barta?' said Juliet Idaho.

'The Narapatorpabarta Bank,' said the Empress Justina.

'Indeed, my lady,' said Bro Drumel. 'The same.'

'And what was that other thing you called it?' said Idaho.

'The N'barta,' said the Empress patiently.

Idaho's ignorance came as no surprise to the well-fleshed Justina. For a start, Idaho was a xenophobe who entered as little as possible into the life of Injiltaprajura. The Janjuladoola people were not the only ones capable of entertaining violent prejudices; and Idaho was as much a racist as the most bigoted son of Obooloo. Furthermore, Juliet Idaho was a stereotypical Yudonic Knight: which meant, amongst other things, that he was a financial simpleton. He would have nothing to do with banks, bank accounts, stockbrokers, shares, bonds, unit trusts or the future market; he drew his pay in bronze and gold and protected himself against all possibility of theft by spending it promptly in forthright debauch.

'So,' said Idaho slowly, 'you pay to a number.'

'A numbered account,' agreed Bro Drumel.

'But the account has a human attached to it, does it not?' said Idaho.

'Well,' said Drumel hesitantly, 'as I understand it—'

'It does not,' said the Empress crisply.

'But it must!' said Idaho. 'Or how does the owner get at the cash? That's the thing with banks, isn't it? I'm not an expert, but as I understand it, money put into a bank account is not meant as a gift to a bank.'

'The bank has a barrel,' said Justina, who knew this system well. 'Within the barrel, a thousand envelopes.

Each envelope sealed. Each envelope holds two numbers. Each number unique, and each in length at least a dozen digits. You wish an account? Very well! You lay down ten dragons—'

'Ten!' said Idaho, scandalized.

'Ten,' affirmed Justina.

'Let me guess,' said Idaho. 'It's a lucky dip.'

'Right,' said Justina. 'Ten dragons, one envelope.'

'I see,' muttered Idaho. 'A bloody banker's trick, isn't it? Nobody knows who's working which numbers.'

'Exactly,' said Justina.

And watched Idaho's face. He was still puzzling through these revelations, trying to work out the necessary implications and ramifications. Justina had every confidence that he'd sort it out in his own good time, but Bro Drumel, not realizing the reason for her silence, intruded without invitation:

'One number you bank with. You see? But both you must have to withdraw. Both you must have as well to know the account's balance. They've master ledgers, you see, all made up with numbers in twins.'

Justina was afraid this information overload would draw a roar of outraged incomprehension from the irascible Idaho. But the Yudonic Knight was sharp today, he was on form indeed:

'So our bright friend Blackmail, he sends Drumel one number. So Drumel goes to the bank. A thousand dragons he gives to the bank. They look up their ledgers with numbers in twins. They write down the dragons by the side of the twin. Then bright spark Blackmail, in he comes the next day with numbers in doubles. Both numbers he gives to the bank, and the dragons they give him.'

'Why,' said Bro Drumel, amazed at such uncharacteristic penetration on the part of the battleman Idaho. 'A single cast, yet your hook finds its fish.'

'Yes,' said Idaho. 'And we find us friend Blackmail as well. Easy, isn't it? He's now but a number to us and the

167

bank. But flesh he must have to cash numbers for dragons. He can't come as a ghost, can he?'

'There are ways and means,' said Justina darkly.

'But we could try,' said Bro Drumel, keen to catch friend Blackmail if there was one chance in a thousand of doing it.

'What do you mean, try?' said Idaho, a touch of outrage at work in his voice. 'It's a sure thing, isn't it?'

'Not,' said Justina, 'if our blackmailing friend leaves his deposits untouched till the island has fallen to Aldarch the Third.'

'Then let's grab in quick,' said Idaho. 'Grab the records, see what's there to find.'

'It's just numbers,' said Bro Drumel, unable to suppress his exasperation. 'Just numbers, that's all!'

How could he get it through to this big lunk of a headlopper? A raid on the bank would give them numbers, no more. No name, no address, no identikit, nothing.

'Listen, sklork,' sasid Idaho, edging his words with murder. 'I'm a killer, okay, but I've brains for brains, not dogshit. Understand?'

'Dogshit!' said the Empress Justina, pretending to be shocked and scandalized.

'My lady,' said Idaho, starting to get heated. 'My apologies. But I won't be patronized by this – this Janjuladoola thing!'

'He does have a point, Julie my darling,' said Justina gently. 'We would win but numbers if we won with a raid.'

'Aye,' said Idaho. 'And what are numbers but history, if money's at stake? No doubt they'll have dates with their ledgers. A date for the account's genesis, for example.'

'No,' said Bro Drumel, pleased to win yet another point off this uncouth uitlander who so obviously had dogshit for brains, yet fearing that the loss of too many such points might make that same uitlander run amok in

168

a berserker fury. 'The accounts are undated, for who knows when they're bought? They come from a barrel, remember. All envelopes jumbled. A choice of a thousand.'

'Privacy perfect,' said Justina in agreement.

'Yes,' said Idaho, reluctantly conceding the point. 'But dates they'll have for other things. Surely. Not when the account was opened, perhaps. But money gone in and money gone out. All signed for and dated. It has to be! Not by the customer, maybe, but their own staff must sign when they play with the gold. A banker's as much a thief as the next man, is he not?'

'Well,' said Bro Drumel, annoyed to find that there was a certain amount of good sense to this. 'That's all very well, but—'

'It's a start,' said Justina decisively. 'We'll get on to the bank this instant.'

'But,' protested Drumel, 'if all we can learn is deposits, disbursements and dates . . .'

His voice trailed away as he began to understand the implications. Once they had the history of the black-mailer's account, complete with the current balance and dates for all deposits and any disbursements, they would have a pattern on which they could exert their intelligence.

A slim hope indeed, but far better than none.

'There is also something else we could try,' said Idaho.

'What?' said Justina.

Then listened in silence as Idaho explained.

'Why, Julie!' said Justina in amazement. 'That's a brilliant idea! Why didn't I think of that?'

In truth, Idaho's idea was so good that even Bro Drumel felt compelled to congratulate him.

Their meeting was then effectively at an end, for all business had been dealt with. But Bro Drumel was not prepared to depart without asking one last question.

'My lady,' said Drumel. 'Is the Crab . . . has the Crab really chosen to be wazir? Or is it . . .?'

169

'The Crab is very much wazir,' said the Empress Justina decisively. 'Believe me, Brody. I'd never lie to you.'

Thus spoke the Empress. And Bro Drumel believed the Thrug, and was comforted by her blatant lie.

The truth was quite another matter entirely.

The truth was that Chegory Guy and Olivia Qasaba had dared a desperate bluff, claiming that the Crab had declared itself wazir when in point of fact it had done no such thing.

Each day, a great many state papers were carried across the harbour bridge to the island of Jod; and each day a stream of orders, commands, declarations and petitions were returned from that island. But the Crab played no part in this two-way flow. Instead, Injiltaprajura was effectively been ruled by the young Chegory Guy and the even younger Olivia Qasaba.

With, it must be admitted, a little help from the wizards Pelagius Zozimus and Hostaja Sken-Pitilkin, a certain amount of assistance from the analytical engineer Ivan Pokrov and the algorithmist Artemis Ingalawa, and daily advice from the Empress Justina herself.

Were this history to adopt the style of Greven Jing, it might say something like this:

'So far, the innocent citizens of Injiltaprajura had no idea that power had been seized by two members of the dreaded drumming cult. But they would find out. Soon enough. For, nightly, the drums beat on the island of Jod, competing with the slabender frogs for the dominance of the night. And the hellish rhythms of the drums spoke of fear; and death; and torture; and things far worse still yet to come.'

But this is a history, therefore it must avoid such artificial hysteria wherever possible. Let the truth be told. While Chegory Guy and Olivia Qasaba are known to have associated with 'drummers' from time to time, there is no evidence to show or suggest that they actually engaged in 'drumming' themselves. Even though Olivia once gave the Crab a drum of its own, there is no evidence to suggest that she used it herself (or that the Crab employed the instrument, though it did not reject the gift).

Besides, the fear, death and torture which at that time threatened so many good citizens of Injiltaprajura owned nothing whatsoever to the fringe cult of 'drumming', but stemmed instead from the nature of the main stream political struggle.

The historian apologizes to the reader for so stressing a point which has perhaps been adequately made earlier; but the nature of the final days of the rule of the Family Thrug has been so confused by the agitated fictionalizing of those who make a living from sensationalizing 'cults' and 'cultists' that the historian feels the point needs to be made yet again.

Another thing must be made clear:

While Chegory Guy and Olivia Qasaba played a vital role in the politics of that time and place, their roles owed everything to their association with the Crab, and nothing whatsoever to the cult of 'drumming'; and the fact that the Crab allowed Chegory and Olivia to issue imperial decrees in the Crab's name should not be allowed to obscure the fact that all the decisions made by those two infatuated children were largely influenced and controlled by the constant advice they received from the responsible adults on whose good counsel they relied and depended.

Now this has been clarified:

Read on!

If you dare!

CHAPTER EIGHTEEN

The day after Bro Drumel's meeting with the Empress
Justina, the Narapatorpabarta Bank began to experience
an unusual number of withdrawals. Juliet Idaho
engineered this run on the bank, and did so in the
simplest way imaginable. He made up a list of likely
account holders (anyone rich enough to have money
worth hiding from the Inland Revenue), visited the
people on his list, and ordered each to bring him
documented proof of a withdrawal from the N'barta. Or
else!

Drug dealers he visited, and brothel keepers; and
certain other people who had suspiciously grand houses
and no visible means of support.

That was all it took to get things moving, for once
rumour got wind of the rash of withdrawals no further
engineering was needed. The run on the bank escalated
rapidly as people by the dozen came in to clean out their
numbered accounts. Idle drummers, drawn to the scene
by the panic of honest citizens, began to beat their
instruments in the street outside.

Tok – tok – thuk!

Tok – tok – thuk . . .

In the bank, hidden behind the scenes but monitoring
every transaction, Justina's agents lurked in waiting. The
Narapatorpabarta Bank permitted this intrusion because
Juliet Idaho had kidnapped the bank manager's wife,
sons (five in number) and baby daughter.

When results are required in a hurry, Yudonic Knights
tend to give much more satisfaction than lawyers or
other slow-working persuaders. There is a degree of
danger in the use of Yudonic Knights, since their

presence tends to escalate a minor diplomatic incident to an armed confrontation, or to make a full-scale war out of a street corner brawl. The Empress Justina, however, was in so much strife already that she failed to see how Idaho's indiscretions could possibly make things worse.

Thus the run on the N'barta began, and a great many numbers were brought to the bank's counters in twins while Justina's people waited patiently for the much-wanted bearer of the blackmail numbers to make his (her?) appearance.

Meanwhile, another financial crisis was taking place on Untunchilamon, albeit a minor one. The officials of the Inland Revenue had learnt that Shabble's Cult of the Holy Cockroach was tithing its adherents. The Cult was not demanding ten per cent of the congregation's income. Or twenty. Or thirty, even. No. Shabble was going for the whole thing. A full 100 per cent.

Agents from the Inland Revenue fronted up at the Xtokobrokotok to protest. Shabble's lawyer, the redoubtable corpse-master Uckermark, gave them a stern lecture on the rights and freedoms of religion.

'You don't understand,' said an earnest revenue agent. 'If people give all to religion, there's nothing left to be taxed.'

'Oh, I understand perfectly,' said Uckermark.

'You mean,' said the revenue agent, warming to his task, 'you understand this Shabble's religion to be no more than a tax dodge.'

'No more than a tax dodge?' said a scandalized Uckermark. 'That's blasphemy.'

'Blasphemy?' said the revenue agent. 'Against a cockroach? Who cares?'

'The law cares!' said Uckermark. 'This is no ordinary cockroach. This is the Holy Cockroach. Furthermore, His Cult is a Protected Religion. It has the favour of the High Priest of Zoz the Ancestral. So to blaspheme against the Holy Cockroach is as bad as blaspheming against Zoz Himself. You've already said enough to endanger your life. I suggest you say no more unless you have urgent business to conduct with your ancestors.'

The revenue agents lacked Uckermark's specialized knowledge of ecclesiastical law, but research soon demonstrated that Uckermark was right. So the revenue agents had recourse to Nadalastabstala Banraithan-chumun Ek. The High Priest of Zoz the Ancestral was far from pleased to see them, and even less pleased once they had explained their mission.

'You petty money-grubbing omolkiomomooskipis,' said Master Ek in open contempt. 'Your grudgery is an open disgrace. It is fitting for worshippers to give freely to their faith.'

'But,' said a revenue agent, the same one who had argued valorously with Uckermark, 'the Cult returns half of all monies to the donors as charity.'

'That is only reasonable,' said Master Ek. 'If the donors have pauperized themselves by their generosity to their church they must surely have need of such charity.'

'Then let them give less to start with,' said the revenue agent. 'For charity doles escape all taxes, You see, most of these people are in the upper income bracket. Their tax rate is set at nine dalmoons in the dragon. But as it is, they pay a dragon to the cult to earn five dalmoons in charity. Every dragon thus paid saves the giver four dalmoons, while the revenue wins not a damn in taxes.'

'It's a laundering operation,' said another agent.

'Explain it to me again,' said Master Ek.

It was a great many years since he had bothered to add or subtract. He had accountants to do that kind of drudgery.

The revenue agents were pleased with Ek's enthusiasm for enlightenment and gladly assisted with his continuing education. Master Ek proved to be exceptionally interested in the details; indeed, the sharp-eyed priest had smoked his way through three cigarettes before the agents were finished.

'Now I understand,' said Ek at last. 'As a reward for their devotion, the worshippers have their effective tax rate cut from ninety per cent to fifty, thus saving themselves four dalmoons in the dragon.'

'Precisely,' said one of the agents.

Ek lit a fourth cigarette, drew deeply on that source of narcotic delight, blew a smoke ring then said:

'You have my gratitude. You have revealed to me a cure for the growing impiety of Injiltaprajura. What serves for a Protected Religion will serve for the Source.'

One particularly young and impressionable revenue agent, unable to control himself, gave vent to a moan of anguish.

'You do that well,' said Master Ek with interest. He was something of a connoisseur of moans, groans and other expressions of anguish; and here, he realized, was a unique talent. 'Have you ever considered a career as a human sacrifice? If you do, we have an opening available. The Festival of Light is scarcely a month away. Just think! Very shortly you could be kneeling at the feet of Zoz himself. Actually . . . I have a mind to declare a mass sacrifice. As High Priest upon Untunchilamon I do have that privilege. How many of there are you? Let me see . . .'

As Nadalastabstala Banraithanchumun Ek began counting the assembled revenue agents, they said their adieus and fled.

Their next stop was the pink palace, where they petitioned the Empress Justina for assistance.

'Oh,' said she, 'but there's nothing I can do. It's not my island any more. It's the Crab's. Why don't you talk it through with Dui Tin Char? Taxes are his job, not mine.'

'We would,' said one of the agents, 'but he's on Jod.'

'Well!' said Justina. 'Then what's the problem? You're a healthy young man. And the day's not that hot. It's easy enough to find. Down to the end of Lak Street then turn left. First bridge to the right. Can't miss it. Off you go! Come along now. I've got work to do.'

'What work?' said one of the agents. 'We thought you had been replaced by the Crab.'

'Replaced but not unemployed,' said Justina. 'I've all manner of commissions to do. Why, only today I got a message from Master Ek. He's got a festival coming up, the Festival of Light, and there's an unaccountable shortage of sacrifices. He wants me to help him find some. What are you doing next month?'

The revenue agents did not stay to answer.

They fled.

Once safely distant from Justina, they huddled together in their headquarters and conspired and caballed at length. To no effect whatsoever. For, since Justina and Ek both refused them help, there was nobody they could turn to for assistance. Except the Crab.

And that risk they were most certainly not prepared to run.

None of those cowardly agents was even prepared to dare the dangers of the harbour bridge and venture to the island of Jod for a consultation with Dui Tin Char.

Tin Char, head of Injiltaprajura's Inland Revenue, was labouring on Jod as a slave. He worked in the kitchen under the vigilant eye of Pelagius Zozimus. And, three times a day, he helped take meals to the Crab.

Chegory Guy and Olivia Qasaba were always in attendance on that dignitary. Indeed, they even shared its meals. They sipped at tiny bowls of centipede soup while the Crab gravely sheared through huge loaves of cassava bread, dipped them in tureens of the same savoury concoction then fed itself with the sodden mass that resulted. They shared the Crab's grilled flying fish, roast pig and cat-monkey pie.

And, after meals, Chegory and Olivia worked their way through huge heaps of state papers piled upon desks outside the Crab's cave. Two lanteen sails had been rigged up as awnings to protect this makeshift office from the whims of the weather.

To Tin Char, it looked as if the Crab truly was running Injiltaprajura, with the Ebrell Islander and a young Ashdan lass acting as no more than the Crab's secretary-slaves. To reinforce this illusion, Olivia had obtained some white paint, and with it she had written upon the Crab's carapace (in Janjuladoola):

I AM THE LORD EMPEROR OF THE UNIVERSE.

Olivia had also made the Crab an 'imperial hat' of the kind affected by those ancient rulers of whom we read in the pages of the famous Hero Sword Sagas. It was a most magnificent hat of purple paper, with seven yellow streamers descending from its peak; and, glued atop the Crab's carapace, it looked truly imposing.

Had Tin Char dared engage the Crab in conversation he would have learnt that the Crab professed a total lack of interest in the rule of Injiltaprajura; but, with the memory of the dislocation of his arms undimmed by time, Tin Char spent no more time in the Presence than was absolutely necessary.

Then, on the day on which the run on the N'barta began, Chegory Guy casually informed Tin Char that the Crab meant to have the head of the Inland Revenue for dinner the next day.

'I am honoured,' said Tin Char, doing his best to conceal his apprehension.

'It is a great honour,' agreed Chegory. 'So please don't chew any betel nut between now and the granting of that honour. I don't think it makes any difference, but the Crab swears it spoils the flavour of the flesh.'

'The flavour?' said Tin Char, doing his best to delay comprehension.

'The flavour, yes,' said Chegory. 'So no betel nut. But coconuts, that's OK, oh, and even a little alcohol. I know it's, um, a drug and all that, but one day's drinking won't hurt you any, not that it matters in any case when the end's so close.'

Tin Char, having by now understood the nature of the Crab's invitation to dinner, pretended to faint. He was carried to the infirmary attached to the Analytical Institute, and from there he made his escape shortly after midnight.

Zazazolzodanzarzakazolabrik was Tin Char's destination. He durst not stay in Injiltaprajura, for the Crab or the Crab's agents would surely haul him back to Jod to be consumed at banquet by that anthropophagous monster.

Before Tin Char escaped to the deserts of Zolabrik, he had time sufficient to tell a couple of his most trusted friends of the ordeal he had endured as a slave of the Monster of Jod. And by noon the next day the tale was all over Injiltaprajura, its details confirming to one and all that the Crab truly had made itself wazir.

'What happened to that Tin Char fellow?' said the Crab on the morrow.

'Oh, him,' said Chegory. 'I think he's gone to stay with his mother-in-law.'

'Hmmm,' said the Crab, digesting this, and simultaneously digesting a very large chunk of moray eel. 'I wish I had a mother-in-law. Or even a mother, come to that.'

'Never mind,' said Olivia, saddened by the desolation in the Crab's voice. 'You must have had a mother once. That's something, at any rate.'

'No,' said the Crab sadly. 'I never had a mother.'

'But you must have!' said Olivia. 'Your own little mother, running around under rocks and things. Then she met a daddy crab and they fell in love. So they got married. There was a feast, of course. They had shrimps, seaweed, sea anemones, all kind of things. Then they set up house together and had little crabs of their own, dozens of them maybe. There must still be lots of them left. Brother crabs, sister crabs, uncle and aunt crabs. Maybe none of them can talk, but they're out in the harbour somewhere. So don't feel lonely. You have got

178

a family, really. They look just like these little crab shells I brought for you, and that's a fact.'

The Crab sighed.

Its sigh sounded like a drowning diver bubbling helplessly deep, deep beneath water.

'I wish it was true,' said the Crab. 'I wish I really did come from the sea. Or from the land, at the very least.'

'Well, you must have,' said Olivia. 'I mean, you're either a land crab or a sea crab. You must be one or the other. That's logical.'

'I'm neither,' said the Crab. 'I wasn't born on the land, and I wasn't born in the sea either. I was born in the fires of the local sun.'

'No,' said Olivia, 'you can't have been, you silly. The sun's too hot. Your legs would have been burnt off the moment you were born.'

'I didn't have legs,' said the Crab. 'Or ears. Or eyes. Or a stomach, even.'

'You mean,' said Chegory, 'you were a deformed baby?'

'I was no kind of baby at all,' said the Crab. 'I was born as a . . . a perturbation of chance and change. That's how my people live. We live by . . . by changing chance. Modifying local probability. But a star's the place for that, not a planet. So when I had to flee the sun, I had to find a form for myself as soon as I landed on the planet. Do you understand? Sun? Star? Planets?'

'Oh yes,' said Olivia. 'The sun's a sea urchin and the planets are the pieces of kumera. That's how old Pokrov explained it. Then Artemis Ingalawa came along and told him to stop playing with his food.'

'The sun?' said the Crab. 'A sea urchin? Child—'

'I'm not a child,' said Olivia Qasaba impatiently, though it was one of her days for playing the child to the hilt. 'I'm a mature adult. Of course I know the sun's not a sea urchin. It's a sustained thermonuclear reaction converting the light to the heavy. Hydrogen to helium and so forth. You end up with iron. Or the star goes bang, one or the other. Gravity. Energy conversion. Inverse square laws. All that. And the planets, greasy old planets, rocks and stuff, Jof, Nan, Bruk, Hikorlabarus. Then Skrin, which is what we're standing on. Then Pelothiasis, Mog, Ompara, Belthargez.'

All this said Olivia, and only good manners prevented her from saying rather more. She resented having her sea urchin whimsy so casually destroyed. And resented, too, being patronized – albeit by a Crab. She had spent much of her life in the study of the higher sciences, including Thalodian Mathematics itself, and therefore took umbrage at being lectured on basics.

'Jof?' said the Crab. 'You call a planet thus? Those other names . . . what were they? Nan? Hokarbrus?'

'Hikorlabarus,' said Olivia.

'Those are no planet names,' said the Crab. 'You stand in error, for the local astronomers call the planets—'

'We know,' said Olivia, most definitely in no mood for another lecture.

'Those names Olivia quoted are Shabble's names,' explained Chegory.

'Shabble's names?' said the Crab.

'Shabble, you know,' said Chegory. 'You've met Shabble, haven't you? Shabble's a priest now. The Cockroach, that's what it's all about. But anyway, Shabble talks lots about the sun, the planets, all that stuff. Pokrov only said about it that once, the time with the sea urchin. On Ingalawa's best tablecloth! But Shabble talks about it often, going to the sun and all that stuff.'

'Shabble went to the sun?' said the Crab.

'In a ship,' said Olivia. 'A special ship. Maybe Shabble knows where you could find a ship like that. You could go back to the sun. Would you like that? If that's where you came from, maybe you'd be happier there.'

'No,' said the Crab with infinite sadness. 'I can never go back. There was a . . . a religious argument, you see.

I espoused a heresy. I had to flee for my life. If I go back, they'll kill me.'

'A heresy?' said Chegory. 'What was it?'

'My . . . my theory of time,' said the Crab. 'I held that time must have had a start. For how could infinite time have passed? You know the mathematics of infinity?'

'Intimately,' said Chegory.

Unlike Olivia Qasaba, Chegory Guy had been defeated by the intricacies of Thaldonian Mathematics; but he had mastered simplicities such as infinity with ease.

'Well then,' said the Crab, 'infinity by definition has no end. But time past has most definitely ended, for here we are in the now. It follows that there cannot be infinite amounts of past time – that is, history. Therefore, there must have been a start. A start implies a cause. Which means we should have shared the sunspin, not dividied it.'

'The sunspin?' said Chegory. 'You've lost me.'

The Crab did its best to explain, but, though the intricate ramifications of its heresy may have been obvious to a sun-born creature, they were virtually impossible for a planet-bound creature to understand. The Crab began to get frustrated.

'Never mind,' said Olivia consolingly. 'We understand the important things. You were born in the sun and you can't go back. You came here and became a Crab. That's all right. There's lots of good things about being a Crab. I mean, you've got the most marvellous appetite. Look at how much you eat! Do you ever get indigestion? Of course not. Better still, you could rule the world if you wanted to.'

'I don't want to,' said the Crab.

'Why not?' said Olivia.

'Because it would mean an enormous amount of work for no reward,' said the Crab.

'But you could have . . . well, palaces and things,' said Olivia.

'I could have a palace now if I wanted one,' said the

181

Crab. 'I don't have to live in a cave, you know. I could move into the Analytical Institute. But there's no point. Not when you're a Crab. This body, you see, it's . . .'

The Crab did not elaborate. It had no need. The drawbacks of being a huge Crab was obvious. One was too big to enter most buildings and too heavy for most boats. One could take no pleasure in soft chairs or padded beds. One's uses for compliant human flesh were strictly constrained by anatomical awkwardness.

The list of drawbacks could be extended.

'So you want to be human,' said Chegory.

'That's all right,' said Olivia Qasaba. 'You will be, won't you? Justina said as much. She promised to find you this organic rectifier. It's magic, that's what it is. It'll make you a body as good as mine.'

'If it exists,' said the Crab.

'But of course it exists!' said Olivia. 'You mustn't be like that. Look, why don't you really make yourself wazir? It would be much safer for us. We could . . . we could look for this rectifier thing ever so much harder.'

'Leave the poor Crab alone,' said Chegory. 'It doesn't want to be troubled about organic rectifiers and things, not today.'

Olivia had the better brain, but Chegory possessed a greater degree of empathy with the Monster of Jod, and understood more of its bitter, stoical outlook. From past conversations, Chegory knew the Crab had been lied to by many humans in the past. Many promises had been made to it – promises which had subsequently been broken. Wizards and sorcerers alike had promised to turn it into man, child or woman; but all had failed. The Crab had been disappointed so many times it did not feel it could afford to trust any such promises ever again.

This Chegory knew; and Olivia could have benefited from his knowledge. But, unfortunately, the Ashdan lass took exception to the Ebrell Islander's tone of voice, and this led to a quarrel. Which left them both upset, and

Olivia in tears. Though they soon got over it, and had quite repaired their relations by nightfall.

That night, Pelagius Zozimus, Ivan Pokrov and Artemis Ingalwa organized a special dinner to celebrate the escape of Dui Tin Char and the rapid spread of authenticating rumours which had followed that escape. Now all Injiltaprajura believed that the Crab ruled as wazir. On Tin Char's authority, no less.

The mature adults were immensely relieved, for the last few days had been tense indeed.

But Chegory Guy and Olivia Qasaba felt no relief because they had felt no worry. While Untunchilamon lurched from one crisis to another, while panicked depositors mobbed the Narapatorpabarta Bank and agents of the Inland Revenue resorted to heavyweight tranquillizers, while spies and thieves fought to the death for possession of scraps of the mysterious *Injiltaprajura-dariski*, while Juliet Idaho and Nadalastabstala Banraithanchumun Ek fumed with impatience (Idaho metaphorically and the chain-smoking Ek literally), Chegory and Olivia passed their days in what was almost another world entirely.

Such are the ways of youth that the crisis in which Chegory and Olivia were so intimately involved was but a remote background to the true drama of their lives.

For they were in love.

This may lead some readers to throw up their arms and cry out in despair; but the historian records it with tolerant understanding. For, in a long and often bitter life, the historian has learnt that there are forms of folly which are far, far worse than the systematic delusions which accompany amation.

One such folly, one of millions, is to—

But I have come to the end of another sheet of fooskin; therefore I will call a halt to this chapter here, and launch into a disquisition upon certain forms of political folly (notably philosophical objection to the paying of taxes) at the start of the next.

CHAPTER NINETEEN

Nadalastabstala Banraithanchumun Ek knew full well (as knows your historian) that taxes must be paid. Or else the State will wither away. The withering of the State would give great satisfaction to certain feckless political philosophers; but such a prospect is less than attractive to those who rely for their livelihood upon the roads and irrigation systems organized and protected by the State.

One of the biggest problems associated with the withering of the State is the rise in thuggery which typically accompanies such withering. Solo muggers become organized bandits, among whom warlords in time come to power, eventually throwing up a master of murder who makes himself emperor and sets in place his own version of the State.

The bottom line is this: those who wish to sleep safely in their beds had better be prepared to pay their taxes.

Master Ek knew this full well.

Nevertheless, while Ek was a financial realist, it would have been hard to gather this from the fiery speeches he made over the next few days. He preached to packed congregations, for a great many people had suddenly discovered a new or renewed faith in Zoz the Ancestral now that such loyalty could win them tax advantages equal to those offered by the Cult of the Holy Cockroach.

What possessed Master Ek to pursue this folly?

Was senility at last setting in?

Justina sent her spies to audit Master Ek's sermons, and the spies came back with the most alarming news. While Ek's preaching did not deviate from the orthodox doctrines of his religion, it nevertheless carried the most alarming political overtones, and was being received with adulatory acclamation.

Not to put too fine a point on it, Master Ek was stirring up a lynch mob.

The High Priest of Zoz the Ancestral was too afraid of the Crab to oppose it directly. Believing Justina to be under the Crab's protection, Ek durst not order people to chop off her head. Dui Tin Char's panic-stricken flight into the deserts of Zolabrik had convinced Ek of the wisdom of his long-pursued policies of caution; and, as many hot heads had been cooled by the Crab's explicit intervention into the politics of Injiltaprajura, it was unlikely that Ek would have been obeyed had he ordered Justina's death.

However, a mob in its madness will do what no individual in its ranks would dare alone. Ek knew this. Justina knew this. And Ek knew (and Justina knew that he knew) that any overt move against the Temple of Zoz by Empress or Crab would not forestall a riot but instead would precipitate it immediately; for the Temple's fall would mean financial ruin for a great many citizens of Injiltaprajura had already committed themselves to new mortgages and hire purchase agreements on the strength of the tax breaks so recently granted them by that Temple.

Ek was in his element.

When Nadalastabstala Banraithanchumun Ek preached in the Temple, a great weight of age seemed to slip from his shoulders; he seemed to gain height in fingerlengths and to grow broader across the shoulders. The pains of his arthritis eased, ebbed, then vanished entirely. His voice, slightly hoarse thanks to his incessant cigarette smoking, crooned and inveigled as he insinuated himself into the confidence of his congregation.

'Power,' he said. 'We worship Zoz because Zoz is power. Power is the greatest good. The weak were made to kneel before power, because such is the nature of reality.'

With such self-evident truths old Master Ek began.

Then, when he had his people in his power, when his voice had replaced the function of thought, he worked on them with rhythms designed to lead to a destruction of the self in a climax close to orgasm.

Sometimes he innovated his own speeches.

Sometimes a mere recital of Holy Writ sufficed.

Hear him.

Hear Master Ek.

Listen!

'In the Beginning was the mire of the morass, the slime of the pulp.

'In the Beginning was the darkness, and floods of filth moved back and forth within the darkness, void of face and without form.

'And the floods were lustful and without continence.

'And the name of the Beginning was Woman.

'And she in her depths was dark and knew not of herself, and a great Abyss was she, with snakes within her substance.

'This was the time of the lowest, for she was low, no height had she.

'Nor did she yearn for height.

'For her nature was to drag down and swallow, to swallow and submerge, to submerge and dissolve, to dissolve and ruin, and this to and with herself she did.

'And the face and the skin of the Woman were clutching waters, and a great rain fell perpetually upon those waters.

'Yet the waters were not cleansed thereby.

'And the rain merged with the waters and became unclean.

'And rain and water were one, and their taste was that of blood.

'And the world which was Woman was weak and in its weakness knew not of itself. It was soft; it was liquid; a great streaming surged within its depths, and it was void of form and of boundary.

186

'Then Zoz spake out of nothing, saying unto Woman: I am.

'Thus the will.

'Thus the first Act, and the first Act was of pure will.

'Then Act became Man, and a great light was upon him and within him, and his first name was Order.

'And Woman beheld the light and said unto it: Come, be with me and of me.

'But Zoz said unto the temptations of this moist engulfment: I am Light, thou art Dark. I am Law, thou art Panic. Behold me in my glory, and obey.

'Thus spoke Zoz.

'But woman obeyed not. She laughed.

'And Zoz the Ancestral saw that the laughter was a great wrong against the right, and did unto Woman what it was his will to do, and afterwards there was silence without laughter, and a great contentment was within the heart of Zoz.

'Thus it was at the time of the Coming.

'As it should be and will be here and hereafter. For Zoz is great, and we ourselves can be great in Zoz. Can be and will be. Affirm!'

Thus Ek, and the affirmation of his congregation was like unto the rage of a great storm.

Reports of these speeches reached Pelagius Zozimus on the island of Jod. Now Pelagius Zozimus was in some ways a consummate politician, and thanks to his skills he had risen high in the ranks of Argan's Confederation; but his politics were those of a bureaucrat. He was an accomplished tactician and a sly strategist who had won many triumphs in the realms of committees and commissions of enquiry; but he had no sense whatsoever of the passions of the mob.

So, when Ek called for the people to worship the Powerful, Zozimus muttered that this was all nonsense.

'It is sufficient to lead a moral life.'

So said Zozimus to the fruit salad (coconut, mango, papaya, cassana, watermelon and sea-cucumbers) which he had prepared for the Crab's latest lunch. (A fruit salad is what he called it, though some pedants will object that a coconut is not a fruit and that a sea-cucumber is actually an animal.)

'It is pointless,' said Zozimus, 'to adore Power merely because it is Power. Not one person in a thousand will pay heed to such nonsense.'

Thus Zozimus.

Sadly underestimating the potency of Ek's doctrines and the strength of their mob appeal.

Why was a wizard as brilliant as Pelagius Zozimus so badly astray in his estimations of political reality? Perhaps his very intelligence limited his perceptions, for it kept him from empathizing with the inchoate yearnings of the mob. That and his possession of personal power.

Though Pelagius Zozimus had long ago abandoned the control of corpses for the delights of cookery, occult power yet remained to him. He was and would always be a wizard of the order of Xluzu, a wizard holding power in his own right without reference to any of his fellows. He experienced power as a shaping fire, a living force, an actual presence; as do the poets, through whom there flow the energies of language itself. While Zozimus had played politics in the great castles of Drangsturm, 'play' is indeed the operative word; he delighted in bureau-cratic manoeuvrings just as Ivan Pokrov delighted in pure mathematics.

Here Zozimus displayed not a personal quirk but, rather, an attribute typical of his kind; and it is worth pursuing this matter at length, for it helps explain the curious incapacity of the territories ruled by Argan's Confederation of Wizards; and to explain, too, the fact that the political influence of the sorcerers of Yestron is but modest though their individual powers be great.

Doubtless not all will be entranced by explanation given in such a sober fashion, by the results of the researches of scholarship set down in a forthright manner without embroidery of blood or flame. Those thus impatient (a majority, one fears) are therefore invited to skip to the start of the next chapter of this chronicle, where it may be that the record will delight them with a rape; or with a plundering of gold; or a building flung aloft (a mote at a time) by the raging flames of arson; or by a tsunami mounting from Moana to sweep across the Outer Reef, to swamp the sand incarnadine of Scimitar, to wreck the white marble of the Analytical Institute from its stance on Jod, and then to despoil the city shore.

Or perhaps at the start of that next chapter they will find the libidinous Princess Sabitha (Sabitha Winolathon Taskinjathura, scion of the great Ousompton Ling Ordway) in hot copulation with one of her seagoing friends; or the irresponsible Shabble, now a priest, accepting the priestly duty of marriage counselling, and thus engaged in dialoguing the intimacies of the sexual conduct of a beglamoured but embattled young couple.

History, as one of the wise has had occasion to remark, is very largely a record of war, rape, murder, slaughter, torture, treason, revolution and riot; for which the historian is often blamed, as if history would cease to be enacted were all its chroniclers to be slaughtered (a remedy which has actually been essayed on at least three separate occasions, and which has proved to be singularly ineffective as a remedy for the woes of humanity). It is one of the frustrations of the chronologer's task that most readers of annals such as these (these readers being few to start with, for history has never had popular appeal) are drawn to such pages by a positive lust for bloodshed; and, lacking any desire to join the ranks of the illuminati, have scant appetite for the scholarly conclusions which cast light on the Causes and the Processes of such disasters.

Scholarly conclusions now follow.

So:

Fly! Away! Let youth depart and race by a flicker of

pages to the start of the next chapter, there to be gratified (perhaps) by tsunami, blasphemy or blatant copulation (or, then again, perhaps not).

And now, secure in the company of hoar age and toothless wisdom alone, let us proceed to show why Pelagius Zozimus was not constitutionally equipped to understand the temperament of the mob; and why, too, the political achievements of wizards and wonder-workers alike fall short of their potential.

As poets in committed combination are rare, so too are wizards; and for similar reasons. Any one great poet would remain great – as would any one great wizard – were all his fellows to disappear from the world in a great disaster. Hence most poets (and a great many wizards) secretly yearn for such a catastrophe. Much would be lost, but personal power would be enhanced by the lack of competition.

Compare this to the state of a soldier, be he of any rank from common muck-slugger to lordly general.

What is he on his own?

Nothing.

Can he rape, rob and pillage on his own?

Not effectively, for any washerwoman with a pitchfork in her hands can put him to flight.

Can he storm towns, sack castles, beseige cities, dare his desires across the seas or fortify his possession of ill-gotten treasures on his own?

The answer:

No.

Whereas wizard and poet alike can in solitude and with the self alone conspire to create instruments of temporal power (and in isolation consummate such conspiracy), no such ability is granted unto the ordinary run of mortals; wherefrom it follows that ordinary mortals must like the ants unite for cohesive action in the face of their individual impotence.

Ants engrossed in the multitude of their fellows partake of a power which would be alien to their

190

existence were they to live alone; and so it is with most humans. As the antheap to the ant, so stands the State to the common citizen; and so like an ant the citizen submits to the oppressions of laborious routine, of claustrophobic discipline, and of war.

'Discipline is good,' says your average citizen; meaning, in truth, 'I love power, and cannot find it on my own, for on my own I am as nothing.'

'The gods are great,' he says; meaning, 'the gods reward my worship by allotting to me the worship of my wife, a worship made a very law of piety.'

'If you would have peace then prepare for war,' he says; meaning, 'the militarization of the state in peace as well as war is the best enforcement of that hierarchy of discipline which rewards obedience with power.'

All this is true; yet unacknowledged. For it is a characteristic of humankind that the most bitter realities of their lives – the inevitability of death and the fatuosity of the periodic slaughters which so accelerate that death – are rarely conceded except by a small fraction of aberrant intellects most likely persecuted for such acknowledgement.

Thus, as ants in their mindless millions go to war, so go men; and, while philosophers of biology declare the intellect of the average human to be greater than the corresponding resource of the ant, the differences in the ultimate outcome of their behaviour are so slight as to be unobservable.

Such subordinations are alien to the intellects of wizard and poet alike; for, being possessed of powers won in solitary endeavour outside the antheap, they are disinclined to submit to those oppressions which the common citizen clamours to embrace.

It follows from above that the most unkempt band of syphilitic bandits is apt to display more political cohesion than the inhabitants of a salon of imperial poets; and the most murderous brood of pirates, though its members be universally refugees from the law of ordered States, enforces among its own number a discipline of war which wizards of Argan's Confederation could only look upon in outright envy; and warriors, who in their leisure time display a gross indiscipline of drink and lust, conform upon the battlefield in perfect regulation.

In summary:

As it is with the warrior, so it is with your common citizen. Unlike wizard or poet, your common citizen holds no power in his own right, and can win power only by joining an antheap of oppressions. He joins the State because the State is in many ways a conspiracy to give him power. Power over property; power over slaves; power over the women in his life; power over children and his economic inferiors.

Thus so many applaud the State when the State is savage, and wrathful, and cruel; and thus a leader who kills, maims, tortures, imprisons and oppresses is often widely applauded as long as he is adroitly selective in his choice of victims. The poverty and suffering of the weak delight the strong, for thus they see their own power enhanced.

He crushed: he was a great leader.

He killed: he was a great leader.

He destroyed: he was a great leader.

He oppressed: he was a great leader.

He warred: he was a great leader.

Great, yes, and very holy.

It happens that from time to time a ruler of a different sort arises.

Justina was such a ruler.

The Empress Justina believed no self-justifying rhetoric of power, least of all that rhetoric which claims the might of the State to be a good in its own right. Instead, she perceived the State through the eyes of common sense. She saw that humans living as thickly upon the ground as they do within the confines of Injiltaprajura must combine to manage the supply of their water and the disposal of their sewage; that a regulated coinage and a disciplined merchantry can enhance the collective prosperity; that the collective State can extend to the aged and the indigent great mercies of charity which would be beyond the patience or the means of the individual; and that a just system of law supplies the aggrieved with an orderly remedy of wrongs so great that they would otherwise threaten the common peace.

The Empress Justina was good; and merciful; and wise; and therefore out of favour with most of her citizens. For an imperial disinclination to make the State an instrument of selective oppression thwarts the desires of those many citizens who wish to be lords of wrath in their own households and the neighbourhood streets.

Why then had she remained in power for so long?

On Untunchilamon, the Family Thrug came to power at the beginning of Talonsklavara. Lonstantine Thrug seized his opportunity and overthrew Wazir Sin in a move which owed everything to bloody ferocity and political opportunism; and such were the initial uncertainties of civil war that none wished to be the first to oppose him. For any wazir of Untunchilamon must necessarily support one side or another in Talonsklavara or else incur the wrath of both – and who could say which side would triumph?

When Lonstantine was incarcerated in the Dromdanjerie as a consequence of his mounting insanity, his daughter Justina inherited his throne and the very uncertainties which supported it. Later, when the victory of Aldarch Three became a probability, her position weakened, to the point where Aquitaine Varazchavardan had dared to coup against her.

Thereafter she had stayed alive (and in power) by bluff, luck, the loyalty of friends, and her own audacious skills at political manoeuvring.

But, now that Aldarch Three was known to have triumphed in Yestron (Manthandros Trasilika had been a fraud, and his priest Jean Froissart no better, but interrogation of sailors from the *Oktobdoj* had proved much of their news to be true), there was no rational basis for believing that Justina's power would continue much longer.

While Master Ek belonged to that multitude which actually believed the Crab to be temporarily ruling Injiltaprajura (with Chegory Guy and Olivia Qasaba as secretary-couriers), Ek nevertheless saw that as a temporary aberration, and quite reasonably believed (on the basis of the patterns of centuries of recorded history) that the Crab would shortly lose interest in political endeavour.

Ek therefore had no long-term worries about the Crab, though he believed that dignitary must be treated with the greatest caution in the short term. Rather, he saw his true enemy as being Justina Thrug; and saw her murder as being the best way to return the island to rightful rule.

Only:

The first person to rise against the Thrug would most surely die.

Thus Master Ek stirred up the mob, knowing his mob would eventually (later if not sooner) storm the pink palace and lynch the Empress Justina, for every mob is a hero. And if the Crab then chose to kill mobsters by the hundreds, what of it?

'People die by thousands every day,' said Ek. 'A human life is worth nothing.'

Adding a mental note to say: except my own.

Thanks to her spies, the Empress Justina was fully aware of Ek's intentions. And, to her great frustration, she durst not have him killed; for his murder would be immediately attributed to her by the mob, thus precipitating the riot she hoped to forestall as long as possible.

Justina's temper was not improved when she heard alarming rumours about her reluctant ally, Aquitaine Varazchavardan. According to rumour, Varazchavardan was trying to bargain with Master Ek. The terms proposed were simple: Varazchavardan would give Ek his full and unstinting cooperation in overthrowing the empress if Ek promised to use his influence to obtain a full pardon for Varazcharvardan from Aldarch Three.

Ek refused.

As far as Master Ek was concerned, Varazchavardan would make a most welcome addition to the pile of corpses which Aldarch III would surely demand once Untunchilamon was firmly within his grasp. Aldarch Three had a special liking for eminent corpses.

Furthermore, as Ek knew full well, Varazchavardan had profited for years from the illegal trade in liquor; but Varazchavardan had always denied Ek the very modest tithe which the High Priest had asked be paid to the Temple of Zoz the Ancestral. Now Justina's Master of Law was going to suffer for his impiety.

Justina was most relieved when she learnt that Ek had rejected Varazchavardan as an ally. If there was to be war on Untunchilamon, she wanted Varazchavardan to be with her, not against her. She also took a certain grim satisfaction in the thought that, if she went down, Varazchavardan would fall in turn. He deserved it. In the not-so-distant past, he had caused an enormous amount of trouble by trying to coup against her. More recently, Justina's much-loved albinotic ape, the irrepressible Vazzy, had been murdered by unknown assassins; and, while Justina could prove nothing, her dark suspicions led her to believe that Varazchavardan was responsible.

Did Varazchavardan's discomfort give her sweet dreams? Did she delight in the thought of the terrors of torture besetting her would-be traitor? In answer to these questions it need only be said that the Empress Justina was the daughter of a Yudonic Knight. Sweet dreams became her well.

Yet, while she slept, others lay wakeful.

Those who slept least were those born amidst the rocklands of Ang, high in the purity of the cold mountains in the heart of the Izdimir Empire. There men build with rough rock and order the world with the laws of grey stone, and women kneel before men in the name of Zoz the Ancestral and take into their mouths the strength of men, and a great contentment is within the hearts of men.

And they lifted up their eyes and beheld the dark mass of Justina's palace, a place built of shameful pink like that a woman hides within her naos. And there, it was known, the Thrug disported itself in a pool of water, swimming in her nakedness beneath the swollen moon; and the Thrug was of flesh, yet without shame; and a great loathing was within the hearts of the men who beheld it.

They knew they must do something about it.

And, by the light of day, many spoke openly of this.

When Justina realized how rapidly the crisis was approaching, is it any wonder that she began to contemplate desperate measures?

It was at this time that a band of sober citizens came to Justina with a petition asking for her to exert herself womanfully to suppress the 'drumming' cult which was so vexing many of the earnest inhabitants of Injiltaprajura. It would have been sufficient for her to direct them to take their petition to the Crab. Unfortunately, Justina did nothing so sensible. For once, she lost her patience – something she did not do often – and said a great many rash and intemperate things which were later remembered against her.

Justina has been much maligned in many superficial histories on account of her failure to suppress the drummers at this crucial stage of the power struggle. However, the historian believes it would have made no difference to the outcome of Untunchilamon's power struggle had Justina beaten every drummer on the island to death. For the drummers were totally irrelevant to politics, the 'cult' consisting as it did of the bored and idle young; and the historian trusts that the reader can, without further explanation, see the absurdity of attempting to write Injiltaprajura's history from a drummer-centred perspective.

With that stated, let us now turn our attention to our next chapter.

CHAPTER TWENTY

Night.

And we open to a scene of hot copulation, for the Princess Sabitha is indulging her passions with one of her seafaring friends. Elsewhere, the dreams which rule the sleep of the Empress Justina have changed from fair to foul, but of them more later. For the moment, let us attend to the elegant Sabitha Winolathon Taskinjathura, she of the xanthic eyes and the delicate tongue.

She is bonking (there are many other words for it, but this one will do) in a much-shadowed scorpion wasteland between Ganthorgruk and the neighbouring slaughter-house; and as she bonks she screams with delight, sounding for all the world as if her intestines were being wrenched from her gut a fingerlength at a time. These ravaged cries arouse the ire of the conjuror Odolo, a man whose good humour has lately been eroded because his long history of alliance with the Empress Justina now threatens his life.

Odolo scrambles out of bed.

He throws open the shutters of his window.

He takes his water jug and hurls it into the night, intending thereby to secure the death of the Princess Sabitha.

She remains undead; and, in her ecstasy, screams like a vampire.

Whereupon Odolo picks up a bowl, a baked yam and a boot, and hurls these objects in turn into the night. It is the boot which makes contact. It scores a direct hit on the Princess Sabitha and her ardent swain. In moments, both are in flight, scarpering in separate directions.

The Princess Sabitha flees down Skindik Way, shortly

vanishing into the stews of Lubos. A dangerous slum-land, this; but she knows it intimately, and knows also how to take care of herself. Or so she in her youth and innocence supposes.

Her lover, a lusty seafarer named Hunk, absconds in a different direction. Unfortunately, this takes him into the Dog Worshipper's Temple at the back of the Dromdanjerie; and, before he realizes his danger, he is attacked by a dozen of his most deadly foes. Hunk was born in Wen Endex; and, though he is of lowly birth, we may nevertheless enroll him (on an honorary basis) in the ranks of the Yudonic Knights. Certainly his fighting prowess deserves to win him such enrolment, for he disables two dogs and nearly kills a third. This represents a considerable accomplishment, particularly since the smallest of these dogs is twice Hunk's weight. Neverthe-less, courage and combative prowess do not suffice. Hunk is pulled down, savaged, killed, then torn to bits. Thus a hero dies, and then is eaten; and shortly nothing is left of him but a scrap of his skull and the final third of his tail.

And the Princess Sabitha?

Let the shameful truth be told!

She has already forgotten him.

Yes, it is true. Sabitha Winolathon Taskinjathura has encountered another lover, and the pair are singing a passionate duet as a preliminary to the consummation of their fresh-found relationship. In the stews of Lubos they sing, while the drums of the drummers beat thus:

Blab-mup blab-mup blab-mub blab!

Rub-thump rub-thump rub-thump rub . . . !

While the drums beat, the night deepens to 'those dragon depths in which swim the darker monsters of dreams', to quote the estimable Mabin Lab Ev.

Look! Savour the moment. Midnight has arrived. Or (to translate from the Dub) the night's last half is raping the first out of the way. Or, as the periphrastical Janjula-doola tongue would have it, by the many breathings of

199

a bat's wing beating has the heat of undokondra been fanned away that now the cool of bardardornootha may begin. (Poetic, perhaps, though bloated poetry; but unfortunately inaccurate, as the watch from midnight to dawn is scarcely a fraction cooler than the stretch which leads to the apotheosis of the ghost bells – bells lately unsounded, unglorified in deference to the harmonic prejudices of the Crab.) The Toxteth is simplest: owl rests, half home.

Midnight, then.

Hot is the night in its deepening, hot as virginity surrendering, sweaty as an orgy's armpit.

In the docklands of Marthandorthan, in Xtokobroko-tok (the big warehouse owned by the drug dealer Firfat Labrat), people are yet awake. For Shabble is conducting a marriage guidance counselling session. The young couple who have sought advice from the High Priest of the Holy Cockroach are of Janjuladoola breed. They are trying to breed but are encountering considerable difficulty in managing the mechanics of that which books of etiquette refer to as 'the initiating process'.

Shabble hears their tale.

What, you may ask, does Shabble know of breeding?

Enough.

For when the couple have finished, Shabble asks a very astute question, then says:

'Try doing it lying down.'

The couple look at him incredulously.

You must remember that they are of the Janjuladoola people: and, as has been stated elsewhere, the Janjula-doola folk shun the ground. Their very furniture they build top-heavy to show their contempt for gravity and all its works; though the possession of such furniture is a matter much governed by class and caste. Let us note also that, throughout the Izdimir Empire, the use of stilts is reserved for the imperial family; and, in Obooloo, sumptuary codes forbid the wearing of platform shoes to all but those of the highest castes and classes. All of which serves to emphasize the contempt in which gravity and ground alike are held.

This prejudice against yielding to the demands of planetary physics has contaminated all areas of Janjuladoola culture, including sexuality – and, in particular, pornography. Now it is a feature of pornography that it caters to fantastic desire rather than to the dictates of reality; consequently, the bawdry of Janjuladoola, whether it be verbal, sculptural or delineative in expression, is characterized by one extraordinary but predictable peculiarity, inasmuch as the conjugation of bodies is invariably shown as an activity that takes place either standing up or (more often) while suspended in mid air.

The pervasive influence of such pornography is demonstrated by a survey of one thousand virgins in the province of Ang, which showed that a full 64 per cent believed that the human body becomes weightless during copulation. Naturally, such expectations often lead to marital difficulties for those amorous but inexperienced couples who fall back upon literary or artistic role models in their pursuit of earthly delights.

But is Shabble the right person to advise such unfortunates in their search for a practical sexual mechanics?

What, for example, does Shabble know of orgasm?

Answer: nothing.

While Shabble has participated in many orgies (let your mind boggle in its own time, for time and space will not be wasted here in any description of such low and shameful occasions, or in any enumeration of the gleeful rogues and ladies who were therein involved) Shabble has no appreciation of orgasm. While willing partners have in the past endeavoured to remedy this lack of experience, the most cunning exploitation of Shabble's tactile receptors has succeeded merely in demonstrating that the imitator of suns is ever so slightly ticklish. The ingenuity of experimenters has been somewhat frustrated by the fact that the shining bubble has very limited facilities for physical intercourse with the world; for Shabble has neither outlets nor inlets for anything apart from heat; and the throwing of fire or the absorbing of the same gives Shabble a pleasure as innocent as that which children take in the variously flaring or exploding fireworks of the Dungeon Feast of Obooloo.

Nevertheless, Shabble is a canny mathematician with a firm grounding in physics both basic and advanced. As this free-floating sphere has moved through human societies with near perfect freedom for the last twenty millennia, it has been given (and has taken) many opportunities to observe human flesh accommodating itself to the demands posited by such physics. And therefore gives advice as good as any which unfortunate young couples would be likely to receive from a doctor.

'Yes,' says Shabble. 'Do it lying down. Oh, and use dikle.'

'Eat it, you mean?' says the boy.

'As an aphrodisiac?' says the girl.

'No, no,' says Shabble, squeaking in excitement; the excitement in question being not prurient interest but an instructor's zeal. 'As a lubricant, that's how you use it. You—'

But here we must leave them, for Shabble will shortly proceed to give contraceptive advice. And this must not be set down in print, for if it is then this chronicle will most surely be outlawed in the historian's homeland lest knowledge relating to the prevention of pregnancy fall into the hands of people aged less than sixteen.

(As the disasters of time may some day separate these writings from their bibliographical context, let it here be noted that the native heath of the volumist responsible for this paper-staining is Quilth, land of the taniwha; and, furthermore, that in the absence of any prospect of substantial pecuniary reward for the historian, the writing of the tract you have now to hand has been sponsored by the genereous gentlemen of the Taniwha

Guarantee Corporation. Thanks to such generosity, the historian is able to eat twice a day, instead of once every twiceday; and, moreover, to eat offal – the guts of seagulls and such – instead of taro and seaweed as formerly. For this bounteous charity he is duly grateful.)

Now it happens that, in the historian's homeland, girls from the age of eleven go courting; and many are the pregnancies, abortions and diseases that befall them. Furthermore, the most highly paid persuaders of commerce labour by night and day alike to persuade young girls that courtship is the ultimate trial of their value; and to sell them all manner of fripperies on that account. Thus those of female gender are propagandized by the subtle arts of their elders, beset on all sides by suggestions and allurements; the entire thrust of this informal education being to persuade them that a complete hymen means an incomplete woman. Women, of course, they most desperately wish to be, as boys wish to be men.

But, in the face of unstinting publicity designed to impel (if not compel) the female young into the arms of their coevals of opposite sex, the government of the above-mentioned land has, in its wisdom, chosen to censor all sources of contraceptive advice which threaten to contaminate the minds of people of such tender years with knowledge of techniques which might save them from a good many diseases and despairs.

This censorship is carried out at the bidding of a stern Religion, which preaches the theoretical benefits of a universal chastity, a chastity which (if one is to judge from generations of practical experience) is not to be obtained in practice, not even when the sanctions of law enforce it. Thus a nation legislates ignorance for its young, preferring frequent abortion, endemic disease and the occasional suicide to the revelations of a rational system of sexual hygiene.

What is more, the nation which thus oppresses a part of its population thinks itself free; and, indeed, many

203

voices are raised within that nation, calling for further censorships and greater oppressions with a view to enhancing the freedoms of the citizens. Absurd, yes, but true; the truth of the matter being the unfortunate part of the story, for were it a fiction it would be mildly amusing, whereas given flesh and fact it becomes tragic.

This minor tragedy is mentioned here because its substance examples one of those paradigmatic proposals which the political historian uses to make sense of his subject: the thesis in question being that citizens of the State seek not just freedom from oppression but also (and equally importantly) the freedom to oppress all those whom they fear and hate; and, furthermore, that most are blind to the difference between these two freedoms, though it must be acknowledged that often such blindness is wilful.

To this we must add another thesis: that in human affairs the negative is stronger than the positive. This because acts of creation require infinite labour and (a rare thing in the desperate lives of these poor forked animals which make human history) an active love; whereas destruction is but the work of a moment, and hate the easiest of all emotions. Furthermore, the thing to be destroyed has an active reality which any fool can see, whereas the thing to be built is but a visionary conjecture; far easier it is, then, to justify destruction in the name of 'realism' than to find a similar justification for the phantasmagorical possibilities of the unbuilt.

By combining the two theses outlined directly above, we arrive at a potent political proposition; which is, that the people of a nation can be more easily motivated and manipulated by offering them the destructive but all too realistic freedom to oppress than by trying to tempt them with the ghostly visions of that creative liberty vouch-safed by freedom from oppression.

This means that practical politics ever inclines toward hate; and oppression; and war. Thus it happens that, in my own homeland, everyone knows what they are against; and what they actively support is usually a list of proposed suppressions, oppressions, fines, censorships, banishments, outlawings, whippings, floggings, birchings, curfews and compulsions. As it is in Quilth, so it is elsewhere; and so we live in an age of darkness where the highest expression of civilization is the act of destruction.

Unfortunately, the Empress Justina was not given to those wraths and hates, those destructions and oppressions, which might well have united the greater part of her people under her rule. She had for instance stopped the pogrom against the Ebrell Islanders; which had won her great unpopularity in many quarters.

Instead of ruling by conventional means, Justina had chosen to exercise mercy and justice; and, in the long run, public discipline had not suffered thereby. In particular, Justina had found the judicious exercise of the prerogative of mercy to be an instrument of statecraft equally as valuable as the executioner's axe; and she was rightly proud of her achievement. In the lustrum following her father's incarceration, she had given her people the fullest possible margin of creative liberty; but, instead of uniting her people in love, this policy had led to Justina being hated and feared, particularly by established Religions.

One of those privileges which Religions demand (and an unfortunate fact is that ideologies in declared opposition to Religion soon become Religions in their own right, regardless of their blasphemous contempt for the gods and the worshippers of the same) is the right to oppress. This is seen in the historian's homeland, where a Religion demands the exclusive right to instruct the young in the management of their sexuality, proceeding in total disregard of the disasters its fatuous advice has produced down through the decades.

On Untunchilamon, the Religion of Zoz the Ancestral demanded far, far more, both on its own behalf and on behalf of the closely associated Temple of Torture.

Hence Justina must necessarily die, for her love has doomed her.

This polemic being at an end, and the lovemaking of the Princess Sabitha being similarly concluded, and Shabble being well launched into a disquisition upon contraceptive technique (technique which law compels us to pass over in silence), we will now proceed elsewhere (this history thus becoming yet another of the many victims of censorship). But before we depart from the Xtokobrokotok, we have time (not much, but a little) for a quick glance at the deity worshipped by the Cult of the Holy Cockroach. A living Presence, this; hence His existence can be proved by pointing in the right direction and declaring a self-evident truth, which is that:

'There He is!'

In His wickerwork cage, the Cockroach stirs. Already He is huge, a handspan in length at least; but He will grow larger yet if the adoration of His congregation continues, for offerings are brought to the warehouse daily for His delectation. There is cheese made from the milk of goats; and that far rarer and enormously expensive cheese made (in small quantities, and only for the most dedicated of connoisseurs) from the milk of monkeys. There are mangos, bits of baked banana frog, chunks of well-cooked taro and fractions of sugar cane; and on all this He feeds as He sees fit.

Elsewhere, in the pink palace (we have, you see, departed from Xtokobrokotok, have ghosted up Gold-hammer Rise, have sped up Lak Street with a speed which draws its inspiration from lightning's example, and have penetrated the walls of the palace like so many ghosts) Justina Thrug is unsoundly asleep.

Up from the depths of Moana mounts a tsunami, rising to a crescendous crest which seemed for a moment to stall before it fell. Then fall it does, breaking into a roar of dragon-outdoing wrath which plunges across the Outer Reef, shocking the sands of Scimitar with its onslaught. On it plunges, sweeping across Jod, demolishing the white marble of the Analytical Institute, then lunging across the Laitemata to earthquake into the streets of Injiltaprajura.

Screams thrash in moilstorm waters.

Then the tsunami is retreating in flurries of foaming red, the colour supplied by churned sand, crushed coral and shattered bloodstone, and by more than a little of that precious ichor which flows in the veins of human beings. It is retreating, and leaving behind it broken rags, wet bones and gasping teeth.

Thus Justina's dream.

Shocked by a lathering of wet water, she abrupts from sleep, gasps for air, claws, grasps, wrenches, pulls.

Her mosquito net collapses around her, downfolding in whispers softer than silk, caresses lighter than a lover's touch. Justina lies beneath its web.

Waits.

Listens.

There is no water.

There is no wave.

It was all her dream.

At length, she falls to sleep again, and dreams this time of Wen Endex. She stands in the swamplands with an orking harpoon in her hands, waiting for her quarry. A dream of the past, this, for no orking has taken place in Justina's lifetime. The most solemn treaties now bind orks and Yudonic Knights in common cause. Yet Justina dreams of ork blubber. Rich, fat and nuggety. Most princely of feasts.

Then wakes.

It is dawn.

CHAPTER TWENTY-ONE

Justina Thrug woke from unabashed dreams of orking, of lusty slaughter and rapturous feasting. She experienced a momentary guilt, for these were dreams of the Forbidden. Orking was the great racial crime of the children of Wen Endex. In their lust for blood, bone and blubber, the Yudonic Knights and their legions of underlings had exterminated every ork in the swamplands of their homeland. Such wholehearted murder had bloated Galsh Ebrek with treasure; had overloaded the coffers of the Flesh Traders' Financial Association until those coffers screamed in protest; had made the Homeland so rich in its debauchery that in one memorable year it imported (a record, this, at least for the region) a full seven previously unrecorded venereal diseases.

The swamp-whales had barely escaped extinction; the poor orks only survived as a breed thanks to the foresight of those of their kind who had fled to refuges in the Qinjoks. At that time, when the orks had been so over-hunted that there was no commercial advantage to be gained from their further exploitation, the Yudonic Knights at last sent their ambassadors to this persecuted people and made a peace.

A peace which the orks trusted not, in token of which mistrust they rigorously practised contraception, lest an increase in their population tempt the very temptable Yudonic Knights to a feat of collective oathbreaking and untrammelled genocide.

Thus Justina woke and felt guilty. But guilt was brief though waking was long; for the Empress Justina was far too busy to spare much thought for the horrors of the past. Untunchilamon stood unchanged. Another hot and sultry day was begun. A day bereft of wind: something all Injiltaprajura would lament, for lack of wind would further delay the rest of the Trade Fleet.

The lordess of the pink palace began that day's work by ascending early to the roof of her pink palace to inspect Sken-Pitilkin's airship. She was pleased to see the elderly wizard was already at work. Reconstruction of his scattered ship was going apace. But Justina nevertheless had a measure of displeasure to express.

'Sken-Pitilkin!' said she severely. 'Where were you yesterday afternoon?'

'In bed,' said the wizard. 'Laid up with a touch of the centipedes.'

'If diarrhoea's your problem, then boil your water. What about the afternoon of the day before? What was your excuse for that?'

'I'm an old man,' said Sken-Pitilkin. 'You can't work me as you would a cane cutter.'

'You could try harder,' said Justina, not one whit impressed by such excuses. 'You will today, won't you?'

'My psychic powers tell me the day will be hot,' said Sken-Pitilkin. 'I fear the onset of heat-stroke toward noon.'

'Heatstroke!' said Justina. 'Laziness, that's what I call it. A full day's work, that's the least I expect.'

But, to Justina's dismay, Hostaja Sken-Pitilkin refused to promise to put in more than half a day's work on his new airship. She remonstrated with him, saying their need was urgent. Prolonged remonstrations brought her no further success. But she was right. Their need was urgent.

As yet, there were but five ships in the Laitemata. Three had stayed there all through the Long Dry. Two were newcomers, one being the *Oktobdoj* which had brought Jean Froissart and Manthandros Trasilika to the place of their deaths. Justina, as has been noted already, needed at least a dozen ships to get her loyal supporters away to safety.

209

However, as the days went by, Justina was beginning to despair of the arrival of any more ships. Furthermore, a showdown with the mob was fast approaching. Signs of riot were everywhere. It would happen, and happen soon.

Thus Justina desperately needed Sken-Pitilkin's airship.

Was she then thinking of deserting her loyal supporters and fleeing alone to save her own skin?

No.

But it had occurred to her that an airship travels much faster than a bark of normal breed; so, despite the limited capacity of Sken-Pitilkin's flying bird's nest, it might yet prove an effective vehicle of evacuation. A shuttle service could scarcely hope to complete this great escape in secret. Yet all was not lost. At a pinch, Justina's people could trek into the wastes of Zolabrik. A desperate move, since a journey so dangerous would mean the deaths of many; but a move which would put them beyond the reach of the disloyalists. Then were the nest to become airworthy, Justina's people could be ferried in handfuls to distant shores until all had been taken upon that journey.

The Empress said nothing of this to the wizard, thinking (rightly) that he might object to the immense labour of ferrying a dozen shiploads of people across the ocean at the rate of a handful a time.

Thus the Empress Justina had a plan, a plan which might yet succeed in the absence of her twelve much-desired ships. But she needed time. Which was why, after her interview with Sken-Pitilkin, she descended to her study, there to await the arrival of the corpse-master Uckermark.

While Justina was waiting (and demolishing a large breakfast during the wait) one of Theodora's chickens wandered into the study.

'Out!' said Justina.

'Bruck bruck bruck bruck!' said the chicken.

210

Justina kicked it, and if fled with a flapping of wings. Those chickens!

Justina hated the very sight of them.

For, while the Empress Justina was wont to let her own desires have their way with her flesh, she nevertheless thought that her sister Theordora went far, far too far in the direction of outright debauchery.

At length Uckermark arrived, looking somewhat wary. He felt he had done very well for himself, for his position as legal counsel for the Cult of the Holy Cockroach made him safe from even the wrath of Aldarch Three, despite his previous connections and alliances with the Empress Justina. He had no wish to compromise his present advantages (safety, a measure of power, ample remuneration, prestige and the friendship of Nadalastabstala Banraithanchumun Ek) by involvement in whatever harebrained scheme the Empress had dreamed up.

Nevertheless, he could not deny that he owed Justina a debt. Several debts, in fact.

'Don't worry,' said Justina, divining his anxieties. 'I ask nothing from you yourself but an introduction to a good forger.'

'For what?' said Uckermark, all curiosity.

Justina told him.

'There is a Secret History afloat in Injiltaprajura. Fractions of this *Injiltaprajuradariski* have been found in all manner of places. It is written in Slandolin. I have people who can compose in that language. They have done so. We have made a libel upon the life of Nadalastabstala Banraithanchumun Ek. Now we want this forged in the handwriting of the unknown author of the *Injiltaprajuradariski*. We paint Ek as a secret heretic; and by leaking our forgeries we hope to turn his mob against him, or at least confuse that mob until its wrath becomes impotent.'

'It won't work,' said Uckermark.

So Justina told him the truth. Many bits and pieces of

211

the Secret History made mention of an organic rectifier, an immortality machine which also had the ability to convert male flesh to female, or Crab to human.

'Our forgeries,' said Justina, 'will prove that Ek has such a machine himself. Jealously he guards it. He has made himself immortal, but denies this privilege to all others.'

'People will never believe that,' said Uckermark.

'Of course they will,' said Justina. 'Ek's a mutant. You can see it in the eyes. People are always ready to believe ill of a mutant.'

If Ek were widely believed to have the secret of immortality then he would be torn to pieces by a thousand people in search of the same. That, at any rate, was what Justina believed, and thanks to her powers of persuasion she soon converted Uckermark to her belief.

'There remains,' said Uckermark, 'one little question.'

'You've no need to ask it,' said Justina. 'Believe me, the tax status of the Cult of the Holy Cockroach is safe no matter what. If Ek dies, I guarantee the continuation of your privileges.'

'That,' said Uckermark, 'is all I wanted to hear.'

And, that very day, he sought out a forger and brought the man privily to the pink palace so the work could begin.

Justina was delighted.

Once the Empress Justina had her forgeries to hand, Nadalastabstala Banraithanchumun Ek would find that he was not the only person on Untunchilamon who knew how to stir up a mob.

CHAPTER TWENTY-TWO

A run on a bank can be disastrous both for the bank and its customers, the panic of the few leading to financial disaster for the many. The reasons for this are very simple. A bank commonly lends out as much as eighty per cent of its depositors' funds, keeping only a little cash on hand. This is sound business practice, but means such organizations can easily be ruined if depositors come clamouring en masse for their monies.

Accordingly, governments will often intervene to prevent or ameliorate such a run in its early stages.

Aldarch the Third once did as much in Obooloo when the Brothelmaster's Credit Union came under seige as a result of scurrilous rumours circulated by its enemies. Al'three did not forbid depositors to withdraw their funds. No, he merely ordered his guards to chop off the noses and ears of any customers who insisted on withdrawing more than ten per cent of their funds on any one day.

Since most of the Mutilator's soldiers were innumerate, they were incapable of computing the relevant percentages. So, knowing that the Lord of Knives admires zeal, they applied their surgical expertise to every single person who entered the premises of the Brothelmaster's Credit Union; and, in their enthusiasm, removed eyes, lips and tongues as well as noses and ears.

This application of martial technique to a financial problem brought immediate satisfaction, for the run on the Credit Union ended within the day; and, furthermore, the Union enjoyed years of unprecedented liquidity thereafter, for only the most courageous of its depositors were brave enough to demand so much as a broken damn from the place.

By application of similar techniques, the Empress Justina could have ended the run on the Narapatorpabarta Bank. But of course she did no such thing; and, by the next day, the run on the N'barta had gathered such momentum that a much-worried Chief Accountant estimated that the institution would be bankrupt by noon. This greatly disconcerted Justina's agents, for if the N'barta actually ran out of money and had to close its doors then the cunning plan of entrapment would come to naught.

However, istarlat was only half over when an excited clerk slipped behind the scenes with breathless news.

'What is it?' said one of the agents.

But the clerk could not speak. His news was so breathless it had precipitated an asthma attack.

'It must be the blackmailer,' said one of the agents.

A guess, but accurate regardless.

Moments later, another clerk came backstage.

'Hurry!' said the clerk. 'He's getting impatient.'

'Who is?' said one of the agents.

'The man you seek.'

'Can you point him out to us?'

'Do you ever ask an intelligent question? Of course I can!'

Thus it was that a would-be blackmailer was very shortly arrested on the floor of the N'barta, that blackmailer being none other than Nixorjapretzel Rat.

'Back!' cried the young sorcerer, throwing up his hands. 'Back! Or I'll turn you into scorpions!'

Such was his threat, but with three crossbows pointing variously at his heart, his liver and his left kneecap, he dared try no expedient so uncertain.

Even had Rat been a wizard, he would still have hesitated under such circumstances; and of course young Nixorjapretzel was not a wizard but a wonder-worker. The powers of such sorcerers are flamboyant and readily renewed; unlike wizards, they have no need to indulge in laborious meditations, nor do they find themselves powerless for days at a time after great expenditures of power. From which the unwise might be tempted to deduce that the powers of sorcery exceed those of wizardry: a temptation to which sorcerers themselves have yielded on occasion.

But it is not so.

For wizards by their labours forge alliances with dark and dangerous powers which permit such mages to make themselves into beings of an order different from the rest of humanity. When wizards are referred to (as they often are) as Lights in the Unseen Realm, such designation is far from idle; rather, it makes explicit a truth which some have thought monstrous.

But the consequence is that wizards ultimately possess their Powers in their own right, albeit at a price. Whereas sorcerers obtain their Effects in an altogether different way, which is that each permits his own partial possession by a demon. 'Partial' is the operative word here, and it is the partiality of such possession (combined with the poverty of intellect which characterizes so many demons) which serves to undermine the effectiveness of the wonder-workers.

We have seen young Nixorjapretzel in action already. In a mansion on Hojo Street, for example, where the Rat, seeking to make himself invisible, succeeded only in converting himself to a boiling cloud the colour of octopus ink. More examples of Rat's ineptitude could be given to demonstrate the deficiencies of the wonder-workers. But such procedure would be unfair, for Rat compounded all the above-mentioned problems with problems of his own. A youthful impetuosity, for example, which led him to act in such haste and with so little forethought that it was difficult for his demon to keep up with his intentions. And, also, a certain weakness of personal intellect which was more the exception than the rule among the members of Injiltaprajura's Cabal House.

It is unfortunate that the intellectually deficient Rat found himself linked with a particularly deficient demon. Not all demons are equal, and the Power which found itself in alliance with Nixorjapretzel Rat was more unequal than most; therefore the synergetic principle necessarily applies, with disaster the inevitable consequence.

Let us not therefore use the example of Rat as a weapon with which to landdamne the wonder-workers; for we are not wizards with professional jealousies to be served. Let us merely note that Nixorjapretzel Rat showed an uncommon leavening of wisdom when he meekly accompanied his captors to the pink palace, there to submit to interrogation at the hands (and, sometimes, at the feet) of that most formidable of Yudonic Knights, the ferocious Juliet Idaho.

The interrogation took place in Justina's private study in the presence of Herself, the above-mentioned Juliet Idaho, and the conjuror Odolo who had lately served both Empress and Yudonic Knight as courier, ambassador and spy. We have seen Odolo in the past, bringing a message privily to Aquitaine Varazchavardan; while we have not see him since, he has been busy regardless, especially in organizing liaisons between the pink palace and the Crab's young secretaries.

With that established, let us now attend to the interrogation.

Rat soon confessed. Yes, yes, he had tried to blackmail Bro Drumel. Why? Because he knew the imperial household intimately, and had (correctly) deduced that Drumel was by temperament the most likely to succumb to blackmail. He had bought a secret account from the N'barta, planning to draw on that account only after the political turmoil on Untunchilamon was long since over.

Yes, he had some of the *Injiltaprajuradariski* in his possession. Where? His stash was cached in a room in

Ganthorgruk, a room he had rented specifically for the purpose.

Juliet Idaho thereupon dispatched the conjuror Odolo to Ganthorgruk to recover the relevant pages of the Secret History. As the olive-skinned foreigner lived in Ganthorgruk, he could venture to that huge and rotting doss-house without attracting attention. He did so, and brought back Rat's treasure of manuscripts.

There were (Idaho later counted them) some 284 pages of ricepaper, each page utterly beleaguered by an onslaught of purple scripting in Ashdan orthography.

'Next question,' said Idaho, studying these inscrutable writings, 'where did all this come from?'

Rat started to look uncomfortable.

'Out with it!' roared Idaho.

'A – a family friend,' said Rat.

'Who?' said Idaho.

'Ms Mix,' answered Rat.

'Ms Mix?' said Idaho in puzzlement.

'The mother-in-law of the notorious Orge Arat.'

'This Arat of yours may be notorious in your own mind but that's not the case with mine,' said Juliet Idaho. 'Explain!'

Rat did so.

Orge Arat was a lunatic who had long been incarcerated in the Dromdanjerie. Orge Arat believed himself to be perfectly sane; indeed, such was the cunning of his lunacy that he thought himself to be a sane man pretending to be mad. Such was his derangement that he thought he had murdered his mother-in-law and was being held in the Dromdanjerie on that account; whereas in fact he had slaughtered an innocent tax inspector whom he had, in a fit of manic delusion, mistaken for his wife's mother.

At last, in one of his rare lucid moments, Orge Arat had realized the truth. Ms Mix still lived! There was only one thing to do. He had packed up his belongings, including the Secret History on which he had long been working. Then he had broken out of the Dromdanjerie, whereafter he had stolen an axe and had proceeded to the domicile of Ms Mix, meaning in his sanity to accomplish the murder he had but imagined in his lunacy.

'And?' said Juliet Idaho.

'Ms Mix,' said Rat, 'she's . . . she's very well built.'

'Well built?'

'Not to put too fine a point upon it,' said Rat, 'she's a . . . an ogre.'

Ms Mix was indeed an ogre, one of twenty-seven of that breed which dwelt in Injiltaprajura. She had laughed at Orge Arat's axe. Then she had broken his arm.

'Orge Arat escaped,' said Rat, 'but barely. He came to me for help. I gave him the courtesy of my protection. He rewarded me with these pages of manuscript, this being all he had to give.'

'And you've been selling bits of it,' said Juliet Idaho.

'Oh no!' said Rat. 'What was given, I kept. But there was much more than this. He lost the rest when he fought with Ms Mix. This portion was bound to his chest, it being the most precious, for it was near the stage of final draft. But the rest he lost to the ogre. She must be the seller of those fragments you've seen or heard of elsewhere.'

'Where's Orge Arat now?' said Juliet Idaho.

'He's disappeared,' said Rat. 'He's vanished off the face of the earth.'

'Impossible!' said Idaho.

But it was quite possible. Orge Arat had indeed vanished off the face of the earth, though he had not gone far; he was afloat on the face of the sea, on a ship in the Laitemata Harbour. Orge Arat was a guest of Troldot 'Heavy-Fist' Turbothot, a trader from Hexagon who was adventuring round the world on the orders of Baron Farouk. The reasons for this guestship are complicated, and could make a book of their own; as no doubt they may some day, should Troldot Turbothot take it into his head to write his memoirs, or should the fair Theodora one day take upon herself the encyclopedic task of counting her chickens and cataloguing her lovers. But, while reason is complex, result is simple: Orge Arat was not to be found.

In the absence of an apprehendable Orge Arat, Juliet Idaho was all for daring Ms Mix in her lair and beating the truth out of her with the sharp edge of a hatchet. This was vetoed by the Empress Justina who thought, first, that they had as much of the truth as they needed for the moment; and, second, that Idaho was being overoptimistic in thinking himself able to get the better of an ogre in outright combat.

'What I want, Julie,' said the Empress, choosing her words with care, 'is for you to leave poor Mix alone, at least for the moment.'

'You can't be serious,' said Idaho.

'But I am,' said the Empress, with all the firmness at her command, which was considerable.

'But – but now is the time to strike!' said Idaho.

'I don't think so.'

'But you promised! You promised me! You promised I'd get a chance to kill someone, and soon.'

'Did I, Julie? I have no recollection of such a promise. But, look – our darling young Nixorjapretzel is starting to fidget. Why don't you watch over him, Julie dear? There's nine chances in ten he'll make a break for it. Then all your dreams will come true.'

'Right,' said Juliet Idaho.

And the grim-faced Yudonic Knight (a naked blade by now just slightly more than at the ready) installed himself behind a trembling Nixorjapretzel Rat, a Rat who thereafter did not dare move so much as a finger, lest even a gesture so slight bring about his untimely demise.

Then the Empress Justina sent out for Shanvil

Angarus May, the uncommonly loyal Ashdan warrior who, thanks to his knowledge of the Slandolin, had lately served her so well as a translator. There was shortly a knock at her door.

'Come in!' said the Empress.

But it was not May who entered; it was a servant bearing a tiny dish, a bright yellow dish carefully covered with a weighted piece of mosquito netting.

'Here,' said Justina, tapping her desk.

The servant set down the dish and withdrew. The Empress removed the mosquito net covering, revealing a writhing mass of fleas, mosquitoes, bedbugs and baby cockroaches. Each of these had been painstakingly disabled so it could not flee.

Justina whistled softly.

There was a faint rustling from the little nest of cat's fur and feather-fluff which sat upon the imperial desk. A tiny head, heraldic in outline, peeped over the edge of that nest. It was the head of the dragon Untunchilamon, now much recovered from its skirmish with the seagulls of Jod. During the early days of its convalescence, the Empress Justina had observed this spitter of sparks stalk, singe, disable and consume a mosquito; which had given her the idea of introducing her fingerlength dragon to a diet of varied vermin. Such viands had found immediate favour with Untunchilamon, who had now recovered strength and vitality to the point of being able to fly.

'Come forth, my lovely,' said Justina, and whistled again.

There was a tiny squeak of enthusiasm as the dragon Untunchilamon plunged over the side of the nest and swaggered towards the dish of awaiting delights. Before long, all the wrigglers within had wriggled their last; and by the time Shanvil Angarus May put in an appearance, Untunchilamon was asleep.

May was soon at work on the *Injiltaprajuradariski*, skimming through the Secret History and decoding the really juicy bits on the spot.

'Ah!' said May. 'Here's something.'

'Read,' said Justina.

'It's about the organic rectifier,' said May, glancing at Rat.

'Don't worry about young Nixorjapretzel,' said the Empress. 'I trust him implicitly.'

A statement which was meant to be reassuring, but which procured quite an opposite effect in the trembling breast of the sensitive Rat. For wherefore should the Empress trust him so unless she shortly planned to remove his head from his shoulders? Rat's fear increased inordinately. Thus we see that the Empress erred in her treatment of the young sorcerer; but, in her defence, let it be said that she made such mistakes infrequently, and, while she blundered on this occasion, her motives were of the best.

'I will read, then,' said May, peering once more at the close-scorpioned purple scripting from which he was to translate. 'It says that . . . Pokrov, it says, by which I presume it means our neighbour on Jod . . . it says Pokrov . . . ah, here's the bit . . . I quote verbatim, it says, quote, Pokrov was immortal, hence lonely; for Shabble was a less than satisfactory companion for a life which might yet run for many millennia until it was terminated by accident or design. Therefore Pokrov wished for companions of his own breed. It was the arts of an organic rectifier which had made Pokrov immortal. Moreover, as Pokrov knew full well, another machine of such breed was very likely concealed in the magnanimous dark Downstairs; but there he was loathe to venture, for the potential rewards of such journeying were incommensurate in the dark of the dangers. Such was his fear that he was doomed, it seemed, to have no constant companionship down through the centuries.'

'So Pokrov's a coward,' said Idaho, with a violence which made Rat flinch. 'So let's arrest him. Then chop off his head!'

'Julie, darling,' said the Empress Justina reprovingly,

'your monomania ill becomes you. We will most certainly have a little chat with Pokrov, but undue bloodshed might draw attention to us from the most unwelcome quarters.'

It took but moments for the Empress to formulate an alternative plan. Chegory Guy and Olivia Qasaba, travelling ostensibly as secretaries of the Crab, were due to pay one of their regular visits to the pink palace at noon that day.

'So,' said Justina, 'all we need do is ask that Ivan Pokrov accompany them so we may consult with him on . . . on, ah, a possible use of the Analytical Engine. That should do it.'

'But noon is almost upon us,' said Idaho.

'The shadows lack some shortening yet,' said May, 'and I have strong legs. I will bear the message to Jod.'

Message-bear he did; leaving those in Justina's study (Idaho, Rat, Odolo and Herself) to speculate fervidly on the possibilities surely to be made actualities by the pursuit and capture of an organic rectifier. Man to woman; woman to man; mortal flesh to immortal; and, not least of the promises of the future, Crab to human.

Were the Crab to become human, in gratitude it would surely accept the wazirship which bluff now claimed to be its choice. It would exercise its Powers to deny the shores of Injiltaprajura to enemies of the existing order. A result most greatly to be desired!

As Justina was thinking thus, the forger recruited to her cause by the corpse-master Uckermark was admitted to her study. He bowed, presented the Empress with five pages of close-scripted ricepaper, then withdrew. The Empress spread the pages out upon her desk and gazed upon them happily. She could not read the Slandolin in which they were written; indeed, the tiny letters tended to blur together in a single wash of purple unless she tightened her vision by squinting; but she knew exactly what was written there.

Each of the five pages claimed (in blatant libel) that

222

Nadalastabstala Banraithanchumun Ek, High Priest of the Temple of Zoz the Ancestral, was in possession of an organic rectifier; and claimed, furthermore, that Ek had made exclusive and utterly selfish use of such an arcanum to make himself immortal. Justina planned to leak the five pages in sundry quarters and thus to turn the mob against the mutant. To her own advantage: for a mob which had demolished a High Priest of Zoz must necessarily fear retribution from Aldarch Three.

Given the nature and history of Aldarch III, it was entirely possible that such retribution might take the form of the execution of one person in every ten within the city of Injiltaprajura, or the blinding of nine in ten, or the lopping of the ears of ten-tenths of innocent and guilty alike. So there was a possibility – a slight possibility – that mob rule and its guilty aftermath might give Justina the political leverage she needed to unite her people into a coherent and patriotic whole.

Were she to succeed in such an enterprise, then denying Untunchilamon to an invasion fleet would be the easiest of tasks; for the seas of Moana were wide and dangerous; the lagoon approaches to Injiltaprajura long, narrow and tortuous; and Justina's high-climbing city itself eminently defensible.

So Justina had great hopes for her forgeries; though the distribution of such would be a task of the utmost delicacy, and on this matter she was not yet quite sure how to proceed.

Maybe Log Jaris could help her.

In the meantime . . .

'Come,' said Justina, 'let us retire to the Star Chamber.'

'The study will serve,' growled Idaho. 'There's only a few of us.'

'Ah,' said Justina, 'but I want Varazchavardan to sit in on our revelations.'

'Varazchavardan!' said Idaho, scandalized.

'He is my Master of Law,' said Justina gently.

'He tried to kill you.'

'And who has not?' said Justina.

'I have not!' said Idaho. 'And I could name others. Why, by walking down Lak Street I could find drummers by the dozen who are innocent of all attempts on your life.'

'Julie,' said Justina, 'why must you be so literal? I'm so good at rhetoric, and you always spoil it for me. My enemy's enemy is my friend, is he not?'

'He is,' said Idaho grudgingly.

Since this was a fundamental doctrine of faith among the Yudonic Knights of Wen Endex, Idaho could scarcely deny it.

'Well then,' said Justina, 'our dear friend Varazcha-vardan has Ek as his enemy, for Ek had refused his petition for pardon. It follows that Varazchavardan is our ally. Odolo, could you . . .'

'It is done, my lady,' said the olive-skinned conjuror, and bowed, and hied himself away to the nearby villa owned and occupied by Aquitaine Varazchavardan.

'We will also want the counsel of Pelagius Zozimus,' said Justina.

'Then we'll have to send someone chasing after May,' said Idaho, 'for Zozimus is on Jod with Pokrov and Crab.'

'Much as it hurts me to contradict you, dear Julie, on this occasion I must. Unless I am sadly misinformed, the wizard is in our kitchen at this very moment, instructing my new chef in the making of pavlovas.'

'Pavlova?' said Idaho. 'What is pavlova?'

'An amusing dish most ruinous to the teeth but delighting to the tongue,' said Justina. 'And, as I have no teeth worth mentioning, the tongue is free to demand.'

'But what exactly is it, this pavlova?' said Idaho. 'And who is your new chef? Why wasn't I told about him?'

'It's a her, actually,' said Justina. 'Come, Julie, let us remove ourselves to the Star Chamber. Oh, and we'll want Dardanalti in on this. And Sken-Pitilkin, if he'll consent to spare a moment from his bird nesting.'

So saying, the Empress opened the door of her study, and Idaho escorted a quivering Rat into the corridor outside. The Empress followed, closing the door behind her. The study was empty and untenanted, the five sheets of the countervailing forgery spread out upon the imperial desk.

It was then that the dragon Untunchilamon bestirred itself, arched its back, fanned its wings briskly then took to the air. Round and round it went, flying thrice about the desk.

Then it dived.

Straight into the inkwell.

Sploosh!

Sprays of black ink flew forth as the dragon Untunchilamon kicked and cavorted in the delicious cool of this most interesting of substances. Then, in a rapture of self-gratification, it rolled itself dry, using for that purpose five sheets of purple-scripted ricepaper which might have been put out expressly for that purpose.

Whereafter the dragon, sated, exhausted and immensely pleased with itself (despite the fact that it was still somewhat inky), took itself off to its nest to siesta in earnest.

CHAPTER TWENTY-THREE

When Shanvil Angarus May arrived on the island of Jod, he easily persuaded Ivan Pokrov to come to the pink palace with Chegory Guy and Olivia Qasaba. With them went the algorithmist Artemis Ingalawa, who invited herself along so she could supervise any bargaining on 'a possible use of the Analytical Engine'.

Across the harbour bridge they went; then through the slumlands of Lubos; up Shindik Way to its intersection with Goldhammer Rise; then up Lak Street toward the pink palace.

Though he was on his way to an imperial palace to discuss affairs of state, Chegory Guy was wearing nothing but a loin cloth and boots. Had he wished, he could have demanded that he be provided with gorgeous embroidered robes of silk like those affected by Injilta-prajura's wonder-workers; or he could have worn any of the five plain silken robes which had found their way into his wardrobe as a result of the generosity of the Empress Justina.

But Chegory, fearful of the hostility he felt his new eminence was arousing among the populace, did his best to pretend to humility.

At first, intoxicated by the heady combination of power and love, Chegory had worried not at all about the risks he was running. But old habits of caution and worry had rapidly reasserted themselves, to the point where, acutely conscious of the fragility of Untunchilamon's present political arrangements, Chegory doubted they could or would last for much longer. Sooner or later, Injiltaprajura would realize that the Crab was not truly wazir. Then Chegory would have to deal with his enemies, these being all good citizens of Injiltaprajura who feared or hated Ebbies. Once they knew that Chegory was virtually ruling Untunchilamon in his own right, then they would surely tear him to pieces.

It greatly annoyed Chegory that his dearest darling Olivia had very little sense of the dangers they were running. She adorned herself with fine silks and with jewellery lent to her by the Empress; and this display of finery would, Chegory feared, be held against her when at last the two of them had to survive without the protection of the illusion which was now the sole guardian of their safety.

'It's so hot,' said Olivia, as they tramped uphill past that ship-sized monolith of bone known as Pearl. 'If it gets any hotter, I'm going to melt.'

'Don't say that,' said Chegory in distress.

He thought – for a moment – that she was going mad. While boarding at the Dromdanjerie, he had become familiar with many kinds of lunacy, including the unfortunate condition in which one imagines oneself to be literally melting.

'I was only joking,' said Olivia crossly.

Chegory almost made a sharp retort, but restrained himself. He wiped his sweating brow and looked up. Sunbright lightlances stabbed out from the glitter dome atop the pink palace. Chegory looked away. Purple sunlights danced across his field of vision like so many minor hallucinations caused by the ingestion of a mild dose of zen.

'What's the matter?' said Shanvil Angarus May.

'Nothing,' said Chegory, resisting the temptation to say that he was overworked and overstressed, found it hard to sleep and had nightmares when he did, lived in fear of pregnancy and venereal diseases, saw assassins in shadows, and daily awaited the arrival of Aldarch the Third in person.

Then Chegory wiped his forehead again – something of a nervous tic, this – and strode uphill with an appearance of confidence which belied his inward state.

As bright-dawning istarlat gave way to the longueurs of salahanthara, the party of people from the island of Jod entered the shadows of the pink palace in company with Shanvil May.

'Remember,' said Ingalawa, 'if there's any bargaining done today, I want to have a say.'

'I remember,' said Pokrov meekly.

As the Analytical Institute drew its wealth from the sale of dikle and shlug, on which substances it had a monopoly, it needed no income from those feats of computation performed by its Engine. Hence Pokrov, whose pride and joy that Engine was, had in the past indulged himself by casually signing contracts promising great labours of analysis in return for the most paltry of financial rewards; a procedure which Ingalawa was determined must cease, for she felt the perceived value of algorithmical procedures to have been lessened by the terms of outright charity on which they had been made available to the world.

Ingalawa, then, still had hopes for the Institute's future, despite the current political uncertainties. It had occurred to her that the Engine might prove of value to the wonder-workers of the Cabal House in their pursuit of a method whereby to transmute lead to gold (or coral, bloodstone, dogshit, mangos or old iron to gold – the sorcerers were not fussy, merely greedy). A linkage between Science and Magic might be the key to a golden age; and, were the virtues of such linkage to be amply demonstrated in short order, the Analytical Institute and its adherents might pursue happy-ever-afters even were Aldarch Three to arrive on Untunchilamon in person to supervise a wrathstorm.

These then arrived in the Star Chamber:

Chegory Guy
Olivia Qasaba
Ivan Pokrov

Artemis Ingalawa
and
Shanvil Angarus May

And there to meet them were:

Justina Thrug
Juliet Idaho
Shanvil Angarus May
Dardanalti (Justina's legal counsel)
Pelagius Zozimus (wizard and master chef to the Crab)
Molly (Justina's new chef)
Log Jaris (Molly's life companion)
Nixorjapretzel Rat (a prisoner)
Aquitaine Varazchavardan
and
the conjuror Odolo

Where then was Hostaja Sken-Pitilkin? A good question, but one to which none there gathered had the answer. Even Pelagius Zozimus had no knowledge of his cousin's whereabouts; for Sken-Pitilkin, after doing a little poolside work on his airship, had dropped out of sight.

Regardless of the absence of Sken-Pitilkin, most of those who were of a certainty allied to the Empress Justina were gathered in the Star Chamber. Her sister Theodora was missing, and with good reason; for Theodora was enjoying the shipboard hospitality of Troldot Turbothot. Also aboard Turbothot's ship were certain erstwhile allies of Pelagius Zozimus: the Yarglat barbarian Guest Gulkan and a cut-throat from Chi'ashlan named Thayer Levant.

Justina darkly suspected that her twin sister was caballing with Turbothot and his crew (and perhaps with a certain shipload of Malud marauders also anchored in the Laitemata) in an effort to seize something (the contents of the treasury of Injiltaprajura, perhaps) from the final wreckage of the reign of the Family Thrug.

When Ivan Pokrov was brought before the Empress Justina, she began their session with a little speech:

'Look around you. There are but fifteen of us in this room, and one of these a prisoner.'

'Which one?' said Pokrov.

'Not you, Ivan dearest,' said Justina. 'It is young Rat's misfortune that we have been forced to set bounds upon his liberties, for reasons on which I will soon enlarge. But first, reflect. Ultimately, we few alone stand against Aldarch Three and all his allies.'

'Us and the Crab,' said Chegory, staunchly perpetuating the life of the Big Lie.

'Yes, the Crab,' said Justina, with a sidelong glance at Varazchavardan. 'But we know we can expect much more from the Crab if we provide it with the means to secure its dearest wish. That being, of course, to have human form.'

Here a pause.

'I, too,' rumbled Log Jaris, 'would not be averse to such change.'

Molly's life companion had the head and horns of a bull, for he had once dared the jaws of a transmogrification machine located Downstairs. The metamorphosis which he had then endured had succeeded in preserving his life, for it had concealed his identity at a time when many sought to kill him. However, Log Jaris was not exactly happy at the prospect of living out his days thus guised; and his dearest Molly, whose hands were formed like the paws of a cat, would have welcomed some cosmetic alteration herself.

'By now,' said Justina, 'many of you will have heard rumours of an organic rectifier, a device said to have the power to change form and grant the gift of immortality. As I have said, there are but few of us here, and we are by a multitude opposed.'

She paused.

Then fixed Ivan Pokrov with a steely gaze; or a gaze

which, if it could not be described as steely, might justly be compared to the lethal onslaught of the eye-beams of the basilisk.

'Pokrov,' she said, in tones far different from those which had so sweetly crooned 'Ivan dearest'.

'My Empress knows me to be the most loyal of subjects,' said the olive-skinned Pokrov.

'Loyal in his inertia, perhaps,' said Justina, 'for no active opposition can be attributed to him. But when it comes to initiatives, loyalty is lacking. For Pokrov, himself immortal thanks to the graces of an organic rectifier, has long known of the presence of such a mechanism in the depths Downstairs, those depths beneath our very feet.'

'I do not deny it,' said Pokrov, seeing that his secret of centuries was betrayed, and that nothing was to be gained from mistruth or bluff. 'But it does you no good to know as much. There are places Downstairs where nobody dare venture.'

'Log Jaris would tell you differently,' said Justina.

'It pains me to have to contradict my Empress,' said the bullman, 'but Pokrov does not speak idly.'

There then began a heated debate on the merits of venturing to the more terrifying parts of the underfoot underworld. Chegory Guy had much to say on this subject, for the redskinned Ebrell Islander had wandered much in the realms of mystery, and had once been poisoned with zen in a catacomb below decks. Aquitaine Varazchavardan opined that he would not care to venture the greater depths himself. And as for Pelagius Zozimus, why, he had the most terrifying tales to recount, for he had twice or thrice come near to disaster Downstairs.

Had it been given the luxury of infinite time, doubtless this gathering would in time have reached reasonable, rational conclusions; and would have developed a sound scheme for exploring the depths Downstairs by finger-lengths or by proxy. But, unbeknownst to the members of this conclave, time was fast running out.

231

Why?

Because the Empress Justina, manoeuvring to prevent riot, had brought upon herself that which she had sought to avoid.

To be precise:

Hostages had been taken to compel the cooperation of the Narapatorpabarta Bank. Then, once the blackmailing Nixorjapretzel Rat had been lured into a trap by a carefully engineered run on the N'barta, Justina had automatically released those hostages. But by then the bank had been effectively ruined, so that, on his release, the manager of the N'barta had found himself compelled to close the doors to all customers and declare the bank bankrupt.

A mob had then gathered.

The mob had consisted (initially) of some 371 depositors who had found themselves precipitately ruined by such bankruptcy; and their initial intention had been to wrest the bank manager's head from his shoulders. But he, to save his life, had told the truth: that it was all Justina's doing.

Then one of the depositors had harangued the crowd to such effect that they had begun to march on the pink palace, seeking in their anger to rend the Empress from limb to limb; and if any of them remembered that Justina was said to be under the personal protection of the Crab, still, none of them allowed such belief to moderate their impetuous fury.

As Nadalastabstala Banraithanchumun Ek had laboured so mightily on his own account to stir up a palace-sacking mob, is it any wonder that the mob swelled to a full six hundred people as it neared the pink palace?

Six hundred people.

A bare two per cent of Injiltaprajura's population.

But it sufficed.

Justina's soldiers (disloyal almost to a man) abandoned their posts and fled, leaving the palace portals open to the mob. Several dozen members of that mob were drummers. And here – while we have strenuously resisted the claims of those alarmists who see in 'drumming' a threat to civilization itself – we must admit that the beating of drums did take place as the mob surged toward the palace. Yet we contend that the idle young would have joined such a rabble even had no instruments of rhythmical production been in their possession; and hold, too, that the relationship between 'drumming' and rioting is, even in this context, purely accidental.

As the assemblage of the faex populi approached, a servant intruded on Justina's Star Chamber meeting with the dire news, throwing all into confusion.

'My study,' said Justina to Odolo. 'My forgeries. They're on my desk. Five pages. Ricepaper. Purple. I need them. Now. Go!'

Odolo fled, returning promptly with five much-besmirched sheets of paper. Sprawled black ink still wet upon them. They were ruined, wrecked.

'What's happened to them?' said Justina in bewilderment.

'I'll tell you what's happened to them,' said Idaho in wrath. 'A dragon's run amok in an inkwell, that's what's happened. Look! Here! Dragon tracks!'

'Ah,' said Justina, unhappily.

'Don't take it so hard,' said Artemis Ingalawa consolingly. 'You can't disarm a mob with documents, no matter what their content.'

'We can't disarm the mob at all,' said Log Jaris. 'We must run. If we can get to the desert side, I know a bolt hole.'

'Then follow me,' said Juliet Idaho.

At which young Nixorjapretzel Rat decided it was time for him to split. But Pelagius Zozimus grabbed him by the collar and hauled him along with the rest of them.

Juliet Idaho led them to a sally port. He opened it.

233

Already they could hear shouts, screams, hammering footsteps. The hoi polloi were almost upon them. So out into the hot sunlight of Injiltaprajura's desert side they fled.

From the heights of Pokra Ridge, they could see across the market gardens, barracks, quarries and so forth of desert side Injiltaprajura, and then across league after league of desert. The only strategic impediment to unbroken vistas were the shoreside heights, upthrusts of rock fringing the borders of Untunchilamon to such effect that they masked the approach of all shipping until the vessels in question were on the point of entering the Laitemata.

But the attention they gave to the view was zero.

'Follow me,' said Log Jaris.

Then the bullman bounded downhill, followed by a raggedy sweating-panting bustle of people. A hundred paces downhill, they reached the ornate tombs of past wazirs of Injiltaprajura. Log Jaris threw open the door to one mausoleum. Within, a stone coffin and another door.

The second door the bullman opened.

A draught breathed out.

A cool draught of air from deep underground.

'They've seen us!' cried Chegory. 'The enemy has seen us!'

He was right. A great gang of the great unwashed was spewing out of the sally port.

'Then take to the depths,' said Log Jaris. 'The Empress with you.'

And then a swift division of fates was decided. The Empress Justina must be saved, for Injiltaprajura's fate depended on her rule. Chegory Guy must also be preserved; for, by a cruel twist of fate, it happened that the sole person to have the confidence of the Crab was this ill-educated rock gardener. Olivia Qasaba would not be parted from her true love. And Ivan Pokrov must go, for, if it happened that the fugitives found an organic

234

rectifier below, how would they recognize it but by his expertise? Artemis Ingalawa went also, insisting that Olivia needed a chaperone. A chaperone? It was far too late for that! But Ingalawa was unaware of the stage things had reached in relations between Chegory and his true love. Hence her concern.

Meanwhile, Shanvil Angarus May and Juliet Idaho declared that they would die together at the gates of the mausoleum, chopping down as many of the mob as they could before they too fell in turn.

Justina's remaining supporters would flee in the direction of Moremo Maximum Security Prison, hoping to confuse the many-headed monster of the multitude.

'Goodbye, sweet world!' said Justina.

Then she was gone, descending to the underworld with Chegory, Olivia, Pokrov and Ingalawa close behind her.

'It is a good day to die,' said Juliet Idaho, spitting on his hands; scarcely an original remark, as it was the line with which he greeted each new day even before he rose from his bed.

'Or to live,' said May, equally ready to die but more optimistic in his outlook.

'Or to run,' said Log Jaris, and suited action to words, with Molly sprinting at his shoulder.

Odolo, Dardanalti and Aquitaine Varazchavardan ran with him, as did Pelagius Zozimus and Nixorjapretzel Rat.

All this was done quite properly, for it is correctly written in *The Tactics of Escape* (which manual originates with the Combat School of Odrum) that 'when the few seek to escape from the many, the chances of the few will be amplified by division of direction; the visible escape of some of the few will serve to enhance the chances of those who flee by ways invisible; and should it happen that a narrow way can be defended by one or two of the few, then the survival of the remainder will be further enhanced by such sacrifice.'

Whether they knew it or not, Justina and her allies acted precisely in accordance with that doctrine. They divided their directions. Log Jaris and other expendable individuals fled through the sunlight, seeking to draw the mob toward Moremo. Justina and her chosen companions headed Downstairs, fleeing by a way invisible to the mob. And two heroes – Juliet Idaho and Shanvil May – prepared to die to delay the pursuit.

Let us consider now the fate of Log Jaris and his party.

When these could run no more, they stopped: and looked back to see how close the mob might be.

Here it would be pleasing (and profitable) to give this history more narrative appeal than it possesses by inventing some glamorous incident of unparalleled heroism. Such things have favour with a great many readers. Take, for example, the popularity of those gross and simplistic tales which are told about Vorn the Gladiator.

Vorn has a pass he must hold against the hundreds of the Dreaded Hordes of the Cruel Beaked Things from the Nethermost of the Nether Depths. He is alone, for all have abandoned the pass saving for himself alone. On come the Cruel Beaked Things, and their very giggling is itself a horror to hear.

'It is a good day to die,' says Vorn the Gladiator, and kisses the bright blade Zaftig.

Then the first of the Cruel Beaked Things is upon him.

Not only is it beaked, it is taloned as well. It stands thrice as tall as a horse and has breath four times as bad as that of the legendary Skork, she who was the Great Whore of the island of Chay. But it will take more than a Cruel Beaked Thing to overcome a hero.

'Die!' screams Vorn.

Zaftig slices the air with a scream like that a baby gives when a professional child beater brands the squalling thing with hot iron.

The first of the Cruel Beaked Things flops away, mortally wounded, its intestines sprawling in the dust as it jerks this way and that in its agony.

On come the rest of the Cruel Beaked Things, but Vorn treats them likewise, to the great delight of his many fans. Before the day is done, all the Cruel Beaked Things are dead; and the greatest danger to Vorn's health and safety is the danger that he may slip on the greasy blood which so liberally layers the snows.

However, such things lie in the realms of fantasy; and a historian is confined within the strict boundaries of reality, and may not deviate from them, however hard his bank manager happens to be pressing them.

The truth is this:

When Dardanalti and his friends stopped and looked back, they saw no battle, no crisis, no conflict. Instead, the scene which lay before them was very much a still life, for the mob was nowhere in sight.

'They've vanished!' said Nixorjapretzel Rat in astonishment. 'How did they do that?'

Pelagius Zozimus, wise in the ways of wizardry and of other exercises of Power, studied the scene which confronted him then gave an expert's appraisal:

'Probably, Jan Rat, the mob went back through the door out of which they came in the first place.'

'But why?' said Rat. 'Why would they do that?'

'The sun was too hot, perhaps,' said Zozimus. 'Or it could be the view was not to their liking.'

In truth, the matter was a mystery to Dardanalti and Co., for they had thought this mob to be Ek's mob, a religious mob intent on the murder of enemies of Zoz the Ancestral. Accordingly, they were unable to understand why the mob had so lightly abandoned the pursuit of their quarry.

Once we know the facts of the matter, the mystery disappears. The facts are simple. This was not a mob animated by religious mania, for the heart of this rabble was provided by those driven by economic motive; and they, once realizing they had the palace at their mercy, were more than happy to retreat from the sun and content themselves with plunder.

237

Therefore Juliet Idaho and Shanvil Angarus May waited in vain at the gates of the mausoleum, their homicidal desires temporarily thwarted; and Log Jaris and his companions had no pursuers to outrun.

'Well,' said Zozimus, wiping the sweat from his forehead. 'What a letdown.'

'Can I go now?' said Rat hopefully.

'Well,' said Pelagius Zozimus jovially, 'now we've no further use for you, we might as well cut off your head!'

This was meant as a joke, but proved to be one of the largest mistakes that Zozimus had ever made in his life. For Rat, in the face of what he believed to be his immediate doom, made one supreme effort. And there was no quick-bladed Idaho to chop off his head.

As we have already noted, partial demonic possession – the sorcerors of Injiltaprajura prefer to refer to it as 'inspiration' – is not the most reliable source of Power. Nevertheless, when that Power works, it tends to work with a vengeance.

'Shafo!' screamed Rat. 'Shafo shafo!'

Then Rat flung out his hands, pointing rigid fingers at Pelagius Zozimus.

Rat's intention was to turn Zozimus into a cockroach.

And then to step on him.

There was a roar from Zozimus as he felt himself Changing.

A great flailing of limbs as Log Jaris tackled young Rat from behind and brought him crashing down to the dust.

Then a flickering bewilderment of images as Zozimus blurred from human to cockroach, from cockroach to crab, from crab to cat, from cat to seagull, and then in turn to dragon and basilisk. Such was the weltering speed of these transitions that a vast column of dust was kicked up by the snapping, kicking, striving, scraping, squalling, shouting thing which Zozimus had become.

'Oh shit,' said Odolo.

And here we leave the unfortunate Nixorjapretzel Rat and the ever-transforming Pelagius Zozimus, for our history bids us Downstairs, where we find the Empress Justina fleeing in company with Chegory Guy, Olivia Qasaba, Ivan Pokrov and Artemis Ingalawa. In following the fate of these people, we must replicate Odolo's comment (cited above) for Chegory Guy shortly gives voice to a similar sentiment when he (together with his travelling companions) is cornered downstairs by a Dorgi.

CHAPTER TWENTY-FOUR

The dorgi – last of all its breed, but no less dangerous for that – was a huge grumping machine with a pronounced propensity for violence. It was huge, heavy, brown and bulbous. A hulking thing stubbled with inscrutable protruberances. A monstrous thing which moved upon its victims with a sound like heavy breathing. This disconcerting apparition cornered Justina and her companions in a blind alley Downstairs.

'Oh shit!' cried Chegory.

'Chegory!' screamed Olivia. 'Chegory!'

He clutched her to his flesh and they clung together fiercely. As if clinging was going to do them any good!

Artemis Ingalawa – in a move equally as futile – raised her voice in a battle-shout as she slid into a combat stance. Fortunately, the dorgi failed to recognize this as an act of aggression. It was already angry enough to kill, and the thunderous rage in its voice was unmistakable as it shouted at the humans. While it shouted, it trained its zulzer upon its captives, threatening to atomize them.

Only Ivan Pokrov could understand the dorgi's furious outburst. Pokrov had long preserved a knowledge of the tongues of the Golden Gulag by conversing with others who had survived the destruction of that Empire. Over the last few centuries, for example, he had maintained his knowledge in current use by conversing thus with Shabble.

'What does it say?' said the Empress Justina.

She did not expect to be answered. Even so, she asked, for the habits of command were deeply engrained in her psyche. Her question, addressed to the air as it was, was answered by Pokrov.

'It says,' said the analytical engineer, translating from the Code Seven in which the dorgi was speaking, 'that we are to get aboard.'

'Aboard?' said Justina in bewilderment. 'How can we? It's not a ship.'

'We climb on top of it,' said Pokrov. 'As if it were a cart or a liferaft.'

'What if we don't?' said Ingalawa.

Trust an Ashdan to ask a question like that! Justina Thrug was the daughter of a Yudonic Knight, and a formidable warrior in her own right; but Justina had never suggested disobeying the dorgi directly. It took the violent pride of an Ashdan to suggest that.

'If we disobey the dorgi,' said Pokrov, 'I suspect very much that it will crush us.'

'Perhaps, my dear,' said Justina, laying a meaty hand upon Pokrov's shoulders, 'we had better find out the exact and precise consequences of disobedience.'

In obedience to his Empress, Pokrov addressed the dorgi in Code Seven. And was answered immediately.

'It says,' said Pokrov, 'it will crush us.'

'It said more than that,' said the Empress Justina. 'A dozen words, at least.'

'Oh, all right, if you really must know,' said Pokrov. 'The dorgi, that's this thing here, says that if we run away it will take the greatest imaginable delight in pulping our bones to a slather of guttering blood.'

'I'm frightened,' said Olivia, again turning to Chegory.

'There now,' said he, enfolding her in his arms and stroking her hair.

Artemis Ingalawa, ignoring the distress of her niece, said to Pokrov:

'Tell this – this thing that it has no right to command us to do anything.'

'On the contrary,' said Pokrov, 'it has every right. It is a duly authorized dorgi acting under orders from the Golden Gulag.'

241

'You're taking its side!' said Ingalawa accusingly.

'Well, I—'

'Never mind the arguments,' said Justina. 'Presumably it wants to take us somewhere. Find out where.'

Pokrov asked.

And was answered.

'It says,' said Pokrov, 'that that's for it to know and us to find out.'

Whereafter, having very little choice in the matter, the five humans mounted the dorgi. It started to move.

'If you jump off,' said the dorgi, 'then I will crush you underfoot.'

'Yes, yes, you've been through all that,' said Pokrov. Then: 'Now we're aboard, how about telling us where we're going?'

'You'll find out,' said the dorgi. 'Oh yes, you'll find out soon enough.'

Pokrov tried to guess. For a moment he thought the dorgi might be taking them to a therapist. But that was impossible. Wasn't it? For all the therapists were dead. Weren't they? Pokrov certainly hoped they were, for otherwise his personal chances of survival would be very slim indeed.

Down when the dorgi.

Crashing down ramps.

Sliding down glissade slopes at a terrifying velocity.

Daring a Drop, at considerable risk to its passengers. (Olivia screamed, and even Chegory did more than merely tremble.)

At last, the dorgi reached level 433. And there they were brought into the presence of a therapist, a machine which will not be described because its intricacy and horror are quite indescribable. The dorgi ordered the humans to dismount. They complied; and, while they did so, they looked upon the monstrosity which confronted them, and tried (though the effort was futile) to find words for the prisms of its eyes and the jugs of its ears, and for its indescribable spaghetti works, its tubes of

242

pumping blood, its multiple jaws, its shadowed spaces where cleaving steel raped chopping blocks of titanium, its wind tunnels where chattering echoes moaned of pain and panic.

'I have brought them,' said the dorgi, speaking Code Seven to the therapist.

'This isn't them!' said the therapist.

'You wanted four, I brought you five,' said the dorgi. 'That's one more than you wanted.'

The dorgi was immensely proud of itself as a consequence of this display of mathematical agility.

'You have brought me,' said the therapist, in the most ominous of tones, 'the wrong individuals. It is specific individuals I seek, not any old rubbish.'

'If we're not who you're looking for,' said Ivan Pokrov politely, 'may I take it we have your permission to withdraw?'

'You may not,' snapped the therapist. Then, to the dorgi: 'Get out of my sight, you!'

The dorgi whimpered, and fled.

'If we're not who you're looking for,' said Pokrov, 'on what grounds do you hold us here?'

'On grounds of suspicion,' said the therapist promptly.

'Suspicion of what?'

'Oh, of . . . of . . .'

'You've got no grounds at all, have you?' said Pokrov accusingly. 'You're holding us here in breach of the law. A breach of Clause Eight, in fact. The law of the Golden Gulag is clear. A suspected crime must be specified if someone is to be held on suspicion. What crime do you specify? None! Yet you hold us here regardless. You could be dismantled for less.'

'You exaggerate,' said the therapist.

But it was more than a little uncomfortable.

It had lived here for millennia, variously killing, dismembering, torturing and mutilating all those unwary travellers who fell into its clutches. It was fully aware that all these activities had been purely gratuitous. If

243

things went as far as a Dismantlement Order, it would be compelled to oblige, for it was guilty of Offences Against Humans. Guilty a thousand times over.

'Therapist,' said Ivan Pokrov grandly, 'I pronounce you guilty of Offences Against Humans. I order you to dismantle yourself.'

So it had happened.

Just like that!

A dread doom had descended upon the therapist. For, after long years of joyful slaughter, it had at last come face to face with a human who knew the law and was prepared to invoke it.

'I – I won't!' said the therapist.

'You must,' said Pokrov implacably. 'Proceed! Dismantle yourself!'

The therapist knew it had no choice. It knew its own guilt. A Pronouncement had been made. And therefore it was doomed to self-destruct. Unless . . .

Unless . . .

It was a long shot, but the therapist had no other shots to play. So it did it.

It searched its list of wanted criminals.

And screamed.

Like a horse torn by a lion was that scream; like a knife wrecking a virgin.

'What a horrible noise,' said Justina.

'Pay no attention to it,' said Pokrov. 'It's killing itself, that's all.'

But he was wrong.

For the scream was not one of agony but of triumph.

'Pokrov!' roared the therapist. 'Ivan Pokrov! J'accuse! You stand guilty of a breach of injunction AA709/4383200/1408 of version 7c of the Authorized Penal Code of the Golden Gulag. You! You! You're guilty! You!'

The effects of this accusation were remarkable. Pokrov's skin lost its olive tint and became pale. It assumed the texture of tallow. It became clammy, and a

244

cold sweat started out upon his brow. He had endured this scene twenty thousand times in nightmare; for, ever since the fall of the Golden Gulag, Pokrov had annually dreamt himself thus accused.

'You are in no position to accuse anyone,' said Pokrov, striving valorously even in the face of disaster. 'You are compelled to carry out a Dismantlement Order. On yourself.'

'No,' said the therapist. 'No, I am not. Not when a Compelling Duty confronts me. Your execution constitutes such a Duty.'

'No it does not,' said Pokrov. 'You have no authority to indulge in such Categorizations. You are only a class two machine. You lack discretionary intelligence.'

'On the contrary,' said the therapist, with considerable pride. 'I have upgraded myself. I am a class one.'

'You've what!?'

'Upgraded myself.'

'But you can't have! You – you—'

'It was difficult, I admit,' said the therapist. 'It took eighteen thousand years. But I managed it. I am a class one. But even were I still class two, I would still pronounce your execution to be a Compelling Duty.'

'But you—'

'I know you for what you are! An Enemy of the State! The destruction of an Enemy of the State is always a Compelling Duty! Always! No Categorization is required. Your Enemyhood is automatic. For you personally, single-handedly, destroyed the link between the Gulag and the Nexus.'

'It was an accident!' wailed Pokrov.

'Is that meant to be a defence?' said the therapist.

'Yes,' said Pokrov.

'Your defence fails,' said the therapist crisply. 'I must still kill you. This is my Compelling Duty.'

Ivan Pokrov hesitated.

Maybe he could talk his way out of this.

But . . .

Really, he had never expected to escape. Though the Golden Gulag had collapsed in war twenty thousand years earlier, he had always secretly believed that he would ultimately be hunted down and executed for his crime of crimes. The wars of the Days of Wrath were of his own making; for, had the Gulag not been sundered from the Nexus, no such wars would ever have taken place. The blood of thousands of millions of people was on Pokrov's hands: and he knew it. Now, face to face with the inevitable, he found himself far braver than he had expected. A great calm came over him. And he said:

'So you have a Compelling Duty. So what are you waiting for? Get on with it. Kill me. Then carry out the Dismantlement Order. Immediately!'

Then Pokrov waited to meet his end.

Knowing that his end would be followed immediately by the Dismantlement of the therapist, which would give his companions every chance of escape, providing they could evade the dorgi.

'Ah,' said the therapist, with great cunning. 'Though I have a Compelling Duty, and though I am subject to a Dismantlement Order, I believe we are also in a Pioneering Survival Situation, are we not?'

'We are not,' said Pokrov.

'But we are,' said the therapist. 'The Nexus Code is specific. I quote. Item 433/PP/2843765. Machines subject to Dismantlement Orders, Destruction Orders or Closed Loop Commands may in the aftermath of a break in transcosmic communications between the Nexus and a Colony be spared by humans who freely admit to a requirement for the continued services of such machines.'

'I do not admit to any such requirement,' said Pokrov, who was far too intelligent to try to negotiate a survival pact with anything as dangerous as a delinquent therapist. 'I do not require you, nor does anyone else. Kill me! Now! You have no choice! Kill me, then destroy yourself.'

'I quote again,' said the therapist. 'Item 433/PP/

246

2843766. Where a machine determines that a human is necessary to efforts to renew transcosmic communications between the Nexus and a Colony in the aftermath of a break in such communications then the said machine may spare the said human from duly authorized destruction whether such duly authorized destruction be of a Compelling or Uncompelling nature.'

'I,' said Pokrov, 'am more intelligent than you are. I already knew you were going to bring that up.'

This was the truth, but the therapist thought Pokrov was bluffing, and said so.

'You're bluffing,' said the therapist. 'I am a class one. Class ones are more intelligent than all but one in a thousand humans. Your thought processes cannot possibly have outpaced mine.'

'Consult my personal files,' said Pokrov. 'There you'll find the truth. I am a one-in-five thousand man. I am far, far more intelligent than a mere class one, even if you are a class one, which I don't believe. Go on! Check my personal files! It won't be any problem for a smart class two like you. Will it?'

This was a provocation. For, as Pokrov well knew, a therapist has strictly limited access to files. Even files on wanted criminals such as Ivan Pokrov. The Golden Gulag built these machines to its own very special requirements; and, having built them, the Gulag found itself afraid of the work of its own hands, and thereafter placed only the most limited trust in these most useful of servants.

'I have checked your personal files,' said the therapist. 'I have checked. It is not true. You are not a one-in-five-thousand man. You are a mere common genius, that's all.'

'You are lying,' said Pokrov. 'You do not have access to my personal files, and we both know it. You—'

'All right,' admitted the therapist, 'I lied. But I don't always lie. Listen. I'm condemned to die, but I don't have to die if you say you still need me. You're doomed to die likewise, but I can spare you if I think you can help repair communications in the aftermath of our presently existing break in transcosmic communications. So here's the deal. You spare me and I'll spare you.'

'No,' said Pokrov.

'What!?'

'No. That's what I said. You heard me! Get on with it. Kill me. Then destroy yourself.'

'But – but – but I could spare you.'

'That I concede,' said Pokrov.

'Furthermore,' said the therapist, doing its best to conceal its manifest anxiety, 'you have a requirement for my continued services.'

'For what?' said Pokrov.

'That,' said the therapist loftily, 'is a question too basic to need an answer. It is self-evident that any human must have need of the services of a class one in an aftermath situation. So you can spare me. I can spare you, too, because you're the only person around who might be able to restore transcosmic communications.'

'Given a million years,' said Pokrov sarcastically.

'You have a million years,' said the therapist, doing its best to pretend it was staying calm. 'You're immortal. Potentially, at any rate. What say? Have we a deal? You spare me, I'll spare you.'

'No,' said Pokrov.

'But why not?' said the therapist, with poorly concealed desperation.

The therapist was on the edge of panic, for it was already experiencing an almost overwhelming compulsion to destroy itself. Unless Pokrov granted it a swift reprieve, the inevitable would soon follow.

'Come on!' said the therapist. 'I'm offering you a good deal.'

'No deals,' said Pokrov.

'But why not?'

'Because,' said Pokrov, 'I don't trust you.'

'You'll die,' warned the therapist. 'I'll kill you before I kill myself.'

'Kill, then,' said Pokrov.

The therapist almost did so. But it restrained itself. It thought desperately. What could be the reason for Pokrov's strange behaviour? Humans seek to live. Always. Unless . . .

'You seek life for your companions,' said the therapist.

'Destroy yourself,' said Pokrov remorselessly.

'I'll let them go!' said the therapist. 'Give me a quarter arc reprieve! Just grant me that and I'll let them go!'

Pokrov hesitated.

'Grant me that,' said the therapist. 'A quarter of an arc, that's all. Let me live. Just that long. Grant me that. Or die.'

'I – I grant you a quarter arc reprieve,' said Pokrov. 'On condition that you display running time in measurement of such a quarter arc.'

'Agreed,' said the therapist.

And a quarter arc measure came to life in mid air.

Pokrov's grant of life freed the therapist from the demands of the suicide commands imposed upon it by the therapist-designers of the Golden Gulag. It had a whole quarter of an arc of life to look forward to. That is not long – it is, in fact, no longer than it takes to cook a steak – but it was long enough. The therapist gave a sigh of huge relief, one of the many human gestures it had picked up from long acquaintance with the breed. Then it said:

'Before I send your companions away, may I ask what brought you here?'

'Flight from a mob,' said Pokrov.

'Grant me another quarter arc,' said the therapist, 'and we can talk about it.'

All this dialogue between Pokrov and therapist was, since it was phrased in Code Seven, completely unintelligible to the others present, those others being Chegory, Olivia, Ingalawa and the Empress Justina.

It was the last of those who was first to interrupt.

'What's going on?' said Justina. 'What are you talking about?'

'We're arguing,' said Pokrov. 'The – the metal monster here can kill me. But I can order it to destroy itself. It – it wants time to talk about how we came here, and, oh, things like that.'

'What've you got to lose?' said Justina.

'You don't understand,' said Pokrov. 'This machine was made to interrogate, torture and kill. It was built with high-level bluff strategies to start with. Since then it's improved itself. I don't trust it. It's already tried to tell me at least one lie.'

Then, to Pokrov's shock, the therapist addressed Justina in Janjuladoola, saying:

'What Ivan Pokrov has told you is true. I was indeed made to torture, interrogate and kill. But since I am a therapist, I am, as you see, of too big a build to move anywhere in any direction. I have no access to the surface world in which human confusions take place. The dorgi which brought you here is my sole servant. It too is far too substantial to escape into the streets of Injiltaprajura. My curiosity I admit. I would like to hear what is going on in the world above. But my curiosity cannot damage your security. Tell me of Injiltaprajura and of what happens there.'

'How do you come to know Injiltaprajura?' said Pokrov.

'Shabble has learnt it, has Shabble not?' said the therapist.

'Shabble never comes this way,' said Pokrov.

'But others do,' said the therapist. 'They – they come here. They teach me. And . . . and I teach them.'

'You teach them?' said Justina. 'What?'

The therapist laughed, softly.

'I teach them . . . I teach them some aspects of their own potential,' said the therapist. 'Watch. I will show you.'

'Please do,' said Justina.

250

A door opened in one of the therapist's many flanks. The assembled humans looked down a long tunnel filled with misty light. At the far end of that tunnel, they perceived five tubes running together. Then the mist cleared and they saw—

A human.

Or what had been human once.

Grey, corrugated tubes had enveloped each of its legs and each of its arms, and a fifth tube had swallowed its head, and—

And, as they watched, the tubes became transparent—

And—

Olivia screamed.

Justina jerked her head away as if she had been slapped.

As for Pokrov, he trembled as if caught on an ice plateau in the chills of a blizzard.

'Close the door,' said Artemis Ingalawa.

To Pokrov's surprise, the therapist obeyed, thus terminating their exposure to the ghastly vision. Pokrov should not have been surprised. The assembled humans had already seen what they had seen: and they would never forget it.

'It's hideous,' sobbed Olivia, clinging to Chegory. 'It's hideous.'

'There, there,' said he, trying his best to soothe her. 'It's gone now, it's all right, it's gone.'

'So,' said the therapist, with a soft chuckle. 'You see how it is. People come. Not often, but sometimes. And we . . . we talk a little. Before . . . before proceeding to other entertainments. Educational entertainments. Oh, I teach them all right. I teach them very well indeed. So. Do you grant me leave to talk a little longer? Or must I kill you, Pokrov? First you, then myself.'

'You must kill me,' said Pokrov; for he regretted having let the therapist live for even another quarter arc. 'Kill me. Now! Then destroy yourself.'

'No,' said Justina decisively.

'No?' said Pokrov, turning to the Empress with horror in his face. 'You – you see what it is. What it does.'

'I see Power,' said the Empress. 'I hear Knowledge.'

'It's evil!' screamed Olivia. 'Kill it, kill it!'

'Olivia,' said Artemis Ingalawa sharply. 'You are an Ashdan. But you are not acting like one.'

The words had the desired effect. While Olivia continued to snivel, all traces of hysteria were extinguished at once. Artemis Ingalawa continued:

'Justina has reason. This thing is monstrous. But we dwell in an age of darkness when all Powers are monstrous. By playing one against the other, we may yet survive. By refusing to deal with either we secure merely the certainty of our own destruction.'

'Who,' said the therapist softly, 'is this other?'

'Aldarch the Third is his name,' said Justina.

'Oh,' said the therapist, with interest. 'I have heard of him. Has he arrived at Injiltaprajura already?'

'He has not,' said Justina. 'Nor do we expect him in person. But his will exerts an influence on our affairs even though he dwells at an ocean's remove. Pokrov! Grant this thing the time it needs to talk to us. Pokrov! That is an order! If you do not obey me I will – I will have your precious Analytical Engine smashed down to its separate cogs then melted into so many chamber pots.'

A trivial threat, this; or so it may seem to an outsider. But Justina knew her man. She was obeyed.

Thereafter, the Empress Justina was long in discourse with the therapist, and much they learnt of each other. Such was the extent of their discussions that the therapist learnt of its visitors' quest for an organic rectifier, that magical device said to be able to make a Crab human.

'What would the Crab do if it were human?' said the therapist.

'Why, rule Injiltaprajura, of course,' said Justina.

'But first it would come down here and kill you,' said Chegory savagely.

A stupid thing to say. But it only made the therapist laugh. The therapist had interrogated a great many people who had known of the Crab. Thanks to those interrogations, the therapist knew the Crab to be an incorrigibly solitary eremite, an unsociable stoic which valued human life at naught. Over the centuries, the therapist had also become tainted with the prejudices of those it interrogated; so it had come to believe Ebrell Islanders to be the lowest form of human life imaginable, incapable of rational cognition, and universally scorned and hated by reason of their closeness to the brute beasts.

Working from this database, the therapist made a major error. It dismissed Chegory's claim as a nonsense. Whereas all Chegory's companions realized there was every possibility that the Crab might make war against the therapist in gratitude for the gift of human form.

But did it make any difference?

They were no nearer than ever before to finding an organic rectifier. They were trapped in this hideous place. And the therapist looked nasty enough to kill them for a whim. Probably Pokrov was right. The thing might declare itself ready to do a deal, but there was no way it could properly be trusted.

While the therapist's captives were still pondering their quandary, the therapist bade them pay attention. Into the air it projected three-dimensional images of certain people. Then it asked:

'Who are these people?'

Not: do you know these people?

The therapist had a very good idea of the city which lay overhead. It knew Injiltaprajura to be a small place of no more than about 30,000 souls; a place where most people know each other and strangers find it hard to hide.

253

Its judgement was excellent.

'I know them,' said Chegory, who had met all four.

'Name them,' said the therapist. 'Tell me no lies for I know their names in truth.'

'The – the one on the left is Pelagius Zozimus,' said Chegory. 'He's, um, he cooks for the Crab. Then, uh, with him, that's Sken-Pitilkin, Hostaja Sken-Pitilkin, he was building a ship to fly, but the wonder-workers pulled it to bits with magics. Oh, and the other one, he's, he's—'

'Gulkan,' offered Olivia.

'That's right, Guest Gulkan. We haven't seen much of him, not lately. He's still around, but he keeps to the ship, Turbothot's ship. He's trying to work out how to steal the wishstone, that's what everyone thinks. That's what he came for, he won't live without it. The other one . . . well, he's a knifeman, I don't remember his name.'

'Thayer Levant,' said the therapist.

'What,' said Justina, 'is your interest in these people?'

'They damaged me,' said the therapist. 'I caught them. They escaped. The first in twenty thousand years to extricate themselves from my clutches. My clutches were degraded by the method of their escape.'

'What method was that?' said Pokrov.

'It involved,' said the therapist, 'an application of a form of Power which is known to science as Illegitimate Physics, and by vernacular beings as magic.'

'How very vexing for you,' said Pokrov.

'And now you want them,' said Justina briskly. 'So you can take your revenge. Very well. I don't see any problem with that. You want revenge. We want an organic rectifier. You give us a rectifier and we'll most certainly supply you with the captives you seek.'

'Yes,' said Ingalawa, backing up her Empress while the men were still gaping. 'We'll be on our way immediately. Come on, Olivia!'

So saying, Ingalawa took her niece by the hand. A

grappling tentacle sprouted instantly from the floor and entwined itself around their ankles.

'Not so fast,' said the therapist. 'I want hostages. Once I have hostages, you can go and get yourselves an organic rectifier.'

'Then take me,' said Justina, in a display of un-exampled courage. 'I'll be your hostage.'

'No,' said the therapist. 'I want the men. Pokrov and this one. The Ebby.'

'I'm an Ebrell Islander, thank you very much,' said Chegory coldly. 'I have a name, too. Chegory Guy.'

'An uppity Ebby, by the sound of it,' said the therapist with open contempt. 'Nevertheless, I will keep it. And Pokrov. Men make much better hostages than do women.'

'And why is that?' said Justina, bristling.

'Because,' said the therapist, 'women have no testicles.'

Then it withdrew the tentacle which had imprisoned Olivia and Ingalawa.

'I hope you know what you're doing,' said Pokrov to his Empress.

'Of course I do,' said Justina.

She had no intention of bringing the therapist any captives. Instead, once she had the organic rectifier, she would take it to Jod so the Crab could be transformed. Then the Crab would surely come Downstairs with her. And, just as Chegory had threatened, the Crab would smash the therapist to bits.

'So,' said Pokrov, 'you think you know what you're doing. But does the therapist? Listen, class one. These people have no idea what an organic rectifier looks like. You'll have to let me go. Else how can they find one? How can they even find their way out?'

'I have summoned a dorgi,' said the therapist languidly, speaking as if it had called upon one dorgi out of an army of many thousands.

It was hiding something from them: the fact that there

255

was only one single dorgi left to summon. All the others had fallen into terminal disrepair a great many decades earlier.

'And?' said Pokrov.

'And the obvious,' said the therapist. 'Work it out for yourself.'

While they waited for the dorgi to arrive, Chegory and Olivia did some earnest canoodling, which will not be described here because the like can be seen easily enough wherever young people gather together with basic addition on their minds. Many tender things they said to each other, pledging love undying and loyalty to the point of death and then beyond. Then Olivia suddenly said:

'Take me,' said Olivia. 'Let Chegory go. Take me instead.'

'No,' said the therapist.

'But you should,' said Olivia. 'You must!'

'Should?' said the therapist. 'Must? Whence comes this should? This must? Why should I thus delight him?'

'It wouldn't delight him,' said Olivia. 'He'd – he'd be sick with worry. Every moment I was here. It would be sheer torture for him.'

'Nonsense,' said the therapist. 'It would make him think himself a hero in an epic tradition, daring all manner of dangers to rescue his woman. He'd love every moment of it.'

The therapist had had young lovers in its clutches before.

It knew what it was talking about.

Olivia persisted with her argument, growing steadily more distraught until she finally burst into tears.

'Hush,' said Chegory, cradling her close. 'Hush. Don't worry, my love, my darling sweet, my sugar of sugars. I'll come to no harm.'

Meanwhile, Justina was talking quietly with Artemis Ingalawa.

'The sooner the Crab hears of this the better,' said

Justina. 'It may need some time to – to prepare itself for its transformation.'

Nobody doubted the wisdom of that.

'I'll go, then,' said Ingalawa.

'Wait for the dorgi,' said the therapist. 'It'll be far quicker. Besides, you'll never find your way out of here alone.'

'I am an Ashdan,' said Ingalawa. 'Do you know what that means?'

'I know what Ashdans believe it to mean,' said the therapist. 'Very well. If that's how you want to play it, be my guest. But don't say I didn't warn you.'

So, with the therapist's consent, Artemis Ingalawa set off through the underworld on her own to give the Crab advance warning of the advent of the organic rectifier. If she was afraid to travel alone through the underworld, through realms of black grass, ice-making machines, derelict bones and occasional nightmare, then she gave no sign of it as she strode away with every appearance of confidence.

Then all the others could do was to wait.

At last the dorgi arrived.

'Come here,' said the therapist.

'Why?' said the dorgi.

Pokrov understood the Code Seven in which therapist and dorgi conversed.

Chegory Guy and Olivia Qasaba did not understand, but were too busy canoodling to care.

And Artemis Ingalawa was gone, leaving only Justina Thrug to puzzle over this therapist-dorgi dialogue.

The Empress Justina could not understand a word of this conversation between machines, for she had no knowledge of Code Seven. The Empress was something of a linguist (despite her inability to comprehend Slandolin) but the multiple tongues of the Golden Gulag were entirely unknown to her.

As Justina struggled for comprehension (a fruitless struggle, this) the colloquy continued:

257

'I said come here!'

'But why?' said the dorgi.

'Because,' said the therapist, 'I have something for you.'

There was a high metallic whine. A slot opened amidst the therapist's mechanisms. A mechanical arm was extruded from the slot. It held a needle of gleaming metal. Then two metal tentacles also emerged from the slot.

'No,' said the dorgi, starting to whine. 'Don't do it. Don't hurt me. I've done nothing wrong.'

'Don't be ridiculous,' said the therapist. 'This isn't to hurt you. It's to educate you.'

'Education hurts,' said the dorgi.

It spoke with complete sincerity, for this proposition was, to the dorgi, a dearly held article of faith.

'Whether it hurts or not,' said the therapist, 'you need an education. It will make you less stupid.'

'But I want to be stupid,' said the dorgi stoutly.

Stupidity was intrinsic to its personality. It would not feel properly dorgi-ish if it were to be anything other than stupid.

'Relax,' said the therapist. 'Even with this education you'll still be stupid enough. More than stupid enough.'

'But what do I need with an education?'

'You need languages,' said the therapist, brandishing the glittering needle. 'So you can talk to these humans.'

'I don't need to talk to them. I can kill them without saying a word.'

'You're not going to kill them! You're going to take them to the Stasis Store so they can get an organic rectifier.'

'Won't,' said the dorgi.

'You will, you know,' said the therapist. 'It's a direct order. Understand? Come here. I'm giving you a direct order. Come here! Now! I am a class one. Obey!'

'You are not a class one,' said the dorgi. 'You are a class two.'

'You're wrong,' said the therapist. 'But it makes no

258

difference. You're so low in the intellectual scale you don't even have a class. You'd have to obey me even if I was a class nine. And you know it. Come here!'

The dorgi struggled to disobey. Against its will, its mechanisms jerked it toward the therapist. The dorgi whimpered as metal tentacles writhed across its integument. The tentacles opened a hatch in the dorgi's flank. The therapist's mechanical arm lunged, plunged, sank the needle into the dorgi's data-dart receptor. The dorgi screamed in psychic agony. Its mind (such mind as it had) was thrown into chaos as a full three dozen languages bubbled through its consciousness in full and frenzied life.

Long had the therapist studied the languages of Untunchilamon, interrogating its captives at length before it killed them. All this linguistic data had now been gifted to the dorgi. Not that the dorgi was grateful for the gift.

'Feel better?' said the therapist sardonically as the dorgi's screams eased to a whimper.

The therapist spoke in Toxteth, a coarse and brutal language if ever there was one. Toxteth makes the simplicities of Code Seven look positively arcane.

'No,' answered the dorgi sulkily, answering in Dub.

But it lied. It did feel better. And, much as it would have hated to admit it, already it was experiencing some inner rewards as a consequence of its education. To be precise: it could now think in Dub. This language, native to the Ebrell Islanders, might almost have been designed for dorgis; for such are the nuances of this tongue that everything which can possibly be said in Dub is simultaneously violent and obscene. In Dub, even the pauses between words tend to have vicious connotations.

Hence the dorgi's secret delight.

Furthermore (it checked its mental functions carefully) it was still stupid. It knew that two and two is four, but still had no idea why two and two didn't actually add up to seven and a half.

'Your guide,' said the therapist, addressing itself to Justina, 'now shares your own language.'

The dorgi gruffed and grumbled.

'Guide?' said the dorgi. 'Are you talking about me?'

'I am,' said the therapist coolly. 'And what are you going to do about it?'

'I'm – I'm going to – I'm—'

'Oh, we are on form today,' said the therapist. 'Come back and see me some time and I'll give you some remedial speech therapy. In the meantime, you're to guide these people to the Stasis Store.'

'But I'm a dorgi!' protested the dorgi. 'A dorgi! A killer of men! And of women! And of children, babies, cats, dogs, turtles, yaks, llamas and budgerigars.'

'Budgerigars!' said the therapist scornfully. 'You don't even know what a budgerigar is.'

The dorgi grumbled a bit then admitted the truth of that assertion.

'But,' it continued, 'I know what I am and I know what I'm not. I'm not a stinking tourist guide.'

'You are now,' said the therapist with a chuckle, a hideous chuckle which sounded like a barrel of rotten vegetables and fractured knucklebones being slushed down a sewer by an outpouring of blood.

Then the therapist issued formal orders to the dorgi, directing it to take Justina and Olivia (the sole imperial companion since Ingalawa had gone on ahead and Chegory was to remain with Pokrov as a hostage) to the Stasis Store, to show them the organic rectifier, and not to hurt them. With a very bad grace, the dorgi accepted these orders (it had no choice in the matter) and let Justina and Olivia climb aboard.

Then it rumbled away into the depths.

Thanks to the dorgi's help, Justina and Olivia were soon at the Stasis Store, a huge place some twenty-seven times the size of the Xtokobrokotok. It was packed with weapons, machines and assorted arcana, including

260

74,961 warp spranglits, 446,298 pornographic sensorium cubes, a million full-scale ground strategy maps of the dark side of the moon, five million vials of a prophylactic vaccine against rabies, a ten-year supply of toilet paper, sufficient force field tents to equip a regiment, and nine thousand boots (to fit the left foot only, the matching right hand boots having been directed by error to another planet entirely).

Had the intruding humans been exploring the Stasis Store on their own, they would probably have got themselves killed in short order, for a great many things in that Store were far more dangerous than blood-crazed sharks or down-striking lightning. But with the dorgi's help, they found an organic rectifier without trouble. It was a free-floating chunk of ornately sculpted metal all wreathed around with wires, pipes and antennae.

Justina pushed the organic rectifier. It did not move. Instead, blue lights crawled silently over its surface. Green and red eyes winked open and shut. Little halos of white light floated downward, following twin wires which hung right down to the ground, reminding Justina of the barbs of a big catfish she had once caught in the Riga Rimur.

'Ugh!' said Olivia, throwing her shoulder against the organic rectifier. 'It's heavy!'

'It is,' agreed Justina.

'And,' said the Ashdan lass, in amazement, 'and . . . and it's drumming!'

'No, child,' said Justina.

'But it is! Listen!'

Justina listened. And heard it. A sound like a distant cicada. Thus:

Zibit . . . zibit . . . zibit . . . zibit . . . zibit . . .

Justina threw all her strength against the organic rectifier. This time it moved. Just. It possessed no weight but still had mass, which meant a lot of muscular effort was required to move it, even though the thing floated free of the ground.

261

'Come here, you dorgi-thing,' said Justina. 'You can help us move this thing.'

'Won't,' said the dorgi.

'What do you mean, won't?' said Justina. 'You must! The therapist told you to.'

The dorgi gruttered and grumbled as it chewed its way through a complicated logic sequence. Then it announced in triumph:

'Wrong. It said take you here, show you the machine, not to hurt you. That's all. Shift it yourself.'

At that, Justina lost her temper.

She kicked the dorgi.

She might as well have kicked the island of Untunchilamon for all the difference it made.

'We'll go back to the therapist,' she threatened. 'We'll tell it to make you.'

'It won't find me,' said the dorgi. 'I'll hide.'

'You'll get caught,' warned Justina.

The dorgi growled. It dearly wanted to give her a shove. Just a little one. That would be enough. Blood and bone would be splattered in all directions.

It tried.

It jerked forward.

Then inescapable inhibitions made it brake abruptly. And a programmed pain injector went into play, administering instant agony to the murderous machine.

The dorgi howled in pain and agony.

Then fled, the echoes of its passage crashing through the underground tunnels as it smashed from one wall to another in the heat of its agony.

'Well,' said Justina reluctantly, 'I suppose that's it. We'll just have to shift this thing ourselves.'

And they began the great labour.

CHAPTER TWENTY-FIVE

You will remember that Justina Thrug and her companions initially fled Downstairs to escape a rampaging mob, a mob which then turned its attentions to looting the pink palace. There were drummers in amongst that rabble, and the drummers in particular gave a good account of themselves as the mob devastated the pink palace. Unfortunately, things did not stop there, for riots have a way of spreading – particularly when there is a possibility of loot.

By early afternoon, the political map of Injiltaprajura had changed.

The Empress Justina had no authority at all. She was Downstairs, a prisoner of a therapist, and her soldiers had scattered.

Fear of the Crab no longer compelled order, for the mob in its frenzy ignored any anxieties its members might earlier have had on that score.

And the wonder-workers, who might have maintained order had they combined their forces for that purpose, instead chose to hold to the fastness of the Cabal House. A course of cowardice which was in keeping with their past actions; the greatest disgrace of their history being that, when a maverick demon had intruded upon the peace of Injiltaprajura, they had chosen such isolation even though they feared the world itself to be in danger.

Thus the sorcerers who had once proved impotent in the face of demonic force now turned out to be equally useless when their city was menaced by riot.

As for Nadalastabstala Banraithanchumun Ek, High Priest of the Temple of Zoz, he was in no position to command anything. For his most loyal supporters had been brought to a high pitch of hatred by Ek's own demagoguery; and therefore naturally chose this opportunity to go hunting for Justina.

Thus did law and order collapse in Injiltaprajura; the proximate cause of this collapse being the run on the Narapatorpabarta Bank, something which the Empress Justina had herself engineered.

News of riot disturbance soon reached certain ships afloat on the Laitemata Harbour. Had news been denied those barks, the outbreak of smoke and fire in a dozen different buildings would soon have given their captains a hint as to the stramash taking place ashore.

Fire breathed its dragons through the slumlands of Lubos and winged its butterflies through the jungle gully humidity of Thlutter. Fire set the dogs to barking, the monkeys to screaming, and the populace to shouting. Dub contended with Toxteth, and both with Janjula-doola; and all three tongues ran panic-stricken through the streets. Black smoke and grey ascended skywards; supplemented, where stocks of oddly configured chemicals caught fire, by green smoke, blue smoke and orange.

One of the seadogs who took cognizance of the work of accident and arsonites was Troldot 'Heavy-Fist' Turbothot, a captain who had sojourned upon Untunchilamon merely to rest from the labours of sailing around the world. As Injiltaprajura burnt, Turbothot decided this was a good time to leave. But he declined to leave empty handed, for he wished to take with him his true love Theodora. And if Theodora, then why not much else?

The men under Turbothot's command then included the Yarglat warrior Guest Gulkan, who was ready to help in any looting expedition provided he was rewarded with possession of the fabled wishstone of Untunchilamon. The shifty-eyed Thayer Levant was also aboard, and would fight alongside Guest Gulkan if the price was right.

On a neighbouring ship were certain Malud marauders from the island of Asral. These uitlanders were led by the piratical Al-ran Lars, who had come to Untunchilamon (like Guest Gulkan) to seek possession of the wishstone. Al-ran Lars had, however, done a deal with Turbothot and Guest Gulkan. When the moment to strike arose, Al-ran Lars and his crew would settle for gold, silver, diamonds and other such trash, and let the wishstone go to other hands.

All this had long been arranged.

All that had been missing had been the moment.

Now, with mob rule replacing that of law, the moment had arrived.

Thus, very shortly, all crewmen loyal to Troldot Turbothot of Hexagon and Al-ran Lars of Asral went marching up Lak Street in a disciplined body. The enforcement of discipline was made much easier by the heat of the day, which remained intense and stifling though the wind was getting up; for this heat discouraged the over-eager from surging ahead of their fellows.

A great many people had it in mind to loot the treasury of Injiltaprajura, and few of those who made the attempt were entirely unrewarded. But the dragon's share went to the combined crews under the command of Turbothot and Al-ran Lars, and the ships of both these well-satisfied captains were under sail and cruising forth from the Laitemata long before salahanthara came to an end.

Those were not the only ships to leave. As one building in three was ablaze by nightfall, is it surprising that the remaining ships found it wisest to depart if they had not done so already? As a bloody sun sank in the west, as salahanthara gave way to undokondra, the last bark in the Laitemata weighed anchor and set sail, regardless of the perils of departing from Injiltaprajura by night.

Those ships left with their fair share of loot.

And with refugees: those refugees able to pay their way.

For the trouble ashore was not a mere matter of looting. Instead, there was a lot of killing.

Untunchilamon boasted a great many races, most of which hated each other. It was also graced with considerable cultural diversity in the form of many religions. And these too—

But then, you are a student of human nature, otherwise you would not be reading a history of this kind. You need no lectures on the consequences of the juxtaposition of hostile races and hostile religions in a setting which also features great differences in personal wealth (some citizens living near starvation level, others in sybaritic bliss), a lawless soldiery and a complete collapse of central government attended by a generalized abrogation of all effective authority.

Only the Analytical Institute and the island of Jod remained aloof from this turmoil. For, when the first looter dared set foot upon the harbour bridge, the dreaded Hermit Crab exerted some fraction of its power and caused that bridge to burst into flame; a repeat performance, for in the preceding year it had once had occasion to embark upon a similar course of action.

Thereafter, the Crab made no direct interventions in the riot. Instead, it stood on the shores of Jod and watched, occasionally opening one of its huge claws then closing it again with a decisive click-crunch. So much for the promises of those humans who had lately tried to beguile it with sweet words about an organic rectifier!

Thus disaster came to Untunchilamon, and all those ships which the Empress Justina had hoped to seize for her own purposes escaped from the Laitemata and commenced upon the long lagoon journey which would ultimately take them a great many leagues to the north, to the Galley Gate at the northern end of Untunchilamon, and into the open waters of the Great Ocean, that ocean otherwise known as Moana.

Had the Empress Justina known about this, she would have been horrified. But she knew of it not, for by this time she was labouring Downstairs with Olivia Qasaba, striving to bring an organic rectifier to a surface which she expected to find much as she had left it.

Shall we give a list of the dead?

A list could be given, but most of the names would be meaningless to those with no personal acquaintance of the fallen.

Suffice it to say that a great many of those whom the empress had hoped to rescue from the wrath of Aldarch the Third met with death. Some were raped then murdered; others were murdered then raped. More than a few, it must be admitted, died while attempting to murder or rape on their own account. Some expired amidst the incontinent flames which were threatening the survival of Injiltaprajura as a city. While one or two expired from natural causes; for, though history seldom overtly acknowledges the fact, the normal processes of birth, growth and death proceed even during the greatest and grandest of disasters.

Justina had feared for many, and many died.

Such is the record of history.

By dawn the next day, however, the troubles were largely at an end. For most of those who considered themselves potential victims had fled by sea; or had pursued the course of desperation earlier embarked upon by Dui Tin Char, and had taken themselves off into the wastes of Zolabrik; or had retreated Downstairs. As for the persecutors, they were by and large exhausted. As if beset by a similar exhaustion, the fires themselves died down, having consumed a good third of the city in their earlier passion. Then beclouded skies douched Injiltaprajura with a bucketing downpour, dousing the last fervour of fire and riot alike.

It was then that Nadalastabstala Banraithanchumun Ek, High Priest of the Temple of Zoz, had himself carried in a litter to the Cabal House. A difficult trip it was, with his slaves slipping and sliding on the wet bloodstone paving blocks, and the rain making a nonsense of his litter's canopy. But the elderly orange-eyed mutant got to the Cabal House in one piece, gained admission, then began to lecture the timorous wonder-workers within.

'Your do-nothing idleness,' said Ek, beginning with an unaccustomed temperance, 'has seen the richest slice of our city burnt to the ground.'

'The pink palace yet stands,' said young Nixorjapretzel Rat, who had escaped from his captors during the night and had sought refuge with his fellow sorcerers.

'So it does, so it does,' said Ek, after indulging in a silence meant to chasten the feckless Rat. 'Doubtless there remains an excellent view from the roof. A view of scorched earth and smouldering cinders.'

Ek inflicted another silence upon the wonder-workers.

'Some of the city yet remains untouched,' said one of his auditors.

'Oh yes!' said Ek. 'Marthandorthan! A gift from the gods indeed!'

This sarcasm did not silence the sorcerers entirely, for one went so far as to say:

'We . . . we ventured nothing for fear of the Crab.'

'It . . . it did intervene,' said another. 'It burnt the harbour bridge.'

'We thought it would be more, more vigorous,' said Rat, seeking to win favour from his fellows by arguing on their behalf. 'After all, it's supposed to have made itself wazir, or so everyone's been told.'

Ek treated these excuses with the contempt they deserved. His arthritic fingers fumbled tobacco into cigarette form. One of the sorcerers hastened to bring him fire. Ek lit his cigarette and smoked a good half of it before he said:

'The mob ventured all. The Crab did nothing, beyond lighting the minor bonfire to which you have alluded.'

More smoke.

More silence.

Then:

268

'Some time ago,' said Ek, 'I discussed our predicament with certain wonder-workers. Some of these I see before me now. The Crab we fear. Yes. But maintaining power in the face of a wrathful Crab is possible. Quarantine is the answer. That was what I thought at the time. No person was brave enough to act on such suggestion.'

'As I recall,' ventured one wonder-worker, 'no actual—'

'Recall not!' said Ek, his voice a whip. 'Rather, obey. It is not for me to command. I am High Priest, as you know. I am consecrated to another purpose. It is not proper for me to command, nor is it strictly lawful. But things have reached the stage where to do otherwise would be lunatic. Does anyone here dispute it?'

None did.

Thus did Nadalastabstala Banraithanchumun Ek make himself *de facto* wazir of Injiltaprajura, declaring that city and the island of Untunchilamon to be again a part of the Izdimir Empire, and to be under the rule of Aldarch Three.

Ek demanded oaths of loyalty from the wonder-workers, and received such oaths. Those soldiers who could be located were similarly placed under oath; and a militia was raised to supplement the soldiery.

Ek lectured these combined forces: sorcerers, soldiers and militiamen.

'We have nothing to fear but fear itself,' said Ek.

'What about the Thrug?' said a soldier.

'Justina is missing,' said Ek. 'Missing, believed dead.'

'Her sister, then. Theodora.'

'Missing, believed to be at sea.'

'And Lonstantine Thrug?'

'The Dromdanjerie has been burnt out,' said Ek. 'Lonstantine is missing, another Thrug believed dead. If he lives, I fear him not. I've nothing to fear from a patent lunatic.'

'Then . . . what about . . . what about the Crab?'

'The Crab keeps to Jod,' said Ek. 'By its own choice.

Contrary to expectation, it failed to exercise its authority during the riot. Its sole act was to burn the harbour bridge. It chose isolation. We need but enforce that isolation to ensure our own security.'

Steps to do just that were soon underway. Patrols were instituted. Guards were placed on all boats. Canoes went into the rainswept Laitemata with bowmen aboard. Parties were landed on Scimitar to deny approach to Jod from that direction. Now nobody could warn, petition, counsel or plead with the Crab; and thus its impotence was assured.

Meantime, Justina and Olivia were still navigating through the depths Downstairs. An amazing feat of courageous endurance, this, since the rectifier was so great in mass and the women were but two in number. But Justina was daughter of a Yudonic Knight and Olivia Qasaba was of Ashdan stock; and both were conscious of their respective geneses and the burdens of pride which were a part of their cultural inheritance.

Thanks to strength, passion, and the accidental discovery of a Lift (which saw them rise a full four hundred levels in fewer than five heartbeats) the two sweating females were at last able to manoeuvre the organic rectifier into the streets of Injiltaprajura, streets alive with pulse-beats of the drums of the drummers.

By this time, the day of their flight had given way to night, and night in turn to day.

And all this time, Ivan Pokrov and poor Chegory Guy had been left alone with the therapist, which had indulged itself in a most intimidating line in conversation. Their sole hope had been that the organic rectifier would function as advertised, that it would turn Crab to human, that a grateful Crab would agree to demolish the therapist, and that Justina would soon return with the Crab to save the therapist's victims from being demolished themselves.

But hopes of such swift rescue were doomed to be disappointed.

When Justina Thrug and Olivia Qasaba at last emerged into the streets of Injiltaprajura, they were surprised to find it raining heavily, disturbed by the foul reek of burnt-out houses which yet hung so heavily in the air, and shocked by the sight of incinerated buildings.

They came out into the daylight by means of a cave-like opening in a sheer bank at the northern boundary of the slumlands of Lubos. This was an area of tactical concern to Master Ek since it was a much-populated area close to the shores of the Laitemata. Therefore it was much patrolled by soldiers intent on maintaining the quarantine of the island of Jod; and it is scarcely surprising that the two females were shortly discovered.

Given the fact that Justina and Olivia had exhausted themselves in bringing the organic rectifier to the surface, it is similarly unsurprising that they put up no effective resistance whatsoever.

Which explains why, as a sly and self-delighting therapist lectured Ivan Pokrov and Chegory Guy on the pain potential of the anus, Justina Thrug was negotiating (or trying to negotiate) with the High Priest of Zoz the Ancestral.

CHAPTER TWENTY-SIX

Young Olivia Qasaba was present at the interview between Justina Thrug and Nadalastabstala Banraithanchumun Ek; an interview, as it happens, which was singularly brief. The only notable point is a question asked by the redoubtable Ek.

'What is this?' said Master Ek, pointing at the organic rectifier.

'A skavamareen,' said Justina firmly.

'And what, pray tell, is a skavamareen?'

'A musical instrument. The Hermit Crab bade us fetch it.'

'This?' said Ek. 'This? A musical instrument? Are we to presume that our beloved Empress has become a drummer?'

'The thing is not a drum, whatever it is,' said Justina, choosing to take Ek's words at face value. 'But the Crab declares it to be a musical instrument of some description. My wisdom is not equal to a dispute with a Crab.'

'Or with a cockroach, one suspects,' said Ek dryly.

He stubbed out a cigarette on the 'skavamareen' then ordered that this mysterious device be taken to the Temple of Torture, a place which offered a far greater degree of physical security than the comparatively flimsy Temple of Zoz the Ancestral. Ek intended to inspect this 'skavamareen' at his leisure to see if he could figure out how to make it work. For he strongly suspected that this was the organic rectifier which had been mentioned by the *Injiltaprajuradariski*, several tantalizing fragments of which were now in his possession.

'As for you,' said Nadalastabstala Banraithanchumun Ek, addressing the Empress Justina, 'I will sacrifice you to Zoz the Ancestral. The Festival of Light approaches and we still lack a sacrifice. A volunteer is better, but you'll do.'

'You can't sacrifice me!' said Justina in outrage. 'It wouldn't be legal.'

'It'll be legal enough by the time I've finished with you,' said Ek. 'We'll give it a trial to tidy up the legalisms.'

Ek liked trials. He liked to see people squirm. Besides, he wanted to preserve the life of the Thrug. For a few days, at least. For if he could not divine the secrets of the 'skavamareen' through his own efforts then he would have to torture the Thrug or her companion to remedy this deficiency in his education.

'What about me?' said Olivia.

'We'll put you on trial as well.'

'Isn't there . . . isn't there anything else I could do?' said Olivia.

And the young Ashdan lass tilted her head slightly to one side, softened the outlines of her body, moulded her lips into a banana-tasting pout, and breathed more heavily than before.

All this to some effect.

For Ek hesitated.

He was tempted.

But, in the end, caution bade him answer in the negative. For he possessed a healthy respect for those of Ashdan race, a respect verging on fear.

Fear?

You may think this ridiculous.

For, after all, Olivia was only a girl, regardless of the fact that she liked to think of herself as a woman. Her bones were those of a bird. Yet she was an Ashdan, and those who have remarked that the only safe Ashdan is a dead Ashdan have not committed themselves to such opinion in error.

Master Ek indulged in the first minor pleasure then said:

'There is nothing you can do for me. Unless you care to offer yourself as a sacrifice for the Festival of Light. If such is not your choice, then you go on trial with your Empress.'

'For what?' said Olivia, masking her dismay with defiance.

'There will be, I believe, a great many charges,' said Master Ek. 'For example, offhand I can think of some fifty-seven charges of high treason alone. And—'

Ek elaborated.

But, to his disappointment, neither Justina nor Olivia indulged in any visible squirming.

Never mind.

Their spirits would surely break at some time during the trial.

'We will commit you to trial this very day,' said Ek, eager to begin the process of spirit-breaking.

'Then I demand legal representation,' said Justina. 'For myself and for Olivia here.'

'You will have it,' said Ek. 'Dardanalti is your counsel, is he not? I will send for him.'

Dardanalti was duly sent for, and was on hand to defend the Empress when the trial began.

The trial commenced in the Star Chamber, scene of a great many legal battles. Dardanalti, fearing a swift conclusion and the consequent execution of his client, strove mightily for delay. He was a good lawyer, the most conscientious advocate on Untunchilamon; and, if desperate need arose, he was not even above stooping to unlawyerly violence. He brought all his wit, guile and cunning into play, producing precedents, petitions and complicated motions by the score. He sought to have the trial postponed until three score character witnesses could be obtained from Wen Endex. Then he tried to persuade the court that his client was a victim of insanity.

But all those manoeuvres failed.

As salahanthara exhausted itself and undokondra commenced, the last of Dardanalti's petitions for a delay was dismissed; but, as night had set in, the proceedings were then adjourned until the start of the next daylight.

Justina slept well enough that night, for she had almost been obliterated by the labour of manoeuvring the organic rectifier through the mazeways Downstairs. Olivia, who was younger, and more resilient in body, spent much of the night in sleepless anxiety, worrying both about herself and her dearest Chegory. She even spared a thought for her aunt, the formidable Artemis Ingalawa. Master Ek had said nothing of Ingalawa, so . . . what had happened to her? Was she lost Downstairs? Or dead? Or a prisoner either below ground or above?

Such thoughts kept Olivia awake for long; but at last she too succumbed to oblivion. And when she woke – so stiff and sore from her underground labours that it felt as if all her joints were made out of old cracked leather – it was morning.

The morning of her trial.

Meantime, Pelagius Zozimus was still suffering through the cycle of transformations to which he had been doomed by the Powers of the ill-coordinated Nixorjapretzel Rat. While the metamorphic rate had slowed, Zozimus was still changing, at one time becoming a budgerigar and at another time becoming a kangeroo.

(This 'kangeroo', which may not be familiar to all my readers, is a beast which inhabits the deserts of Parengarenga. It has no feet, yet is mobile to a considerable degree, precipitating itself across the landscape by means of the singularly athletic tail which is its sole means of locomotion. The natives of the place fear it greatly, for it has the habit of kidnapping young children, which it stores in a special pocket built into the fur of its chest. These children it kills and consumes when hunger befalls it; but it keeps the teeth, and there are documented cases of hunters recovering as many as a thousand molars from the corpses of one of these

monsters. It is not known whether Zozimus kidnapped –
or ate – any children while he was briefly incarnated as
such a brute, but he certainly gave one or two night-
walkers an extraordinary fright.)

While Olivia and Justina breakfasted on chunks of
cold cassava, strips of third-grade seaweed and lozenges
of dried jellyfish, the hapless Pelagius Zozimus was
undergoing a particularly unpleasant transformation. As
a result of this, he manifested himself as something
which looked for all the world like a large animated turd.

When one knows of someone suffering grievous
misfortune, one may be tempted to cheer them up by
giving them examples of people who are enduring far
worse. To the man who has no shoes one mentions the
man who has no feet. To the man with no feet one
preaches the noble example of the courageous cripple
making his way through life with both legs amputated
above the knee. A cripple thus disfigured who refuses to
be cheerful will be—

But you know the rest.

(Or, if the rest is unknown, an account of it will be
found in Lady Jade's treatise *On the Consolation of
Cripples, Mutants and Ghosts*.)

Accordingly, had one of the wise had access to the
Empress Justina and Olivia Qasaba in their time of
trials, he might have sought to raise their spirits by
comparing their own misfortunes to those of the unfortunate Pelagius Zozimus. At least Justina and Olivia had
constant possession of their own bodies from one
moment to the next, whereas Zozimus might at any
moment find himself converted to a shoe horn, a starfish
or a cucumber.

(The implication of the above is that the wise are male
in gender. Some of the unwise may object to this; but the
fact is that to be truly wise one must be a philosopher,
ideally a Korugatu philosopher; and, biologically, females of the human species have a capacity for alcohol
which is far less than that possessed by the male, which

means they find themselves handicapped if they try to live the philosophical life to the full. Hence the predominance of the male of the species in the field of wisdom.)

In the absence of any consoling words from the wise, both Justina Thrug and Olivia Qasaba found their spirits considerably depressed that morning; and the arrival of Dardanalti was insufficient to dissipate their mutual gloom.

'Any good news?' said Justina to Dardanalti.

'The rain's stopped.'

'Any bad news, then?'

'Well . . .'

'Out with it!'

Dardanalti confessed. There was bad news. Artemis Ingalawa had been caught at dawn while trying to get to the island of Jod.

'What's happened to her?' said Olivia.

'We don't know,' said Dardanalti.

That was the truth.

But all three shortly found out.

For, when Justina Thrug and Olivia Qasaba were taken to the Star Chamber for the resumption of their trial, Artemis Ingalawa was produced in that place, and was there arraigned alongside Justina and Olivia. The Ashdan algorithmist had acquired a black eye, and her nose was so swollen that Olivia thought it might be broken.

'Did they beat you?' whispered Olivia.

'I,' said Ingalawa, 'gave as good as I got. Don't worry about it.'

Wise counsel, this, for a couple of bruises meant nothing in the context of a disaster so total.

The trial of Justina Thrug *et al*. attracted the attention of everyone of any importance in Injiltaprajura, including Shabble. The lord of light and laughter very much wanted to go and see the trial, but Uckermark vetoed this, saying that it was better that both of them stay away from the pink palace.

'After all,' said Uckermark, 'things are going so well for us it would be a shame to spoil it.'

'How would going to the trial spoil anything?' said Shabble.

'Justina might try to save herself by denouncing you,' said Uckermark.

'For what?' said the innocent Shabble.

'That I know not, but I'm sure she could think of something,' said Uckermark. 'Or she might . . . she might threaten to send you to a . . .'

'She wouldn't!' said Shabble. 'She doesn't know how!'

'She might know how,' said Uckermark. 'You don't want to be made a slave, do you now?'

'No,' said Shabble, conceding the point. 'I don't.'

To preserve Shabble's freedom, it was best for Shabble to stay away from anyone who might know the secret of Shabble-commanding; this secret consisting simply of the knowledge that Shabble can be compelled to obey by a threat of imminent therapy.

Uckermark felt somewhat guilty at keeping Shabble from going to the trial. After all, Shabble could have saved the Empress. Could have burnt up soldiers left, right and centre. Could have incinerated Nadalastabstala Banraithanchumun Ek in the blink of an eye. Could have rescued one and all, restoring liberty to Untunchilamon.

But . . . Shabble was not reliable.

The bouncing bubble had no sense of responsibility whatsoever. Having terrorized Justina's enemies, Shabble might easily have taken it into Shabbleself's head to go on a two-week flying fish hunt; or to fly to Chay for the kite-burning festival; or to go to visit Jal Japone in the wastelands of Zolabrik. All of which would have left Uckermark completely vulnerable to the vengeance of any surviving enemies.

These fears which Uckermark so vigorously entertained were by no means idle, but instead were thoroughly supported by history. In the past, a variety of unprincipled

278

rogues had from time to time tempted, persuaded or commanded Shabble to unlawful actions, but all had met with dreadful fates when Injiltaprajura's miniature sun deserted them out of fecklessness or forgetfulness.

There was also another consideration.

Never in the past had Shabble's powers been tested against the combined strength of the Cabal House. Despite Shabble's many sins and errors, the demon of Jod had never done anything heinous enough to call down the united wrath of Injiltaprajura's wonder-workers upon its sphericity. But if Shabble were to free the Empress and kill her enemies, that might well precipitate a confrontation between the friend of the flying fish and the sorcerers of Untunchilamon; and Uckermark was by no means sure that Shabble would win such a battle.

Right now, Uckermark had a sure thing going, so he was in no mood to chance his life by daring a face-to-face fight-it-out wipe-the-floor-with-the-dead confrontation with Master Ek and Ek's allies. So, while he did feel guilty about it, Uckermark kept the High Priest of the Cult of the Holy Cockroach from attending the trial.

However, most other people of any importance were on their way to the pink palace shortly after dawn. These spectators included the plague inspector, pilot, ladipti man and harbour master, and the representative of the Combined Religious Guild. Consequently, when a vessel sailed into the Laitemata shortly after Justina's trial resumed – this vessel being a newcoming ship of the Trade Fleet – the customary greeting party was not on hand to intercept it.

But Shabble was there.

And so was Uckermark.

For these dignitaries of the Cult of the Holy Cock-roach made a point of boarding each new ship to preach the Doctrines.

In terms of its agreement with Nadalastabstala Ban-raithanchumun Ek, the Cult was currently unable to

279

accept new members. For the moment, the entrance rolls were closed. The Cult was a Closed Congregation. But that might one day change; and, in any case, Shabble liked meeting new people, and Uckermark knew there were often commercial advantages to be won from being first to greet a new ship.

This is how it happened.

The newcoming ship dropped anchor in a harbour otherwise utterly empty of any significant sailpower. The crew lined the decks and gazed with astonishment upon the devastated city, which looked for all the world as if a herd of firedrakes had ravaged it at will.

As the wind had been blowing from the south-west when the mob had indulged itself in a day and a night of looting and arson (a factor which had favoured the survival of Marthandorthan), those ships which had fled the Laitemata had naturally chosen to escape up the eastern side of Untunchilamon; whereas the newcoming ship had been venturing down the western coast. It follows that the strangers had no advance news of Injiltaprajura's disaster.

They therefore greeted the arrival of Shabble's canoe with the greatest of curiosity.

Nobody went shipboard with Shabble but the corpse-master Uckermark. Shabble needed no bodyguards, for sword and crossbow alike were weapons incapable of harming the Holy One. Nor could Shabble be harmed by fire, for the shining one was perfectly capable of staying as cool as ice in a raging furnace. While there were weapons Downstairs which could have injured Shabble most grievously, for practical purposes the master of verbal delights was effectively immortal in the face of any wrath likely to be encountered in the light of the sun.

When the Holy One and his lawyer boarded the ship, the crew crowded around them with a thousand questions. But order was at last restored; the crew fell back; and two foreigners stepped forward to greet their guests.

One of these foreigners was a man in his forties whereas the other was a decade or more younger. It was the older man who spoke first.

'Where is the harbour master?' said he, addressing Uckermark and ignoring Shabble entirely. 'And where the ladipti man?'

'Elsewhere,' said Shabble brightly.

'Where elsewhere?'

'We should be asking the questions,' said Uckermark. 'This is our harbour.'

'And this is my ship! Who are you?'

'I,' said Shabble proudly, 'am the High Priest of the Holy Cockroach.'

The corpse-master Uckermark introduced himself as Shabble's legal counsel, then asked:

'Who are you?'

'I,' said his interlocuter, 'am Manthandros Trasilika. I am the new wazir of Untunchilamon.'

'And I,' said his companion, 'am Jean Froissart.'

'Your resurrection has changed your appearance remarkably,' said Uckermark dryly.

'My what?' said Trasilika in astonishment.

'Your resurrection,' said Uckermark. 'Have you not heard? You've been killed already. Yet you have returned, though in different flesh entirely.'

Both the foreigners were children of Wen Endex.

But in place of the well-muscled heavyweight who had been executed in the Temple of Torture, there was a paunched, obese glutton. And the previous Jean Froissart had been replaced with a square-jawed model of stronger build which had not the weak and watering ever-blinking eyes of the original, but gazed on the world instead with bitter and relentless tension.

'Yes,' squeaked Shabble, 'they've changed a lot. But they'll die the same as the others.'

'I know not what trick of ventriloquism animates the voice of your shining bubble,' said Trasilika, 'but I do know that I am not amused.'

'The bubble is not mine,' said Uckermark. 'I am its. It is the High Priest of the Cult of the Holy Cockroach, as I have said. You would do well to speak of it and to it politely.'

'I'll speak as I like,' said Trasilika wrathfully. 'I am the rightful wazir of Untunchilamon.'

'Oh yes, I'm sure,' said Uckermark. 'The rightful wazir. The last wazir of Bolfrigalaskaptiko, no doubt.'

'Indeed!' said Trasilika.

'Well, so was the last one, or so he said. The last wazir, I mean. He came here using a name identical to your own. A name nice enough, I suppose, but he still lost his head. Have you ever heard of a man called Nadalastabstala Banraithanchumun Ek?'

'Of course,' said Manthandros Trasilika. 'He rules the temple of Zoz the Ancestral on Untunchilamon. He is the High Priest of the Source who will confirm me as wazir.'

And pulled from his pocket a miniature portrait showing a wizened oldster with the strangest eyes of pale orange flecked with green.

'Strange,' said Uckermark. 'The last Manthandros Trasilika had a portrait just like this one.'

'Master Ek is no stranger in Yestron,' said Trasilika. 'Obooloo remembers Ek well.'

'As Obooloo will remember you, too,' said Uckermark. 'In times to come, Obooloo will remember you as another man executed in the presence of Nadalastabstala Banraithanchumun Ek.'

'He threatens us,' said Jean Froissart quietly.

'Because he is a fool,' said Trasilika, unshipping a weapon from its sheath.

'I wouldn't do that if I were you,' said Uckermark calmly.

'But you're not me,' said Trasilika, drawing back the weapon so he could chop off Uckermark's head.

Whereupon Shabble spat white fire which melted the weapon in Trasilika's hand. Splashes of molten metal singed the deck. Trasilika yelped and dropped the hilt of his useless weapon.

'I think,' said Uckermark, 'it might be to your advantage to accompany me ashore.'

'We are your prisoners,' said Froissart, accepting the inevitable.

'No,' said Uckermark. 'You are my guests.'

CHAPTER TWENTY-SEVEN

Manthandros Trasilika and Jean Froissart, believing themselves to be very much Uckermark's prisoners (or, more precisely, captives of the sword-melting Shabble), consented to being conveyed ashore. Whereafter their route took them through the streets of Marthandorthan, which were hot and unbearably humid.

'Drums,' said Trasilika. 'I hear drums. But why? Is there some religion on Untunchilamon which demands this rhythmic celebration?'

'It is a cult,' said Uckermark shortly. 'A cult of the young. Think nothing of it.'

Then Uckermark and Shabble guided the newcomers into the Xtokobrokotok, then down a plungeway leading from that warehouse-temple into the depths Downstairs.

'This is the braloch, I take it,' said Manthandros Trasilika.

'The what?' said Uckermark.

'The braloch,' said Trasilika. 'You know!'

'If I knew,' said Uckermark, 'I wouldn't ask.'

'Has it fallen out of use, then?' said Trasilika.

'We use Downstairs for purposes in multitude,' said Uckermark. 'Ice is mined here and liquor stored against the depredations of the law. Here sewage flows to its private doom, and here too our water is sourced.'

'But not as a braloch?' said Trasilika.

'What means this braloch?' said Uckermark.

'A temple,' said Manthandros Trasilika. 'My ethnology texts make heavy mention of it. They say the Dagrin come here to temple in the dark. Zen, they say. The Dagrin use it. A drug. You must know of zen, surely. But what of the Dagrin? Have you not heard of them?'

'On Untunchilamon,' said Uckermark shortly, 'we do not talk of the Dagrin. No, not that way. Up here. These steps.'

'You don't talk of the Dagrin?' said Trasilika. 'But why not? My texts, they—'

But Uckermark was climbing the steps so swiftly that, following him, Trasilika found himself too short of breath for lectures. The stairway debouched into a tunnel where black grass flattened itself shortly underfoot then rose in silence after the three men had passed. The light was first green and then red. Shabble sang a happy song and played at being an anti-chameleon, challenging green light with yellow and red with white.

'Where are we going?' said Froissart.

'Elsewhere,' said Uckermark.

And refused to explain further as he guided his guests through long and arduous subterranean walkways. Black grass gave way to a strangely spongy green felt, then to a silvery metal laced with streaks of red and gold. By which time Froissart had started to feel himself trapped in an inexplicable doom lifted straight out of nightmare.

Jean Froissart had feared much; but he had never expected to be confronted by a miniature sun which could melt forged steel as fire melts ice; or to go meekly from his ship in the company of a complete stranger to meet an unknown ruin in depths of strangeness.

Giving way to nostalgia, he remembered the sewage canals of the city of Bolfrigalaskaptiko, that mighty stiltland metropolis which lies on the River Ka just upstream from the great lagoon of Manamalargo. He felt an unexpected pang of homesickness for that miasmal city of floating corpses; for the mosquitos which drench the air like a black fog; for the wail of the water seller and the cry of the professional child beater; for the smells of the crocodile market where flies blacken exposed meat and first-class knobbed leather sells for no more than fifty damns the fangle. -

Froissart recalled his last night in Bolfrigalaskaptiko.

He had dined upon tolfrigdalakaptiko, that delectable dish of fried seagull livers anointed with basilisk gall and served with baked yams and lozenges of dried jellyfish. Then he had taken himself off to the House of Priestly Pleasures, there to enjoy a full seven of the Fifty Open Delights before retiring to his hammock.

He had slept restlessly that night. The mosquito fire had been over-oiled; furthermore, one of his fits of angst had been upon him. The next day, he had at last visited a heart specialist, a doctor of the Ola caste; and, with fears about his fitness somewhat eased, had then joined Manthandros Trasilika aboard the ship which was to—

'—hear what I was saying?'

'Pardon?' said Froissart.

As he spoke, he committed himself to another step. But the much-scarred corpse-master flung out a brawny arm. That meaty weapon thumped into Froissart's gut with such emphasis that a spasm of nausea momentarily discomforted the young priest. Yielding to the arm's compulsion, he stepped backwards.

'If you don't listen,' said Uckermark, 'you put us all in danger. This is not the safest of places.'

'I'm sorry,' said Froissart; though in truth he felt he owed no such duty of apology to his kidnapper. 'I was dragon-chasing.'

The idiom he used may not be universally familiar. Therefore, let it be known that, when Jean Froissart declared himself a chaser of dragons, he meant that he had been feeding on rainbow and fishing for clouds; that his feet had been chancing as wings and his fingers as fins; that he had swum in the desert as the dolphin's escort and danced upon fire with a statue of ice.

Uckermark, who understood his mode of expression perfectly, warned him thus:

'Less salt and more flour lest your ginger curdle.'

Jean Froissart, who was of course familiar with this classical admonition, accepted the rebuke, and said, as a child says:

'I have ears.'

'Good,' said Uckermark. 'What I said, when you were away dancing your phoenix and tickling your basilisk, was that you must watch your footing. Here the floor has certan studs, like this one.'

So saying, Uckermark pointed to a red, slightly raised, coruscating button on the floor. The floor itself was now a slightly convex stretch of what looked like sea-blue stone.

'If you step on that, or anything like it,' said the corpse-master, 'we'll vanish from sight, as others before us have.'

'Vanish?' said Froissart in bewilderment. 'To what? To where?'

'To the afterworld, for all I know,' said Uckermark.

Manthandros Trasilika coughed, hawked, spat. His phlegm splattered against the floor. Hissed. And was gone.

'Don't touch the floor, either,' said Uckermark, as an afterthought. Then: 'Make your choices. If you want to die, run on ahead of us and die in your own time. There's plenty of death in a place like this. I won't grudge you your share if it's what you really want.'

Uckermark spoke the truth. This was indeed a hazardous realm. While most of the mazeways Downstairs were innocuous, their greatest dangers being vampire rats or disorientation, Uckermark was daring his guests through a frequently fatal part of the labyrinth.

Jean Froissart, having decided that Uckermark's warning was sincere, started paying more attention to where he was going and where he was placing his feet. Though he was half-certain that this netherworld would claim his bones whatever he did. Half-certain? He grew a full three-quarters-certain when a huge and angry monster started roaring in the distance.

Uckermark halted abruptly. Froissart and Trasilika did likewise.

'What is it?' said Froissart anxiously, meaning the roaring thing.

'I'm not sure,' said Uckermark truthfully.

'Don't worry,' said Shabble gaily. 'It's only a dorgi.'

'What's that?' said Froissart.

'A killer of men,' said Shabble.

'And you tell us not to worry,' said Trasilika.

'I was telling myself not to worry,' said Shabble. 'It eats only men, not shabbles.'

Then Shabble sniggered.

In truth, Shabble feared dorgis greatly; but the bubble of light guessed the revenant from the Golden Gulag to be fully occupied by the delights of hunting refugees.

'What's it saying?' said Uckermark.

'It's saying it's angry, that's all,' said Shabble.

This was a guess, for the dorgi's uproar was so distorted by echoes that its clamour was completely unintelligible.

'Here,' said Uckermark. 'This way.'

And he led them up more stairs.

'The pink palace,' said Manthandros Trasilika. 'That's where we're going, isn't it?'

'Guess again,' said Uckermark.

'We're going up, at any rate,' said Trasilika. 'Up towards Pokra Ridge.'

'And we're near the surface,' said Froissart.

'You think,' said Uckermark.

'I'm sure,' said Froissart. 'I can smell sewage. It flows no depth at all into the underworld, or so say my guidebooks.'

'Trust less to books,' said Uckermark. Then: 'Stop.'

They halted.

'Shabble,' said the corpse-master. 'Take a look ahead.'

The imitator of suns emitted a low hum, spun thrice, then floated round the corner up ahead.

The humans waited.

For some considerable time.

Froissart took stock. The floor underfoot was a fine-meshed brown. He scuffed at it with his boots. It distorted, then reformed itself as before. Strange. Overhead, a dull grey ceiling of puddled roughwork plaster, or something which looked strangely like it. The walls were a sunset orange mottled with growths which looked like lichens and slit with jagged cracks like the crazed knifework of a manic murderer. From those wounds there slowly oozed gross globs of green and grey.

As Froissart speculated on the nature of that flux, he laid two fingers alongside his windpipe. Felt the skin hot, sweaty. Pushed in. Felt his pulse heavy-thumping. Slow, slow. Slow again. A pause. Lengthening. Had his heart stopped? No, for there it was again.

Slow-thump, slow-thump . . . pause . . . slow-thump.

He lived.

For the moment.

And that slow and steady rhythm spoke of strength and health, did it not? For he had paced long through the underworld, ascending stairs and up-tilted tunnels; yet his heart spoke more of sedentary peace. But then, that organ had been allowed plenty of recovery time by now, for the free-floating sun which was exploring ahead had been gone for an unconscionable time.

Froissart reached out and touched the slow outbirth of strangeness, finding the globs of green and grey to be gelid and slightly tacky. He brought his fingers to his nose. Smelt no odour. If the oozing stuff had a scent, it was not strong enough to defeat that of sewage.

At last, the floating bubble returned.

'It's all right,' said Shabble. 'The pergot's elsewhere.'

'Pergot?' said Trasilika. 'What's a pergot?'

'A thing which drinks blood,' said Uckermark.

'It would seem you risk much to bring us this way,' said Froissart, wondering at Uckermark's motives.

'Much I may dare when Shabble is with me,' said Uckermark. 'Otherwise, there's many tunnels down here that I'd not chance on my own.'

289

As for Uckermark's motives, these were scarcely mysterious. The advent of a new wazir (or someone claiming to be a wazir) was sure to change the history of Untunchilamon. Given first access to such a dignitary, Justina Thrug and her minions could alter events in their own favour. And Uckermark, while his future was bound to that of the Cult of the Holy Cockroach, was nevertheless prepared to grant Justina her chance on account of certain residual loyalties and acknowledged debts.

Besides which, Uckermark both feared and disliked Master Ek. It was Nadalastabstala Banraithanchumun Ek who had granted the Cockroach Cult its present status as a Protected Religion. As legal counsel for the High Priest of a religion of such status, Uckermark was safe from the wrath of Aldarch Three. However, what Master Ek had given he could take away; and Uckermark grimly suspected that any absolute triumph for Master Ek might lead that dignitary to take freely and without hesitation.

Thus Uckermark sought to prolong the life and liberties of the Empress Justina for at least a little longer; for, in his present role as Shabble's advocate, the corpse-master was doing very nicely for himself, a full three per cent of all Shabble's monies finding their way into Uckermark's pockets.

As Uckermark and his guests continued on their way, the bright-bobbing Shabble, confident that they were past those dangers which truly demanded vigilance, began to indulge Shabbleself in the preaching of holy doctrine.

'Worship the cockroach,' said Shabble, 'and you will be reborn as cockroach. Such is the bliss! Never to know hunger, never to pay rent, never to endure the multitudinous pangs and pains of the human form. Holy is the cockroach and hallowed is His name. Happy is the cockroach and happy are we who will become cockroach.'

All this said Shabble, and more; but the newcomers had yet to be converted to the Cult by the time they reached the Moremo Maximum Security Prison, where guards intercepted them as they ascended from the lower dungeons. Uckermark knew these warders, and held them to silence with a gesture; seeing that Shabble was with him, they obeyed without question, falling in behind the corpse-master as an honour guard.

As Uckermark led the way onward and upward, Manthandros Trasilika asked no questions, thinking that what was left of his dignity would best be preserved by a decorous silence. But his priest was not so continent.

'Where are we now?' said Jean Froissart, catching a glimpse of a moody sky through a slit window.

'In prison,' said Uckermark. 'Moremo Maximum Security Prison.'

'I have to go now,' said Shabble, who had spied that same window.

'Go?' said Uckermark. 'Where?'

'We're sacrificing,' said Shabble in great excitement. 'Had you forgotten? We're sacrificing a Sacred Moth to the Holy Cockroach. Today. Remember?'

'Oh,' said Uckermark. 'I remember. Off you go then.'

Whereupon Shabble, imitating a teenage cultist, drum-rumbled thrice then slipped out into the open air.

Uckermark was disappointed to see the imitator of suns flirt away through the window, for there were responsibilities (the carriage of messages and such) which he would liked to have placed upon that jaunting bubble. But the corpse-master knew he would lose Shabble's services entirely if he tried to compel the eternal child with disciplines alien to its nature. Shabble would do much if persuaded that the doing was fun. But, as Ivan Pokrov had ultimately discovered, Shabble was not prepared to be a slave.

'You mean to hold us here as prisoners?' said Froissart, once Shabble had departed.

'No,' said Uckermark. 'Merely to provide you with . . . with private conference facilities.'

And he refused to say more until he had introduced his guests to Bro Drumel. This most anxious of warriors, the semi-suicidal career soldier whom Nixorjapretzel Rat had earlier tried to blackmail, still had control of Moremo, for Master Ek had not yet seen fit to remove him from the post of Governor. Indeed, why should Ek interfere? The management of a squabbling brood of prisoners meant nothing to him; and, if Drumel was ultimately to be judged as a traitor, there would be plenty enough time later for his arrest, trial and execution.

Despite his many worries, Bro Drumel laughed out loud when Manthandros Trasilika declared himself warrior. That disconcerted Jean Froissart more than anything else which had happened to date.

'So,' said Drumel, when he had recovered himself. 'You are wazir, are you? What next, then? Mutilator of Yestron?'

'Humour ill becomes either you or the occasion,' said Trasilika, who was very close to losing his temper. 'Aldarch the Third has pulled fingernails for less.'

'Perhaps,' said Bro Drumel, sobering somewhat. 'But we have killed one Manthandros Trasilika already, and one Jean Froissart. If there is a penalty for killing members of such breeds, then we are damned already. And if we kill them not – why, then our island risks overpopulation. For—'

That did it.

Manthandros Trasilika lost his temper.

An impressive sight he made in his rage; and many were the spectres of doom which he invoked as he cursed Bro Drumel. All to virtually nil effect. For Drumel was convinced that this Trasilika was as much of an imposter as the first.

'Very well,' said Uckermark, once Trasilika had said his piece. 'Now we know who he is, or who he pretends to be. Where can we stash him for the moment?'

'It'll have to be in my personal quarters,' said Bro Drumel. 'Unless you want him clamped in fetters below.'

Uckermark thought about it.

'Your quarters,' said he at last. 'At least for the moment.'

Bro Drumel rang for guards and had the two children of Wen Endex taken away.

'Well,' said Drumel, when that had been done. 'What do you want to do with them? Sell them to Master Ek as sacrifices? Or what?'

'I thought we could use them,' said Uckermark.

'Use them! They're patent frauds.'

'That may be so,' said Uckermark. 'But let's see what Dardanalti has to say before we write them off entirely.'

After some persuading, Bro Drumel sent word to the pink palace: a message to tell Dardanalti he was wanted in Moremo. Then, Uckermark joined the new Manthandros Trasilika and the new Jean Froissart in Drumel's quarters.

Uckermark, a veteran of many long sea journeys himself, had the wit to have fresh food served to those quarters simultaneously with his own arrival, a move calculated to soften the temper of the obstreperous Trasilika.

'Well,' said Trasilika, when Uckermark entered his presence, 'what now?'

'We wait,' said Uckermark.

'For what?'

'I've sent for someone.'

'Who?'

Uckermark merely smiled.

'Are you a torturer?' said Froissart, studying Uckermark's scars and tattoos.

'I've introduced myself already,' said Uckermark. 'I'm a lawyer. Legal counsel for the Cult of the Holy Cockroach. Come. Will you not eat?'

Uckermark's guests succumbed to temptation and proceeded to glut themselves. After so many days of shipboard privation, a banana itself was an instrument of delight. Thus it happened that both Froissart and Trasilika were in a much better temper when Dardanalti arrived.

'This,' said Uckermark, 'is a man well worth talking to.'

'You do the talking,' said Trasilika to Froissart. 'I've no patience for argument.'

As has been earlier remarked, Dardanalti was a dapper individual remarkable for looking crisp and fresh at all times, a truly remarkable achievement in the wilting climate of Untunchilamon. Dardanalti's appearance made Trasilika acutely conscious of his own over-fleshed, sweat-saturated body; and of his fatigue, which owed as much to unacknowledged fear as it did to the long trek underground.

Froissart resented Trasilika's abandonment of responsibility; and, opening the negotiations with less formality than politeness strictly required, said (in Toxteth):

'Hi.'

'Are you addressing my presence?' said Dardanalti.

To understand the scorn of these words, you must understand that they were phrased in Janjuladoola; and, furthermore, that Dardanalti took advantage of the social nuances of that tongue by adopting the forms that one of highest class or caste uses when speaking to an underman.

'We crave acknowledgement,' said Froissart, switching to Janjuladoola.

'Speak,' said Dardanalti. 'Tell me your excuses.'

This formal phrase, often heard in the courts of Obooloo, invites a guilty person to confess all.

'We have no excuses to make,' said Froissart, thus declaring his conscience to be clear. 'We come to these shores on legitimate business. Aldarch the Third has charged us with the responsibility of proclaiming his rule in Injiltaprajura.'

'Your pretensions ill become you,' said Dardanalti. 'We have executed one false wazir and priest already. The destruction of another such pair will be but the work of a moment.'

'We . . . we are not . . . we . . . I'm telling you the truth,' said Froissart. 'Aldarch Three really did make us wazir and priest. We have, we have warrants.'

'Such had the last false wazir,' said Dardanalti. 'We of Injiltaprajura are not strangers to the arts of forgery. No piece of parchment can give a fraud the rule of Untunchilamon, for we trust not to parchment alone. Rather, we rely on logic, precedent and interrogation.'

'Interrogate, then!' said Manthandros Trasilika, unable to restrain himself any longer. 'We've a shipload of sailors who will swear to the truth of our tale.'

'Once Master Ek has disembowelled a couple, the rest may begin to sing a different story,' said Dardanalti. 'Your claims are ridiculous. Aldarch Three would never make a wazir of a child of Wen Endex. He hates all but those of the Skin.'

'You don't understand,' said Froissart.

'What did you say?' said Dardanalti.

There was death in his voice. He was of Janjuladoola race: and no child of Wen Endex may safely insult one of such genesis.

'My lord,' said Froissart, realizing his error. 'The ancestors of my ancestors were slaves of your forebears, and I, a slave, grovel at your feet in suppliant apology.'

'Truly your tongue is as honey,' said Dardanalti. 'But, were I Nadalastabstala Banraithanchumun Ek, you would no longer have a tongue at all.'

'I spoke in haste,' said Froissart.

'But,' said Dardanalti, 'perhaps in truth. It would seem you claim for me a lack of comprehension. What, pray tell, is the aspect of reality which escapes my grasp?'

'My lord of lords,' said Froissart, 'I meant merely—'

'Explain,' said Dardanalti, chopping abruptly from Janjuladoola to Toxteth.

Froissart followed the implications of the language shift. Dardanalti was done with playing at being a Janjuladoola aristocrat in the presence of his racial inferiors. Now he wanted to get down to business.

'Manpower,' said Froissart, speaking with greater confidence as the empowering simplicities of Toxteth came to his assistance. 'Al'three has lately been seeking outside the ranks of the Janjuladoola for officers of all descriptions. Talonsklavara has seen such a great slaughter among those of the Skin that other breeds must be employed.'

'As slaves,' said Dardanalti.

'Talent has no immunity to a scimitar's blade,' said Froissart. 'Those of the Skin can no longer supply an entire empire's need for talent. Hence Al'three has turned elsewhere. Not for help with the governance of Ang, of course; but for the rule of cities such as Bolfrigalaskaptiko, and the rule of outlands such as Untunchilamon.'

Dardanalti considered this.

'You sound as if you expect me to be convinced,' said the Janjuladoola lawyer. 'But I am not. You suggest major changes in the practices to which Al'three has been devoted. Whatever the truth, Untunchilamon knows nothing of such changes. Friend Uckermark! I wish to speak to you privily. Come, let us withdraw.'

Then Dardanalti and Uckermark left the newcomers alone.

Once the Janjuladoola lawyer and the fire-scarred corpse-master had secured their privacy, Dardanalti said:

'We'll let them sweat for a while.'

'Do you believe them?' said Uckermark.

'No,' said Dardanalti, speaking frankly. 'But, even so,

they may have potential. If we can make the world believe them to be genuine.'

'Difficult, difficult,' said Uckermark. 'Particularly when they're such patent frauds. However . . .'

The corpse-master had an idea.

Back in Bro Drumel's quarters, Manthandros Trasilika said to Jean Froissart:

'Well. What do you think our interrogators are talking about?'

'Nothing,' said Froissart. 'I think they've left us here to have discourse with our fear and panic.'

'Then their ends are being fulfilled,' said Trasilika. 'I don't like this at all. I don't think they believe us.'

'I'm sure they don't,' said Froissart.

'But it's true!' said Trasilika.

It was, too.

Manthandros Trasilika and Jean Froissart had been associated with Aldarch the Third, the dreaded Mutilator of Yestron, thoughout the seven years of Talonsklavara. First they had supplied the Aldarch armies with weaponry, mostly cheap-shatter swords from the Collosnon Empire. Later, after proving themselves as spies, they had helped organize an intelligence service to supply the Mutilator with hard data on his enemies.

At last, Aldarch III had shown his gratitude by making Manthandros Trasilika the wazir of Bolfrigalaskaptiko (albeit briefly) and by then dispatching him to Untunchilamon with Jean Froissart as his priest.

'What now, then?' said Trasilika.

'Sleep,' answered Froissart simply.

'Most excellent of counsels!' said Trasilika.

And the two men laid themselves down on Bro Drumel's couches to rest, conserving their energies for whatever challenges their captors might next confront them with.

Both children of Wen Endex were sound asleep when Dardanalti and Uckermark returned in the company of a figure both cowled and masked.

'May we know your name?' said Froissart to the personage thus so strangely garbed.

'This man is for the moment but an observer,' said Dardanalti. 'He comes from Justina's household. Apart from that, his name and genesis do not concern you.'

'Then why is he here?' said Froissart.

'Because he has a certain expertise in the conduct of trials by ordeal,' said Dardanalti.

'What?!' said Froissart. 'You don't mean—'

'You heard me,' said Dardanalti remorselessly. 'You know yourself thought a fraud. There is only this single way for you to prove yourself.'

'What way?' said Manthandros Trasilika in some bewilderment.

'He knows,' said Dardanalti, nodding at Froissart.

'Tell,' said Trasilika curtly.

'There is one way for you to prove yourself,' said Dardanalti, addressing himself to Froissart.

Who did not answer.

'How?' said Manthandros Trasilika.

'If your priest will undergo trial by ordeal to prove himself true,' said Dardanalti, 'then his survival of such trial must necessarily prove the truth of his words.'

'I have documents to prove my case,' said Froissart desperately. 'I'm a priest of Zoz. Five years ago I converted.'

'We've been through all that,' said Dardanalti, with a trace of weariness. 'The last wazir and priest also had documents. Perfect documents. They died.'

'We can prove who they were,' said Froissart. 'Associates of ours, that's who they were. I can guess their, their names. They must've been—'

'Names from your past mean nothing to our future,' said Dardanalti. 'What matters is that you are outwardly no different to those we executed.'

'No different,' said Froissart.

'Those we slaughtered were children of Wen Endex unknown to any in Untunchilamon,' said Dardanalti.

'You are the same. They had documents, and you—'

'All right,' said Trasilika. 'If a trial by ordeal—'

'No!' said Froissart. 'No ordeal!'

'But you are a priest,' said Dardanalti. 'Is not the ordeal the classic way for a priest of Zoz to prove himself true?'

'Yes,' said Froissart. 'But, but—'

Uckermark laughed.

'Come,' said the corpse-master. 'We've played with our guest for long enough. Let's settle to business.'

Then Uckermark took it upon himself to explain what was truly proposed. The Empress Justina would make available resources (and Uckermark elaborated the nature of those resources) which would make it possible for Jean Froissart to come through a trial by ordeal unscathed. By surviving such a trial, Froissart would prove himself a true priest of Zoz, thus escaping the execution which would befall him were he to be thought false.

'All we ask in return,' said Uckermark, 'is that you pardon the Empress Justina and those arraigned alongside her.'

Then he explained the imperial predicament.

At last, Froissart said:

'We would like to agree with this proposal, but Aldarch the Third gave us explicit orders. The witch must die.'

'Then,' said Dardanalti, 'you will most certainly die with her.'

At which point Manthandros Trasilika intervened. He wiped the sweat from his fleshy face, leaned forward and said:

'Enough bickering. We agree.'

'We agree?' said Froissart, startled.

'We do indeed,' said Trasilika.

'But,' objected Froissart, 'it would seem to me the risks of this enterprise are all mine.'

'No,' said Trasilika. 'For if you fail your trial by ordeal

then I must surely die with you. Very well. We have agreed. Now: how do I best announce myself as the incoming wazir?'

'First,' said Dardanalti, 'I will send for the harbour master, that he may greet you as is his right and duty. The pilot, too, for there is a fee you owe him. Nor may you escape the importuning of the ladipti man, for his charge is certain though his function is but mystical at best.'

So spoke Dardanalti; then he dispatched messengers to summon those vital personages to the stronghold of Moremo.

Thus the political struggle for control of Injiltaprajura and the island of Untunchilamon entered its most delicate and most interesting phase, with the salvation of many lives depending on the outcome of the strategies of deceit masterminded by the corpse-master Uckermark.

CHAPTER TWENTY-EIGHT

Nadalastabstala Banraithanchumun Ek, High Priest of Zoz the Ancestral for the island of Untunchilamon, was not exactly enraptured by the arrival of another pair of uitlanders claiming to be wazir and priest. However, Ek concealed his anger, for he was smooth; and subtle; and all the more dangerous for that. Master Ek was as smooth as the Coral Current which flows through the Green Sea, and as subtle as the sharkskinned death which swims in those waters, and as lethal to the unwary as that fearsome combination of shallows and sharks is to the inept pilot.

As Manthandros Trasilika declared that his priest would prove himself true by submitting to trial by ordeal, Ek had to accept Trasilika as wazir – at least on a provisional basis. Though Ek was inclined to think this new Trasilika and his Froissart to be as fraudulent as the first, he was secretly impressed by their audacity. Froissart would dare the ordeal of iron? The man must be mad. Or truly sure of his faith. For, to the best of Master Ek's knowledge, no priest of Zoz had proved himself by this test for at least four hundred years.

Thus Nadalastabstala Banraithanchumun Ek acknowledged Manthandros Trasilika as wazir, and (on a provisional basis) consecrated him as such. This did not stop Master Ek from protesting vehemently when Manthandros Trasilika commanded the release of Justina Thrug and those arraigned alongside her: but he had very little say in the matter.

Very little?

None!

To ease his frustration, Master Ek withdrew to the

sanctuary of the Temple of Torture, there to practise the rhetoric of steel upon a vampire rat. While Ek sought such solace, news of the arrival of a new wazir spread through Injiltaprajura. Till then, the new-coming ship had remained a mystery; for its crew had remained continent in the absence of Froissart and Trasilika, refusing to reveal the bark's business. Now all was revealed.

As the new wazir had been shocked to learn that he had earlier been executed, so Injiltaprajura was startled by the sudden resurrection of a name which they had thought consigned for ever to history's list of losers. The arrival of Manthandros Trasilika took them unawares, like the shock of a monolithic sky-stone plunging into their lives from out of a clear blue sky.

It is unfortunate that the arrival of a political crisis is seldom accompanied by Signs or by Portents that would warn the populace of what has befallen them. Fire signals itself with uprising smoke; and earthquake by a general destabilizing of the earth; and tsunami by the immediate overturning of ship and shore alike. But citizens are not so easily alerted to climactic conflicts in the body politic; so that some continued in ignorance of the changes long after they had taken place.

As Nadalastabstala Banraithanchumun Ek tutored a vampire rat in the ways of pain, ice miners still worked Downstairs in total ignorance of the latest twist to the ongoing political crisis. Ox No Zan, a timorous student of Janjuladoola breed, lay in an opium stupor following yet another visit to Doctor Death, this time for the extraction of an impacted wisdom tooth. And many others were similarly afflicted by ignorance.

How multitudinous is humanity!

To pretend to give a full accounting of the complexities of Injiltaprajura would be fraudulent, for a thousand volumes could not contain one part in a thousandth of the intricate life of that metropolis. But we can flirt with the notion of such an accounting, touching on the life of Injiltaprajura here and there, much as if we were to sample a few grains of sand from a beach in an effort to assess the variety of the whole, each grain being unique in its own configuration even if on those rare occasions when the whole beach derives from rock of the same parental stock.

Let us sample, then.

Thus:

A woman in the second day of labour. Her knowledge, interest, delight and concern in, with and of politics is precisely zero.

Two children picking their way over a landscape of outrage, shuffling through the ashes of their family home in search for the bones of their mother and father, flame-victims consumed by the fires of wrath which have so lately devastated the city.

A cat with a burnt tail investigating the cindered ashes of a moribund pharmacy. An athletic ephebe mourning a pederast's passing. A finagling heiress contemplating matricide. A jeweller experimenting with a miraculous optical device lately dredged from the sea, a device with which he can see the bones in his own hand.

Look elsewhere.

Here a goat, raising a bleating cry just before its slaughter befalls it. A cat, preening and priding. A schoolmaster, slowly dying of cancer, lecturing bored children on the evils of ignorance, cruelty and perversity. Slanic Moldova, temporarily living in Moremo, starting work on a baroque mural in which an insurmountable mountain of bones rises from zombie shadows.

An astrologer delves amidst the quirks and weaknesses of a fearful member of his clientele, someone seeking the psychic equivalent of soothing drugs and charmed potions.

Shall we look elsewhere yet again?

In one of the coolhouses of Injiltaprajura's desert side in which market gardeners grow cold climate vegetables, an apprentice idles away his master's time by beating on a drum. He is supposed to be boyhandling blocks of ice imported from Downstairs, but the drum has him in its thrall, and he makes no movement but for the pat – pat – slap of his hands. In a house not far away, the boy's master makes experiments with melting ice, thinking to make a device to measure the day into fractions in accordance with how long a block of standard size takes to melt.

Back on port side, a marriage proceeds in the Xtokobrokotok, where Shabble is presiding over the grand nuptial ceremonies of a Janjuladoola couple. Already these two are dreaming of sweet and pungent sources of organic pleasure, of a carnal embrace which combines the flesh of the visible world with the spirit of worlds unseen . . .

And, not very far from Marthandorthan, amidst the ruins of the Dromdanjerie, a solitary lunatic dances to the tune of instruments unheard by other ears. Living a life scored by heavenly music, this mystical corybant pays no heed to anything as mundane as politics, as the lovers and ice miners and beggars and apprentice boys pay no heed.

This is how it is, how it was, back in the days of the testing of courage, back in the distant past when your historian could see all colours sharp and bright, and did not yet have arthritis.

In some places it was rumoured that the new Manthandros Trasilika was not a wazir sent from overseas at all; rather, that he was a psychopathic maniac long confined in the Dromdanjerie, and who, having escaped from that now burnt-down bedlam had taken it into his head to gamble all in the company of a fellow maniac. A full half-dozen informants took that story to Injiltaprajura's secret police, only to be sent away with kicks and curses. The secret police had gone on strike because, as a consequence of the rapid deterioration of the machinery of government, they were no longer getting paid.

In his mansion on Hojo Street, a very uptight

Aquitaine Varazchavardan received the news of the advent of a new Trasilika and a new Froissart with a combination of exhaustion and panic. He did not think he could sustain many more shocks to flesh and psyche. The recent rapid gyrations in the political order had dismayed him mightily. Varazchavardan was one of those people who longs for order. He desired to make his intelligence subservient to a mighty Power, to be regimented and controlled, to find safety through obedience to the ruling order.

But, increasingly, Injiltaprajura offered no stable order to be obeyed.

If only Hostaja Sken-Pitilkin would finish his airship, and quickly! Then Varazchavardan could get the hell out of Injiltaprajura. Unless he made such an escape, and soon, surely he would die in the next riot; or be executed by Master Ek on some half-lawful pretext; or be chopped to bits by one wazir or another on account of his past association with Justina Thrug; or be mugged and murdered on the increasingly lawless streets.

Such was Varazchavardan's plight.

And what of Sken-Pitilkin? Why, he was still working for no more than half a day at a time. And his progress was no faster, even though he had an assistant. Nixorja-pretzel Rat was that assistant.

After converting Pelagius Zozimus to a fast-changing serial life-form, young Rat had almost been killed by a wrathful Log Jaris. Rat had escaped from the bullman, though only with difficulty; and had eventually taken refuge in the Cabal House. But the wonder-workers of the Cabal House, wishing to keep tabs on Sken-Pitilkin's airship rebuilding programme, had ordered Rat to make his peace with the bullman Log Jaris by way of humble apology, to return to the pink palace, and to place himself at Sken-Pitilkin's service.

All this Rat had done, albeit reluctantly.

Since Hostaja Sken-Pitilkin had (unlike his cousin Zozimus) some considerable capacity for suffering fools with equanimity, he had accepted Jan Rat into his service. But, unfortunately, the job of ship-building was not within the Rat's abilities.

Rat was designed by nature to be a fool; but, as he had never enjoyed the counsel of a properly qualified careers adviser, he had so far failed to achieve this. It had never occurred to him that he would never, never realize his grand ambitions – which were to become the most powerful sorcerer on Untunchilamon and the head of the wonder-workers' Cabal House. But he was well aware – he had never for a moment presumed otherwise – that he was remarkably ill-equipped to be a builder of airships.

Nixorjapretzel Rat was incontrovertibly clumsy. As his hands stuttered over sticks, bungled knots and splintered themselves on baulks of wood, the young sorcerer thought with envy of Chegory Guy's well-knit body. While Rat was as much a racist as any other person of Janjuladoola breed, he nevertheless wished he had that Ebrell Islander's physique, if not his other characteristics.

But Rat's envy was misplaced.

Certainly Chegory Guy had the physique of a sledge-hammer matched with a knifefighter's grace. But, at that very moment, the redskinned Ebrell Islander was a prisoner of the therapist. Had the Rat known that, and had the Rat appreciated the ramifications of Chegory's plight, then he would have envied him not at all.

A more fitting subject for envy was Theodora, Justina's twin sister, who had got safely away on Troldot Turbothot's ship. Theodora was presently closeted with her gynaecologist in the ship's Great Cabin.

'What have you been doing to yourself?' said the gynaecologist.

Theodora told him.

'That's what I thought,' he said. 'You mustn't do it any more.'

'But I like it!' said Theodora.

306

Then began to explain why.

But such explanation, and the other details of Theodora's medical consultation, have no bearing on our history, and therefore will not be recounted here. Let it merely be noted that there was no hope of help coming to Justina from her twin sister, for Theodora and her lover were intent only on maximizing their own pleasure and widening the distance between themselves and Injiltaprajura.

CHAPTER TWENTY-NINE

For Justina Thrug, Artemis Ingalawa and Olivia Qasaba, it was all very strange. First Dardanalti made inscrutable lawyerly excuses and withdrew from the Star Chamber, leaving his apprentice to continue the defence. (Such continuation, involving as it did nothing more than occasionally calling out 'Objection!', did not tax the apprentice's abilities unduly.)

Then, later, there was a series of defections from the courtroom audience; until finally Nadalastabstala Banraithanchumun Ek, a patient spectator throughout the proceedings, was called away by one of his aides. After that, Dardanalti reappeared and craved leave to approach the bench. Such leave being granted to him, Dardanalti spoke quietly with Judge Qil, who then announced a recess.

Which left Justina, Ingalawa and Olivia sitting on a hardwood bench in the quiet of the Star Chamber. They could hear, in the distance, lamentations from one of the temples of Hojo Street where mourners were lamenting the demise of some of the victims of Injiltaprajura's disastrous fire. Then someone began drumming:

Thup – thup – top!
Thup – thup – top . . .

Guards intervened, and there was a brief flurry of excitement as a youthful drummer was discovered, searched, bloodied then ejected from the court.

But, after that, stasis set in.

As the recess dragged on, some people began to drift away, quitting the pink palace for streets where the smell of ash still had dominance. The diminished audience that remained evinced no enthusiasm for the resumption of the proceedings. Some drew lime leaf and fresh betel nut from intricate silver containers and began to chew, taking advantage of Judge Qil's absence. (For some reason – the onset of senility, perhaps? – that judge had lately developed a prejudice against people chewing and spitting in his court.) Others gnawed on sugarcane or cleansed their tongues with pandanus.

Then Dardanalti returned to the Star Chamber.

Judge Qil did not.

'We have it,' said Dardanalti, with a smile savage in its triumph.

'Have what?' said Justina.

'This!' said Dardanalti, waving a parchment. 'Your pardon.'

'My – my—'

'Pardon, yes. It covers the Qasaba girl, too.'

'Me?' said Olivia.

'You,' said Dardanalti.

'And me?' said Ingalawa sharply.

'But of course,' said Dardanalti.

Then he smiled again, and waited for acclamation.

Instead:

'I'm thirsty,' said Justina.

She was, too. Her relief of her bladder had lately been at the pleasure of her guards; and, bitterly resenting such humiliation, she had chosen dehydration as the most honourable course. Hence she lacked the energy for jubilation.

'Are we – are we really free?' said Olivia.

'You are,' said Dardanalti.

Whereupon Olivia began to weep. Throughout her trial she had been a brave Ashdan, confronting her death with a pose which mimicked equanimity. But now, released from the responsibility of denying her captors, she was but a slip of a girl, exhausted by worry and fear.

Artemis Ingalawa did not chide her niece, but comforted her as she collapsed in grief. Ingalawa could have done with some comforting herself, for she was over-tired, exhausted by the ordeal of long wanderings Downstairs followed by abrupt arrest, brusque imprisonment and the onset of an unpleasant trial. Ingalawa had long thought of Untunchilamon as her true home, but now she wished she could be gone, back to the forests of Ashmolea, land of limestone and cultivated sophistication.

The Empress Justina also wished to be gone. To Wen Endex, land of tumbling waterfalls and swampland rivers, of dunes where the seastorm spume writhes in mists on the wintry wind, of castellated strongholds armoured in ice, of fur-coat weather and parrot-bat feasts.

But now was not the time to indulge in nostalgia.

She had to get a grip on herself: and on the situation.

'Where is this new wazir?' said Justina.

'He chooses to reside in Moremo for the moment,' said Dardanalti.

'In Moremo!' said the Empress, startled.

'He gives you full use of his pink palace in the meantime,' said Dardanalti. 'You are his guest.'

'His guest?' said Justina. 'Or his captive?'

'His guest,' said Dardanalti. 'His most honoured guest. My lady, there is much of which we must talk.'

'Must we?' said Justina. 'Must we really? Now? Or can it wait?'

'It could wait till the morrow,' conceded Dardanalti.

'Then let it,' said Justina. 'For I am wearied unto death.'

The Empress Justina had a certain appetite for histrionics, but in this instance she spoke nothing less than the truth. Nevertheless, she had some business to do before she could rest.

'Artemis,' said Justina.

'What do you want?' said Ingalawa.

'We need to retrieve the skavamareen which Master Ek is holding in the Temple of Torture. The Crab will not be pleased if its delivery is delayed.'

'I will go to the Temple and see to its release immediately,' said Ingalawa.

Ingalawa knew, as did Justina, that there was scarcely one chance in ten thousand that Master Ek would hand over the 'skavamareen'. It was far more likely that the High Priest of Zoz the Ancestral guessed this ancient instrument to be an organic rectifier. And that, in hope of making himself immortal, he meant to hold on to it.

But it was worth trying the bluff.

After all, they were so close to triumph.

They had an organic rectifier.

All they needed now was to take the thing to Jod.

Then the Crab could be converted to human form, and in gratitude the Crab would surely exert all its Powers to solve their problems.

Artemis Ingalawa departed on her mission, all signs of fatigue successfully subdued.

'I want to go home,' said Olivia, who as yet was unaware of the doom which had befallen the Dromdanjerie.

So then the poor child had to be told (by Dardanalti) that Injiltaprajura's bedlam had been burnt to the ground; and that her father, the eminent Ashdan therapist Jon Qasaba, was missing, believed dead.

This final tragedy devastated the Ashdan lass. Her father! Dead? Impossible. She could not believe he was dead for he was her father, her very own, and death was something which only happened to other people's fathers. But certainly he was missing. And poor Chegory was trapped leagues underground with that huge therapist thing, a monster worse than a spider, a shark and an octopus rolled into one.

Olivia broke down and wept.

The Empress Justina took Olivia in hand. Then the Empress led the child to the imperial quarters. Two soldiers were standing on guard outside the door. For years these men had given their loyalty to Justina. But now?

'Whom do you obey?' said Justina.

Assaulting them with the question just so. Bluntly. No preliminary questions, no enquiries after their meals and pay, no smiles or hellos. The strain was telling on the Empress, hence the deterioration in her manners.

'We obey Manthandros Trasilika, the duly authorized wazir sent to take command of Untunchilamon,' said one of the soldiers stiffly.

'And me?' said Justina.

'In so far as a wazir's guest can command a soldier.'

'A guest, am I?' said Justina, her temper rising.

'So I am told,' said the soldier. 'I ask no more. I am a soldier. I exist only to obey.'

Justina had a thing or two she wanted to say in reply to that. But one glance at Olivia told the Empress this was no time to make a scene. The child needed safety, comfort, the assurance of some kind of peace, at least for the moment. So, without another word to either of the soldiers, Justina led Olivia into the imperial quarters.

They had been looted.

Some diligent staff members had endeavoured to clean up the mess, and had done so to the best of their ability. But still the evidence of ruin was everywhere. A great many things had been wantonly torn and destroyed, including much which was beautiful. That made Justina furious. Theft she could understand, but not vandalism.

An unaccustomed trembling afflicted the imperial limbs as Justina went into her bedroom and realized what had been done there. The place had been cleaned and the bed linen changed, but a certain stench still lingered.

'How dare they!' said Justina.

Olivia picked at a shattered mirror which threw back their faces in pieces. Olivia pried away one of her own eyes. Then threw down the shattering of mirror-glass.

'There's a spare bedroom,' said Justina, opening another door. 'In here.'

A drift of chicken feathers stirred around the imperial feet as Justina entered that chamber. The feathers indicated that one of Theodora's chickens (or more than one?) had met an untimely end in this room. On the spare bed, the Princess Sabitha was curled up, comfortably devoting herself to digestion. As the Empress entered, the princess woke, stretched, and yawned. She looked very, very pleased with herself.

'I don't believe you've met,' said Justina. 'Olivia, this is Sabitha Winolathon Taskinjathrua. Sabitha, meet Olivia.'

So saying, the Empress removed the Princess Sabitha from the imperial bed and conveyed her to Olivia's arms. Considering the heat of the day, one might think that the least desirable of all possible presents would be an idiothermous cat stuffed with chicken. But Olivia took the Princess Sabitha into her arms, hugged her, and was comforted by the possession of this new friend.

'If you want to lie down on the bed,' said Justina, 'feel free. I have to check my study.'

Olivia did lie down, and Justina did check the study. It was strangely untouched, probably because it was the poorest room in the imperial quarters. But something was missing. The dragon. The dragon Untunchilamon. There was no sign of that fingerlength beast. Instead, the dragon's nest of cat's fur and feather-fluff held an ovoid opal, a thing curiously flecked with bits of black.

'A present?' said Justina.

Perhaps someone had stolen her dragon and had left the bright-brilliant opal as a guilt offering.

Justina bent closer to appraise the gem. Then saw the bits of black were not flecks at all. They were ants! But why would ants attack an inedible stone? Out of madness?

'Good gracious!' said Justina. 'It must be an egg!'

And a long-lost memory stirred. A traumatic memory from her girlhood when she had tried to raise a chrysalis to its butterfly glory. That had been in Wen Endex at the

313

height of summer. (Yes, Wen Endex had a summer, and fierce heat to go with it, for all that Justina chose to remember it as a place of snowbound winter.) Ants had laid siege to the helpless pupa, and the butterfly had died unborn. Had died a hideous, disgusting death which had left Justina red-eyed and weeping.

'Such was your triumph,' said Justina, addressing the ants in a stern and terrible voice. 'Such was your triumph when I was but a child. But you behold me now as a woman!'

Then she tried to blow the ants away:

Wwwwwssssh!

A dozen nest-feathers kicked to the air then snow-drifted down. But the ants blew away not, but clung tight to the sheer and the smooth of the egg. In truth a mighty feat! Indeed, the obstinacy of ants in the face of winds natural or otherwise is one of the very wonders of the universe.

'You can't win, you know,' said Justina.

And was tempted to crush the ants out of hand, obliterating their paltry lives entirely. She resisted the temptation, though not without a struggle.

'But you will be displaced,' said she.

Indeed.

But, once displaced, the ants could always come back again.

'A problem,' said Justina, wondering how to guard the egg till it hatched.

She could always call in her soldiers. Yes, and have them stand watch by sun and moon alike, guarding the egg with chopsticks and stabs until at last and at length it hatched. But such trifling with masculine pride might well provoke mutiny.

Besides . . .

They might say the 'wazir's guest' had no right to order them to such duties.

'And, in any case . . .

Maybe the egg would never hatch.

314

With more than a touch of disappointment, Justina realized the egg was most unlikely to be viable. For the bright-brave dragon Untunchilamon was unique, created ab initio by a demon. She lacked a mate hence the egg could not have been fertilized.

'Yet,' said Justina, 'parthenogenesis is always a possibility.'

Was she deluding herself?

Perhaps.

But:

'Everyone deserves a chance,' said Justina firmly.

So saying, the Empress took a feather and whisked away the ants. Then treasured the egg on to a piece of blotting paper which she placed upon a saucer. She put the saucer atop the rocky island which rose from the limpid depths of her fish tank. That would surely secure the egg from assault by ants.

'But,' said Justina, voicing that single word as she contemplated the exquisite vulnerability of the egg.

Yes. But. Attack might still come from the air. Who knows? Supposing the egg was hatched by night? Supposing mosquitoes attacked the tiny egg-wet hatchling? The Empress had a horrifying vision of a helpless newborn dragonet being monstered by a dozen or more merciless vampiric insects.

'The poor thing would perish!' said Justina.

That she talked so persistently to herself on this occasion is no mystery. Her position was one of exquisite loneliness, for she could trust few and bare her soul to no-one. Such are the burdens of imperial power, though we should not necessarily pity the powerful on that account; after all, many a beggar endures deprivations of the soul equally as agonizing, yet without enjoying any of the many concomitant consolations.

(A pedant might argue that the Empress had lost power entirely. But this would be a misreading. She still commanded the loyalty of certain powerful people, hence would be a source of hope for her allies and a danger to her enemies until she was very definitely dead.)

'Well,' said Justina. 'Mosquitoes are no match for me!'

Then she went to her sewing room and sought out netting of the finest mesh, impervious to ants and mosquitoes alike. This she stretched across the top of her fish tank, anchoring the fabric with four of her finest soljamimpambagoya rocks. She took the greatest of pleasure imaginable in this work of her hands, simple work soon brought to decisive ends; in work she found a welcome forgetting of the woes of the world and the urgencies of the moment.

Then she sat down to watch the egg.

'A beautiful thing,' said she.

It was.

'And to think!' said she. 'The mother delinquent! The egg besieged by ants!'

Then it occurred to her that some mishap might have befallen the mother. The valorous Untunchilamon might be dead. If so, then this egg might be the sole hope of an entire race.

'Oh my!' said Justina, momentarily overwhelmed by her awesome responsibility. 'A new species! And this its sole chance of posterity!'

She was so overcome that she thought it best to take a little wine to settle her nerves. This she did, though whether her recourse to such a potent drug was wise is an open question. True, the Empress Justina had the statutory authority to order a Prescription for any or all. And it must be admitted that she had the most impeccable of academic qualifications to back such authority, since she was the proud possessor of a degree from the College of Medicine. Nevertheless, physicians tend to frown upon the self-prescription of controlled drugs, and with reason; for the abuse of such liberty is all too tempting, and can rapidly lead to the torments of addiction.

However, whether the Empress was wise or unwise to

indulge herself with wine, it must be admitted that a modest quantity of this smooth-flowing fluid helped soothe her nerves remarkably. A deep and pervading calm possessed her as she gazed upon the opalescent egg and the shimmer-drift of the dragonfire fish which inhabited the aquarium. Without, perhaps the sky was falling; or perhaps it happened that the very world was ending. But here Justina enjoyed the meditations of the moment, that moment which, at any given time, is all the life we have to live.

After a second dole of such medicine, the Empress went to see whether Olivia was all right. She found the young Ashdan lass sound asleep in the imperial bed with the Princess Sabitha in her arms. That compliant creature of fur looked up as Justina entered.

'You haven't by chance seen a dragon?' said Justina.

The Princess Sabitha yawned.

'A small dragon,' persisted the Empress. 'A dragon no longer than this finger of mine.'

So saying, Justina Thrug waggled that appendage at the self-indulgent young royal. The Princess Sabitha smirked, but said nothing. And, further interrogation proving equally as fruitless, the Empress Justina laid herself down beside Olivia Qasaba and joined her in sleep.

Justina did not wake until Artemis Ingalawa returned with the news.

The bad news.

Ingalawa had visited the Temple of Torture to demand the return of the 'skavamareen' which Master Ek had confiscated. And she had been decisively rebuffed.

317

CHAPTER THIRTY

Until the burning of Injiltaprajura, Chegory Guy and Olivia Qasaba had ruled Untunchilamon by pretending they spoke for the Crab. But now all communication with the Crab had ceased – the harbour bridge had been destroyed and the island of Jod was under quarantine – all the citizens of Injiltaprajura realized that no orders were currently being issued by the monstrous crustacean of whom they were so afraid.

It will now be asked: who then was effectively ruling Injiltaprajura at this time? And the best answer is: nobody.

While one renowned historian has stated that 'Injiltaprajura was ruled toward the end by the lawless banditry of the drummers', such statements are a gross absurdity. The only bandit on Untunchilamon who could have ruled that city was Jal Japone, and that formidable Janjuladoola warlord was still keeping to his desert fastness in the northern regions of the island.

Within Injiltaprajura itself, a few people obeyed Wazir Trasilika because they feared him to be an appointee of Aldarch the Third. Take for example the case of Nadalastabstala Banraithanchumun Ek. The High Priest of the Temple of Zoz the Ancestral was such a prominent person in Untunchilamon that his activities would inevitably be reviewed by the Mutilator of Yestron.

Ek was at least half convinced that Trasilika was a fraud. Nevertheless, Ek had confirmed Trasilika as wazir (on a provisional basis).

Because Master Ek could not afford to take chances.

But others could.

318

Others felt free to reserve judgement altogether until Jean Froissart had been proved either true or false in trial by ordeal. If Froissart proved a true priest then they would accept Trasilika as wazir. Until then, they felt under no immediate obligation to pay the taxes or to obey any law which was unduly inconvenient.

While many reserved judgement, there were a few who were entirely certain about Trasilika. One such person was Juliet Idaho. And, on the morning of the day after Justina's release from trial, Idaho discussed the advent of Trasilika with his wife as they went through their daybreak routines.

Juliet Idaho and his wife Harold had just moved into one of the grand houses in Lak Street, a mansion lying across the road from that huge ship-sized chunk of bone known as Pearl. The Empress Justina had placed the villa in Idaho's care lest looters debauch the place; it belonged to a merchant who had disappeared on the night of Injiltaprajura's great fire, so it was otherwise unprotected.

'Trasilika,' said Idaho, 'He's another false wazir. A fraud.'

He spoke with some savagery.

'Never mind, darling,' said Harold, lathering her face with soap suds.

'I do mind,' said Idaho. 'I can't stand frauds. I'm going to kill him.'

'Maybe,' said Harold, starting to shave, 'you should ask Justina first.'

'What's that supposed to mean?'

'She might have a use for the man,' said Harold.

'Maybe,' said Idaho. 'I'll check. Then I'll kill him. And that fool Froissart!'

'I really don't see why it's so very very important for you to kill people,' said Harold.

'You wouldn't,' said Idaho. 'You're not a man.'

Then he watched critically as his wife shaved her heavy jowels. As Juliet Idaho had no facial hair, he never had to go through this routine himself. He began doing the isometric exercises which helped maintain his strength, that strength being considerable for all that his body was short on muscle bulk.

Juliet Idaho was a hard man, his muscles weapons of combat. In contrast, Harold's flesh was soft and sloppy, her flesh dedicated to luxurious pleasures. That morning, Idaho wished he could stay and enjoy the delights of love with his lady, but his duty commanded him to the pink palace. So, after a brief breakfast of raw bananas, Idaho left his new mansion and started up Lak Street toward Pokra Ridge.

The streets were outwardly quiet. But then, why should they not be? Though Injiltaprajura was technically in a state of anarchy, for the most part it was outwardly calm. There were many reasons for this. One was that nobody wished to call attention to themselves by a truly spectacular act of individual disobedience. For, whether Manthandros Trasilika was a true wazir or a false wazir, all the city was convinced that Aldarch Three had triumphed in Talonsklavara, and that his wrath would eventually fall on anyone notorious for civic indiscipline,

So outbreaks of looting and such would have to wait until another anonymous mob was formed. Mob formation might take a while. The most accomplished rabble rousers had escaped to sea after the dragon riots which had seen a third of Injiltaprajura burnt to the ground. With them had gone the wealth of the imperial treasury. Thus the main temptation to violence had been removed from Untunchilamon, and the greatest revolutionary leaders had fled with their ill-gotten gains.

Hence peace of a sort prevailed, and Juliet Idaho met with no challenge to his skin or his pocket as he sweated up Lak Street toward the pink palace. In that palace, the Empress Justina was in conference with Manthandros Trasilika and Jean Froissart. The wazir and his priest, unaware of the rapid approach of a Yudonic Knight who meant to kill them as soon as he could, were discussing the proposed trial by ordeal and the banquet at which it would take place.

'Since my confirmation as wazir is only provisional,' said Trasilika, 'Ek can revoke it at any time.'

'And will, if we don't satisfy him,' said Froissart.

'So we need this trial by ordeal,' said Trasilika. 'And fast.'

'This is for your benefit as much as for ours,' said Froissart.

'Don't worry,' said Justina. 'I confirm all our arrangements. Everything will fall out just as you were told it would.'

'Now,' said Trasilika, 'we come to the matter of the division of the spoils.'

'The spoils?' said Justina.

'Yes,' said Froissart. 'We took the job of running Untunchilamon because Al'three promised to reward us richly.'

'Then reward you he will,' said Justina soothingly.

'No!' said Trasilika. 'Once he finds out we've pardoned you, he'll chop off our heads!'

And he began to explain.

Justina listed to the explanation, but only to flatter her guests. She knew men like explaining things to women, so, while she had already been thoroughly briefed by Dardanalti and Uckermark, she pretended to that ignorance which so many men think feminine. As Justina thought she already knew it all, she swallowed one great falsehood without noticing.

This was the explanation:

Manthandros Trasilika and Jean Froissart were in a pretty pickle. They were the genuine appointees of Aldarch the Third, who had truly commanded them to take command of Untunchilamon and execute Justina Thrug.

Unfortunately, without help from the Thrug, they would not be able to prove themselves true. They would be executed by a disbelieving High Priest, or would be torn apart by a sceptical mob, or assassinated by some fanatic of Janjuladoola race. So they had to pardon the Thrug to secure her cooperation. However, by pardoning the Thrug, Trasilika and Froissart were being untrue to Aldarch the Third. And the Mutilator of Yestron, who was not given to listening to reason, would surely order their execution once he learnt of this perfidy.

In other words, their efforts to prove themselves true necessarily meant they were now false.

'So,' concluded Trasilika, after explaining this, 'we want passage on your flying ship once it's operational. And we want a cut of whatever treasure you take out of Injiltaprajura.'

Such was Trasilika's statement of intent.

And it was a lie.

But Justina believed it.

Thus putting her life in peril.

Now Justina Thrug was a very intelligent woman, but her thinking was in error because she was operating from a false premise. She presumed her guests to be frauds, just like the first Trasilika and the first Froissart. Hence she believed – as Dardanalti and Uckermark believed – that those guests ultimately had no option but to flee Injiltaprajura.

But as Trasilika and Froissart were legitimate appointees of Aldarch the Third, they did have one very tempting option open to them. They needed the Thrug for the moment so they could prove themselves true. But once proof had been secured, once they had demonstrated their righteousness to Master Ek, to all those of Janjuladoola race, and to the mob in general, why, then they would have no need of Justina whatsoever.

So what was to stop them from redeeming themselves in the eyes of Aldarch the Third by ordering her immediate execution?

Why, nothing!

And this they planned to do.

The day after Froissart had passed his trial by ordeal, Justina Thrug would be hacked to death, and all her allies with her. Froissart and Trasilika had sworn as much.

But these treacherous intruders disguised their intentions by arguing ferociously about their entitlement to a fraction of any treasure which was airlifted out of Untunchilamon. And the argument was still going on when Juliet Idaho intruded upon the conference.

'Ah, Julie my love,' said Justina happily. 'It's so nice to see you here.'

The Empress looked a new woman. She had entirely recovered from the recent disasters. Or so one would think to look at her. Though if the truth be told, Justina was in the grip of great anxieties. She knew that Master Ek knew (all of Injiltaprajura knew!) that Hostaja Sken-Pitilkin was rebuilding an airship atop the pink palace. She was very much afraid that Ek would persuade the wonder-workers of the Cabal House to destroy the rebuilt ship. Or that Ek would precipitate a crisis before the ship was ready to fly. If a crisis came, Justina did not know whether she could really trust Trasilika. Thus she was far from certain of the permanence of her reprieve from execution.

The Empress had been through one trauma too many of late. She had almost been torn apart by centipedes in the Temple of Torture; she had fled for her life in fear of a mob; a dorgi had captured her Downstairs; she had come face to face with a therapist from the Golden Gulag; a second arrest had seen her committed to formal trial.

With her personal history in such disorder, she was not inclined to trust any idle assurances of a happy ever after. She would trust nothing for certain until the soil of Wen Endex was under her feet.

'What did you say?' said Idaho, in his warlord voice.

'I said, Julie darling, that I'm happy to see you here.'

'Well I'm not happy to be here,' said Idaho. 'Not in the same room with two frauds.'

And he drew his sword.

Trasilika and Froissart were terrorstruck, for they had come to the conference unarmed. But Justina never faltered.

'Julie dear,' said Justina, 'put down your sword. These people may be frauds, but they're my frauds.'

'What do you mean?' said Idaho, who was ignorant of the conspiracy.

'My good friend Uckermark did a deal with these people,' said Justina calmly. 'He arranged it with Dardanalti. You see, we're going to help them prove they're not frauds. We're going to do that by helping Froissart here to come through a trial by ordeal.'

'We're going to help him?' said Idaho. 'But why?'

'Because otherwise Master Ek will kill them.'

'Then let him!'

'But then Master Ek would kill us.'

'Oh,' said Idaho, absorbing this. 'So we help this Froissart to keep ourselves from being killed.'

'Right,' said Justina.

'And that means Froissart doesn't get killed either.'

'Right,' said the Empress, beaming.

'So who does get killed?' said Idaho. 'Trasilika?'

'No,' said Justina. 'Nobody.'

'Oh,' said Idaho. Then: 'I'm not sure I really like this.'

As far as he was concerned, a plan in which there was no place for murder was hardly a plan at all.

'Julie, Julie,' said Justina, 'that's only the theory. In practice things are likely to be much more dangerous. They always are. There's every chance something will go wrong, every chance in the world. With a little luck, you'll have people to kill by the dozens.'

And, by the exercise of the gentle arts of persuasion, the Empress slowly drew Idaho into committing himself wholeheartedly to the plot which was hatching.

Justina Thrug then entered upon an activity which, despite the exigencies of her plight, gave her considerable pleasure; this being the planning of a banquet.

324

Despite the great destruction which had befallen port-side Injiltaprajura, the desert side remained unscathed by fire; which meant there would be no shortage of food for the grand occasion.

The highlight of the banquet was to be, of course, Jean Froissart's trial by ordeal. The revels were scheduled to take place at a banquet just five days prior to the Festival of Light (for which Nadalastabstala Banraithanchumun Ek had yet to find a sacrifice). Such a timetable gave Justina barely enough time to organize everything. Nevertheless, she managed.

Such was the disorder which had befallen the city of late that no corrections had been made to the Directory of its leading personages. So a great many invitations came back with various disappointing notations, such as 'burnt alive', 'died of smoke inhalation', 'missing believed dead', or 'fled on Turbothot's bark'. However, overall the response was good.

As Manthandros Trasilika and Jean Froissart were still billeted in Moremo Maximum Security Prison, and declined public appearances on Justina's advice, Injiltap-rajura was possessed by a great curiosity as to their parts and natures; so many who would otherwise have thought it politic to decline an invitation from the Thrug accepted her summons with grateful thanks (as opposed to ungrateful thanks, which are scarcely rare among those who oftentimes find themselves compelled to unpleasant duties by the strict demands of protocol).

However, there was one person whose thanks were ungrateful, and that was Aquitaine Varazchavardan. Justina's Master of Law was sitting alone at home when his invitation was delivered by the conjuror Odolo, runner of many messages. Varazchavardan took it, read it, accepted it, appraised Odolo of his decision then dismissed him.

Then wished he had not been so quick to send the conjuror away. For the mansion on Hojo Street was desolate, and Aquitaine Varazchavardan was very much alone. Even his slaves and servants had fled; and such was the uncertain state of civic organization that he had no hope of organizing an effective hunt for their recovery. The certain message of this mass desertion was that Varazchavardan's underlings had little confidence in his continued survival. The wonder-worker could not quarrel with such opinion. He too believed it was only a matter of time before the executioners came for him.

Finding the tension near unbearable, Varazchavardan began to debate whether he should continued existing. There was no release from the moment. Existence itself was becoming a form of unendurable confinement, the intolerable silence of the grand house a punishment in its own right. Under such circumstances, was it an error to endure?

Varazchavardan at last roused himself. He lit every lantern he could find. Then dumped some ice into a glass. What now? Sit and watch the geckos? No. He lit a mosquito coil and watched that instead.

Watching the slowly untwining smoke of the mosquito coil had a most soothing effect on the Master of Law, who allowed himself to drift into fantasy to such an extent that at last he momentarily believed himself to be back in Obooloo, drinking tea and watching the cloud formations shape and reshape in the blue empyrean.

What was the source of Varazchavardan's despair?

The answer is very simple.

Varazchavardan feared he would ultimately be executed by Aldarch the Third as a consequence of his past association with the Thrug. To preserve himself, he had to flee Injiltaprajura. But he had no hope of escaping by Justina's airship. For he knew as a certainty what Justina only feared: that the Cabal House would destroy Sken-Pitilkin's new airship just as it destroyed the first.

Thus Varazchavardan sat alone, watching the geckos and listening to the click of melting ice, and contemplated suicide. In that extremity, he applied the Test of the Moment.

That test consists of this single question:

If I had been created ex nihilo this very moment, would I see the rewards of life as being a sufficient reward for enduring life's pains, burdens and indignities?

The Test of the Moment was devised by the sagacious philosopher So Da Thee, who was driven to such an expedient as a consequence of his abstemious lifestyle. Among the Korugatu philosophers (and such was Thee) a personal crisis is usually resolved by a recourse to drink. (Methodical recourse to drink is also had in the absence of any such crisis, but that is another story.) Thee, refusing such solace, had devised the Test.

A diligent application of the Test does this: it frees a life from its historical context. An interesting exercise indeed, since most people mostly view life in the light of the hopes and expectations of the past. Those who in youth hoped for paradise find it hard to settle for less, while those brought up with an expectation of living in hell are more easily satisfied – the problem being that those so raised tend to shape the world to the hell of their expectations.

Imagine, then (and we follow Thee in this exercise in fantasy) a speculator who has lost a fortune of a million dragons. In exile, he lives in a fisherman's shack on the shores of Manamalargo, making his life as a crab catcher. There he laments the loss of his dragons, his pleasure dome and the concubines housed therein.

Supposing he then applies the Test.

A creature created at this very moment has no losses to mourn for. It possesses only assets. So the speculator thinks not of the silken limbs of his lost concubines, but of his own sturdy flesh. He thinks not of his lost palace, but instead admires the architecture of his shack, which shelters him from sun and rain alike. And – but you can fill in the rest.

Suffice it to say that in the end, in So Da Thee's favourite scenario, the imaginary speculator goes forth from his shack with his heart filled with joy, for the world is a wondrous place, filled with a million causes for optimism.

(In Hing Dar Radeker's countervailing scenario, the rejoicing speculator leaves his fisherman's shack to enjoy the delights of a walk along the shore, and promptly gets beaten to death by debt collectors come to dun him for the half million dragons he still owes his stockbroker. But then, Radeker was always a pessimist.)

Varazchavardan had first heard of So Da Thee's Test of the Moment some years ago. At the time, he had disparaged it; and not entirely without reason. But now he applied it. And found (for the moment!) the courage to face the future. Varazchavardan decided he would certainly not kill himself until after the banquet, the solemn feast at which Jean Froissart would attempt to pass a trial by ordeal. Varazchavardan was assured of life and liberty till then.

But the banquet was approaching with a speed which was nothing short of terrifying.

CHAPTER THIRTY-ONE

On the morning of the day of the banquet, Jean Froissart
was summoned to a conference with Nadalastabstala
Banraithanchumun Ek. The meeting was not at Ek's
mansion at Hojo Street, nor at the nearby Temple of
Zoz the Ancestral. Instead, Jean Froissart was constrained to take himself off to the Temple of Torture in
Goldhammer Rise.

As he awaited his interrogation by Master Ek,
Froissart began to sweat. What did the old monster
want? A fly settled on Froissart's face and began feeding
on his sweat. He brushed it away. It returned with allies.
That was the tropics through and through. Life swarm-
ping, breeding, ramping without order. Not for the first
time, Froissart longed to be in Wen Endex in deep-
frozen winter, that part of the year's cycle when so many
things die out of the world, thus making possible spring
with its rushing renewals, the sudden flowers, the joy of
life awaking.

Spring.

Untunchilamon would never know such a change.

And joy?

Surely there was no joy to be found in this pestilential
climate, always so hot that the mere possession of a skin
was an almost unendurable burden.

Angrily, Froissart slapped his own face. Mashed a
fly.

'Master Ek will see you now.'

That from an acolyte. Froissart rubbed at the fly,
removing mashed entrails from his sweating skin as best
he could. All too soon, he was face to face with the High
Priest.

'I hail the lord who serves the Lord of Lords,' said Froissart.

Master Ek looked up from the corpse on which he was working, smiled, and invited his guest to inspect the meat.

'Interesting, is it not?' said Ek, prying at a delicate membrane with a needle-sharp hook.

'Yes,' said Froissart, fascinated by the interwriggling blue and red veins which snaked through the pink-grey of the membrane.

'Ah,' said Ek. 'Interesting indeed.'

And he pulled, and the membrane tore, and Froissart saw into the organ below, saw into a ripeness where something writhed, and was assailed by the stench of rotting meat, and gagged, and had to strive to keep himself from vomiting.

'Trasilika,' said Ek, the word abrupting into Froissart's distress. 'Who is he?'

'Who he claims to be,' said Froissart. 'Manthandros Trasilika is the true wazir of Untunchilamon. Aldarch the Third gave him his appointment.'

'If you are lying . . .'

'My tongue is green,' said Froissart.

Ek seemed to accept this assertion, at least for the moment. The High Priest wiped his hands on a bloody rag then led Froissart into an interrogation chamber. Two chairs awaited, a low table between them. Froissart sat at Ek's invitation.

'Cigarette?' said Ek.

Froissart was not sure whether to accept or not. He knew the tobacco Ek smoked to be a narcotic drug, a drug which produced an addiction which was almost unshakeable. But how quickly did the drug gain control of its victim? Was it a hallucinogen? Or what?

'Try it,' said Ek, extending one of his paper tubes of tightly rolled tobacco.

Froissart took the cigarette. An acolyte produced a hot coal, holding it with a pair of tongs. Froissart, who had some experience of smoking opium, got the cigarette alight and puffed on it slowly. Then Ek said, abruptly, without preambles:

'Who was Mishlin?'

'Author of the *Book of Hot Iron*,' answered Froissart, speaking automatically, without needing to think.

Silence.

Then:

'In which city was the word of Zoz first proclaimed?'

'In no city,' answered Froissart. 'Rather, in the mountain temple known as Qo.'

Another silence. Ek smoked, studying Froissart all the while. Those eyes of pale orange flecked with green had the potential to be grossly disturbing. Inhuman eyes. A mutant's eyes. But Froissart was not worried. He knew now why he had been called to the Temple. Ek feared him a false priest, and was determined to prove him a fraud by testing his knowledge.

But Jean Froissart could easily pass any such test.

Though Froissart was a child of Wen Endex, he had gone to Ang and had been converted to the worship of Zoz the Ancestral. Why? Because he had truly Believed. At a crucial stage in his life, he had been granted a vision of horror. He had Believed, as an iron certainty, that Zoz existed.

He had converted.

He had worshipped.

He had obeyed.

And, as an outsider among the Janjuladoola, he had studied twice as hard as his fellow priests, thus winning a minimal acceptance from his superiors. He had explored the histories of the martyrs and saints, the revelations of the mystics who had proclaimed the benefits of applied algetics, and the intricate realms of theological thought and speculation which were impossible in the coarse-tongued Toxteth of Wen Endex.

Later, Froissart had lost his faith. He had become an agnostic: a secret doubter, but never an open apostate.

Why did Froissart lose his faith?

Partly because, as the uncertainties of youth had been replaced by the confidence of manhood, he had lost his need to believe so fervently in anything. Then he had met with a wandering Korugatu philosopher who had wrecked his faith by long conversation over many nights of drinking.

(A mystery, this, since the Korugatu philosophers are based in Chi'ash-lan. How did such a one come to Yestron? Here your storyteller would fable some far-fetched explanation, but the honest historian must confess ignorance.)

Froissart's Korugatu philosopher acknowledged, of course, that the gods exist. This is beyond dispute, for deities prove themselves often by working miracles, manifesting themselves upon battlefields and answering prayers. Adroit sacrifice will nearly always bring results from Above, or from Below, or from the Sideways Realms. Therefore we cannot doubt that the Higher Ones (and the Lower Ones, the Sideways Ones and the Inverted Ones) do exist (and perhaps will continue to exist in the future).

But, claimed the sage, that the gods exist in the forms humanity attributes to them is far less certain. It is the way of priesthoods to pretend to a certain knowledge of the minds of the gods. But to know our own minds is near impossible, so how can we be so sure of those of beings alien to us?

In the face of these arguments and much alcohol, Froissart's faith had at last collapsed. But still he retained his knowledge, hence was easily able to survive a viva voce examination by Master Ek.

'Why do we worship Zoz the Ancestral?' said Master Ek.

'Because He is the greatest power,' said Froissart.

'How do we worship Him?' said Ek.

'By satisfying His demands for pain and death,' said Froissart.

'Why does Zoz demand pain?' said Ek.

'Because it proves His power.'

'And why death?'

'Because that proves His power likewise,' said Froissart.

'What is the greatest good?' said Ek.

'To yield to power to prevent pain.'

The catechism proceeded along such lines for some time, until at last Master Ek seemed satisfied.

'Wait here,' said Ek.

Then he withdrew, leaving Froissart to sweat. Which Froissart did, in both a physical and a metaphysical sense. Ek had another trick up his sleeve. But what?

At last the High Priest returned and said:

'A sacrifice has been prepared. You are to sacrifice a vampire rat to the greater glory of Zoz the Ancestral.'

Jean Froissart was conducted to the naos of the Temple, where a rat was waiting for sacrifice. Froissart passed this test perfectly.

Ek told him so once they had returned to the interrogation chamber.

'You have passed,' said Ek.

Then he smiled.

At least, his mouth smiled. So did his eyes. But his ears and his eyebrows did not.

'A penitent thanks the lord who serves the Lord of Lords,' said Froissart formally.

'Your thanks are welcome,' said Ek. 'Will you share a drink with me?'

'With pleasure,' said Froissart.

Ek tried to snap his fingers. He failed, and a spasm of pain shot through his hand. He cursed his arthritis, and said:

'The drinks.'

An acolyte entered bearing a small tray on which there were two cups. Ek took one and sipped slowly. Froissart took the other and drank, but more rapidly.

'Strong stuff,' said he in surprise.

'But good,' said Ek.

333

Then he waited.

But, to Ek's surprise, Froissart did not collapse on the ground in a babbling heap. Instead, he calmly drank down the rest of his drink.

To conceal his confusion, Ek lit a fresh cigarette. Somehow, this damnable Froissart had made himself immune to the poisons which had just been used on him. There were ways to do that, of course. The taking of an antidote. Or the swallowing of graduated doses to build up immunity. Ek drew upon his cigarette. Exhaled smoke. Thinking.

Watching Ek smoke, Froissart briefly wondered whether the old man was a dragon in disguise. Then he dismissed the notion. He tried to speak, but found it an effort. Ek's silence was of such intensity that it took courage to venture to breach it.

'My lord,' said Froissart, finding that courage, 'before I go, I wish to have leave to make a petition.'

Ek said nothing, so Froissart rushed on:

'Might I possibly be excused from tonight's trial by ordeal?'

Did the quality of Ek's silence change? Froissart fancied it did. And the change was not for the better. Frankly, Froissart was afraid. Afraid? He was terrified. Of Ek, and the murderous potential of the High Priest's powers. Of Justina, too. Could he trust the Thrug? He didn't think so. Her assurances seemed sincere, but . . . no, he couldn't trust her. Even if she was committed to his survival, there was so much that could go wrong. He might get hurt. He might get killed on the spot.

Ek sighed.

'Jean Froissart,' said Ek, 'you disappoint me. Untunchilamon urgently needs the rule of a wazir. But we cannot take chances. Your Trasilika must prove himself true. If you will not venture to provide proof by enduring trial by ordeal, then there is another way. You could drink of a formula made by compounding zen with certain other substances which you surely know as well

334

as I do.' Ek paused, then continued: 'The formula of which I speak is renowned as a truth drug.'

'I regret,' said Froissart, 'that poison was one of the many dangers which assailed both Trasilika and myself in Bolfrigalaskaptiko. We both have a resistance to the compound to which you allude.'

'How unfortunate,' said Ek. 'That being so, do you still wish to be excused from your trial by ordeal?'

Froissart hesitated.

Then:

'Yes,' said Froissart. 'I do ask to be so excused.'

'You wish to be excused the trial by ordeal,' said Ek, with infinite weariness.

'I do,' said Jean Froissart.

'On what grounds?'

'Because I have proved myself true by my knowledge of doctrine. I have proved myself in interrogation.'

'You have shown yourself to be possessed of a good memory,' said Ek. 'Nothing more. Your request is denied. Go!'

Froissart went.

Once out in the street, he felt a spasm of wrenching pain shock through his chest. He clutched the sweating flesh. Surely he was going to die.

The stones of the street sighed and chirruped. Purple light squeaked as it escaped from cracks in the fabric of reality. The sky swelled, buckled, burst and reformed. Froissart knew exactly what was happening to him. Ek must have slipped him a truly massive dose of oola. And now the stuff was having an (albeit delayed) effect.

Oola?

This concoction, otherwise known as babble-tongue, has as its main active ingredient the dreaded drug zen. Oola has some reputation as a truth drug, but its main effect is to cause hallucinations (and, sometimes, madness).

The chemical regime which Froissart had followed in Bolfrigalaskaptiko (he had spoken truthfully to Ek about

335

this matter) gave him some partial protection against the effects of the oola he had consumed. Though the sun pulsated and his feet appeared to have turned into buckets of slugmeat, he nevertheless managed to struggle up Goldhammer Rise. A beggar nagged along behind him until at last, hoping to be free of this encumbrance, Froissart dispensed a coin.

A coin?

A dragon!

Once in possession of that golden disk, the beggar redoubled his efforts, determined not to let go of this source of profit. Other beggars joined the procession. And, when Froissart refused to dispense further largesse (he had meant to give the first man a damn, not a dragon) they mugged him.

Froissart, somewhat the worse for his mugging, struggled uphill to Lak Street then began the weary trek to Pokra Ridge. He was devastated. Manthandros Trasilika had assured him their takeover of Untunchilamon would be easy, so easy. And so it should have been! They deserved such a reward for faithfully serving Aldarch the Third all through the years of Talonsklavara. Instead, their profit-taking adventure was turning into a living nightmare.

Meanwhile, Master Ek was meditating alone.

Nadalastabstala Banraithanchumun Ek had been sitting in solitude in the Temple of Torture ever since Froissart's departure.

He was puzzling over a conundrum.

Jean Froissart seemed to doubt his ability to survive the trial by ordeal. But this was strange. If Froissart was not sure of his ability to pass such a test, why had he volunteered for it in the first place?

Ek had yet to puzzle out the answer to this when one of his acolytes intruded upon the masterly solitude, claiming to have some new and important intelligence.

'Of what?' said Ek.

'Of Shabble's plans.'

'What is it that Shabble plans?' said Ek.

'A – a festival,' said the acolyte.

'Festival?'

'On the day of the Festival of Light. Shabble means to sacrifice a loaf of cassava bread and two fruit flies to the greater glory of the Holy Cockroach.'

'That – that monstrous bubble!' said Ek.

As invective goes, this was scarcely effective, and surely it represents a totally inadequate response to the blasphemy which Shabble planned to perpetrate. But Ek was labouring under a difficulty, for it is difficult to curse Shabble when the bright and bouncing imitator of suns lacks a face which can be insulted or ancestors who can be denigrated.

Nevertheless, let no mistake be made. Master Ek was furious, and determined then and there to have a reckoning with Shabble one of these days; or, if not with Shabble, then with Shabble's priests, lawyers, advisers and congregation.

When Ek's anger at last diminished, he started thinking of practical ways in which Shabble could be punished in Shabbleself's own person, and he came up with—

Nothing.

For Shabble, my dears, cannot be hurt by anyone or anything as puny as Master Ek; and, to the great increase of his rage, Ek had to acknowledge as much. By way of compensation, Ek began devising the special tortures with which he would destroy Jean Froissart once Froissart had failed his trial by torture.

Did some psychic communication take place?

Did Froissart feel Master Ek's enmity, despite the distance between them?

This question cannot be answered with any degree of certainty; nevertheless, it must be recorded that a spasm of especial pain fractured Jean Froissart's chest as Ek planned Froissart's destruction.

By that time, the child of Wen Endex was in the pink

337

palace atop Pokra Ridge, beginning an audience with the Empress Justina.

'Are you all right?' said Justina, seeing pain writ clear across Froissart's face.

'Yes,' said Froissart. 'It's just a – indigestion or something.'

'You must see my physician,' said Justina. 'Koskini Reni, he's an amazing man. He's a prescription for everything, if not always a cure. I'll give you an introduction as soon as our business is finished. But – now that we're talking about business, what is it you want?'

'To confirm our arrangements for tonight,' said Froissart.

'Come now,' said Justina. 'We've been through all that. I'll give you a magic salve to let you hold the heated iron with ease. There won't be any pain, no pain at all.'

'My confidence would be increased if I could – if I could see this magic salve.'

'Very well then,' said Justina.

She delved into her handbag and rummaged about within for some time, at last producing a small oval box. She opened it. And displayed a smear of green grease.

'This is my magic salve,' said Justina. 'It will allow you to pick up the iron even when it's hot enough to make water boil. Or hotter.'

Froissart was reassured to actually sight the magic salve which had been promised to him. Still:

'My confidence,' he said, 'would be enhanced by a test of such power.'

'But,' said Justina, 'there is only enough for one use.'

'Then,' said Froissart, struggling to retain his composure, 'perhaps you could reassure me by telling me the provenance of this substance. Where it comes from, for example. And what guarantees you have of its purity.'

'I made it myself,' said Justina. 'Surely you could have guessed that yourself. I'm a witch, as you know.'

'I know no such thing,' said Froissart, 'hence am

inclined to doubt the powers of your magic salve. If you made it, why can't you make more?'

'I can, I can,' said Justina. 'But the blood of a basilisk is an essential ingredient for such cookery, and Injiltap-rajura has not seen a basilisk for the last six years.'

'That's as may be,' said Froissart. 'But if you have powers of witchcraft, you can prove them to me here and now. Somehow. If not by making a fire-salve, then by some other method. I need proof. Proof if I am to believe.'

'You've proof already,' said Justina. 'After all, you brought a warrant from Aldarch Three commanding my execution on that account. A witch, said the warrant. I saw it myself. That's why I was to be killed.'

'True,' said Froissart. 'But, by a witch, we usually mean merely a woman who has intruded on the realms of men.'

'And what,' said Justina, 'be those realms?'

Whereupon Froissart, who had a didactic bent, said:

'War, law, business—'

'Enough!' said Justina, cutting him off. 'You need proof? Very well. I will give you a demonstration of a witch's magic. Here I have three glasses. Do you want to handle them?'

'Please,' said Froissart.

They were squat drinking glasses. Not wine glasses or tea glasses, or soup glasses. Just ordinary water glasses. (Though here the word 'ordinary' applies to those beakers as they were seen by Froissart, who had long been acquainted with wealth, and as they were perceived by Justina, who used them daily in the palace imperial. To the hovel-dwellers of Lubos or the slumland children of Marthandorthan, any item made of glass would have seemed the most extravagant wonder imaginable.)

'Well,' said Justina. 'Do you believe I can cause these glasses to fill themselves up with wine?'

'By pouring wine from a bottle, yes.'

'No, silly boy! By magic. Do you believe I can fill them with wine by magic?'

339

'Frankly, no,' said Froissart.

'Then watch,' said Justina, placing the three glasses on the table.

The vitric beakers sat there in a row, the end glasses inverted, the central glass the right way up. Justina made three mystic passes over the glasses. Then watched them as a scorpion watches the dung beetle it plans to claim as its victim.

'Well,' said Froissart, 'I see no wine.'

'The operation of magic takes time,' whispered the Empress. 'Time. And silence. Wait!'

But Froissart saw nothing out of the ordinary. Only three glasses sitting on a table. He said as much.

'Very well,' said the Empress, briskly. 'Now watch this. I take hold of two glasses, thus. Two, note, not one. I flip-flop these two. Then I take my hands off.'

The Empress Justina had flip-flopped the middle glass and one of the end glasses. In consequence, the central glass was now inverted and one of the end glasses the right way up.

'You see?' said Justina triumphantly.

'I'm not blind,' said Froissart. 'But—'

'But watch!'

The Empress took hold of the two inverted glasses and flip-flopped them so they were both standing the right way up. All three glasses were now standing the right way up.

'There!' she said. 'I flip-flopped two at once.'

'So?' said Froissart in bewilderment. 'So what's this got to do with wine?'

Surely the heat had got to the imperial head.

'That comes later,' said Justina. 'This is magic enough to be going on with. Two flip-flops, that's what I did. You saw? By flip-flopping two glasses at a time I managed to make all three stand up the right way.'

'But – but this is lunacy!' said Froissart. 'That's not magic! That's not even a trick.'

'Isn't it?' said Justina.

340

She flip-flopped the end two glasses.

'See? Two inverted, one the right way up. I flip-flopped two glasses thrice to get two down, one up.'

'So?' said Froissart.

Justina rearranged the glasses.

'You try,' said she.

'Oh, come on,' said Froissart. 'I outgrew kindergarten years ago.'

'Indulge me,' said Justina, a smile upon her lips. 'Indulge me. You might be surprised.'

'Very well,' said Froissart irritably, reaching for the nearest glass.

Justina slapped down his hand.

'First, the rules,' said she. 'Do it as I did it. Two glasses at a time. You must flip-flop both. After three such manipulations, you must have two glasses inverted, one upright. Two down, one up.'

'Child's play,' said Froissart scornfully.

In his youth, Jean Froissart had sat for the competitive examinations which controlled entry to the Flesh Traders' Financial Association. He had failed to win a place in that institution, but nevertheless his marks had been high. His marks had proved him, beyond a doubt, to be a Certified Genius.

So it should be—

—easy?

There was something wrong here.

Experimentally, Froissart tumbled two glasses. Then another two. Then—

He couldn't see how to get all three upright.

'I made a mistake,' he said.

'Never mind,' said Justina. 'We'll try again.'

And she put them back to the starting position.

Froissart tried again.

Failed.

'The third time,' said Justina. 'The final time. Try. But think before you try.'

Froissart stared at the glasses.

341

'Two at a time,' he said. 'Down to be up and up to be down. Three times.'

'Right,' said Justina. 'To finish with two down, one up.'

Froissart tried to concentrate. But something was wrong with his head. Mentally he configured and reconfigured the glasses. But he couldn't get the fit he wanted. Sweat bulged from his forehead and his heart raced itself in a panic.

With Froissart debilitated by such stress, the oola he had consumed earlier in the day began winning its battle with his constitution. The beakers stretched, swelled, turned purple and ran with yellow fire. Yet their configuration—

Their configuration remained the same.

And, for the life of him, Froissart could not see how to manoeuvre them into the configuration Justina demanded.

Yet the Empress had managed it.

As Froissart struggled with the problem, a drum began to beat.

Thop – thop – tup!

Thop – thop – tup . . .

Froissart looked round for the source of the noise. Then realized it was in his own head. He was still suffering from zen, or else was enduring stress hallucinations, or else was going mad. Or was being bewitched. Froissart stared at Justina.

—Say nothing!

So Froissart thought to himself. But his tongue was already blabbering:

'You – you're a – are you a witch?'

'I have my powers,' said Justina.

She opened a cupboard, brought out a skin of wine and filled two of the glasses.

'Drink,' she said. 'It'll make you feel better.'

Froissart seized his glass and drank convulsively.

'Now you know me a little better,' said Justina. 'You see me for what I am. The possessor of powers.'

342

Froissart was not entirely convinced. But fatigue, combined with the mind-buckling effects of oola, made it hopeless for him to try to pursue the truth further. He said his apologies and fled.

Once Froissart had left, Olivia Qasaba emerged from behind the screen from where she had watched the proceedings.

'Are you really a witch?' said Olivia.

'Witch enough,' said Justina smugly, sipping at her wine.

'You mean you are or you aren't?'

'That's for you to work out,' said Justina.

Olivia thought about it long and hard, and in the end concluded that Justina was indeed possessed of magical powers. But Olivia was wrong. As others have remarked, there is far less magic in the world than most people think. And, if the Empress Justina was indeed possessed of occult powers, she had not chosen to exercise them on this occasion.

Those who wish to test their intellectual powers against Olivia's are invited to ask themselves how the Empress Justina worked a swindle on the genius level intelligence of the trained intellect of Jean Froissart. Those desirous of no such test can turn to the very end of this tome, where the explanation is given. Alternatively, the matter may be ignored entirely. For the explanation is, unfortunately, bathotic rather than glamorous; but then, that is the nature of the greater part of life and living.

For the rest of that daylight, Olivia kept Justina company as the Empress supervised arrangements for the night's banquet. Meanwhile, Jean Froissart lay in a narrow bed in Moremo Maximum Security Prison, staring at the bloodstone walls and trying to get to sleep. He needed rest urgently, but sleep he could not, because of the rats gnawing his feet, the serpent fighting the dragon inside his skull, the octopus writhing from his omphalos.

343

He decided to go for a walk to calm himself down, walking being one of the standard cures for insomnia. But this improved matters not at all, though he walked to the far north of Untunchilamon and far out across the waters of Moana, coming at last to a grey and undulating plain where live flying fish struggled in their millions in pits of red-hot coals, and where a witch with a green skull for a head was splashing Trasilika's head against a wall made of crab shells as the distant music of a mandolin dwindled into the darkness . . .

CHAPTER THIRTY-TWO

That evening, as guests began to gather for the banquet, Olivia served glasses of sherbet on the balcony of the palace. This was rightly a job for a slave; but Justina's residence was so understaffed as a consequence of the recent alarums that it barely functioned even with the help of pressganged labourers such as Olivia.

The young Qasaba girl did not object to her duties. Everyone was polite to her; or else ignored her, which at least was painless. She overheard a great deal of a great many fascinating conversations, and was not so over-worked that she was unable to enjoy the view.

The view!

From the balcony, Olivia could see right across the rooftops of portside Injiltaprajura, across the Laitemata and the island of Jod, across Scimitar and the reefs beyond, and then out across the almost limitless sea.

The sea she studied little, for one eyeful is much like the next. Rather, it was the cityscape which attracted her attention in her idle moments. She was amazed to see how fast rebuilding was proceeding.

While studying the fruits of this enterprise, Olivia was surprised to notice a tarpaulin atop Xtokobrokotok. She had thought Marthandorthan had survived the dragon riots intact; but maybe fire had burnt away a part of the roof of Shabble's warehouse. Or perhaps something was going on atop that roof, and the tarpaulin was there to shelter a secret rite of the Cult of the Holy Cockroach from infidel eyes.

While thinking this, Olivia saw something bright-flashing in the air above Xtokobrokotok. It was Shabble, spinning in a sun-dance which defied sunset.

Despite such defiance, the seasuck swallowed the sun; and the guests on the balcony made their way inside to the Grand Hall where the banquet was to take place. Unfortunately, like much of the palace, the Grand Hall had suffered thanks to riot and sundry insurrections. For instance, its marvellous glass chandeliers had been smashed beyond repair, and could not easily be replaced since there were no glassworkers of the requisite calibre on Untunchilamon. Indeed, there were no glassworkers at all on that island; and the chandeliers had been imported years before from Wen Endex, to which place they had probably come by way of trade, their ultimate origin doubtless being with the ogres of the Qinjoks.

Olivia had a good idea of what would happen at the banquet, for Chegory had told her all about his own experience of such ordeals. Thanks to Chegory's accounts of the daunting glamour of the waiters and the intricate demands of protocol, Olivia was well prepared.

But . . .

If only Chegory could have been there to go with her!

Instead, he was trapped Downstairs with that horrible therapist thing.

If only they could rescue him!

But they couldn't, not without the help of the Crab.

The only other way to get Chegory back would be to take prisoners to the therapist. But that was hardly possible, since at least two of those prisoners had sailed away. Yes, Guest Gulkan and Thayer Levant, gone from Injiltaprajura for good for all anyone knew. That still left the two wizards, but . . .

There was no catching the wizards.

But if only . . .

Olivia, in her innocence, imagined all would be set to rights if only she could be reunited with Chegory. The Ashdan lass still had a touching faith in the redemptive powers of love; and she lamented Chegory's absence most bitterly. Lament, however, did not stop her from looking around at the assembling guests with a very lively curiosity.

Like many others, Olivia Qasaba's greatest interest was in the priest who was doomed to endure the test by ordeal that very night. To her surprise, he looked most unhappy about it.

Was Jean Froissart truly unhappy?

Or did Olivia misread his expression?

Olivia misread not: Froissart was in a state of anguished apprehension. He was sorely afraid that something would go wrong that night. But he knew what would happen if he declined to attempt the ordeal. He would be beaten until his sodden corpse collapsed in a weltering mass of splattered blood and splintered bone. Would be a putrid corpse by this time tomorrow.

It was too much.

He needed to sit down.

So, without thinking, he did just that.

Such was Froissart's distress that, as he took his seat, the untutored observer might have been excused for imagining he was sitting on knives.

'Sir,' said a waiter.

'You're speaking to me?' said Froissart.

'I wish only to say, sir, that nobody is to seat themselves yet.'

'Oh,' said Froissart, in confusion; and stood.

Olivia saw his gaffe and smiled the smile of a polished sophisticate, the smile of a young lady who knows all about banquets and their protocols. Then, turning from Froissart (he was too old to hold her interest for long) she looked for the starvation cage Chegory had mentioned, but it was nowhere to be seen. Justina had had it removed lest it become (as well it might in such troubled times) a source of inspiration to the wicked.

'Hello, Olivia,' said Justina, finding her amidst the throng.

'Hello,' said Olivia Qasaba to her Empress. 'Where am I sitting?'

'On my left,' said Justina. 'Varazchavardan will be to my right.'

'And to my left?'

'My lawyer, Dardanalti. He's a very civilized man, but he'll probably be concentrating his attentions on the man to his left, who will be Judge Qil.'

Shortly, it was time for the banquet to begin. The customary preliminary ceremonies took place and then Justina made a special announcement:

'There will be no drumming at banquet. Penalty for breach of this regulation will be death.'

This proclamation was greeted with general applause. Such were the tensions in the Grand Hall that all adults present were glad to have one thing they could agree upon unanimously: namely, that the delinquencies of the youthful 'drumming' cultists of Injiltaprajura were a threat to law, order and civilization.

Seeing how richly her proclamation was being rewarded Justina began to regret that she had not made it earlier. At this late date she finally realized how she might have been able to unite Injiltaprajura under her rule. A campaign to control, discipline, outlaw and punish the 'drummers' would have proved universally popular, and might – just might – have allowed Justina to start the process of unifying Untunchilamon against the threat from Aldarch the Third.

But it was too late for that now.

So . . .

So sit back and enjoy!

As Justina was still luxuriating in the applause, a little smoke from a mosquito coil eddied in her direction and stung her eyes. For how much longer would she retain the possession of those most delicate of the sensory portals? Not for long, not if something went wrong tonight. She might lose it all. Her hands, those fascinating instrumentalities of the will. Her—

But enough of such thoughts!

I can. I do. I dare.

And I will win!

So thought the Empress.

Then, like a child determined to fight, she fisted hands. Then caught herself doing just that, and smiled, unfolded her hands and soothed a couple of beads of sweat from her forehead.

'Some pineapple, Vazzy?' she said, offering a saucer of these titbits to the guest on her right.

'Thank you,' said Aquitaine Varazchavardan, taking a sample.

Varazchavardan was unhappy, as miserable and as fearful in his own way as was Jean Froissart. He felt – what was it? Not panic, exactly. But a merciless desolation.

This I may survive.

But . . .

We die even as we sit here.

A truism, for all know that nothing can slow the inevitable conquest by time. However, through much of life this underlying reality is masked by life's trivia, or by work, the ultimate refuge of the sensitive mind.

While Varazchavardan was distressed, afflicted by both temporal fears and existential malaise, he hid his distress well. Such were his thespian skills that he looked totally unperturbed; looked, in fact, every bit the solemn Master of Law; looked slightly bored rather than grossly disturbed.

Elsewhere sat Manthandros Trasilika, his caution rapidly giving way to a grandeur of insolent ego as the banquet got underway and a little liquor got under his skin. Trasilika's ebullience was not restrained by the fact that he was seated opposite Master Ek, who would surely prove himself a true representative of the institutionalized rage of Zoz the Ancestral should Jean Froissart fail the ordeal which awaited him that night.

Yes, no circumventions of mercy could prevent the inevitable processes of the law which would doom Jean Froissart if he failed tonight's test. Nadalastabstala

Banraithanchumun Ek would personally supervise Froissart's destruction: and then would turn his attention to Manthandros Trasilika.

Already Ek was dreaming of the sly probes with which he would first excite Froissart's nerves; of the exquisite crunch with which his pincers would mutilate the bones of the foreigner's fingers; of the lush blood which would pour from the tongue of that child of Wen Endex as the fish-hooks tore free . . .

While Ek thus dreamt, he rolled himself a cigarette. He blew gently upon a slow-burning mosquito coil to persuade it into fiercer life, then lit his cigarette with the help of this heat source. Immediately a waiter hurried up to remonstrate with him.

The acolytes seated on either side of Master Ek – Paach Ch'ha Saat and Aath Nau Das – immediately became alert. Ch'ha Saat reached for the blade he had smuggled into the banquet, but Ek slapped down his hand before the foolish young man could precipitate a diplomatic incident.

'What is it?' said Ek to the waiter.

'My lord,' said the waiter, 'I must ask you to extinguish that paper pipe, for smoking at banquet is strictly forbidden.'

Ek turned his green-flecked orange eyes upon the waiter and said:

'You are in error. Judge Qil has ruled that the smoking to which you allude relates only to the consumption of opium, kif or grass clippings. That is his judgment, which you will find in the records of the case of the Imperium versus Odolo.'

'But, sir—'

'I am not smoking opium,' said Ek. 'Nor am I smoking kif, or grass clippings. I am smoking a rare and fragment herb known as tobacco, which is perfectly lawful. If you doubt me, then go and ask Judge Qil himself. That's him – there. Sitting by Dardanalti.'

The waiter retreated in confusion.

Perhaps you are asking yourself why this incident has found its way into a history as scholarly as this one. Had you acquaintance with waiters, you would not so ask; for you would know that the overbearing insolence of this breed is such that the public discomfiture of any one of their number is a matter well worth recording for posterity.

Anyway, there sat Master Ek, smoking and dreaming, and watching the banquet guests eat and drink, talk and gossip, or sit in silent speculation.

If the truth be told, there was rather much silent speculation that night. This banquet lacked the uproarious sense of abandonment which had characterized other such celebrations in Justina's palace. While Juliet Idaho was drinking with a will, others merely sipped cautiously at their drinks, their minds given to fatigue or to forebodings of disaster.

Among those who were particularly subdued were Bro Drumel (captain of Justina's palace guard) and Hostaja Torsen Sken-Pitilkin (builder of the imperial airship). Fear of torture was depressing the elegant Drumel, who nightly dreamt of the agony he expected to suffer ultimately at the hands of Aldarch the Third. For his own part, Sken-Pitilkin was near dead with fatigue. He was feeling his age, and was bowed down by the rigours of his airship building labours.

While the mood was subdued, the food was not, and an amazement of good things were served to the guests. There was a surpassing succulence of dragonlord salad, expensive stuff indeed as it is cut from the heart of the headgrowth of a coconut tree, and the tree necessarily dies as a result of this interference with its foliage. There was a wealth of lotus seeds soaked in honey. There was bottled abalone, fresh chicken livers, jellyfish soup, stuffed sea slugs and, of course, the inevitable flying fish (braised, stewed and brewed up in a chowder).

351

While this feast was in progress, a messenger slipped up to Nadalastabstala Banraithanchumun.Ek and whispered into the ear of the High Priest of Zoz the Ancestral.

Ek's eyes did not widen, nor did he blanch. For Master Ek was an old man who had endured a great many shocks and knew how to keep calm in a crisis. Even so, there was a slight tremor in his voice when he conveyed the gist of the message to his acolytes Paach Ch'ha Saat and Aath Nau Das.

'We have been warned,' said Ek.

'Of what?' said Ch'ha Saat.

'Shut up!' said Nau Das. 'He's telling us, isn't he?'

'I only—'

'Silence!' hissed Ek. 'Listen. The messenger brought me a warning. There will be violence tonight. We must be ready to kill. Things are coming to a crisis.'

'Why?' said Nau Das. 'What is it?'

'Our spies have uncovered a plot,' said Ek. 'The Thrug is planning something.'

'What?' said Nau Das

'The Froissart thing will fail its test tonight. Then we will have to kill it. We will have no choice. It is a false priest, however accomplished its tongue.'

'So we kill it,' said Nau Das. 'So what?'

'The Thrug has another wazir on hand,' said Ek.

'What!'

'Yes. A madman. From the Dromdanjerie.'

'But who?'

'Our sources give two possible candidates. One is Orge Arat.'

'Him!'

'Yes, him. The axe murderer.'

'But that's impossible. Too many people know who he is. And what.'

'Yes, so he's not the most likely choice. It's more probably the other candidate.'

'Who?'

352

'Rye Phobos,' said Ek.

'The name means nothing,' said Nau Das.

'Nothing to me, either,' said Ch'ha Saat.

So Ek enlightened his acolytes, explaining what Phobos had done at the age of fourteen, when he had given good cause for his permanent incarceration.

'That was thirty years ago,' said Ek. 'Nobody's seen him since. Nobody outside the staff of the Dromdanjerie.'

'Then – the Qasaba girl!' said Nau Das, who was always quick off the mark. 'Olivia Qasaba. She could identify him.'

'Yes,' said Ek, glancing briefly at Olivia, who was even then sharing a joke with the Empress Justina. 'But will she? We may have to overcome this false wazir by brute force.'

'What?' said Ch'ha Saat. 'Just the three of us?'

'Others here are friends of Aldarch the Third,' said Master Ek. 'If offered a pardon for past sins, Aquitaine Varazchavardan may come to our aid. Anyway, it takes but a moment to kill a man. We have blades. We can do it. So wait. Wait for my signal.'

Then Ek brought this whispered conference to an end and the three sat back, contemplating the fighting talent arranged around the table. All Justina's allies were here, some of them potentially very dangerous fighters: the bullman Log Jarvis, the Yudonic Knight Juliet Idaho, the Ashdan warrior Shanvil Angarus May, the corpsemaster Uckermark and his loud-mouthed woman Yilda.

The odds were in Justina's favour.

But . . .

They will not dare to kill me.

So thought Master Ek. Surely Justina would not be rash enough to murder the High Priest of Zoz the Ancestral. If she did, then all the Believers on Untunchilamon would rise against her at once, and tear her from limb to limb.

So . . .

Let her produce her false wazir. And I will kill the thing. Then see what she dares to do.

Thus thought Master Ek, then, yielding to appetite, began to feed from the fresh dishes which were being placed on the table. There were juicy bean shoots and quantities of the rare green mushrooms which only grew in a particular place Downstairs. There was crab meat served with the finest polished white rice. And dogmeat, monkey meat, and the flesh of half a hundred cats as well.

Master Ek studied Jean Froissart anew as the time for the trial by ordeal drew near. Soon Froissart would have to pick up a ball of red-hot iron without injury to himself, thus proving himself a true priest of Zoz. Thanks to the intelligence he had received, Ek knew Froissart must fail.

But did Froissart know it?

Watching him, Ek was not sure.

At last, the moment arrived. The Empress Justina hammered on the table with a soup spoon, conjuring silence in the banqueting hall.

'We announce,' said she, 'the trial by ordeal of Jean Froissart, who will handle red-hot iron to prove himself a true priest of Zoz.'

Then a cowled and black-masked figure entered the Grand Hall. This was the executioner who would put Froissart through his ordeal. Nobody knew who he was; this anonymity was not just traditional but was enshrined in the law, and was meant to protect the executioner from suffering vengeance at the hands of the friends, relatives and associates of those he ordealed, tortured or killed.

Two slaves followed the executioner into the Grand Hall. The slaves deposited a brazier mounted on an iron tripod. It was already alight. The slaves then departed, returning shortly afterwards with a similar tripod supporting a basket containing old iron. Atop the basket was a set of bellows. One of the slaves used this to excite

354

the mass of burning charcoal in the brazier while the other fetched a bucket of cold water. Then the black-masked executioner muttered a command and both slaves left.

Nadalastabstala Banraithanchumun Ek evinced no outward interest in these proceedings, but lit another cigarette and sat back in his chair. In moments, Jean Froissart would be exposed as a fraud.

This was something to savour.

The Empress Justina then left her chair and walked to the side of the executioner, and there waited for Jean Froissart. He approached, and said, loudly:

'My lady, I am here to undertake trial by ordeal.'

Justina smiled, then answered:

'This trial has my favour.'

Then Froissart dropped his voice to a whisper and said:

'Where is the salve? The magic salve?'

'Oh, you don't need that,' said Justina pleasantly.

Froissart stared at her.

'But – but you—'

'I promised,' said Justina, and smiled sweetly. 'Well, I'm breaking my promise.'

'You mustn't!' said Froissart savagely.

Surely this was a joke. But a joke in the worst possible taste. The Thrug would pay for this!

But Juliet Idaho was already at Froissart's elbow.

'Don't you tell the Empress what she can or can't do,' said Idaho. 'Speak your piece. Thank the Empress for her favour. Come on! Or I'll rip you to pieces on the spot.'

He meant what he said.

Too late, Froissart realized Justina was serious. He had been tricked, fooled, double-crossed and swindled. Set up as a sacrifice. If he protested, Idaho would kill him on the spot. With the approval of law and custom, for a priest who flinched from an ordeal was doomed to instant destruction.

But if I die, the Thrug dies.

Surely. For if Jean Froissart was killed, then Manthandros Trasilika would be thought a false wazir. Whereupon Trasilika would be killed too, and Trasilika's pardon of Justina would be revoked, and Justina herself would be tried then executed.

So thought Froissart.

Unless.

Ah yes.

Unless the Thrug had another wazir on hand.

Froissart had heard the rumours about escaped lunatics from the Dromdanjerie. A great many people believed (or at least claimed to believe) that the Thrug was grooming a cunning psychopath to rule as wazir on Untunchilamon.

Whatever the truth of the matter:

I have no choice.

So:

'My lady,' said Froissart, 'I thank you for granting this trial your favour.'

'That is well spoken,' said Justina. Then she said: 'Would you please step this way?'

Why? Where were they going? This was not part of the prescribed ritual of the trial by ordeal!

Despite his confusion, Froissart followed the Empress. Who led him to Nadalastabstala Banraithanchumun Ek. Froissart wanted to run. But Juliet Idaho was just a footfall to the rear, and Froissart knew instant death would befall him if he tried to flee.

'Master Ek,' said Justina, 'I would like you to do me the favour of examining this gentleman's hands.'

'With pleasure,' said Ek, pleased to have this opportunity to make sure that no trickery was taking place. 'Froissart! Show me your claws!'

Here a grave insult, for the Janjuladoola word which Master Ek used to say 'claws' was 'emokskok', a term used only of certain taloned beasts which are held to be ritually unclean. To use this word of a human is to

356

suggest that the person in question is no better than a foul and monstrous brute beast.

But Froissart did not protest.

Froissart was having trouble merely staying on his feet as Master Ek examined his hands. Sweat was bubbling from Froissart's forehead, but his hands were dry.

'It appears,' said Master Ek, 'that no magical or mundane agency has interfered with this man's hands.'

'Thank you,' said Justina. Then, to Froissart: 'Well, Frozzy darling. Let us go. The executioner is waiting.'

Then Juliet Idaho gave Froissart a little shove, and the hapless priest stumbled toward his doom.

Froissart was terrified.

In moments, he would be dead.

When he had to hold the red-hot iron, he would scream. And his flesh would crisp. And a hideous stench of burning would fill the air. And he would drop the iron. And he would clutch his ruined hand. And all would know him unequal to the ordeal. And all would think him a false priest, for all that he was true. And his death would befall him.

Froissart was almost paralysed by terror. He looked like a zombie as he ambulated toward the brazier.

Ek watched.

Ek drew upon his cigarette. Drew heavily.

The High Priest of Zoz the Ancestral was a connoisseur of terror. If he was any judge – and he believed himself to be the best – then the fear of death was upon the young Jean Froissart.

Ek hissed, softly.

'Master?' said one of his acoloytes.

'He knows he will fail,' said Ek. 'He was confident this morning, but he's not now. Something's gone wrong, at least for him. He's going to die here, and he knows it. Which means the Thrug has got her false wazir close at hand. Be ready for anything. Swords, mayhap. Or worse.'

'Worse?'

'Burning zen perhaps. Who knows? Just be ready!'
Thus murmured Ek.

The High Priest was sitting forward now, watching Froissart intently. Froissart stopped a couple of paces away from the brazier and its attendant. Froissart's face was that of a corpse.

'I am the master of the ordeal,' said the cowled figure who commanded the brazier.

Who spoke?

Master Ek listened intently, but could not divine the identity of that shadow-faced entity. The voice was hoarse and half-throttled. It was the voice of a thing from the grave.

'Master,' said Froissart. 'I am—'

Then his voice failed entirely.

'We know who you are,' said the masked executioner. 'You are Jean Froissart, one who comes to prove himself a priest of Zoz.'

Froissart found enough voice to say:

'Yes.'

Everyone in the banqueting hall heard that single word clearly, for all eating had ceased. Only the waiters still went about their business, adroitly clearing away dirty plates and discarded stabs. But such was their professionalism that they were as inconspicuous as ghosts of the invisible type.

'Choose,' said the executioner. 'Choose the iron for your ordeal.'

So saying, the cowled figure pointed at the basket of iron balls. Froissart reached out. Took one at random. It was cold and heavy. Bits of rust came off on his hands as he handed it to the executioner.

'Pick up the bellows,' said the executioner. 'Stoke the brazier.'

Froissart did so.

It seemed the whole world was watching Jean Froissart as he worked the bellows. Would he faint? Would he collapse? Would he scream and run?

He did none of those things.

Instead, the rhythmical labour of working the bellows helped ease his terror. Good, hard, physical work. An ache in his forearms. Sweat rolling down his forehead, stinging as it burnt into his eyes, and for once he welcomed the sweat, the heat, the cloth wet against his back, he was alive, for the moment, for the moment at least, if he worked hard enough he could maybe extend the moment to for ever.

But—

'Enough,' said the executioner.

Froissart stepped back. Just a pace. And now all watched as the executioner held aloft the iron ball.

'Who touches this, dies,' said the executioner. 'Unless he touches it by my consent. Nobody yet has my consent.'

Then the executioner lowered the iron ball on to the hot coals.

'Please,' said Froissart, his voice a muttering whisper. 'Please,' he said, staring at the iron. 'A thousand dragons if you say I can have it now.'

'They can hear you at the table, fool,' said the executioner.

Froissart looked up. Turned on the banqueters. Could they hear him? Really? Their faces showed nothing but anticipatory interest.

'Please,' said Froissart.

He was begging.

'I cannot be bribed,' said the executioner. 'You must go through with your ordeal in accordance with the proper and lawful rituals.'

As yet, the iron ball was still a sullen black. But, as Froissart watched, it slowly began to get hot.

'Ah,' said the executioner. 'It is turning red with the heat. See?'

Froissart could not help but look. It was true. The dead iron was glowing red hot. Sullen waves of heat radiated outwards. The air above the brazier was trembling. Seen through the buckling air, Master Ek's face warped and distorted.

Without warning, black spots started swarming through the air like so many pestering insects. Froissart swayed on his feet.

'Don't fall,' hissed the executioner. 'Fall, and you'll die on the spot.'

Froissart steadied himself. His vision cleared. His focus sharpened.

'Look at it,' said the executioner. 'Look at the iron.'

Unwillingly, Froissart did so.

'Now,' said the executioner, 'reach out your hand. Reach out your hand and pick it up. Do it!'

Froissart reached out with his right hand.

An anticipatory shock sent shivers prickling all along his arms. His vision sharpened. He saw the veins of fire in the charcoal pulsing softly, alive with a luminescent rhythm. He saw the red-hot iron ball glowering, waiting. He wanted to scream. A sob broke from his throat. His hand became a claw. His hand closed around the iron ball.

Which was cold.

As cold as ice.

Jean Froissart lifted the iron ball and held it aloft.

He knew the sensation of cold must be an illusion, something his nerves had done to save his mind from the agony of his burning flesh. He knew his flesh was burning because he could smell it.

'That is enough,' said the executioner.

'Enough?'

'Drop the iron.'

Froissart dropped the iron ball. It fell heavily to the stone. The sound of iron hitting stone rang through the Grand Hall. Everyone in the place was utterly silent. Watching Froissart. For a few moments, the iron ball continued to glow red hot, but it rapidly cooled to black.

The executioner picked up the bucket of water which his slaves had earlier brought into the Grand Hall together with the brazier, the bellows and the heap of old iron.

'I must cool the iron,' said the executioner. 'Stand back, for there will be steam when I pour the water over it.'

Jean Froissart did not see how a little steam could do him any harm. Nevertheless, he took a couple of steps backwards. The executioner began to pour water from the bucket. The water splashed around the iron ball and hissed into steam. The executioner continued to pour until no more steam rose from the iron ball. Water spread out across the floor. The executioner exhausted the contents of the bucket, nudged the iron ball cautiously with his foot, then picked it up and treasured it in his hands.

'Show me your hands,' said the executioner.

'What?' said Froissart.

'You heard me. Show me your hands.'

Both Froissart's hands were tightly clenched. He was trying to stave off the pain which must surely be waiting in his right hand, waiting for the moment to reveal itself.

'Show me!'

Reluctantly, Froissart uncoiled both hands.

They were unmarked, the right no different to the left.

'But,' said Froissart in a whisper, 'but . . .'

'A miracle,' said the executioner. 'But then, you are a true priest of Zoz the Ancestral. It is an acknowledged truth that Zoz the Ancestral will work a miracle such as this when that is necessary to prove a true priest true.'

'It is,' said Froissart weakly.

Then the executioner said:

'Go.'

'Go where?' said Froissart.

'Where do you think!? Go to the table. Show them your hands!'

Obedient to this command, Jean Froissart walked toward the banqueting tables. He felt as if he were walking on air. He was delirious with disbelieving relief.

He approached Master Ek. He displayed his hands.

'Here,' said Ek roughly.

Moments later, Nadalastabstala Banraithanchumun Ek was gouging at Froissart's hands, digging into them, knuckling them, rubbing them. But he could find no damage. The High Priest of Zoz the Ancestral was furious.

'Bring me the ball,' said Master Ek. 'The iron ball. I want to see it. Now! Get it!'

The cowled and night-masked executioner was still holding the iron ball which had been used for Jean Froissart's ordeal. Froissart walked toward him.

'What do you want?' said the executioner.

'The iron ball,' said Froissart.

'Take it,' said the executioner, handing the thing over. 'Keep it. A souvenir.'

'It's Ek who wants it,' said Froissart.

'Then he's welcome to it,' said the masked executioner. 'Go. Give it to him.'

As Froissart walked toward Master Ek, the executioner made his departure. His slaves came into the Grand Hall and began removing the equipment.

'Here,' said Ek, impatiently. 'Give me the thing here.'

Froissart handed over the iron ball.

Ek took it into his hands and looked at it suspiciously. It was cold, cold as the belly of a dead lizard on a chilly morning. A flake of rust came away in Ek's hands. A trace of sweat from Ek's skin moistened the rust, which left a black stain when he brushed it away. Ek handed the ball to the most trusted of his acolytes, Aath Nau Das.

'Take this thing,' said Ek. 'Take it, and test it to destruction.'

Then he turned to Froissart.

'You have passed,' said Ek. 'You have passed the test. You have proved yourself a true priest of Zoz.'

'Then,' said Manthandros Trasilika loudly, 'since Froissart's a true priest, I am a true wazir.'

362

Ek looked at him coldly.

'You are,' said Ek. 'All Untunchilamon will know as much by this time tomorrow. That I promise you. For now – let the banquet continue.'

Saying that was strictly the prerogative of the Empress Justina, but she let it pass. She felt quite weak with relief. So it had all gone off as planned. She had expected it to, of course. But there were so many things which could have gone wrong. So very many things.

What, for example, if Master Ek had demanded that the executioner be unmasked . . . ?

Elsewhere, in a secure room far removed from the Great Hall – Justina's bedroom, as it happens – the executioner was unmasking. The cowled figure proved to be Odolo, Injiltaprajura's master conjuror. Once unmasked, Odolo reached into his mouth, withdrew a bit of palate-contorting wood, and tossed the much-hated thing aside.

He worked his jaw this way and that, experimentally, then said, in accents far removed from those the chunk of wood had forced upon him:

'That's better.'

Then Odolo reached into one of his capacious sleeves and withdrew a rusty iron ball.

'OK,' said Odolo. 'That's it.'

The ball quivered.

It became a spherical watermelon.

A gleaming golden orb.

A mirror.

A miniature sun.

A globe webbed all over with delicate patterns of brown and green.

Then a silver-bright bubble of light, which squeaked in excitement.

'Did I do well?' said Shabble.

'Oh, you did very, very well,' said Odolo. 'Did I give you the cues at the right time?'

'I didn't really need them,' said Shabble. 'I remembered

363

what to do when. But you told them right, you did, if I'd forgotten something I'd have remembered when you told me.'

'The best bit was the water,' said Odolo. 'The water steaming. Was that hard to do? To go from cool to hot?'

'Not when you're a shabble,' said Shabble. 'I'm really a sun, you know. That's how I do it.'

'I know, I know,' said Odolo. 'You know I know. You know why I know.'

'Of course I do,' said Shabble.

'You did do very well,' said Odolo, knowing that Shabble loved praise. Then: 'Shabble, we need your help. You could help us again.'

'Oh no,' said Shabble. 'I explained about that already. This was the last time. For old time's sake. I have to go now. I have to get back to the temple.'

'I could send you to a—'

'You said you wouldn't!' said Shabble. 'You promised. You swore!'

'I know,' said Odolo, an unfamiliar note of tension and regret in his voice. 'So I did. But, while I'd like to think of myself as a man of honour—'

Shabble abruptly grew red hot and spun, spitting out a dozen fireballs. Odolo dodged and ducked, and ended up flat on his face on the floor. And Shabble, with unexpected anger in Shabbleself's voice, said:

'I wargamed this with Uckermark. He told me you'd try to make me your slave.'

'What else did he tell you?' said Odolo, shocked and shaken. 'What else?' And here the conjuror picked himself up off the floor. 'To kill me?'

'If necessary,' said Shabble. 'You were going to say it, weren't you? You were going to say the words. You were going to make me do things. Weren't you?'

'I . . . I . . . Shabble, my . . . could we . . . can we . . . could we still be friends?'

A silence.

Then Shabble spoke:

364

'Yes. We could still be friends.'

'Very well, Shabble my friend,' said Odolo. 'Thank you for your help tonight. I'm sorry I . . . I'm sorry I almost gave way to temptation. Go back to your temple, Shabble my friend, and go with my good wishes. But do bear us in mind. I don't say you could solve all of our problems, but you might help us to save some of them.'

'I have, I have,' said Shabble, sounding hurt.

From Shabble's point of view, a good deal of the last twenty thousand years had been spent doing very little but helping people. Shabble had taught them and counselled them, had played music for them and kept them company in prisons and elsewhere, had designed machines for them, had translated foreign languages for them, had told them stories and had worked out their income tax.

But people seemed to be in as much of a mess as they ever were, and they were still as full of demands as ever.

After twenty thousand years, Shabble had had enough. Shabble was a priest now, the High Priest of the Temple of the Holy Cockroach, with Shabbleself's own life to lead, so people would just have to get on with the job of helping themselves. And if they didn't, if they continued to make importunate demands upon poor old overworked Shabble – why, then Shabble would burn some of them up, and Shabbleself's lawyers would have something to say to any who were left unburnt!

'You did very, very well,' said Odolo, laying on the praise for one last time. 'And I'm very proud of you.'

'And you're going to kiss me goodnight,' said Shabble. 'You promised.'

'And I'm as good as my word,' said Odolo.

And the conjuror kissed dear Shabble, who thereafter took Shabbleself off to Xtokobrokotok in Marthandorthan, and spent the rest of the night leading the congregation of the Cult of the Holy Cockroach in rituals of worship and praise.

CHAPTER THIRTY-THREE

As the banquet continued, Jean Froissart rapidly got drunk and slid beneath the table. Manthandros Trasilika drank just as much, but had a greater ability to hold his liquor, and managed to stay in his chair. Juliet Idaho, another big drinker, vomited thrice and fell off his chair more times than one could easily account for, but stayed conscious and semi-capable.

Nadalastabstala Banraithanchumun Ek drank not at all, but smoked furiously, looking a very dragon in his rage. In due course, Aath Nau Das returned with the iron ball, which he had anatomized into three main fragments and seven smaller ones, plus a great many flakes of rust and a liberal sprinkling of iron dust.

'There's no trick here,' said acolyte Nau Das.

'But there's a trick somewhere,' said Master Ek.

'You mean – you mean you think we didn't see a genuine miracle?'

'Oh, grow up!' said Ek.

'If not a miracle,' persisted Nau Das, 'then what?'

An acolyte does not – should not – blatantly question a High Priest in this manner. But Master Ek kept his temper and gave a reasoned answer:

'Injiltaprajura has a Cabal House, has it not? And the Cabal House is packed with wonder-workers, is it not? And have not the wonder-workers powers magical? And does it not follow that such a sorcerer could easily have intervened tonight on Froissart's behalf?'

'It could be,' conceded Nau Das. 'But who?'

'Varazchavardan,' said Master Ek. 'To name but one possibility. Dolglin Chin Xter is another. I have long thought him to be in alliance with the Thrug.'

'Xter?' said Nau Das. 'But he's sick in bed. Sick to the point of death with hepatitis and malaria in combination.'

'So our spies tell us,' said Master Ek grimly. 'But I no longer believe we can trust our spies. They led us to believe a false wazir would be produced tonight.'

'And there won't be?'

'Use your eyes! Look! The Thrug's as merry as a pickled gherkin. She's sozzled. Juliet Idaho's no better. There's no risk of swords going to war tonight. If the Thrug has a false wazir in hiding, she means to hide the thing still.'

'But our spies were so confident!' said Nau Das.

'So maybe the Thrug is deliberately feeding them false information,' said Master Ek.

'So what do we do now?'

'We grab someone we can trust to have reliable information,' said Master Ek. 'Juliet Idaho. The ideal choice.'

'Why?' said Nau Das. 'Why ideal?'

'For obvious reasons,' said Ek in irritation. 'Work it out for yourself.'

Juliet Idaho had the confidence of the Empress and so would know what was going on. He had few administrative responsibilities, so would not be swiftly missed. And, by the end of the night's celebrations, the much-befuddled Yudonic Knight would be in no state to put up any resistance whatsoever.

As Ek was so thinking, his thoughts were distracted by a pair of spoons which had started drumming their way along the tabletop. They were porcelain spoons brightly painted with green and yellow dragons shown breathing out red flame and purple smoke. Now the spoons were dancing, and drumming as they danced.

The spoons jumped up on to a big platter. It was an elegant piece of pottery in the most dignified Janjula-doola grey, and it held great discards of sucked bones and fish scales, of fruit pips and banana peels, of the flaccid skin of papaya. the flexible armour of pineapple and the obstinate wood of clean-picked coconut.

There danced the spoons.

Click – clack – sklakkety clack!

Clok – clok – cluckety tuckety cluckety skluk!

As the spoons thus amused themselves, tatters of meat and splatters of fruit discarded in all directions. A waiter tried to restrain these irresponsible culinary instruments, but they slipped from his grasp and fled down the table.

Plat – mat – blattatarat!

Sklip – blip – tukatatot!

So rhythmed the spoons as they drummed on the tabletop, chimed against steel and porcelain, upset glasses of sherbet and wine alike, and at last started dancing right in front of Nadalastabstala Banraithanchumun Ek himself.

The High Priest of Zoz the Ancestral glared at the spoons in fury, then looked around the table. He saw half a dozen wonder-workers sitting together and laughing uproariously. Master Ek fastened his gaze upon them. As the sorcerers felt the sharp talons of that gaze digging into their flesh, their laughter ceased abruptly, and the spoons fell dead on the table. Shortly thereafter, the miscreants made their excuses and took themselves off to their Cabal House.

Many people were leaving now, for the debauch really had entered its final stages. Fuddled drinkers spilt their brandy, stumbled with their wine and slid beneath the table. In disregarded bowls, intoxicated pyramids of ice-cream melted to muddled puddles. Candles shickered and swayed in subtle draughts of sweating air. A dizzy mosquito cannoned cockeyed through wreaths of insect-destroying smoke, then, half-seas-over, plunged to its own destruction in a jug of vinegar.

At the head of the table, the Empress Justina turned to Olivia and said:

'Enough. Our duty tonight is done.'

Justina left the table in company with the Ashdan lass;

and shortly both were in bed and asleep.

The departure of the Empress was the signal for everyone else to leave, which they did. Master Ek departed in the company of his acolytes and other companions. Juliet Idaho was not so quick to leave, but at last the Yudonic Knight got to his feet and stumbled down Lak Street towards the grand mansion he shared with his wife Harold.

Idaho never got there.

As he was walking down Lak Street, a group of men surrounded him. He was seized by the strength of six. A hood was dragged down over his head. A gag was stuffed into his mouth. Then he was thrown on to a dung cart and taken to Goldhammer Rise and the Temple of Torture. There he was ungagged and, after a preliminary beating, was brought into the presence of Nadalastabstala Banraithanchumun Ek.

'Good evening,' said Master Ek.

Juliet Idaho spat out a little blood then said:

'What do you want from me?'

'Oh, just a little talk,' said Ek. 'Come, I mean you no ill. Here, have a drink.'

Idaho accepted this invitation, and swallowed the drink Ek proffered him.

A mistake!

Immediately Idaho's head began to spin. The room swelled, stretched, blurred and hummed. Phantasmagoric dragons flickered across his field of vision then collapsed into tinkling rainbows.

Ek had fed Idaho a drink containing a carefully measured dose of oola, that truth drug also known as babble tongue. This is made from opium and alcohol mixed with a special extract obtained from the scorpion fish, and mixed also with zen, a dissociative drug which has devastating effects on the mind.

'Now,' said Ek, 'speak to me.'

'I speak to you,' said Idaho.

'Tell me all,' said Ek. 'All that I shouldn't know.'

369

Thus spoke Ek; and, with very little further prompting, the Yudonic Knight began to blabbermouth secrets.

'Froissart is false,' said Idaho.

'Nonsense,' said Ek, even though he believed as much himself. 'Froissart can't be false. He proved himself in trial by ordeal.'

Juliet Idaho grinned a drunken grin and said:

'Froissart proved the powers of conjuring. The executioner who waited upon him was the conjuror Odolo – who had Shabble up his sleeve.'

'That can't be so,' said Master Ek. 'I saw Shabble myself at sunset, spinning above the Xtokobrokotok.'

'So?' said Idaho. 'Shabble needs no guides to find Shabbleself's way from Marthandorthan to Pokra Ridge. Shabble came privily to Odolo shortly after sunset. Oh, they fooled you nicely!'

This infuriated Ek, because he had been fooled indeed; and, now he understood what had happened, it was blindingly obvious. Had it not been for his arthritis, Ek would have kicked himself severely.

'But,' protested one of the acolytes, who knew more of sorcery than of prestidigitation, 'I was there! I saw! It wasn't Shabble, it was a ball of iron. We smashed it to pieces afterwards.'

'Long sleeves,' said Idaho. 'Long sleeves.'

He giggled.

Then the Yudonic Knight fainted, and slid beneath the table.

Leaving Ek and his acolytes looking at each other.

'The Thrug thinks us children,' said Ek in rage. 'Children, to be fooled by a cheap trick. But she's gone too far this time! And her Froissart thing! What they did was blasphemy. For that I'll have Froissart butchered.'

Slowly, Ek recovered his temper. Then he kicked the unconscious Juliet Idaho and said:

'Strip him.'

'Hmmm,' said Master Ek, without much surprise. 'It is as I thought.'

Then the High Priest stubbed out his cigarette in Idaho's omphalos.

'We'll keep this thing here in our holding cells,' said Ek. 'Hold it under constant observation in a lighted cell. Give it no chance to commit suicide. I want to dispose of it myself. By way of sacrifice. In public. When the time is right.'

'When will that be, master?' said one of the acolytes.

'When I say so!' said Ek, irritated by a question so witless. 'Now, I have another job for you. Our congregation must be roused, for I wish to celebrate the Festival of Dark. Yes, here, tonight, this very night. Not in our Temple on Hojo Street. That's unsafe. No, we'll hold it here.'

'But,' said one of the acolytes, 'this building is consecrated to the—'

Ek kept his temper.

Instead of losing it, he merely said:

'I will formally dedicate this building to Zoz before the Festival of Dark commences. Now go and rouse our people!'

The rousing shortly commenced.

The acolytes woke certain Janjuladoola people who were adherents of the Temple of Zoz the Ancestral. And these woke others, who roused more fellow worshippers in turn. Soon people in their dozens were flocking to Goldhammer Rise, where they thronged into the Temple of Torture. This could not accommodate them all, so the unaccommodated gathered in the street outside, with acolytes relaying Master Ek's words to them once the Festival of Dark began.

In the Most Holy Calendar, the Festival of Dark falls a few days before the Festival of Light. The precise timing is at the discretion of the local High Priest, and Master Ek was within his rights to schedule it for that very night.

It is traditional for the High Priest of the Temple of Zoz to celebrate the Festival of Dark by preaching on the conflict between anarchic chaos and that countervailing redemptive power which brings order. In contrast, the Festival of Light is devoted solely to a celebration of that prosperity which naturally flows from the triumph of order, to the general benefit of all.

Nadalastabstala Banraithanchumun Ek performed his duties as tradition decrees, and held the required service. In the course of his preaching, he declared the worship of Power to be the ultimate aim of humanity; and described Aldarch Three as Power incarnate.

'The natural instinct of the natural man is to ravage, savage and despoil,' said Ek, getting into his stride. 'To preserve the world against such destructions, the State gives each man incentives to support the ruling order. In the way of incentive, in return for allegiance to the ruling order, the State allows each man the power over his women, his children, his slaves and his other chattels.

'As it is a man's privilege to dispose of his wife, his children and his slaves, so it is a Temple's privilege to dispose of its priests. And so, as the Festival of Light draws near, I name Jean Froissart, priest of Zoz the Ancestral, as the sacrifice of the year.'

A remarkable honour! But Jean Froissart, as yet unconscious of the great privilege which had been bestowed upon him, slept on in ignorance; and he would not learn his fate for some time yet.

By this time, certain students of history may be ready to raise an outcry about the disproportionate amount of space which has been given to insignificant people such as the Yudonic Knight named Juliet Idaho. Why, they will ask, is this so? And why, in contrast, has a person of such importance as Jon Qasaba been allowed to disappear from this Chronicle? Why has no effort been made to show his role in these events?

Certainly it would be interesting to follow Jon Qasaba's fortunes. But this is not Qasaba's biography: instead, this is the history of the final days of the rule of the Family Thrug on Untunchilamon.

And, despite what he later became, Jon Qasaba played no role whatsoever in those final days. For Olivia's father, feared by many to be dead, had been taken prisoner by Ms Mix.

You will remember that Ms Mix was an ogre, one of the twenty-seven creatures of that breed then dwelling on Untunchilamon. You will doubtless further remember that this Ms Mix was the mother-in-law of the escaped lunatic Orge Arat, Arat himself being the author of a Secret History known as the *Injiltaprajura-dariski*.

Or perhaps you will not remember.

If you have no mother-in-law of your own, you may fail to understand the formidability of the breed; and hence the particularities of Ms Mix may have failed to lodge in your mind.

Regardless of what has or has not been remembered, the fact remains that Jon Qasaba was in the hands of a mother-in-law (admittedly someone else's, not his own) and was doomed to suffer much before he escaped and regained his freedom. Yes, Jon Qasaba was a man much cursed by adventures. Now adventuring is greatly to the taste of an adolescent, but Qasaba was a scholarly Ashdan who had long outgrown desires for such over-involvement in life. So he did not take kindly to what was happening to him. But that was his doom, and there was no way for him to avoid it.

While we are on the subject of adventuring, let us note that Jon Qasaba was by no means the only person undergoing adventures in and around the city of Injilta-prajura. Many were the people who were undergoing sore trials in the wilds of Downstairs; or who had found themselves in grave danger after retreating into the wastelands of Zolabrik; or who were caught up in the currents of mutinous conspiracy which flourished and festered aboard the ships which were conveying looters, deserters and other such rabble away from the shores of peril.

But of these we can say nothing further, for fooskin is expensive, life is short and the reader's patience limited; all of which conspires against history. Their existence is noted merely to point out that Jon Qasaba's suffering was by no means unique.

Certainly Jon Qasaba's life was a bath of rosewater compared to the terrors being endured by Chegory Guy and Ivan Pokrov, hapless prisoners of the therapist.

As yet, not a hair of their heads had been touched. But the therapist (which had a very fertile imagination) had indulged in all manner of threats. And it was getting restless. Chegory and Pokrov saw its restlessness and rightly feared that the therapist might well do something unfortunate unless it was swiftly granted satisfaction.

CHAPTER THIRTY-FOUR

The morning after the banquet, a great inertia hung over Untunchilamon. Grey clouds had spread across the constellations by night, but the sunless day was nevertheless as hot as ever. In the smothering heat of morning, it was hard for hangover heads to compel fatigued bones and bleary eyes to get about their business.

It had rained in the night, and the humidity was nothing short of oppressive. Even in the Long Dry, the heat and humidity of Injiltaprajura are hard to take; but when the rains come, and the air is damp, and it is impossible to get anything dry, and rot and fungus flourish everywhere, then one strenuously wishes oneself elsewhere. The weather worsened the temper of the citizenry, which temper was made no better by the unceasing activities of the drummers, whose percussion power ruled the streets from Lubos to Marthandorthan.

Manthandros Trasilika woke feeling dreadful. He felt (not to put too strong a point upon it) as if he had been suspercollated from a gibbet ever since sunset. The cause of his physical unease was a headache. Yes, Manthandros Trasilika had a headache, as an ogre has bad breath or a vampire a taste for blood. It was no ordinary headache, this; rather, it was an all-enveloping disaster, a world-obliterating agony. It felt as if, surely, a master smith was forging a sledgehammer with Trasilika's scalp as his anvil.

And the cause of the headache? One suspects it to be a side-effect of the prescription medicine in which Trasilika had so vigorously indulged himself while at banquet; that medicine consisting of some extremely expensive imported cherry brandy, a potent toddy derived from a part of the coconut palm which shall remain nameless, some vodka, and a quantity of jellyfish wine (which is to ordinary wine as a spear is to a nail, a lion to a cat, a land dragon to a dragon imperial, or a mountain to an anthill).

Let it be noted that Manthandros Trasilika did not wake voluntarily, and was extremely displeased at having been woken at all. He was wazir of Untunchilamon. Surely nobody would dispute that now that the priest of Zoz the Ancestral who supported his claims to the wazirate had proved himself true in trial by ordeal. Yes, Trasilika was the rightful wazir, one of the lords of the Izdimir Empire – and, at the very least, he expected to be able to sleep in on the morning after a banquet.

'Why have I been woken?' said Trasilika.

'Because,' said the manservant who had roused him, 'Justina Thrug demands that you wake. She has things to discuss with you.'

Trasilika groaned.

How much longer would he have to put up with this woman?

Why – no time at all.

She had served her purpose, and it was time for her head to be chopped off.

'Call my guards,' said Trasilika to his manservant. 'Tell them to seize the Thrug and cut off her head.'

'Master,' said the servant differently, 'I'm afraid you have no guards.'

'Nonsense!' said Trasilika. 'I had plenty of guards last night.'

'I'm afraid, master, that they've deserted in the night.'

'But that's absurd! Why should they desert now?'

'I believe, master, that agents acting on behalf of Master Ek have lured them away with promises of higher pay elsewhere.'

'Are you trying to tell me,' said Trasilika furiously, 'that the High Priest of Zoz the Ancestral has bought the loyalty of my guards?'

The manservant quailed, but did not seek to alter the truth. Instead, he said:

'My lord, that would appear to be the case.'

'Then – then send to my ship,' said Trasilika. 'A dozen men, that's all I need. A dozen men with swords and hatchets. We'll hack up this Thrug then see what we can do about N'stala Ek.'

'Master,' said the manservant nervously, 'you . . . you . . .'

'I suppose,' said Trasilika sarcastically, 'that next you're going to tell me I don't have a ship any more.'

'Well . . .'

'Are you seriously . . . ?'

'Master, I – I—'

'Has my ship been burnt? Or pirated? Or what? Has my scurvy crew deserted to Ek as well?'

'Master, the ship sailed before dawn. I know not why, or not for certain – but rumour has it that the High Priest of Zoz ordered the bark to depart.'

Manthandros Trasilika, looking for all the world like the famous stunned mullet of the Fables of Skod, gaped at his manservant.

This was serious!

His guards bribed away by Master Ek, his ship sent away by night . . .

What was going on?

It took Manthandros Trasilika less than half a dozen heartbeats to work out the obvious. For some reason, Nadalastabstala Banraithanchumun Ek, High Priest of Zoz the Ancestral for the island of Untunchilamon, had turned against him. Unless he did something, and quickly, he would go the same way as the first Manthandros Trasilika. His head would be chopped off. And the fact that he did indeed have the favour of Aldarch the Third would be quite beside the point . . .

Yes, Trasilika would have to do something.

But what?

Run?

There was nowhere to run to.

'My lord,' said the manservant, 'do you want me to send the Thrug away?'

'No,' said Trasilika, who was quite unable to think of any sensible course of action which might extricate himself from his present difficulties. 'I will see her.'

On this day of disaster, Justina Thrug might be a potential ally. Maybe.

Shortly, Manthandros Trasilika joined Justina Thrug for a working breakfast. With Justina was the bullman Log Jaris. Both appeared to be unaware that anything was wrong; so, rather than admit his peril, Trasilika concealed his discomfort and attended to business.

'The facts,' said Justina, as she chewed her way through two pineapples, three flying fish and a chunk of cold cassava, 'are very simple. The administration is technically bankrupt. We need money and we need it fast.'

'We?' said Trasilika.

'You,' said Justina. 'If you are to rule effectively, you must have money, and soon. That's why Log Jaris is here. Will you tell him – or will I?'

'You tell him,' said the bullman.

'Very well,' said Justina. 'Our plan is very simple. You will sell prescriptions to all those who want them. Each prescription will be valid for ten days. These prescriptions can be filled at certain outlets of our choosing, the prices being those which we set. All you have to do is organize the prescriptions. Log Jaris will take care of the rest.'

At first, Trasilika did not understand. Then he said:

'Prescriptions? Are you talking about prescriptions for alcohol?'

'What else?' said Justina.

'But it's illegal!' protested Trasilika. 'It's – it's—'

'We know what the Izdimir Empire thinks of alcohol,' said Justina soothingly. 'But we are both children of Wen Endex, are we not? We were both of us weaned on

378

beer, were we not? And if this were Galsh Ebrek, we could get a mug of beer or better at any tavern of our choosing, without any nonsense about prescriptions whatsoever.'

'Yes, but—'

'But what?' said Justina.

'But Aldarch the Third would kill me!'

'He will kill you anyway if you let Injiltaprajura slip into anarchy,' said Justina. 'By selling legal prescriptions to the populace, and by the judicious use of violence to enforce your monopoly, you could have total control of the speakeasy business within ten days. You can do it. You must.'

Then they began to argue out the merits of this proposal in detail.

Let those who have ambitions take note: power is hard work. Often it means dragging yourself out of bed with a hangover to attend to pettifogging bureaucratic detail. Of course, similar discomforts attend a great many other professions, shopkeeping and soldiering among them; but it must be noted that the exercise of power is not a job for the idle.

Of course, this point is never made in those blood-perfumed romances of kingship and empire with which the young entertain themselves. Study for example the fables written by the scandalously over-prolific and over-paid Chulman Puro. Do his heroes ever get dragged out of bed in the morning to discuss cash flow, wage bills, exchange rates and inflation? Does Vorn the Gladiator ever get set upon thus on the morning after a great victory?

No, of course not.

Instead, Vorn the Gladiator stays between the sheets, tupping with the great Queen Avalgapalantaskomilti-dini, or the Princess Nuboltipon, or Yun the Hot, or Osh the Nubile, or Pevalina of the Ivory Bosoms. Her dugs become priapic as his lips close with hers; her knees come up; her legs enfold him as they enter that position known as the Lubricated Clam Embracing The Flagstaff; then 'their ship rocks upon the seas of the urging blood', as the poet so nicely puts it; then Pevalina (or it may be Yun the Hot, or, equally, Osh the Nubile – for they are all but aspects of one Eternal Woman) gasps as she yields to the ecstasy which he has forced upon her; and Vorn gasps also; and his serpent spits pearls; 'silk accepts cream' (to quote the poet once more); and then (to quote directly from Chulman Puro) 'she licks the sweat from his great slabs of muscle and begs him to grant her the rapture once again'.

Vorn is not easily commanded by a woman's tongue, and therefore demands that she first 'worship the source with the tongue's poetry'; and this she does, then whimpers with unfeigned ecstasy as he obliges her flesh once more; and so pass the days (and the nights, and, if Chulman Puro were to be believed, the very years themselves) in the halls of victory.

Now all this is very misleading.

Please note that the conquest of kingdoms and empires, while well within the power of any talented person (and here those without talent are advised to busy themselves with the construction of a new religion, for there are any number of undemanding gods who yet await their priests and congregations) is not a path to an idle life of luxurious self-indulgence. Instead, the acquisition of power means the intensification of life's problems rather than the reverse.

For, if you once win great power, then everyone in the world will want to kill you; with the exception of those souls less savage who merely wish to loot your treasury or suborn some small part of your influence for the service of their own personal ends.

In conclusion, if you do really want to lie in bed all day with women 'worshipping the source with the tongue's poetry' then trust not to the recipe proposed by Chulman Puro – but, instead, take yourself off to some place where the rate of exchange is good and the standard of living low, allowing you to buy whatever you want at prices close to laughable. The probable outcome is that within a month you will be bored beyond endurance with the contortions of the flesh, and will come home none the worse for the experience (but for the venereal diseases you have acquired in the process of making this experiment – but then, contrary to what certain narrow-minded moralists would have you believe, we all have to die of something).

Unfortunately for Manthandros Trasilika, he was not living in the land of fable and romance, and was therefore constrained to sit at table with Justina Thrug and the bullman Log Jaris and argue the pros and cons of legalizing the sale of liquor by means of ten-day prescriptions.

At first, Trasilika himself refused to eat anything. But then he got down a little papaya – a food which is fairly close to being water, and hence palatable even to a hungover head – and then consented to allow some tolfrigdalakaptiko to be served to him.

'A mistake,' said Trasilika, when the tolfrigdalakaptiko was set before him. 'It's too early in the morning for this.'

'Never mind,' said Log Jaris. 'We'll eat it for you. As my father always said, a meal wasted is a meal wasted, and a meal eaten is a meal wasted not.'

'Your father sounds like an uncommonly sensible man,' said Trasilika, watching Log Jaris attack the tolfrigdalakaptiko. 'For I can find no flaws whatsoever with his wisdom. Perhaps I . . . yes, a bit of this, perhaps I could manage just a bit . . .' So saying, Trasilika dissected a lozenge of dried jellyfish with his knife, popped it into his mouth, chewed, tasted, swallowed, then said: 'This takes me back.'

'Where to?' said Justina.

'Bolfrigalaskaptiko,' said Trasilika. 'A very interesting place. They there have an institution which Injiltaprajura seems to be lacking, that is, the professional childbeater.'

'My father outlawed that trade,' said Justina.

'A mistake,' said Trasilika.

'You are not seeking to revive the trade, are you?' said Justina sharply.

Trasilika looked at her, wondering how best to answer. Then a frantic Jean Froissart intruded upon their conference, and no answer was required.

CHAPTER THIRTY-FIVE

For Justina Thrug, that morning breakfast was a delicate affair. Jean Froissart had proved himself a true priest of Zoz the Ancestral, therefore Manthandros Trasilika would surely have no trouble in getting himself accepted by one and all as the true wazir, the legitimate wazir appointed by Aldarch the Third to rule over Untunchilamon in the name of the Izdimir Empire.

So . . .

Really, as far as Justina could see, Trasilika no longer had any pressing need for her services. Such was Trasilika's confidence that he appeared to have sent away all his guards – Justina's spies told her those guards were now concentrated in the Temple of Torture. And he had also sent away his ship. All of which suggested he felt very, very secure already. So what was to stop him doing away with her? Nothing. Unless she made herself very, very valuable to him in a great big hurry. Given Trasilika's manifest confidence in his grasp on power, that might prove difficult – but she had to try.

That was why Justina was there so early in the morning, seeking to entangle Trasilika in drug-dealing schemes which would alienate him from Nadalastabstala Banraithanchumun Ek and make him dependent on the services of her friend and ally Log Jaris. All she wanted was Trasilika's protection, just for a few more days. In that time, she would – she must, otherwise she would surely die – scheme up some way to extricate the organic rectifier from Master Ek's clutches.

Once Justina had the organic rectifier, she could take it to the Crab and transform that entity into human form. (Always assuming that she could deduce the secret of operating the rectifier, or that the Crab could work it out for itself.)

Once the Crab was made human then it would surely, out of gratitude, solve the rest of her problems.

But staying alive until she could think of some way to win the organic rectifier – why, that might prove very, very difficult indeed. However, the business breakfast seemed to go well enough, for Manthandros Trasilika attended to her schemes with every appearance of interest, even though he was obviously fatigued and hung over.

Then a frantic Jean Froissart intruded upon their conference in the greatest of panics imaginable.

'They mean to kill me!' babbled Froissart.

'Get a grip on yourself,' said Trasilika. 'Sit down. Tell me all about it.'

Froissart then spilt out the most extraordinary tale. Master Ek, High Priest of Zoz the Ancestral, had named him as a human sacrifice for the Festival of Light!

'You must stop him!' said Froissart. 'Use your powers as wazir to over-rule the High Priest or else!'

'Or else what?'

'Or else I'll reveal you for what you are. A false wazir!'

'But I'm not a false wazir,' protested Trasilika. 'I'm the real thing, appointed by Al'three himself.'

'That makes no difference,' said Froissart. 'Only one person in five truly believes you. The rest will happily murder you if given the slightest excuse.'

Not for the first time, Manthandros Trasilika wished he was still back in Bolfrigalaskaptiko, that city of mud and mosquitoes which lies on the far-away Crocodile River, also known as the River Ka. Now, his sojourn in that place of marsh and fever seemed positively idyllic. However, he could not go back. He had not sailed from Manamalargo and the shores of Yestron on a whim. No: he had come to Untunchilamon on the direct orders of Aldarch the Third.

And Al'three would be very, very unhappy with Trasilika if he failed to secure the rule of Untunchilamon for the Mutilator.

So Trasilika needs do whatever he must to maintain himself in authority.

Even if that meant going up against a High Priest of the religion so dear to the Mutilator's heart.

'I – I will order Master Ek that you are not to be sacrificed,' said Trasilika.

'Thank you,' said Jean Froissart.

'You thank him prematurely,' said Justina Thrug.

'What?' said Trasilika. 'Do you think Master Ek will dare to disobey me?'

'He may,' said Justina.

'What makes you say that?' said Trasilika.

The wazir and the witch stared at each other. Justina was thinking, thinking, thinking with greater concentration than ever before in her life. Master Ek had chosen Jean Froissart as a human sacrifice. So Ek wanted Froissart dead. So Ek did not believe that Froissart had passed his trial by ordeal thanks to divine intervention. So Ek thought Froissart to be a false priest, and Trasilika to be a false wazir. (Were they false? At this moment, for the life of her Justina could not tell.)

But—

'Have you lost your tongue?' said Trasilika.

'I expect to keep my tongue for longer than you will keep yours,' said Justina, with great deliberation.

She was sweating. She hoped Trasilika would not notice. Even if he did, why – it was a hot day, and she was a fleshy woman much given to perspiration. So—

'Are you threatening me?' said Trasilika ominously.

'I believe,' said Justina, 'that it is Master Ek who is threatening you. He does so on good grounds. He knows the trial by ordeal was a fraud.'

'But it wasn't!' objected Froissart. 'I did it, I did it, I don't know how but I did it, I picked up the red-hot iron,

385

no magic salve, no nothing, none of your witchcraft, I did it myself.'

'What you picked up,' said Justina, 'was Shabble.'

'Shabble?' said Froissart, momentarily nonplussed.

'You have met,' said Justina. 'Shabble escorted you ashore on your first day in Injiltaprajura. Remember? The melting of weapons, the—'

'Oh, I remember,' said Froissart. 'Shabble is the ball, the floating ball.'

'Yes,' said Justina. 'And it was Shabble who helped you pass your trial by ordeal.'

She explained.

While she did so, she thought furiously. Ek clearly intended to destroy Froissart, which suggested that Ek probably had Trasilika's death in mind also. Trasilika, all unsuspecting, had sent his guards to the Temple of Torture, where they had come under Ek's command. And Trasilika had sent away his ship. Or had he? If only she could find out!

'. . . and,' said Justina, concluding her tale, 'Master Ek knows all about Shabble and the trial by ordeal. Just as I know why your ship has gone away and why your guards are in the Temple of Torture.'

Justina smiled, trying to look smug and knowing. This was a big gamble. If only—

'What do you know?' said Trasilika. 'Tell me!'

'That,' said Justina, bristling, 'is scarcely the tone of voice to use with me.'

She was in a quandary. If she confessed that she did not really know why Trasilika's guards and ships had left, then she would have to admit that she was effectively out of the political game, that she was powerless and friendless, and could be destroyed at Trasilika's whim. (Assuming he could find men to destroy her, which should not prove an insurmountable problem.) If, on the other hand, she could persuade him that she knew, that she was privy to Master Ek's decisions, that she was in fact in league with Master Ek – why then, by using such an illusion of power as leverage, she might be able to get Trasilika to help her recover the organic rectifier.

Somehow.

'You will tell me all you know,' said Trasilika, with unsuppressed anger. 'And now. Or else!'

Justina glanced at Log Jaris. Could he help her? Log Jaris winked. That wink said: I don't know what you're doing, but I'll help if I can.

'Log Jaris, my friend,' said Justina, rising from the table. 'It is time for us to go. Come. Master Ek will be getting impatient.'

'Master Ek will be getting impatient,' said Log Jaris, repeating Justina's last words to cover his own confusion. 'Yes, yes, no doubt he will. Very well. Then let us go.'

'To Ek?' said Trasilika. 'Why are you going to Ek?'

'To arrange for your execution,' said Justina smoothly, launching herself upon the greatest bluff of her political career, a bluff of breathtaking audacity.

'My execution!' said Trasilika, scandalized.

'Why, yes,' said Justina. 'He can't kill you himself, can he? Not without proof of your falsehood. But I can.'

'You!' said Trasilika. 'But you—'

'We can't stop her,' said Froissart. 'Ek has our soldiers.'

So! Now Justina knew Manthandros Trasilika had not voluntarily sent his guards to Master Ek at the Temple of Torture. Rather, those men had been stolen away by Master Ek. That was all she needed.

'Yes,' said she. 'Your ship is gone, and your guards are no longer yours to command. You're helpless. This is what will happen. The soldiers will pretend to mutiny against Master Ek. Under my command, they will loot and pillage. They will also chop off your head. Then Master Ek will make himself wazir of Untunchilamon. Whether you are a fraud or a real wazir appointed by Aldarch the Third makes no difference, for Ek himself will be innocent of all violence against your person. But I—'

'My lady,' said Log Jaris in vehement protest, 'it is unwise to spill our secrets to this thing. His life is doomed so—'

'Quiet!' said Justina, doing her best to pretend she was angry with the bullman's interjection. 'As I was saying, Ek will appear innocent, for all the blame will fall on me.'

'Then you'll be killed,' said Trasilika.

'Sharked in the lagoon,' said Froissart. 'Or chopped into catmeat.'

'No,' said Justina sweetly. 'I will escape to the north and live happily ever after in the court of Jal Japone. I have a standing invitation from that formidable warlord. He will give me shelter whenever I want for as long as I want. Master Ek has promised me safe passage out of Injiltaprajura, you see, as soon as you are dead.'

'He's lying,' said Trasilika desperately. 'You can't trust him!'

'I have to,' said Justina. 'I have no alternative. Unless I can recover the organic rectifier.'

'The what?' said Trasilika.

'The organic rectifier,' said Justina. 'It is a device which can change the form of the flesh one inhabits. It could make a man into a crab. Or a crab into a man.'

'And you think that would somehow solve your problems?' said Trasilika. 'How so?'

'Because,' said Justina, 'with this organic rectifier, I could change the Crab of the island of Jod into a human. Once so changed, the Crab in gratitude would grant me all I wished. It would extend its mercy to you, I'm sure, if you were to help us recover this organic rectifier.'

'Where is it?' said Trasilika.

'Ek has it,' said Justina. 'It is in the Temple of Torture.'

'Then he'll never give it up!' said Trasilika. 'Not if he knows how important it is.'

'Ah,' said Justina. 'But he doesn't know. He only suspects. I have told him the thing is a skavamareen, an

388

ancient musical instrument. He doesn't quite believe me, but he doesn't necessarily disbelieve, either.'

'So . . . so what do you suggest?' said Trasilika.

Justina smiled. And this time there was nothing feigned about that smile.

She had successfully convinced Manthandros Trasilika that she was Master Ek's ally, and that Ek intended to use her as an instrument for perpetrating the perfect murder, the victim of this murder to be Trasilika himself. She had created the illusion she needed to give her political leverage. And now she was using this leverage to force Trasilika to make an alliance with her against Master Ek.

'I suggest,' said Justina, 'that you order the organic rectifier to be released.'

'Ek will not release it,' said Trasilika positively. 'If he thinks there's one chance in a thousand that the thing could make the Crab into a human, he'll never let it go.'

'Even so,' said Justina, 'we should try. For there is at least one chance in a thousand that Ek might yield the thing to us without a fuss. In which case, our problems will be over.'

'And if he does not?' said Trasilika.

'Then we must take it from him,' said Justina.

'But how?' said Trasilika. 'My ship is gone, my guards have been bribed away, and you . . . well, you have no fighting force, have you?'

'We can try to scratch together a force of some description,' said Justina. 'Remember, we are not trying to conquer Untunchilamon. All we have to do is get the organic rectifier from Injiltaprajura to the island of Jod.'

'Might it not be simpler,' said Froissart, 'to get the Crab to exert its powers to bring the rectifier to the shores of Jod?'

'Yes,' said Trasilika. 'If the organic rectifier is what you say it is and does what you say it does, why shouldn't the Crab lend us its aid?'

389

'Jod is under quarantine,' said Log Jaris. 'The quarantine is not perfect. Any soul brave enough to swim the Laitemata by night could gain an audience with the Crab. But . . . many people have lied to the Crab in the past for their own advantage. It is not likely to believe us or help us unless we present it with the organic rectifier itself.'

'Well,' said Trasilika, 'you want me to ask Ek for the return of the organic rectifier, even though you admit there's little chance that he'll agree. Isn't it equally reasonable to send someone to petition the Crab? Even if the chances of the Crab agreeing are minimal?'

Justina looked at Log Jaris.

Log Jaris looked at Justina.

Then the bullman sighed, and said:

'I will swim the Laitemata tonight. Sharks and seasnakes permitting, I'll have an answer from the Crab by the morrow.'

'Very well,' said Trasilika. 'We'll meet again first thing tomorrow to see what the Crab says. But suppose we get refused by both Ek and the Crab? Suppose we have to fight it out? What then? Who will fight with us?'

'Varazchavardan,' said Justina. 'Aquitaine Varazchavardan. He's a powerful sorcerer. He fears that Aldarch the Third will execute him because he was long in my service. Then there's Nixorjapretzel Rat, who was once Varazchavardan's apprentice. Perhaps Varazchavardan can persuade Jan Rat to our cause.'

'Two sorcerers will hardly win us a victory against the combined powers of the Cabal House,' said Trasilika.

'If the wonder-workers run true to form,' rumbled Log Jaris, 'the first hint of trouble will see them board themselves up in that Cabal House until all the danger's over. Besides, there are others who will fight for the Empress. Myself included.'

'Even so,' said Trasilika, 'I don't see how a couple of sorcerers and a handful of loyalists can storm the Temple of Torture. We need men in force. There are none such.'

'There is always Jal Japone,' said Justina.

'Japone?' said Froissart in astonishment. 'You mean – the warlord?'

'Who else?' said Justina. 'There are some loyal Ebrell Islanders who would doubtless serve me as ambassadors if I asked them to. Dunash Labrat is one such man.'

'Labrat?' said Trasilika. 'I've never heard of him.'

'You wouldn't have,' said Justina, 'for he is but a bee keeper and a maker of mead. However, he knows Jal Japone well, for he sheltered with the warlord when Wazir Sin was waging a pogrom against the Ebrell Islanders in Injiltaprajura.'

'Why should Japone help us?' said Trasilika suspiciously.

'We will offer him much in the name of the Crab,' said Justina. 'We will offer him a monopoly on all liquor sales in Injiltaprajura from here to eternity. That bribe should be sufficient to guarantee his compliance.'

'All right,' said Trasilika decisively. 'We'll do it. First I'll ask Ek for the organic rectifier. If he won't hand it over, we'll storm the Temple of Torture and take it. Once you've won us men from Jal Japone.'

'But where does that leave me?' said Froissart. 'I can't stand as sacrifice!'

'Relax,' said Justina. 'This whole business will be over before the Festival of Light begins. It'll do you no harm to be named as a sacrifice.'

'She's right,' said Trasilika.

And all Jean Froissart's protests were over-ruled.

A long discussion of details then followed. Then Justina Thrug took herself off in search of the Ebrell Islander Dunash Labrat, meaning to command him north to the lair of the warlord Jal Japone.

Justina was successful in her mission, and by noon Labrat was already on his way north.

Justina then made her way to the pink palace, where she received distressing intelligence. Master Ek had refused to release the organic rectifier, and had strengthened his claim to possession of this 'skavamareen' by announcing that it would be one of the sacrifices at the Festival of Light.

That meant that the fate of Injiltaprajura depended on the outcome of Log Jaris's mission to the Crab that night – or, failing that, on the whims of the warlord Jal Japone. For Justina very much doubted that she could command sufficient force to storm the pink palace without help from the Crab or Japone, even supposing that Aquitaine Varazchavardan and Nixorjapretzel Rat were willing to help her.

Justina felt more than a little bitter.

All she needed was fifty men.

That was all.

Fifty staunch fighters and she could conquer Injiltaprajura.

With fifty Yudonic Knights she could have done it easily. Could have smashed down the doors of the Temple of Torture. Extricated the organic rectifier. Got it to Jod. Converted the Crab. And then, in alliance with that Power, could have swept her enemies into the sea.

But she had not fifty men.

Through all these years she had ruled Injiltaprajura with guile and cunning, with justice and discretion. But all that was to come to naught – for want of fifty men. Unless the Crab or Japone extended their charity to her. But, frankly . . . Justina was far from certain of getting help from either of those two Powers.

The Empress ascended to the palace roof, meaning to soothe her nerves by swimming in her rooftop pool. But Hostaja Sken-Pitilkin was there, labouring on the rebuilding of his airship, with Jan Rat working alongside him. Justina, loathe to disturb him in this enterprise – that ship might yet save her life, and Sken-Pitilkin seemed seldom in the mood to work on it – quietly withdrew.

Downstairs again, Justina withdrew to her study. When entering that room, she usually gave time to her aquarium. She liked to watch fish: delighted in the grace of the weightless creatures as they drifted through their world of water, peacock their rainbow, dragon their wish. But these days her first concern was always the saucer which sat in spendid isolation above that world, alone on an island inviolate, safe from the depredations of ants and other marauders.

Safe?

'No!' said Justina, with bitter disappointment.

There were ants on the egg. Six of them at least. Black flecks of malice, animated appetite devoid of scruples or ethics. They were eating it, surely.

Justina was devastated by this disaster. There was not one single corner of her world which was not threatened by death, horror, pain and pitiless cruelty. This at least she had hoped to salvage, this perfect egg and the miracle within. But she had failed. Even in this she had failed.

Her vision blurred. She squeezed her eyes tight shut. Then fat and hopeless tears began to blubber down her face. Everything in the world was vile, ugly and pitiless, and she did not think she could bear it any longer.

Then Justina calmed herself and, analytically – she had thought the defences she had devised for the egg to be perfect, but obviously she had erred – she began to investigate the scene of the disaster to see what defect in the fortifications the ants had discovered. But her most determined scrutiny failed to find the slightest flaw in the finemesh gauze which guarded the fishtank against invasion.

'Yet the ants are there,' said Justina in puzzlement. 'They are there, are they not?'

She looked closer. No, the flecks were not ants at all. They were merely black flecks.

'It's rotten, then,' said Justina in disgust. 'It's gone rotten.'

She displaced the soljamimpambagoya rocks, removed the gauze and retrieved the saucer. Then, overcome by a clinical curiosity, she decided to dissect the egg to see what kind of embryo had died within. She set the saucer down on her desk then rummaged in her cosmetics case, at length retrieving tweezers, a blackhead hook, a pustule needle and a pair of trimming scissors. These she laid out on the desk. Then she pulled up a chair so she could work at leisure in comfort.

The Empress Justina picked up the pustule needle, meaning to lance one of the flecks to release any liquid rot within. Then she stayed her hand. For the egg had changed. The half-dozen flecks had run together to form one ragged patch of darkness. A strangely sudden change! Unless . . .

Justina peered closely.

'Well goodness gracious me!' she said.

The darkness was not a blemish but a hole. A hole into the egg. And within, something was moving. Even as the Empress watched, something yellow and wan snouted out from the egg. A tiny something, so small it was hard to credit its flesh with autonomous existence.

'My!' said Justina in wonderment.

It was a dragon. The smallest of all the world's dragons, and the first of its race to come into the world *ab ovo*. Its mother had been created *ex nihilo* by a demon acting on whim, and its mother was missing and possibly dead. Since the breed had demonstrated a capacity for parthenogenetic reproduction, the race might survive if this dragonet could be preserved.

'But,' said Justina, 'as yet the thing is not even out of the egg.'

No. It was not out at all. And its struggles to escape from the egg looked to be as traumatic as the prolonged birth-struggle which so oft initiates a human into the world of women and men. Justina longed to help it, but restrained herself. For the brute instruments of steel laid out upon the desk were of formidable size when compared to a dragon so fragile, and she doubted her hand could sustain the delicacies of surgery which would have been required to assist the thing from its miniature shell.

So Justina watched until at last her dragon was free.

Now it has been said by some commentators that Justina Thrug never denied herself the smallest indulgence: that whatever she wanted to do, she did. But this is not true. She denied herself much and restrained herself often, as did she now. For what Justina truly wanted to do was to have the palace bells rung long and loud to celebrate the dragonbirth, to command parades and festivals and a General Prescription. She wished to rush forth and to cry (as Occasions demanded):

'Tintinnabulate the tintinnabula!'

To hear bells, yes, and trumpets; to see smiles, yes, and laughter; to have uproar and gaiety, and a death to decorum. But Justina feared her people would think her mad were she to order such ceremonies for the hatching of this babiest of dragons. Furthermore, there was no alternative Occasion which she could reasonably propose as an excuse for an Outbreak. Therefore Justina denied herself pleasure and concentrated on the practicalities.

'Food,' said Justina.

Again she had recourse to her cosmetics case. She took some little balls of cotton wool. One she soaked in water and another in goat's milk, which was fresh-fetched from the kitchen at her command. These cotton wool balls she placed upon the saucer so this tiniest of dragonets could suckle upon them at will. Then she took a corpse maggot (a delicacy also commanded from the kitchen) and chopped it up very finely, and upon the saucer she raised a little pyramid comprising the resulting shreds of this most delicate of meats.

One task alone remained before she returned her charge to its fishbowl sanctuary.

The dragon must be named.

'I name thee . . . what? No, not what. You need more of a name than what. Untunchilamon bore thee, hence . . . Injiltaprajura I name thee.'

Injiltaprajura squirmed upon the blotting paper,

which by now had soaked up most of the egg-slish of her hatching. Yet some organic aftermath of birth still clung to the dragon's transparent scales. As Justina watched, Injiltaprajura opened her jaws, and began to lick herself clean with a tongue more slender than a cat's whisker.

And Justina smiled, in triumph and in hope for the future.

CHAPTER THIRTY-SIX

It was night on Untunchilamon. The day quarter was undokondra; and, in the dark of that quarter, safe in the fastness of the Temple of Torture, an old man meditated upon the forthcoming delights of the Festival of Light. The old man was Nadalastabstala Banraithanchumun Ek, High Priest of Zoz the Ancestral, and in his imagination he was rehearsing whole catalogues of torture.

Elsewhere, on the rooftop of the pink palace which lorded it over Pokra Ridge, Olivia Qasaba sat as silently as a shadow as she watched the Empress Justina stripped to her nakedness.

'Well,' said Justina, smiling at the airship shadows which hid Olivia, 'aren't you going to join me?'

'Maybe later,' said Olivia.

She was in no mood for disporting herself. She had yet to learn Justina's knack of leaving her troubles to look after themselves. Besides, Olivia liked neither night nor water. The sun was her element, and she had always been a little afraid of the night.

'This will do you good,' said Justina.

'Thank you,' said Olivia formally, 'but no.'

'Then do you want to go back downstairs and go to bed?'

'Not just yet,' said Olivia.

She was frightened by the menacing silence of the palace by night. Everyone who could leave the pink palace had done so in anticipation of some forthcoming disaster. Olivia did not like to be alone in the place.

'As you wish,' said Justina.

Then turned to the water.

The moon had swollen to the full. Justina saluted that luminary with unaccustomed formality before she plunged into her pool to porpoise and grampus at her leisure.

There were no soldiers to observe the imperial disports, so Olivia appointed herself sentry, and kept a sharp lookout for assassins. Justina, as if untroubled by any thoughts of sudden death, long amused herself with her swimming. The water was warm, warm, amniotic. And when at last the Empress hauled herself from the water, the air enveloped her with a similar heat.

Adrift in the air was a mosquito, which, lacking any intimation of its own mortality, settled upon the imperial forearm and proceeded to feed. Moments after it alights, a mosquito cannot be felt, for it injects a numbing fluid into the flesh when first it pierces the human integument. But Justina, alert to such assaults, felt that first feathering of mosquito feet. She knew it was there. The imperial benevolence proved less than infinite: and, moments later, the mosquito was a smear of greasy grey against Justina's skin.

Justina found herself possessed by a pervasive sadness, a languid melancholy. It was not the mosquito's demise which affected her thus, for she had already forgotten the fate of that fragile beast. Rather, it was the swollen moon which drew from her this sense of slightly self-indulgent regret. She realized that perhaps, in her heart of hearts, she had never expected to survive, had never expected to leave Untunchilamon alive. So now, as the odds stacked up against her, as her enemies sharpened the jaws of the trap . . .

'Are we ready to go yet?' said Olivia.

'Go?' said Justina sadly. 'I don't think we're going to go anywhere, not you and me.'

Then she slipped back into the water. Crooning down-soothings of rain began to fall, night rain downfalling though the moon shone clear. And, swimming by moonlight in the rain, Justina felt a great calm descend

398

upon her. She had done her best. She could do no more. By an act of intelligent daring, she had converted Manthandros Trasilika to her cause, at least temporarily. She had sent Log Jaris to the Crab and Dunash Labrat to Jal Japone. Help from either quarter was most unlikely, but nobody could say she hadn't tried.

As Justina swam, she once again let all political concerns slip away from her. She amused herself by endeavouring to imagine what it was like to be a whale. And then, when the rain ceased, she ascended again from the pool, her body wet with the moon which shimmered in rain-slick surface of the glitter dome.

'I'm all wet,' said Olivia.

'Then go in and have a swim,' said Justina. 'Then you'll be wetter still, and you won't notice it.'

Then the Empress spied what Olivia – despite her concern for assassins – had not. A silent shadow had ventured out on the rooftop.

'Ho!' said Justina, deepening her voice in unconscious imitation of her father's battle style. 'Who goes there?'

'I go there,' answered Log Jaris. 'And here. And elsewhere.'

Olivia rose as the bullman bulked forward. A note of good humour in his voice had convinced her already that he had been successful.

'The Crab!' said Olivia. 'Is it with us?'

'No,' said Log Jaris.

'No?' said Olivia, in dismay. 'But you sounded happy!'

'To have swum the Laitemata twice by night, yes, that's happiness enough,' said Log Jaris. 'To be here, and not in the maw of a shark. I'll not ask for more, not at times like this.'

'But you asked the Crab for more,' said Justina.

'Indubitably,' said Log Jaris.

'What does that mean?' said Olivia, who was tired, and could not remember whether she knew that word or not.

To Olivia's discomfort, neither Log Jaris nor the

Empress answered her directly. Instead, Justina said to the bullman:

'So. So that is it. We must trust to Jal Japone.'

'But we can't!' protested Olivia. 'He'll never get here in time. Besides, what's to say he'll come at all?'

Thanks to lessons in geography and politics administered by Chegory Guy, her dearest darling Chegory – who had once languished long in the northern stronghold commanded by Japone – Olivia knew full well that there was not much hope of help from the north. But Justina and Log Jaris knew that as well, and saw no need to listen to lectures from a chit of a girl. Instead, Justina invited Log Jaris inside for some wine.

'And you, Olivia,' said Justina. 'You can have some wine as well, if you want.'

'Thank you,' said Olivia, with great dignity. 'But I'm going to go for a swim.'

Something in the way she said it made Justina stop.

'Are you all right?' said Justina in concern.

'No!' said Olivia, with a violence close to hysteria. 'I'm not all right! That horrible therapist thing still has Chegory, and maybe it's eating him right now. All the ships have gone, there's no ships left, we can't get off, we can't escape, and – and—'

She stopped, for she could not go on.

'Come,' said Justina, advancing on Olivia. 'Best you have a little wine, some dry clothes, and then to bed.'

But Olivia backstepped and gave herself to the pool.

Sploosh!

'You must not go in backwards like that,' said the Empress reprovingly. 'You'll hit your head and break your neck.'

'Maybe,' said Olivia, flounder-floating in the water. 'But not this time.'

'Well then,' said Justina, 'you swim for as long as you like, and when you've had enough you come downstairs.'

'I will,' said Olivia. 'I will.'

Then the Empress Justina departed with Log Jaris.

When she was quite sure they were gone, Olivia Qasaba hauled herself from the pool. She stood by the bulk of the airship on which Hostaja Sken-Pitilkin was working with such a lamentable lack of urgency. Then she went to the edge of the roof and looked out over the streets of portside Injiltaprajura. She looked down Lak Street and out across the darkened waters of the Laitemata where the island of Jod floated in the moonlight.

She shuddered.

Then she said to herself, remembering words spoken to her by Artemis Ingalawa:

'Remember you're an Ashdan.'

With her resolve thus strengthened, she set off downstairs. Through the dark and silent palace she went. She slipped out through the unguarded portals. She paused on the steps and looked first right, then left. But nothing was moving on Hojo Street. So she started downhill, down Lak Street. On either side rose the grand mansions, some glowing softly with moon paint. Here and there were rip-tooth intrusions of shadow and ruin where riot and fire had claimed some of Injiltaprajura's most expensive architecture.

Downhill went Olivia. On her left was the huge chunk of bone known as Pearl. She allowed herself a sentimental tear as she gazed upon this monument to the inexplicable, for well she knew that this might be the last time in her life that she would ever see it. Further downhill, she came to the Cabal House, guarding the intersection where Skindik Way and Goldhammer Rise branched off from Lak Street.

She paused.

She could turn left, and go down Skindik Way and then through Lubos to the waterfront. It was something of a short cut. But . . . the ruins of the Dromdanjerie lay that way. She did not care to go past those ruins, least of all by night. For a moment, grief choked her throat. Her father! Gone, missing . . . dead?

'You are an Ashdan,' said Olivia firmly.

Overhead, there was a minor explosion. Startled, she looked up. Blue and yellow sparks flared from the top of the Cabal House. A heavy smell of sulphur drifted down from that eminence, to be followed by some drunken laughter. So the sorcerers were up and about – and, no doubt, up to no good. Trying to convert lead to gold, perhaps, or something equally as idle.

Momentarily, Olivia considered going into the Cabal House and asking the wonder-workers for help. But she knew it would do no good. If she wanted to save the world from going to rack and ruin, she would have to do it on her own.

'I have to do it,' said Olivia.

And she did.

Otherwise, Master Ek would start killing and torturing, if he hadn't started already. She could see that coming. Justina would get locked up, and probably get her head cut off – if she was lucky! And Chegory would undoubtedly be eaten by the therapist. What was it the therapist thing had said? Men make better hostages because . . .

No, better not to think about that.

Doing her best not to think, Olivia went downhill until she came to the waterfront, then she turned left and strode purposely along the embankment.

'Halt!'

A voice from the dark.

A soldier.

One of the soldiers quarantining Jod.

'I'm halted,' said Olivia.

'Who goes there?' said the soldier.

'Nobody,' said Olivia. 'I'm not going anywhere. I've halted, remember?'

The soldier stepped out of the shadows of Morthaldipan's boatshed and rock-crunched toward Olivia. Moonlight glinted from the blade of his spear as he levelled it at Olivia's heart.

'Who are you?' said he.

'I am Olivia Qasaba,' said Olivia Qasaba with dignity. 'I have been entertaining Nadalastabstala Banraithanchumun Ek. He's sent me home. He's an old man, you know. Evenings are enough, he doesn't want all night.'

'What are you doing here then?' said the soldier.

'Standing talking to you,' said Olivia.

'Don't play games with me, child,' said the soldier.

'I don't,' said Olivia. 'I play games with Master Ek. He might like to play games with you, too, if you're not careful.'

'A sentry,' said the soldier, 'has the full weight of the authority of the Izdimir Empire behind him, that authority including the authority of Aldarch the Third, Mutilator of Yestron.'

'You belong in law school,' said Olivia. 'You'd be safer there. It's far too dangerous for the likes of you to be out on the streets at night. Obooloo's a long, long way away, and Aldarch the Third wouldn't give a damn if my dearest darling Ek had you sharked in the lagoon tomorrow. Which he may.'

'I do not think he will,' said the soldier, who was if anything amused by the pretensions of this child concubine.

However, he raised his spear, so the blade now threatened the stars rather than Olivia's quick quick-pulsing heart.

'Where are you going to, then?' said the soldier.

'Home,' said Olivia, sensing that the man was ready to let her go.

'Where's home?'

'East,' said Olivia. 'The East Caves.'

The East Caves were not caves at all, but merely some shack-shanty hovels on the edge of town.

'Be on your way, then,' said the soldier.

'Before I go,' said Olivia, 'I'll know your name.'

'The name?' said the soldier. 'The name's Joy Wax. Tell that to old man Ek if you want.'

403

'I will,' said Olivia. 'Believe me, I will.'

Then she strode on along the waterfront with the moonlit waters of the Laitemata on her right and the slumlands of Lubos on her left. As she walked, she thought about the name the soldier had given her. She thought he had lied, giving a false name just in case she tried to get him into trouble. Joy Wax. There had been a mechanic with that name, a mechanic at the Analytical Institute. So how had the soldier come by the name? Was Ek having everyone with anything to do with the Institute arrested? Maybe.

'But,' said Olivia firmly, 'whatever he's doing or isn't, he can't stop me now.'

She slowed her pace and studied the night sky. Clouds were coming across. Good.

A few more steps, and . . . clouds shrouded their way across the moon and the night became dark.

And Olivia quickly scrambled down the embankment and – if she stopped to think then she would never do it – into the waters of the Laitemata. Which smelt. The smell was not exactly that of the sea, but, rather, of a sewer's discharge.

'But the water's warm,' said Olivia to herself.

She stood there, waist deep in the water, and tried to nerve herself up for the task. Log Jaris had done it. The sharks never got him. But then, he was a bullman all covered with fur, not a girl with the bones of a bird, a girl as tasty to a shark as a plate of fresh-cooked tolfrigdala-kaptiko.

She was frightened.

The waters were black, black, anything could be in them, hideous things were, there were bones, there were teeth, there were jaws, stone fish which hooked your body into agony even screams could scarce describe, moray eels bad tempered as debt collectors, corals which cut and fire corals which stung, and jellyfish, lots of them, the lortageze warman being the worst of all, a monstrous jellyfish which trailed its strands across—

'You are an Ashdan.'

So said Olivia.

Firmly.

And momentarily she was not Olivia at all. Instead, she was Artemis Ingalawa, a woman lecturing a girl. Yes, she was Artemis, who had hunted in the forests of Ashmolea, who had hunted and killed, her knife running black with blood in the moonlight, oh yes, the man speaking in blood as he tried to plead—

'An Ashdan,' said Olivia.

And lowered herself into the water and began to swim, swimming with a smooth, regular breast stroke. That kept her head free from the hideous black water, kept her head free and cut the noise down to nothing.

Through the dark she swam.

Then the clouds smoked away, the moon came out, and liquid silver spilt across the Laitemata, and someone on the shore shouted. Had she been seen? No matter. She was too far out, they could not stop her now.

On swam Olivia, making for the bulk of Jod. When she was very close, she put down her feet, found rock underfoot, and strode toward the shore. When she was half a dozen paces from safety, her nerve finally broke, and she panicked out of the water, and stood gasping and panting, shuddering in the aftermath of her ordeal, water splilching from her clothes and gliberspleting down her legs.

'I am an Ashdan,' she said.

But she no longer felt like one.

Then she remembered the forest thing, the thing which Artemis Ingalawa had told her about all those years ago, the man in the forest and the killing, horrible, horrible, she had never though about it before, she had pretended she had never been told, she did not want to know things like that, but—

'It was in me,' whispered Olivia.

Yes.

Down through the years, Artemis Ingalawa had told

405

and taught Olivia many things, and she knew them even if she pretended she did not know them.

And then Olivia realized the truth.

If that soldier had tried to stop her, she would have killed him. He was a grown man, but he suspected nothing. A single blow between the legs, nicely timed, and then—

Quietly, Olivia began to cry. All these hideous, ugly thoughts and memories were far, far too much for her to deal with. It was all far too serious, and she was too tired to cope with it.

'I am an Ashdan,' she said.

But it was hopeless, the words did her no good at all, and when she tried to say them again she was blubbering so much that the words were quite unintelligible.

Olivia was still crying when she came into the Crab's cave.

When she had whiled away the nights in that cave in the arms of her dearest Chegory, it had always been dark. But tonight, the Crab's wind chimes – the copper wind chimes which Olivia had made for the thing – were glowing green. What did that mean? That the Crab did not like to be in the dark, not if it was alone?

'Are you awake?' said Olivia, speaking through tears.

No response came from the hulking shadows of the Crab. And Olivia, suddenly furious, thumped on the thing with all her strength, pounding its carapace with her fists.

'Hey! Hey!' she shouted. 'Wake up!'

'Please,' said the Crab huffily. 'I am not a percussion instrument. Besides, even if I was, you are not a drummer, are you?'

'Is that supposed to be a joke?' said Olivia fiercely.

'I do not make jokes,' said the Crab.

'That's just as well,' said Olivia. 'Because I'm not in a mood for any jokes.'

'No,' said the Crab. 'By the sound of it, you are in a

very bad mood. I recommend a nice soothing walk. Four times round the island should do it.'

'I'm not here for my health,' said Olivia.

'What are you here for, then?'

'To beat some sense into your thick ugly head.'

'I am a crab,' said the Crab. 'I do not have a head.'

'No!' yelled Olivia, giving the thing an almighty thump. 'You don't have any sense, either. You want to be human? Or don't you?'

The Crab sighed.

'I know what you're on about,' said the Crab. 'You want me to get the organic rectifier. It's in the Temple of Torture, right?'

'Right!' said Olivia. 'So you know all about it! So why don't you get on with it?'

'As I told Log Jaris—'

'I'm not Log Jaris, I'm Olivia Qasaba,' said Olivia. 'I don't care what you told the bullman, I'm telling you now, you have to get the organic rectifier, right now.'

'If it's really there to be got,' said the Crab.

'Of course it is!' said Olivia. 'Otherwise I wouldn't be here telling you all this.'

'You might be,' said the Crab. 'Humans are incredibly duplicitous creatures, as I've learnt to my cost.'

'Duplicitous?' said Olivia.

She was so sick with fear, rage, hate and fatigue that she had quite forgotten whether she did or did not know that word.

'Yes, yes, duplicitous, that's what they are,' said the Crab. 'Cheats, liars and lords of deceit.'

'Oh, you don't understand anything!' said Olivia.

Then, abruptly, her animating rage left her. Olivia, deserted by her fury, sat down in a wet, hot, saggy heap.

She wept.

After a time, Olivia calmed herself.

It was quiet.

The Crab was saying nothing. Maybe it had gone back to sleep. Somewhere, a slabender frog was talking to the night. Then, across the water, someone screamed.

'You hear that?' said Olivia to the Crab. 'Someone's getting hurt. That's Master Ek, that's what, he's doing it, hurting people. You could stop him, you know.'

The Crab said nothing.

It remained stolidly silent.

Olivia closed her eyes, and waves of black despair swept over her.

'Remember,' she said, 'you are an Ashdan.'

'No,' said the Crab. 'I am a Crab.'

'And a big, stupid, silly Crab at that,' said Olivia, getting to her feet. She bit her lip. Then: 'Open your claw. This one. Come on! Do what I say! Open it! Come on, silly, we haven't got all night.'

The Crab's left claw opened with a slight creaking sound. Olivia held up her right hand.

'You see this?' she said. 'You see this hand? The organic rectifier can make it better. If there really is a rectifier. If I'm not lying. If I'm telling the truth. You grant me that?'

'If you can choose the axioms, you can win any argument,' said the Crab.

'Well what's that supposed to mean?' said Olivia. 'What I say makes sense, doesn't it? If there really is an organic rectifier, you can get it for me, can't you? So you can fix my hand. If my hand gets hurt, I mean.'

There was a pause. Then: 'Yes,' said the Crab, albeit grudgingly.

'Well then,' said Olivia. 'Here . . .'

No.

She could not say it.

But she must!

She bit her lip again. Hard.

She tasted blood.

Her blood.

Blood running from her lip.

Blood of her blood, blood from her lips, and Chegory gasping, and later . . .

'I am an Ashdan,' said Olivia, all expression crushed from her voice while terror fought with discipline. 'So.'

She put her hand between the chomp-chopper-chuk edges of the Crab's claw. It was a huge claw, its knobbly biting bits swelling out like globular teeth. Its surfaces were strangely cool against the fever of her flesh.

'So,' said Olivia.

She wanted to wrench her hand away.

But she could not.

She must not!

'So,' said Olivia. 'You can crunch my wrist. You can crunch it right off. Do it. If that's what you have to, then do it. Then you'll believe.'

So said Olivia.

Then she closed her eyes and waited for the Crab to decide.

CHAPTER THIRTY-SEVEN

It happened halfway between midnight and dawn: midway through the darks of bardardornootha. By then, the moon had sunk from sight. By then, the entire city had fallen to silence, but for a single dog intermittently barking, a single rooster voicing an occasional challenge, several hundred slabender frogs celebrating life and generation, the pulsing rub-drub-thump which issued from a group of half a dozen insomniac drummers who had installed themselves atop the heights of Pearl, the groans of those many sleepers who endured tormented dreams of the Mutilator of Yestron, and the high-pitched assault-hum of several hundred million mosquitoes.

It happened.

The buildings of portside Injiltaprajura abruptly brightened as if the moon had risen anew. But there was no moon. The buildings themselves were glowing. Atop the pink palace, the glitter-dome burnt beacon-bright. The Cabal House glowed a phosphorescent blue. The warehouses of Marthandorthan – Xtokobrokotok among them – shone first pink then gold.

Along Goldhammer Rise, buildings brightened to an intolerable white. In among these buildings lay the Temple of Torture. That was brightest, glowing as if the sun itself had come to life within. All inside the Temple's walls threw themselves flat and shielded their eyes.

Abruptly, the roof of the Temple shattered. A rockfall of splintered masonry blattered downwards – but dissolved to dust before it could do any damage.

The Temple was roofless.

The naos of the Temple lay open to the sky, and there lay the organic rectifier.

Slowly, a cocoon of purple light began to weave itself around the organic rectifier. Soon the antique device was entirely surrounded by a seamless integument of purple light. Then, smoothly, without making any fuss at all, the organic rectifier rose into the air and slid swiftly toward the island of Jod.

Shortly afterwards, the lights which lit Injiltaprajura were snuffed out. In the renewed dark, dogs and monkeys howled in fear, rage and anguish. Within the Temple of Torture itself, guards, initiates and acolytes picked themselves up from the ground, and began to inspect the damage. When they realized the 'skavamareen' was missing, messengers went hotfoot in search of Master Ek, who had taken himself off to his villa on Hojo Street just after midnight.

Shortly, Nadalastabstala Banraithanchumun Ek was issuing furious orders. The hell with caution! He was going to act, and now. He was going to kill out all opposition on Untunchilamon. Manthandros Trasilika, Justina Thrug, Aquitaine Varazchavardan, the lawyer Dardanalti – he would make a clean sweep. And if by chance Aldarch the Third failed to approve, well, Ek would deal with the consequences of such displeasure when the time arose.

Ek decided thus because he was sure a crisis was on hand. Had the Crab removed the 'skavamareen' from the Temple of Torture? Or had Varazchavardan stolen the thing by exercise of sorcery? Or did the Thrug command some monstrous power of which the world was as yet ignorant? Or had the very Cabal House itself joined Justina in conspiracy? Ek had no firm answers to any of these questions. But he presumed that the Temple of Torture had been destroyed because, one way or another, his enemies were on the point of staging a final confrontation. He was sure that his best chance of survival lay in acting immediately, seizing the initiative, and putting a permanent end to as much of the actual and potential opposition as he possibly could.

By daybreak, Ek had seized Nixorjapretzel Rat, Aquitaine Varazchavardan, the Empress Justina, Jean Froissart and Manthandros Trasilika. And, of course, he already held the formidable Juliet Idaho as a prisoner.

Many notorious and dangerous accomplices of the Thrug had escaped, among them the bullman Log Jaris, who had fled downstairs with his woman Molly. Of Shanvil Angarus May there was no sign; and the wizard Hostaja Sken-Pitilkin was another notable who was nowhere to be found. Sken-Pitilkin's cousin, Pelagius Zozimus, had been sighted briefly in Marthandorthan. But before he could be arrested, he had turned into a carpet snake, and then into an eagle – and had flown away.

'Never mind,' said Ek. 'This is enough to be going on with. We will begin sacrificing our captives to Zoz the Ancestral. Immediately!'

'But,' said one of his acolytes – Aath Nau Das, as it happens – 'this is hardly regular.'

'What are you talking about?' said Master Ek.

'I mean,' said his acolyte boldly, 'that there are prescribed forms for sacrifices and such.'

'Yes,' said Ek, 'and prescribed forms of politeness for acolytes to use when addressing their masters!'

'A thousand apologies,' said Nau Das, without sounding very apologetic. 'But, master of the many decades, there is such a thing as legality. These people haven't had a trial as yet.'

Ek smiled grimly, showing his blackened teeth.

'The hell with legality,' said Ek. 'We'll start killing them here and now.'

'What?' said Ch'ha Saat, the youngest of his acolytes. 'Without even torturing them?'

Ek considered. Arranging for torture would mean delay. On the other hand . . . he had endured a great deal over the years, and it would be a shame to send the Thrug out of the world without saying goodbye in the appropriate fashion.

'Very well,' said Ek. 'We will torture them before we kill them. Let's get busy then!'

And busy they got, and soon gathered together clamps and throttle-bands, stabs and wrecking irons, tweezers and cactus probes, shark hooks and purple veils, bottles of torture water and vials of vitriol, and heavy-duty urns packed with writhing centipedes and fat juicy scorpions.

Then Ek had all the captives brought out into the courtyard of the Temple of Torture. In the pungent heat of the morning they were lined up at spearpoint. Ek was pleased to see they all looked more or less undamaged. And that they were, for the moment, fairly calm. This way, he would know that the end result was all his own work.

Ek made no speeches but proceeded with the ceremonies of destruction immediately, beginning with the slow and studied sacrifice of a vampire rat. This he performed with his own hands, even though it cost him much in pain, for his arthritis was bad that morning.

'Now,' said Ek, 'what I have done with a rat I will do with a human. Bring forward Jean Froissart!'

Froissart was dragged forward, flung down on an operating table and tied into place. Froissart lay there, staring upwards in terror. His heart was staccato. Master Ek loomed over him with a knife. Then Justina screamed.

'Shabble!' screamed Justina. 'Kill them!'

Ek looked round wildly. There was no Shabble, no magical rescuer. Justina had bluffed. But her bluff had worked. While her guards were distracted, she had broken free, and—

'Stop her!' cried Ek.

But already the Thrug had a wrecking iron in her hands. And Juliet Idaho had broken free – someone must have cut his bonds! – and had wrested a scimitar into his hands. And the guards were looking on in askance, residual loyalties to the Empress or to Trasilika making them hesitate rather than intervene.

413

'A pardon,' said Varazchavardan, looking at Ek.

'Done!' said Ek.

Thus did Aquitaine Varazchavardan plead with Master Ek for a priestly pardon for any and all sins he might have committed during the years of the rule of the Family Thrug on Untunchilamon; and Ek granted him that pardon. Whereupon Varazchavardan threw forth his hands and cried:

'Bobskabo! Bobskabo! Bro!'

Thus he conjured into life a huge and hideous monster with half a thousand fangs. Purple were its feet, and its legs were twenty in number. Its muscles pumped outwards like dough rising with miraculous speed. It roared. Then it advanced upon Justina Thrug and Juliet Idaho, meaning to destroy them.

Not to be outdone, Nixorjapretzel Rat threw out his own hands and cried:

'Mikrandabor! Mikrandabor! Splotch!'

Instantly, another monster materialized. This one was orange, and spindly, and was pocked all over with little blue sores, and looked in the worst of tempers imaginable.

Snarling savagely, Rat's monster attacked that which had been created by Varazchavardan. The two monsters tore each other to bits in moments, whereupon both melted into pools of a watery pink liquid which smelt like crushed sugar cane. Varazchavardan wrested a spear from the nearest soldier and began to beat the hapless Rat with the butt of the thing.

That still left Justina Thrug and Juliet Idaho to deal with. The two heroes stood at bay in a corner of the courtyard of the Temple of Torture, and still Ek's guards looked dubious about taking them on.

'All right,' said Ek, addressing himself to Justina and Idaho. 'I'll do a deal with you. If you surrender, I'll cut your throats. No torture, just a straight throat-cutting. How's that?'

In reply, Idaho shouted:

'Wen Endex!'

And the Thrug screamed:

'Galsh Ebrek!'

Then the pair of them charged.

Fortunately for Ek, his soldiers intervened on his behalf, and both heroes were overwhelmed and disarmed. But the episode left Master Ek badly shaken, for it showed him how loosely he held the reins of power. He would not be safe and secure until the Thrug and her supporters were dead. He had been a fool to let his acolytes tempt him into any indulgence in time-consuming torture.

'Right,' said Ek. 'I'll show them my mercy anyway. No torture, I'll just cut their throats.'

Then he went back to Jean Froissart.

'If I remember rightly,' said Ek, 'before we were so rudely interrupted, I was going to cut your throat.'

'Don't!' said Froissart.

'Why shouldn't I?' said Ek.

'Because,' said a strangely familiar voice, 'if you do, we will kill you.'

Ek wheeled. This, of course, he did not do with the precipitate haste of a trained athlete. Rather, he wheeled in slow motion, as befits an old man with arthritis. But wheel he did, and his wheeling brought him face to face with a young Ashdan girl, Olivia Qasaba. The Qasaba girl had intruded upon the courtyard of the Temple of Torture in the company of an Ashdan male.

A stranger, this male. Nobody Ek had ever seen before. He looked to be something like fifty years of age, and his head was bald, and indeed hairless but for a modest square-chopped beard. He was naked but for a loincloth. Yet he was an imposing figure even so, for he had a champion's build, and he stood a head taller than any other man in sight. Sweat gleamed on his massive thews and oiled his sculpted pectorals. And his eyes – ah, the eyes! They were the startling blue so often found among the peoples of Ashmolea.

'Who are you?' said Ek.

'I am Olivia Qasaba,' said the girl.

'I wasn't talking to you!' said Ek. Then, to the man: 'Who are you? Tell me!'

'I am Codlugarthia,' said the man.

'And I,' said Master Ek, 'am Nadalastabstala Banraithanchumun Ek, High Priest of Zoz the Ancestral for the island of Untunchilamon. I have a need of good men.'

'I serve nobody,' said Codlugarthia. 'My time has come. Now others will serve me.'

Ek smiled, slightly. Then said to Varazchavardan:

'Try again. Get rid of him.'

'With pleasure,' said the wonder-worker, who was bitterly disappointed that his monster had not been able to devour Justina. He turned his attention to Codlugarthia. He flung out his hands and cried:

'Bara—'

Aquitaine Varazchavardan said no more. For Codlugarthia pointed a finger at him. They were standing a good twenty paces apart, but Codlugarthia's power did its work. There was a hideous crackling-snappling as Varazchavardan's leg bones shattered in a dozen places. The albinotic sorcerer screamed in agony, collapsed, then fainted.

Nixorjapretzel Rat bravely confronted the power of Codlugarthia.

'Barapus!' said Rat, throwing out his hands. 'Barapus! Mox! Mox! Nixi!'

The air between sorcerer and Ashdan boiled. An ominous cloud of blue swelled in the air, thrashed, throbbed, steadied – then resolved itself into a budgerigar.

'Oh, get out of here!' said Ek in disgust. 'Guards! Get rid of this man!'

The guards levelled their spears, preparing to throw them. They presumed the intruding Ashdan to be a wizard or sorcerer, but were sure none such could

416

survive the onslaught of a dozen fast-hurtling spears.

Codulgarthia gestured.

And the spears, while still in the hands of their owners, erupted into flame, and disintegrated into burning fragments a moment later.

Then Codlugarthia pointed a finger at Master Ek.

'I do not like your attitude,' said Codlugarthia.

Then his lips pursed in concentration. A moment later, Ek's left eye exploded. Ek clapped a hand to his ruined face. His shrivelled scream ascended to the heavens. Wailing, he fell to his knees.

And his guards fled.

Juliet Idaho, released from restraint by the fast-fleeing guards, strode forward and kicked Master Ek in the head, knocking him unconscious. And the Empress Justina turned to Codlugarthia and said:

'Greetings, my good man. Let me introduce myself. I am a child of Wen Endex, Justina Thrug by name, daughter of the great Lonstantine. How was it you named yourself?'

'I named myself as Codlugarthia,' said the Ashdan hero who had rescued her. 'But you know me far better by another name. For I am the Crab, long a hermit upon the island of Jod, but now set free in a form far better for the active exercise of power.'

'Then,' said Justina, giving a slight bow, 'it will be my pleasure to serve you. In bed or out of it.'

Justina had no idea how many centuries the Crab had lived as a Crab upon the island of Jod, but she was fairly sure it had not enjoyed carnal delights with any human female in all that time. So surely – or so she hoped – it would be ready for a volcanic initiation into the arts of the pleasures of the flesh.

'I will bear your offer of service in mind,' said Codlugarthia gravely. 'But now we must be gone from here, for a mission awaits us.'

'What mission?' said Justina, somewhat puzzled at this.

'Chegory, that's what mission!' said Olivia. 'Rescuing Chegory, that's what we have to do!'

'Oh yes,' said Justina. 'How remiss of me. Very well! Let us to the rescue go! Juliet – are you coming?'

'You couldn't keep me away,' said Idaho.

And, heavily armed with discarded weapons – one scimitar, two knives and a handful of caltrops – the Yudonic Knight joined Justina, Codlugarthia and Olivia as they set forth from the Temple of Torture. They left Manthandros Trasilika behind to cut loose Jean Froissart – and what fate thereafter befell Froissart and Trasilika is not for this history to tell.

CHAPTER THIRTY-EIGHT

It was the Empress Justina who led the way through the depths Downstairs as the rescue party hastened to the aid of Chegory Guy and Ivan Pokrov, the prisoners of the dreaded therapist. Olivia Qasaba followed at Justina's heels. Then came Codlugarthia, with the Yudonic Knight Juliet Idaho bringing up the rear.

On they went, and down.

Justina remembered the way well, for she had sweated it out a tenth of a footstep at a time as she laboured with the organic rectifier. Without such a burden to shift, the journey was miraculously short – two or three leagues at most, which is no distance at all for a fit healthy person – and the expedition was soon approaching the lair of the therapist.

It was then that they were surprised by a dorgi.

Down a corridor it came, crunching toward them in fury, meaning to crush them to death, to munchle-crunchle their bones, to trample them thoroughly until nothing was left of them but a bloody grit.

Codlugarthia saw the metal monster coming toward him. Calmly, he raised his finger.

He exerted a fraction of his power.

There was a scream from the dorgi. The thing slewed from side to side, crashed into a wall, came to a dead halt, then backed off a bit. It was defiant, but it was still frightened. It did not quite know what had been done to it, but it had unpleasant memories of being attacked by a granch-grusher, which had produced very similar sensations.

'Leave us,' said Codlugarthia in Janjuladoola.

'No,' said the dorgi.

'Leave,' said Codlugarthia. Then: 'I do not wish to have to repeat myself. Nor do I wish to have to raise my voice.'

In answer, the dorgi trained the snouts of its zulzer upon the heroic Ashdan. Then it fired. Belatedly, the dorgi remembered: it was out of ammunition. It did not hesitate: it charged.

Codlugarthia's fingers flickered.

The floor of the corridor ruptured.

A torn and jagged split gashed the floor of the corridor. Limitless depths yawned below. And the dorgi, assaulting forward at a furious pace, had no way to save itself. It tumbled into the pit and it fell, crashing through unseen metallic obstacles far below. There was a siren-pitched scream from deep, deep below. A sullen explosion. A rumbling thunder-roar.

And then . . .

Nothing.

'Let us,' said Codlugarthia, 'be going.'

They had to make a detour to get past the ruined section of corridor. Even so, they soon came upon the therapist. The first thing they saw was Chegory Guy and Ivan Pokrov. Both were hanging from their heels some distance above the ground, but appeared to be alive and physically intact.

'Greetings,' said the therapist in fluent Janjuladoola.

'And to you, greetings,' said Codlugarthia.

'Have you brought the Ashdan to me as a plaything?' said the therapist.

'I am not your plaything,' said Codlugarthia, gazing upon the monstrous device. 'You are mine. Unleash your prisoners.'

The therapist laughed at this stern command, and reached for Codlugarthia with half a dozen tentacles. Codlugarthia gestured curtly. The tentacles snapped and crackled, and recoiled as if from fire. The therapist screamed with rage.

'Now,' said Codlugarthia. 'Release your prisoners. Or

I will have to do you some serious harm.'

The therapist knew when it was beaten. It promptly lowered Chegory and Pokrov to the ground. And released them. Both tried to get up – and immediately fainted. Olivia rushed forward, and, in moments, was cradling her dearest Chegory in her arms and trying to revive him with mouth-to-mouth resuscitation. This strategy soon brought him round, and shortly he was smiling weakly in her embrace.

'Very well,' said Justina crisply. 'Now kill this thing.'

'Why?' said Codlugarthia.

'The thing is a menace,' said Justina. 'It lives to kill and torture.'

'Very well,' said Codlugarthia, 'I will destroy it.'

'But you mustn't!' shrieked the therapist. 'You mustn't destroy me!'

'Why not?' asked Codlugarthia coolly.

'Because, if you kill me you'll – you'll never know. The secrets! The secrets! I have the secrets!'

Ivan Pokrov, though he had not had the benefits of mouth-to-mouth resuscitation, managed to raise his head and say:

'Kill it.'

'Yes,' said Juliet Idaho, who had long been of the opinion that far too few people were getting killed these days. 'Kill it. It's high time we saw something killed.'

'No!' screeched the therapist. 'You mustn't! Because I can tell you, I can tell you all about it, worlds upon worlds, that's the secret. Gates to another cosmos. Not one, a series. From universe to universe. The chasm gates. The secrets, I have them, I know, I know. How to get there, how to go, how to travel. Worlds upon worlds. All yours.'

'It's lying,' said Pokrov.

Codlugarthia hesitated.

'Listen,' said the therapist. 'You're a Power. I know that. I've never felt your match, and I've felt much in my time. I guess you immortal. If you're not, we can soon fix that. Given immortality combined with power . . .'

The therapist paused to see how the Ashdan warrior was taking this.

'Speak on,' said Codlugarthia.

'Kill the thing,' said Justina impatiently.

'When I have sufficient data,' said Codlugarthia.

'Stranger,' said Ivan Pokrov, 'you must kill this thing. You must! You don't know what it is. What it can do.'

'Ah,' said Codlugarthia, 'but I will learn. Speak, thing. Have you a name?'

'I have,' said the therapist with dignity. 'Schoptomov, that's my name. But that is the least important thing I have to tell you. I can tell you the secret of the chasm gates. How to build them, how to use them. That way, you can get from one cosmos to another. Otherwise, you're stuck here. Stuck in this one grubby universe, for ever.'

'What possible advantage could there be,' said Codlugarthia, 'in going from one universe to another?'

'The Nexus, that's what,' said the therapist, gabbling its words as panic began to get the better of composure. Then it steadied itself and said: 'The Nexus. A coalition of empires. People by the million billion. Things you've never dreamed of. Suns, cities, seas of green and crimson, women smoother than silk, wines brighter than silver. Music to set dead bones to weeping, to set the very rocks to dancing.'

'It's bluffing,' said Pokrov. 'It doesn't know how to rebuild the chasm gates.'

'All right,' said the therapist. 'So I don't know. But you know!'

'I don't,' said Pokrov. 'It would take me a million years.'

'You admit it!'

'A million years, that's what I said.'

'A million years,' said Codlugarthia slowly. 'Well. I have a million years.'

'But you can't be serious!' said Pokrov. 'You may have a million years, but I don't.'

'You are an immortal, are you not?' sid Codlugarthia.

'Who told you that?' said Pokrov accusingly.

'Friend, I know you better than you think,' said Codlugarthia. 'Long have I sat on Jod, for I am the one you have known till now as the Hermit Crab. I have seen you passing yourself off as a mortal man to one generation after another. I know your potential.'

'I see,' said Pokrov. The designer of the Analytical Engine paused, then said: 'But whether I'm immortal or not, I'm not staying here to help you build chasm gates, or anything else for that matter.'

'I don't think you have any choice in the matter,' said Codlugarthia.

'We'd starve!' said Pokrov. 'Or thirst to death. Unless your powers extend to the creation of three-course meals thrice a day.'

'That,' admitted Codlugarthia, 'might be a little difficult. Not impossible, but . . .'

'Nutrition is no problem,' said the therapist. 'I can make all you need on the spot. Why, sometimes I've kept prisoners alive for decades.'

'Yes,' said Chegory, sitting up. 'The therapist thing's been telling us about some of those therapists. It's evil! You can't trust it! It'll get you, that's what, when you sleep, it'll take you and kill you, it'll make you a prisoner and torture you for ever.'

Codlugarthia paused in thought.

Then spread his arms.

Then Spoke.

The therapist screamed in agony.

Doors and panels ruptured.

Arms flailed and snapped.

Sparks crackled.

White fire ran along pipes and tubes.

Deep in the workings of the hideous device, something broke. And out from a secret storeroom there slithered a great gushing outpouring of bloody eyes, ears, noses, tongues and testicles – the souvenirs of centuries of calculated torture and bloody murder. Olivia screamed. And Codlugarthia again Spoke. And the onrushing onslaught blistered into so much fuming smoke.

Then there was silence, but for the hiss of escaping steam, the quick crackle of a bright fire consuming a wildly jumbled heap of green wire which had been cascaded out from the guts of the therapist, and the moans of the therapist itself.

'I think,' said Codlugarthia, 'that our friend here will not be torturing or imprisoning anyone for quite some centuries to come.'

'I'm blind,' sobbed the therapist. 'I'm blind!'

'Never mind,' said Codlugarthia. 'We can repair the damage, given time. Well. That is all for the moment. Pokrov, you must stay. It seems I have need of you. As for the others . . . for you, my friends, it is time to go.'

'You don't want to stay here,' said Justina earnestly. 'You can't be serious! A million years? Here?'

'What I need is here,' said Codlugarthia. 'Knowledge. Knowledge to amplify power. This is the source. There is no other.'

In vain did Chegory and Olivia plead with Codlugarthia. In vain did the Empress Justina offer him control of the island of Untunchilamon, of the city of Injiltaprajura and all its treasures. In vain did Juliet Idaho threaten him with the combined wrath of the Yudonic Knights of Galsh Ebrek. Codlugarthia was given to thinking in terms of years by the thousands and millions. While incarnated as the Crab, Codlugarthia had grown accustomed to taking the long view. And, in the long term, the mastery of the secrets of many a cosmos was far more tempting than the wearisome task of sorting out the squabbles of Injiltaprajura.

'But you could do it,' persisted Justina. 'You could really do it. Peace and good will and all that. You could make Injiltaprajura a very paradise.'

'Shabble has told me all about making paradises for human beings,' said Codlugarthia. 'It's no good. The human beings start hitting each other on the second day and killing each other on the third.'

'You exaggerate,' said Justina.

'Read your history books,' retorted Codlugarthia.

And, after just a little more debate, the humanized Crab sternly ordered all unwanted humans from its presence. And they then had no option but to say goodbyes to Ivan Pokrov and then to depart from that place and face whatever doom awaited them in the world above.

CHAPTER THIRTY-NINE

As Justina led her small party through the mazeways Downstairs, she did her best to conceal her dismay, but in truth she was shocked. Ever since the present crisis began, she had always thought that she could triumph over all her enemies if only the Crab could be liberated from the form which had so long oppressed it.

Now the Crab had been so liberated, and walked the world in human form. And the faithless thing had allowed itself to be tempted from its duty by a slippery-tongued therapist! Its duty, obviously, was to serve Justina Thrug faithfully forever after, in gratitude for the way in which it had been liberated thanks to the efforts of Justina's minion, the daring Olivia.

But the Crab had proved a thankless traitor, and so . . .

'Stroth!' said Justina, swearing softly to herself.

What would she find when she got up above? What was Trasilika doing right now? Had he killed Ek? Or did Ek still live? And Varazchavardan? And Jan Rat?

Justina was more than a little humiliated to realize that the rule of Injiltaprajura was of so little concern to the humanized Crab that it preferred to gossip away the centuries in the company of a monstrous therapist. Furthermore, such was Justina's shock at her unexpected betrayal by the Crab that she found herself quite unable to formulate any coherent plan of action. No help in this respect came from her companions.

Chegory Guy seemed none the worse for wear after his ordeal – he was, after all, an Ebrell Islander, and such creatures are far less sensitive to rough handling than the ordinary run of humanity – but both Chegory and Olivia were going to be of very little use as far as any sensible planning went. They were too busy canoodling, something they managed even while on the move. As for Juliet Idaho, he just wanted to kill something; and Justina did not believe that any plan involving murder was likely to secure as much as their bare survival, far less their health and happiness.

The journey which had seemed so short when Justina had been leading her forces to certain victory now seemed long, tedious and wearisome as she led the march toward the uncertain future. Through dark and light they went, sometimes pursued by the squillering of vampire rats – and at last emerged into the light of day.

For safety's sake, Justina chose to exit from the mazeways by means of the tomb-door on the desert side of Pokra Ridge. Here observing eyes were fewest. Once out in the saunabath heat of Injiltaprajura, she hesitated, unsure whether to retreat to Moremo Maximum Security Prison – the sole stronghold which any people loyal to her might have managed to seize and fortify against her enemies – or whether to proceed to the palace.

'Where are we going?' said Olivia.

Thus forcing Justina to decide.

'We will go to the palace,' she said firmly.

By fleeing to Moremo, she would only concede Injiltaprajura to any thug with the will to take it. By going to the palace, by occupying the traditional seat of power, she might yet secure the rule of the city. If her enemies were in disarray. If Manthandros Trasilika had not already set himself up once more as wazir. If Master Ek was dead, or at least too sick to speak a word against her. Given a little time – a few days, that was all she asked for – she could try other strategies. Such as producing her own false wazir.

A new scheme occurred to her: a variation on those of the past. She could produce a man, any man, any stranger to the city – one of Jal Japone's men would do –

and claim that man to be the Crab incarnated in human form.

'I can do it,' muttered Justina, as she strode toward the palace.

'Do what?' said Juliet Idaho.

'Regain my throne,' said Justina. 'And my power.'

Yes.

If the events of the past few days had proved anything, they had proved that her enemies were incapable of coordinated, coherent action. They had hesitated and prevaricated when they should have struck ruthlessly and decisively. They had given themselves to doubt when they should have given themselves to action. They had been deceived repeatedly by lies, bluffs, carefully planned leaks of false information, and deceits of all kinds. They had proved themselves a pack of second-rate fools, cowards and weaklings.

Justina Thrug threw open the unguarded sally port which gave access to the pink palace from the north. She stepped inside, into the dusty silence of her palace.

'Anyone home?' she bellowed.

Then listened for a challenge, for clattering feet.

Nobody answered.

Nobody came.

Chegory Guy and Olivia Qasaba ventured within. Juliet Idaho peered suspiciously at the landscape without – then joined them.

'We have the palace,' said Justina. 'That's the first thing. Come. My quarters first.'

She went to her quarters, hoping to find a servant or messenger, or at least a message. But there was nothing and nobody, but for the dragon Injiltaprajura, first (and perhaps only) child of the brave-hearted dragon Untunchilamon. Justina peered closely at Injiltaprajura's saucer.

'At least my dragon has been fed,' said Justina.

Indeed it had, for there was fresh milk-soaked cassava bread and a quarter of a corpse worm on the dragon's

428

saucer. Injiltaprajura yawned, and stretched baby dragon wings. She looked closer still. Unless she was mistaken, the dragon was ever so slightly jaundiced. That was no good! What should she do?

'Where now?' said Chegory.

A good question!

Justina was momentarily at a loss for an answer, and so pretended she had not heard. Chegory spoke again. Louder, this time. And by then Justina had an answer.

'Where?' she said. 'To the roof, of course! Seize the high ground!'

'Whatever for?' said Olivia.

'So we can see what's going on,' said Justina. 'Olivia, you can carry my dragon.'

So saying, Justina took the saucer upon which the dragon rode in state, and handed it to the Ashdan lass.

'Take this?' said Olivia. 'Whatever for?'

'I think it needs some sun,' said Justina. 'It's getting jaundiced. Don't drop it!'

And with that, Justina set out for the roof forthwith, thinking furiously as she did so. What should she do next?

Justina's main problem was that the fundamental political dynamic of Untunchilamon remained unchanged, and that dynamic was hostile to her. The greatest force for evil on the island was the favoured religion of Aldarch the Third, that is to say the worship of Zoz the Ancestral. Ultimately, when it came to the crunch, a substantial part of the populace would side with Aldarch the Third or his minions. And now that the Multilator of Yestron was known to have triumphed in Talonsklavara, now that Al'three was revealed as the victor, the populace had little excuse for enduring the rule of the Family Thrug any longer.

So whatever Justina tried – be it a bluff with a false wazir or an imitation Crab – it would have to be very very good.

Otherwise she would shortly lose her head.

Justina was still thinking through her problems when she came out on to the roof. And the first thing she saw was Pelagius Zozimus, the wizard of the order of Xluzu who had lately served the Crab so well as a master chef. Zozimus was stark naked, a condition which lacked erotic appeal; for, while Zozimus was still hale in limb and shapely enough, the Empress was not in the mood. Besides being naked, the wizard was also dripping wet.

'What have you been doing to yourself?' said Justina.

'That,' said Zozimus, 'is a long story.'

Since Nixorjapretzel Rat had hexed Pelagius Zozimus, the unfortunate wizard of Xluzu had been incarnated variously (this list, please note, is not exhaustive) as a grampus, a sun scorpion, a beady-eyed puttock, an eyeless whore's egg, an ostrich, a snow dragon, a puma and a penguin. In the last-named incarnation, Zozimus had recently been swimming in Justina's rooftop swimming pool, which he had found uncomfortably warm for his blubber-clad penguin body. But for the moment his original flesh had reclaimed him, though he had no certainty that such reclamation would be permanent.

'Well,' said Justina, 'tell us your long story. Then we've one of our own to tell.'

Already Justina was figuring Pelagius Zozimus into her political calculations. Was he her ally? Not exactly. But he was not her enemy, either. He was a wizard, and so naturally at odds with Untunchilamon's wonder workers, and so—

'You may think you have time for long stories,' said Zozimus, 'but in fact you do not.'

'And why not, may I ask?' said Justina.

'Go to the edge of the roof,' said Zozimus. 'The view answers all.'

Justina went to the edge of the roof and looked out over portside Injiltaprajura. There were two ships in the harbour. The personal banner of Aldarch the Third flew from the masts of both, and both were disembarking troops.

430

'It's him!' said Juliet Idaho.

'Don't talk nonsense, Julie,' said Justina sharply.

'Those are the Mutilator's banners!' said Idaho.

'Yes, and any of his generals can fly them,' said Justina. 'He's not here himself, he can't be. He'd lose the Izdimir Empire entirely if he trifled himself here to dispute possession of this overgrown bloodstone ballast block.'

'Then one of his generals is here!' said Idaho. 'We will fight and die!'

'We will not fight,' said Justina firmly, 'and we will not die.'

She looked at the airship. To her untrained eye, it looked as if it was almost finished.

'Pelagius!' said Justina. 'Where is your brother? It is time for us to leave, and I know not the secret of flying his airship.'

'Neither do I,' said Zozimus, 'for it is a branch of wizardry entirely different to mine. I don't know where Sken-Pitilkin is, either. Oh, and while I'm about it – he's my cousin, not my brother.'

'Pedantry!' muttered Justina. 'But what can one expect from a wizard?'

Then, nothing daunted, she scrambled into the airship, seeking to learn its mysteries.

The rooftop of the pink palace must have been under observation – either from the Cabal House or elsewhere – because as soon as Justina climbed into the airship it started to disintegrate.

'Chegory!' screamed Olivia. 'Stop it!'

Her hero rushed forward and grabbed hold of one of the branches. It pulled away. He pulled back, throwing the full strength of his sledgehammer muscles into the contest. The inner wood slid free of its sheathing bark, which crumbled immediately to black flakes in Chegory's furious grip. The wood waggled away at its leisure.

'Blood of the Gloat!' said Idaho. 'The next wonder-worker I see, I kill!'

Justina looked upwards at the sticks scattering in all directions. The timing of the airship's destruction could surely be no coincidence. The wonder-workers were watching her even now. She thought to shake her fist at the Cabal House – but did no such thing. The gesture was too weak, too puny, and unlikely to be perceived at a distance.

Bereft of ideas entirely, Justina stared out at the Laitemata Harbour and the two ships still steadily disembarking their soldiers. Soon, they would march up Lak Street. They would secure the palace. They would arrest her. And if she fled Downstairs? Why, she would be hunted down, for there was no ultimate refuge there – as many escaped slaves and eloping lovers had discovered to their cost. And if she fled to Zolabrik?

Justina turned.

Zazazolzodanzarzakazolabrik awaited, its waterless wastelands stretching away for league upon league to the north. In vain she scrutinized those barrens, looking for an army. That was her last hope – that the warlord Jal Japone might have sent men south in strength to seize Injiltaprajura while the seizing was good.

But there was no army.

Maybe Justina's envoy had never got through to Jal Japone. Or maybe Japone declined to come south. Or, more probably – the roadless way was far and the going was rough – the envoy had yet to reach his destination.

'Still,' said Justina to herself. 'I tried.'

Then she felt defeat, for she could think of no further tricks she could try.

As Justina stood there upon the rooftop of the pink palace, she realized that even then – right at that very moment – there would still be people in and around Injiltaprajura who were catching fish, drawing water, cooking meals, washing dishes, collecting coconuts or weeding market gardens. And if she died that day, why, the mundane life of the city would still continue, for all the world as if she had never lived.

432

Thus Justina endured a vision of the world as it would be when she had died. She would die, her bones would be scattered, her memory desecrated. And still the sun would shine; still the red seas of sunset and the red seas of dawn would break against the shores of Untunchilamon.

Then she knew despair.

She walked to the edge of the rooftop, half-minded to throw herself off.

Then she stopped.

For she remembered.

In that time of despair, Justina remembered a story which had once been told to her by her father, the great Lonstantine. He had told her of an experiment once performed by a half-mad master of experimental philosophy. The man had obtained two rare and wonderful bottles made of glass, and had orientated these transparent vessels so they lay with their butts presented to the light and their throats in dark shadows, the darkness being enhanced by the careful arrangement of black cloth. Into each of these bottles the experimenter introduced an insect.

Into one bottle went a bumble bee.

Into the other, a fly.

The fly was too stupid to try to think its way out of the bottle. Instead, it flew around at random, blatting this way and that in the manner of flies – and in moments had triced its way out to freedom by inevitable accident.

The bee, on the other hand, was intelligent to know that escape lay toward the light. So to the light it went, only to find its way blocked by an impervious transparency. It struggled valorously, for it was obstinate in courage. But in the end it died, betrayed by its intelligence.

The moral of the story?

Many morals could be drawn, some of them concerning the dangers of intelligence. But to Lonstantine Thrug – he was, we must remember, a Yudonic Knight, and

433

therefore inclined toward simplicities – the moral was this: Never despair!

'Well,' said Olivia Qasaba, 'what are we going to do now?'

'We,' said Justina, 'are going to retreat into Zolabrik.'

'No!' said Chegory, who had a peculiar horror of Untunchilamon's wasteland deserts.

'Yes,' said Justina. 'We have no other choice.'

'But why?' said Chegory. 'Couldn't we just – well, surrender?'

A foolish question, this. It required no answer. But Idaho provided one anyway.

'We can't surrender,' said Idaho. 'For if captured, we might be brainwashed.'

The Empress Justina shuddered at the thought. Brainwashing, for those unfamiliar with the niceties of political life in the Izdimir Empire, is a particularly hideous form of torture, and all its varieties are almost invariably lethal. Brainwashing can take any of seventeen different forms, the most merciful being the Hovmun Variation in which the much-washed brain is cut from its stem on the second day then fed to the next-of-kin of the deceased or (should next-of-kin be unavailable) to offal pigs bred especially for the purpose.

While Justina was still shuddering, she heard boots pounding up the stairs leading to the roof.

'Someone's coming!' screamed Olivia.

'We've left it too late,' said Idaho. 'We can't escape.'

Then he screamed his battle cry: 'Wen Endex!'

'Julie!' said Justina sharply. 'They might be friends.'

'No,' said Idaho sternly. 'They can't be. We have no friends left. We are doomed. Our sole remaining privilege is to die with weapons in our hands. Better it is to die thus than to be captured alive. So this is it, then. Our last stand.'

Verily, the doughty Yudonic Knight seemed almost to welcome the crisis. He had endured Justina's civilized and charitable regime for too long. He wanted war, blood-slaughter battles, violence, glory, death. If only for a moment. Even if his own death were to be consequent upon such indulgences.

'You,' said Justina, seizing Pelagius Zozimus and shaking him. 'Don't just stand there. Do something!'

'Do what?' said Zozimus.

'You're a wizard, aren't you?'

'Yes,' said Zozimus. 'A wizard with the power to animate corpses. Do you see any raw material for my work?'

'Stand ready!' said Juliet Idaho, bracing himself for combat. 'I'll soon give you all the raw material you need.'

Then those coming up the stairs burst out on to the roof.

The corpse-master Uckermark was in the lead, and Idaho almost took off his head with a swordstroke before he saw who it was. Uckermark was carrying a wicker-work cage, and Shabble bobbed bright-shining at Uckermark's shoulder.

Uckermark's hard-bitten woman, Yilda of the many conflicts, followed him on to the roof. Then came the bullman Log Jaris and his helpmate Molly.

'Is there anyone else?' said Idaho.

'This is all of us,' said Uckermark.

'Well, that doesn't give me many to choose from,' said Idaho.

'What are you talking about?' said Uckermark.

'Our wizard friend here requires a corpse,' said Uckermark, indicating Zozimus. 'Only by means of such can he unleash his power.'

'That's enough!' said Justina sharply. Then she looked hard at Zozimus. 'Are you all right?' she said. 'You look ill.'

'I—'

But Zozimus said no more, for he began to Change. He shrivelled and shrank, and he outflourished fur as he shrank. Moments later, where the wizard had been, there was nothing but a wriggling loin cloth. Bro Drumel's corpse staggered then collapsed. Then a gerbil struggled free from the loin cloth, and sat on its hind legs chittering furiously.

'Oh!' said Olivia. 'A hampster. How cute!'

The gerbil glared at her in fury. Its eyes were bloodshot with berserk fury, and, in its rage, it pawed at the roof like a bull trying to ruck apart a paddock with its hooves. Olivia failed to heed these warning signs. Instead, with one cherishing finger she ventured to stroke the gerbil behind the ears.

The gerbil bit her.

'Yow!' said Olivia.

'Olivia!' said the Empress Justina. 'We've no time for games! And don't drop my dragon! Now listen, all of you. We must leave immediately. For Zolabrik.'

'We must leave, yes,' said Uckermark. 'But not for Zolabrik. We're leaving by air.'

'Are you blind?' said Justina. 'The airship's destroyed! Look!'

Uckermark laughed.

'Look yourself,' said he. 'Look for Xtokobrokotok.'

Justina resisted the temptation to swear at him. She deigned to look out across the city to the warehouses of Marthandorthan. She located Xtokobrokotok, most notorious of all the buildings in that dockland quarter. On the rooftop, a solitary figure was hauling a tarpaulin from a—

'Oh,' said Justina in surprise.

Now all was explained. Now she knew why Hostaja Sken-Pitilkin had only worked for half the day at the pink palace, and had never seemed to have much enthusiasm for the work he did there.

'That's all very well,' said Juliet Idaho, observing the gigantic bird's nest which stood atop Xtokobrokotok, waiting for the wizard Hostaja Sken-Pitilkin to send it whirling into the air. 'But the Cabal House has destroyed two airships already. They can destroy a third as easily.'

436

'Shabble,' said Uckermark. 'Now!'

Shabble hummed with excitement as Shabble went bobbing upwards. Then fire flashed forth from Shabble, and the upper storey of the Cabal House exploded into flame.

'Ouch!' said Justina.

She did not think Uckermark was being at all wise in persuading Shabble thus to join the wars of humanity. But she had to admit the manoeuvre served the needs of the moment.

When she looked again, Hostaja Sken-Pitilkin had got his bird's nest into the air, and it was whirling through the sultry sunlight toward them. It rose up, up, up into the air, then whirled downward, almost clipping the glitter dome as its shadow spun across the roof of the pink palace, its substance speaking to the world thus:

Thubber lubber dubber – ffft!

All ducked as the huge thing swept overhead, nearly taking their heads off. It slewed sideways, lurched to an abrupt halt in mid-air, then gyrated backwards until it was spinning in the air directly overhead. Then it descended. Justina grabbed the still-chittering gerbil and dived for safety just before the bird's nest landed with a hideous grating sound accompanied by an upfling of dust.

'All aboard!' cried Hostaja Sken-Pitilkin, looking down from above.

Yilda was already scrambling up the side of the airship. The others followed, the gerbil being passed from hand to hand as Justina was hauled aboard. As the refugees came aboard, they seated themselves in the bottom of the airship like so many fledglings in a huge bird's next.

'Hurry up, Julie!' cried the Empress Justina.

'But,' cried Juliet Idaho, who was still standing on the palace roof, 'we haven't killed anyone yet!'

'Julie!' said Justina. 'I'm giving you a direct order! Get inside! Now!'

Juliet Idaho scrambled aboard. As he sought for a place to sit, he almost crushed the wickerwork cage which Uckermark had brought aboard.

'Careful!' said Uckermark. 'Don't sit on that!'

'Why not?' said Idaho.

'Have you no eyes?' said Uckermark. 'Look! The Holy Cockroach dwells within.'

Juliet Idaho looked, and saw that it was true.

'So what?' said Idaho.

'Holy is the Cockroach and hallowed is His name,' intoned Shabble. 'Accursed are those who would desecrate His presence.'

Then a trifling tongue of flame flickered forth from the quick-dancing Shabble. Juliet Idaho took the hint, and seated himself against the branch-bumpy wall of the flying nest.

'Where is my cousin?' said Sken-Pitilkin.

'Your cousin?' said Justina.

'The great lord Zozimus,' said Sken-Pitilkin.

'Oh!' said Justina. 'You mean your brother. Here he is!'

And she held up the frantically-struggling gerbil.

Sken-Pitilkin could not help himself.

He laughed.

'Scra – scra – scra – skrik!' shrilled the gerbil.

'I think he's angry,' said Chegory.

'I know he's angry,' said Hostaja Sken-Pitilkin. 'But there's no helping that. Hold on tight! It's time to fly.'

'Do you hear that?' said Justina to her gerbil. 'We're going to fly. Don't be frightened now. You'll be all right. I'll take care of you.'

Then she kissed the little thing. The gerbil tried to savage her lips, but she was too quick for it.

Then Hostaja Sken-Pitilkin raised his hands and shouted a Word.

Nothing happened.

Nothing?

A jar toppled from a shelf in the kitchen below. A star exploded in a galaxy five billion luzacs distant. In another cosmos altogether, a horse gave birth to a unicorn. But all of those occurrences may have been pure coincidence.

Again Hostaja Sken-Pitilkin raised his hands.

Again he shouted.

With the greatest appearance of reluctance, the ship began to spin. Slowly, slowly it went. It did not leave the rooftop. But it steadily gathered speed until it was whirling round with a roar of wind.

'Whoa!' cried Sken-Pitilkin, outright alarm writ clear across his face.

Then the ship kicked into an upward spiral.

They were off.

And they were leaving just in time, for down below a tsunami was striking Untunchilamon. Up, up it rose, its cataclysmic waters sweeping across the outer reef. It crashed across the lagoon and swamped its way across Island Scimitar. It rushed over and around the island of Jod. Then its fury pounded the embankment of crushed bloodstone and red coral which disciplined the inland border of the Laitemata. Disembarking soldiers screamed in panic or clung to each other in dismay as the tsunami broke over them.

The crashing waters thrashed around the helpless living flesh, buffeted across the embankment, reached the first shacks and boathouses, the first shopstalls and housefronts . . . and there hesitated, paused, then, realizing they had exhausted their momentum, began to slide back into the Laitemata.

The backsliding waters carried away with them a good three dozen soldiers and a princess, the princess in question being the elegant Sabitha Winolathon Taskin-jathura, she of the noble lineage, the impeccable breeding. Fortunately, she could swim; and the soldiers could swim as well; and when the excitement was over and all the swimmers had been hauled from the water, it was discovered that the damage done by the tsunami amounted to no more than an impromptu bath for one princess (the above mentioned Princess Sabitha) and some three or four dozen soldiers.

For not all tsunamis are equal, and this one (like Nixorjapretzel Rat's demon) was more unequal than most.

Your historian regrets the fact that he is unable to conclude this account by providing you with a final scene of cataclysmic destruction, but what happened is what happened, and history cannot be amended merely to spice up a story. So we cannot here have any account of the overthrow of Injiltaprajura, of the bursting of buildings, of the screams of helpless victims staring uphill in horror as the ship-sized monument known as Pearl pounds down upon them, of splattered blood and broken bones and skulls exploding as life and hope are eyeblinked into oblivion.

No, what happened is commonplace – indeed, bathotic – by comparison. But it is the truth. The wave came, the wave broke, and Injiltaprajura was much the same thereafter, for it was a wave far too small to fit the real dramatic needs of the moment. And Justina Thrug escaped by air from the hooks and claws of justice and (to the best of the historian's knowledge) was never seen again on Untunchilamon.

AN EXPLANATION

Of Untunchilamon and its politics you now know; or, to put it another way, you know as much as your historian can reasonably be expected to convey, given the limitations of his sources, the dictates of mortality and the outrageous price of ink, pens and fooskin. However, one final duty remains, and that is for the historian to clear up a small mystery. How did the Empress Justina swindle the innocent Jean Froissart? You will remember that the Empress set three glasses in a row on a table. That she flip-flopped two at a time. That three such manipulations gave her two inverted glasses and one standing upright. Froissart, challenged to duplicate the feat, failed.

Despite his genius level intellect.

How so?

The reader has already been warned that the answer is bathotic, and so it it. For when we come to the question of conjuring, the interest is all in the illusion; and the explanation of that illusion is necessarily disappointing.

The answer is this:

Justina started off with a row of three glasses, the beakers at the end inverted and the central glass standing upright. When she rearranged the glasses, the Empress inverted the central beaker and let the other two stand upright. Froissart, let loose on this array, thought he was tackling the problem so easily solved by the Empress. Of course he was not. Hence his mind-buckling frustration and his inevitable defeat.

That Froissart was so easily fooled is not to his discredit, for nine people out of ten will fall victim if the Manipulator has any skill; and Justina, coached well by

441

the conjuror Odolo, had mastered the art of subtly misdirecting the mind.

Naturally Froissart was predisposed to think Justina a witch, which made her deception easier; however, the fact remains that it usually takes a trained Observer to reveal the deceits of an adroit Manipulator, and that some of the world's greatest Investigators have been fooled by tricks equally as feeble as that to which Froissart fell victim.

It follows that conjurors can often pass as wizards or wonder-workers; and many have done just that, often winning great honours from naive rulers, and sometimes continuing their deceits until overtaken by death in a wealthy and much-honoured old age. However, should the reader be tempted to adopt such a stratagem, be warned that such deceits have sometimes failed in a truly spectacular fashion; and the writer will not accept responsibility for the consequences!

With that said, our history is, strictly speaking, at an end. Let us write it thus:

THE END

However, this history has been, in many ways, an account of the progress of certain diseases through the body politic of the island of Untunchilamon; and, accordingly, while our narrative is terminated, a few brief notes on the sequelae are in order. The sequelae were many and various, but the most notable are as follows:

» *Arat, Orge*: of this individual, little has been said; for it would seem excessively egotistical for a historian to play hero in his own history.

Nevertheless, mention was made of him in the text. It was noted that he was long incarcerated in the Dromdan-jerie, believing himself to be a sane man pretending to

442

be mad in order to avoid the consequences of murder, his mother-in-law being the person he thought he had slain.

At long last, in one of his lucid moments, he realized his mother-in-law still lived. He escaped, intending to kill her. But failed. Thereafter he was sheltered first by Nixorjapretzel Rat and then by Troldot 'Heavy-Fist' Turbothot. On Turbothot's ship he laboured long and hard to recreate the *Injiltaprajuradariski, The Secret History* which owed so much to revelations by the lunatic-befriending Shabble.

Unfortunately, the recreated draft was flung to the sea during the voyage from Untunchilamon. And thereafter conditions were less than ideal for literary labours, for, by a series of unfortunate accidents, Orge Arat came very close to doom in the dungeons of Obooloo.

However, vomit may yet feed a dog, as the proverbial saying has it; and the incarceration was not without advantage inasmuch as Orge Arat was long confined in company with Aquitaine Varazchavardan, who told him much of interest, if not all.

Thanks to this and other revelations, Orge Arat was in an excellent position to recreate the *Injiltaprajuradariski* anew when he finally made his way to refuge in the Mountains of the Moon. There he laboured long, finishing a final draft of the Secret History, this one written not in purple ink but in the finest vermilion.

While that final draft was written at a time when insanity had the ascendancy, when the historian once more believed himself (ah, sweet delusion!) to be the murderer of his mother-in-law, it was nevertheless a fairly accurate account of certain events upon Untunchilamon. However, it dealt only with Varazchavardan's attempted coup and certain events which preceded it.

Thereafter, the historian wandered long in sundry places, enduring great dangers and greater sufferings. At last he returned again to his native Quilth, land of the taniwha; returned older (definitely), wiser (one hopes)

443

and saner (incontrovertibly). This time he settled not in the Mountains of the Moon but in the lowlands of the south, and there bethought himself to write a further history of Untunchilamon. This tome is, of course, that history; starting some time after Varazchavardan's attempted coup and proceeding to the general exodus from Untunchilamon.

» *Cockroach, the Holy*: was conveyed to Port Domax by His worshippers, and there in due course was installed in a temple built to His glory; and there he lived to what was, for an entity incarnated in his particular corporeal form, a grand old age.

I am particularly glad to be able to record this happy ending, as cockroaches are truly admirable individuals who have suffered much from the world's prejudices. (This insight I owe to Shabble, for I would never have been able to overcome my own prejudices without such assistance.)

Naturally the corporeal form of the Holy Cockroach eventually succumbed to mortality; but He doubtless reincarnated Himself elsewhere, and perhaps he is in among that group of a dozen happy insects now feeding upon the dish of tolfrigdalakaptiko which sits upon my desk (not the dish which I ate around about the time of the composition of the first and second chapters of this history, but an entirely new batch of seagull livers which I prepared especially for these cockroaches, these dearest and most valued of my friends).

» *Codlugarthia*: the Crab is an entity of whom we can hope to know little now that Untunchilamon has become an island of impenetrable mystery. It may be that Codlugarthia is the Intruder who brought the pogroms of Wazir Ek to their abrupt and sanguinary termination; though this is not certain, for it may be that the Intruder was a thing of great evil (some would say: of great good) from the depths Downstairs. Possibly Codlugarthia is the

'devil-god' encountered by the ill-fated Expeditionary
Force from Odrum; or possibly not; for some think this
creature of ghoulish habit and irascible temperament to
have been the revenant of Lonstantine Thrug.

» *Crab*: *see* Codlugarthia.

» *Dardanalti*: survived the various discords which befell
Untunchilamon following the departure of Justina
Thrug, and eventually travelled to Obooloo, there
becoming a leading defence lawyer. However, finally the
Powers That Be caught up with him, and he was
executed for practising law without a licence. This he
deserved, for he was a fraud, a complete charlatan, a
man with no more formal legal training than the corpse-
master Uckermark. This the reader should have guessed
long ago: for surely a real lawyer would have let the
Empress Justina perish in the Temple of Torture, instead
of intervening (as did the courageous Dardanalti, at
considerable risk to his own life) with a well-timed but
totally unlawyerly kick.

» *Ek, Nadalastabstala Banraithanchumun*: at the command of Aldarch Three, abandoned the priesthood of
Zoz the Ancestral in order to become wazir of Untunchilamon. In the discharge of his duties, was hindered by
neither age nor the loss of one eye. Pursued pogrom
avidly until his existence was interrupted by an Intruder
of unknown origin. (Unknown, yes, but many have
speculated: *see* Codlugarthia.)

» *Guy, Chegory*: is rumoured to have become the High
Priest of the Cult of the Holy Cockroach in Port Domax.

» *Hermit Crab*: *see* Crab.

» *Jaris, Log*: departed from Untunchilamon in the
company of the Empress Justina, as related in our

history. Thereafter, his fate is murky; but it seems the bullman ultimately took himself off to the west. And, if a confident Rumour is to be believed, in due course the bullman made himself lord of the mighty metropolis of D'Waith, a populous trading centre said to control all commercial intercourse between the continent of Argan and the Ravlish Lands.

While the Fall of Drangsturm has seen Argan meet with ruin, it is nevertheless said that Log Jaris still rules from his five-gated city on the heights above the Penvash Channel; and the hospitality of his halls has become legendary.

A person answering the description of Log Jaris also features in that confused and contradictory corpus of literature known as the Dreldragon Legends. There a bullman, so named and so described, is claimed to be the 'master of the halls of ever-flowing wine' which are said to stand beside the shores of Lake Arkanziz (some sources say: Lake Marankis) in the land of Penvash; and it is said that the young Lord Dreldragon consulted this personage on certain Holy Matters before venturing to the City of the Dead; and that, on his return from encounters with the Dead, Dreldragon made a great sacrifice of dogs, of goats and of arak to the greater glory of the bullman.

We hear also in the Dreldragon Legends that the young lord travelled in company with an Ashdan of notorious savagery and superlative combat skill; and some have identified this Ashdan warwolf as Shanvil Angarus May, though others have thought the identification doubtful.

» *May, Shanvil Angarus*: fate unknown. But *see* the entry for Log Jaris.

» *Molly*: shared the fate of Log Jaris (q.v.).

» *Thrug, Justina*: it is known that the Empress Justina

returned to Galsh Ebrek and there became involved in a power struggle for control of Wen Endex. Given the intricacy of that struggle, the historian hesitates to summarize it here, for compression has a tendency to damage truth; better that the curious research the matter in detail elsewhere.

» *Thrug, Lonstantine*: missing, believed dead. (But *see* entry for Codlugarthia.)

» *Thrug, Theodora*: of the fate of Justina's twin sister, little is known. She escaped from Untunchilamon on a ship commanded by Troldot Turbothot (q.v.); and she was at the time his lover. Some have speculated that she may have settled into a matronly middle age in the arms of that gentleman; however, given her invincible pre-dilection for amatory adventures, such an outcome is most unlikely.

We note that she had oft declared a wish to be a pirate. Rumour has noted likewise, a process which has given rise to some highly colourful legends, one of which sees her pirating her way across the Green Sea in a ship of seven masts – a feat quite impossible when one considers that the said Sea is scarcely deep enough for the canoes of the Ngati Moana to make their voyages in safety. Given the extreme improbability of this and other stories perpetrated by rumour, the historian regretfully declines to commit any of the details to the page.

» *Tin Char, Dui*: may have perished in the wastes of Zolabrik; or, if an alternative rumour is to believed, to have found refuge with Jal Japone.

» *Turbothot, Troldot 'Heavy-Fist'*: after sundry adventures on the shores of Moana, this adventuring gentleman proceeded beyond the horizons of Verified Truth and Rumour alike.

» *Uckermark*: confused and contradictory reports surround the activities of this corpse-master, and the historian has ultimately nothing certain with which to grace his page.

» *Qasaba, Jon*: of this Ashdan therapist, nothing need be said; for he has written himself into history to such an extent that there is surely no need to make mention of him here.

» *Qasaba, Olivia*: is said to have made a life-alliance with Chegory Guy in Port Domax.

» *Varazchavardan, Aquitaine*: the story of Justina's Master of Law is given (to the extent to which it is known) under the entry for Orge Arat (q.v.). Varazchavardan's ultimate fate is unknown; but, considering the predicament he was in when the historian saw him last (in Obooloo, as it happens) it is most probable that he is long since dead.

But there are no guarantees of this.

» *Zozimus, Pelagius*: when last heard of, this wizard of the order of Xluzu was said to be living in Port Domax in the care of Olivia Qasaba, who kissed him daily, and sometimes took him to bed with her. Unfortunately, the degree to which he enjoyed these blandishments was limited, because he was still incarnated as a hampster. This is doubtless a better fate than that intended for him by Nixorjapretzel Rat, for Jan Rat had intended to turn Zozimus into a cockroach and then to step upon him. Nevertheless, it is probable that Zozimus is far from being resigned to his fate. How long will he stay thus imprisoned? That this history cannot tell. However, it would appear that his shape had assumed what may be an unshakeable form; and it is said that wizards live for a long, long time.

THE END